WELCOME TO THE DUNGEON

It is a cave from which the unwary can fall into the sky of an alien world.

It is an ocean of monsters, dotted with islands of deadly danger.

It is a world of captives seeking an escape from the strange prison that transcends time and space.

From a subterranean maze to the jaws of doom, this is the quest of Clive Folliot, explorer and hero!

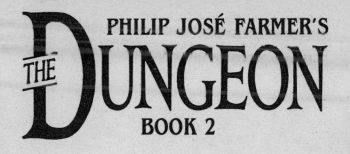

PHILIP JOSÉ FARMER'S
THE DUNGEON
BOOK 2

THE
DARK
ABYSS
■
Bruce Coville

A BYRON PREISS BOOK

BANTAM BOOKS
TORONTO • NEW YORK • LONDON • SYDNEY • AUCKLAND

THE DARK ABYSS

A Bantam Spectra Book / February 1989

*Special thanks to Lou Aronica, Shawna McCarthy,
David M. Harris, and Mary Higgins.*

*Cover and interior art by Robert Gould.
Book and cover design by Alex Jay/Studio J.*

THE DUNGEON *is a trademark of Byron Preiss Visual Publications, Inc.*

ISBN 0-553-27640-9

Published simultaneously in the United States and Canada

---

*Bantam Books are published by Bantam Books, a division of Bantam
Doubleday Dell Publishing Group, Inc. Its trademark, consisting of
the words "Bantam Books" and the portrayal of a rooster, is Registered
in U.S. Patent and Trademark Office and in other countries. Marca
Registrada. Bantam Books, 666 Fifth Avenue, New York, New York 10103.*

PRINTED IN THE UNITED STATES OF AMERICA

O   0 9 8 7 6 5 4 3 2 1

for
Barbara Block

▪ Foreword ▪

Books should burn, not be burned.

What they do or is done to them depends upon the reader, the person who holds the book in his or her hand. Some books do indeed radiate a high heat, and blaze with a light that blinds but which, paradoxically, enables you to see as you never saw before. Some books glow with a gentle warmth, and you want to relish the mild fire again and again. Some are matches that drive away the cold and dark within a small area. These, when extinguished, cannot be relit. You light another match—that is, read another book—enjoy the not-too-bright light and faint fire. When it's out, you can't relight it, and you don't want to do so.

Then there are books that feel soggy when you first open them and are dripping by the time you finish them, if you do. They have put out whatever fire was in your mind.

Others, I'm sorry to say, give a pain akin to hemorrhoids.

The strange thing about all this is that the same book can turn into a soaked lump in the hands of one reader but be a blaze in the mind of another reader.

My own viewpoint is that a book can be judged objectively. Not, though, by any member of Homo sapiens. Perhaps, in heaven, there is an angel who, though among the elect, must still pay for his sins on Earth. He's given the job of reading every work of fiction produced on Earth. He must write reviews of these, all stored in celestial disks. All excellencies are noted. So are all flaws. Another angel, his sins even greater, must rewrite the stories to divine standards. When the original author gets to heaven, he or she must read the reviews and rewrites of his works. That's pain enough to reverberate through eternity. But this is, after all, heaven. The rewriter angel pats the sobbing creature on the head and says, "There, there. You did your best. That's what counts up here."

If the author asks what happens to writers who did not do their best, the angel says nothing but points to "down below." Way down below.

The above fantasy came to me as I sat down to write this foreword. Until my *tochis* touched the chair, I had no idea of what was roiling in the hinterlands of my brain, such as it is. But contact with the seat of the chair was a spark emitted by the closing of a switch. Truth will out, however strange its form.

What gave birth to the above was, I think, an eagerness and a sharp-edged curiosity to see the final result of this many-volumed book. *The Black Tower,* volume I of *The Dungeon* series, by Richard Lupoff, will be out in a few months. (I am writing the foreword for this second volume on April 27, 1988.) On my desk is a reproduction of the cover, superbly done by Robert Gould. I have not seen the interior illustrations, but I expect them to match the cover. This more than hints at the mystery and great adventure and the gruesome quest of the hero and the even more gruesome things beyond that phallic-shaped keyhole through which the hero (or is he the villain?) is about to enter. He is looking behind him to catch sight of anyone trying to sneak up on him. He is also looking at you, the reader, and daring you to follow him.

While I write this introduction to the book at hand, the Canadian Brass Basin Street group is playing "That's a Plenty" on my CFD 5. The music glows with satisfaction and joy, delight in the plenum of life. I hope that you find this volume and the preceding one—and the entire single book composed of these volumes—as full of joy in the many-faceted jewel of life as "That's a Plenty." I am optimistic that you will because of my own feeling that the *The Dungeon* is a plenum slowly filling with golden liquor. That is, it's not yet a plenum but has the potential of being one. The characters are certainly not enjoying themselves, but the reader should relish the adventure.

The writers, too, relish their project. They, like me, know the classics of both mainstream and science fiction, and they know the pulp works. My adventure stories have been a fusion of the forward-rushing spirit of the pulps tempered by the classics. Lupoff and Coville have the same approach, not because they were told to emulate mine but because they naturally would do so. And they are assured a place in heaven. They always do their best. No hackwork for them.

The aim of these is to enflesh, as it were, the *geist* infusing my works. Their works are not spinoffs of my fiction. They do not continue the worlds or characters I have created in earlier books. They do not attempt to imitate my style, which would be difficult, anyway, because I have more than one.

These *Dungeon* writers are feeding on the psyche, the philosophy, the themes of my science fiction adventure stories, though they will, of course, introduce their own during their development of their own works. Every person is unique. He or she has his own brand of amazing grace.

(I must note a side thought, the admirable restraint of Lupoff and Coville in not emulating my unfortunate penchant for puns. They've got class.)

What are the themes, the philosophy, the spirit of my works?

They are:

1. Always, well, almost always, the drive of the protagonist from the Known to the Unknown. Richard Francis Burton, the main character in my Riverworld series, says, "Some of you have asked why we should set out for a goal that lies we know not how far away or that might not even exist. I will tell you that we are setting sail because the unknown exists and we would make it the known. That's all!"

It is not really *all*, but that desire is the prime drive.

2. For every current, there is a countercurrent. Thus, our *Dungeon* protagonist, Clive Folliot, is the reverse of the uneasy-at-home and ever-wandering Burton. He finds himself in the Unknown, not because he longed to know it but because he was compelled to find his lost twin. If it were not for that unavoidable quest, he would have been content to stay embedded in the Known. There is no indication so far that he has any wish to reside here (the Unknown) or to push on into it because he has a Burtonian curiosity.

But, by battling to rescue his twin and get back to the Earth he knew, he drives ever deeper into the dangerous and shadowy Unknown. However, only by striving to know the Unknown may a person really know the Known. That which had not been explored, but is now experienced, throws light on what we thought we knew but really did not know. The shadows of each realm are erased by the light each throws on the other. Unfortunately, as always happens in this check-and-balance universe of ours (and those of others, I'm sure), the two lights also cause more shadows. These had always existed but were not seen before the two lights crossed like swords of reality.

There is no end to the darkness which, at times, enables us to sleep and, at other times, keeps us wide awake and trembling.

The Dungeon is a world in which sleep, though often much needed, is unsafe.

I don't know how this series is going to end. I suspect that Folliot's character is going to change (for the better). He will not be exactly the same man he was when he plunged into the otherworld. He may even find that the Earth he knew is repulsive and go forth from the world of the Black Tower to look for a world better than either of the two he knows. Or thinks he knows.

3. The dark continents of the physical world and of the mind of Homo sapiens. My protagonists often venture not only into the rock hardness of the unexplored but, while doing this, are on a safari into their own minds. They are penetrating two dark Africas. The lions and leopards, the cannibals, the hardships and

fevers, the lost races and cities of gold that are palpable are paralleled by those in the hero's psyche. In these situations, however, the physical and the mental are parallels that do meet.

Mainstream literature is Euclidean geometry; science fiction and fantasy, Riemannian. Mainstream is the algebra of the Known; science fiction and fantasy, of the Unknown.

The Dungeon has humans from many eras and non-humans/near-humans from many time periods and spatial locations. All brought together by some mysterious power(s) for some purpose unseen by those who have been transported. Or maybe the power(s) are doing this just for sinister fun or lust for power. Or maybe the bringing together of so many disparates is the result of some as yet unknown natural phenomenon. In any event, the Dungeonworld is very unpleasant for the involuntary immigrants. It makes urban Detroit look like a picnic at Sunnybrook Farm. The ruler of this world has many affinities with Ivan the Terrible. And, for all I know, Ivan may be the menacing power behind the dark throne.

4. Things are never what they seem. That is an oft-recurring theme in my stories. That idea is by no means original, but I base my premise on what I have observed on Earth. Even if nobody had ever put this forth, I would have formulated it. I did so when very young and before I read the books which had the premise. Thus, my own characters and those in this series often misread entities and situations. Sometimes, this is because the entities are purposely deceptive. Just as in real life. Or the protagonist does not know enough about the mess he's in to gauge its causes and complications correctly. Just as in real life. Also, the protagonist may not know his own true identity, not in the sense of being an amnesiac or the lost heir to millions but in the sense that he deceives himself. Self-images that have little to do with the person's real character are endemic among Homo sapiens. This self-deceiving can get you into more trouble than other people cause you or wish to cause you.

The first two volumes of this extended book show that clearly enough. Our hero is lucky in that others are diligent, even eager, to point out the difference between his idea of what he is and what they think is his true persona. They work on him like an ancient Olmec rubbing a well-formed statue from a block of crude jade.

5. Archetypes. Sometimes, rereading my own works, I recognize that I have unconsciously written something that came up through a direct pipeline from the hindbrain. These are archetypal images and situations. Some are personal icons; some, those which Jung and others attribute to humankind's collective unconscious. The two *Dungeon* volumes resonate with these. Item: the raft floating through twin cliffs in this work. These reflect the narrow gate of hell, the choice between Scylla and Charybdis. Or, if you wish, the strait passage from womb to birth or from death to the afterlife. And there are, in both works, trolls under the bridge. How often, during a troubled sleep, has my mind, fishing in the deep dark moat around the black tower of night, hooked into one of the nightmare creatures. And then watched, terror stricken, these creatures unhook themselves and leap at me just before I awoke.

Also, I notice on rereading my works that I have used the underground motif, the tunnels and caves deep beneath the earth, too often for it to be coincidental. Though, maybe that's because most of my writing has been done in basements.

6. The grand adventure. No matter what my main theme, that is the drive of all my longer works.

There are other elements I could expand in this essay: nonhuman-human sex (some of that in Coville's work), the multilevels of plot and character (in both volumes), the questions of the existence of free will and of the afterlife (are Fols adventures making him less of a socially conditioned robot, and is the Dungeon-world another universe or an afterlife, a real Hell?), the condemnation and praise of religion, sometimes in the same book, and other elements I won't mention in this essay. The big thing is the story. We're just like the cavemen who huddled before the fire at night and listened to the tribe's story-teller. Their stories and ours may be somewhat different. But ours takes the form of the big leap into the Unknown and the battle for survival against the exotic others (though this includes one's self) and the mystery to be explained.

Always, in both a plot sense and a religious sense, The Mystery.

CHAPTER ONE

Flight

Some are called to the Dungeon
Still others come by choice;
Yet before the end each must heed
The power of His dark voice.

The words were uttered in a way that made Clive Folliot think of a priest offering an invocation. But any aura of holiness about the man who had spoken them was dispelled by the gleaming American Navy Colt revolver he was pointing at Clive's chest.

Without taking his eyes from Clive, the stranger reached down with his free hand and closed the large, leatherbound book in which he had been writing. Clive could see powerful muscles move and shift beneath the man's beautifully tailored, Victorian-era jacket.

"Where is my brother?" asked Clive.

The man shrugged. "Your twin is too curious for his own good. Eventually, of course, he will pay a heavy price for that trait."

Clive Folliot stared into the stranger's eyes, gray eyes into green. "And what will that price be?" he asked. As he spoke he wondered—not for the first time—what Neville's recklessness had gotten them into.

The man ignored Clive's question. "Take off the crown," he said, gesturing toward Clive's forehead with the barrel of the revolver.

Clive hesitated. Other than the fact that it had been placed upon his head by two women he cared for—'Nrrc'kth and Annabelle Leigh—the crown had no personal value to him. However, the fact that it had begun to glow when it touched his brow had convinced the residents of this strange castle that Clive was their true ruler—a belief he could surely use to his advantage if he managed to get out of this room alive.

"Hurry!" said the stranger, waving his gun. "I'm in no mood to wait."

As if to emphasize his point, he tightened his finger on the trigger of the revolver. But as he did so, he broke eye contact for the first time since he had stood up, glancing beyond Clive to the open door where he had entered.

Was there a hint of nervousness in his glance?

Clive raised his hands to lift the crown. Though he moved slowly, his mind was racing. If the man wanted the crown, it must have some significance, some meaning beyond just this castle.

Could it be a key to the mysteries of the Dungeon?

Clive found himself less and less willing to hand over the crown.

"Do I have to kill you?" asked the stranger, in a tone so civilized he might have been asking if Clive preferred one lump of sugar or two.

Clive took the crown from his head. He was interested to see that it still glowed; he had assumed that when he removed it it would become invisible once more, as it had been when worn by Annie.

Holding the crown before him, he stepped toward the man. As he moved, he tried to gauge the man's strength and speed, wondering if he could manage to strike away the pistol and fight him hand to hand.

"Stop there," said the man, waving the gun once more. With his free hand, he lifted the large book in which he had been writing. "Put the crown here," he said.

Clive placed the crown on the cover of the book. He tensed his muscles, preparing to make his move. But to his astonishment the man closed his eyes, whispered a word, and began to fade out of sight.

"Wait!" yelled Clive. He lunged toward the stranger. It was too late: man, crown, book, and revolver had all vanished. Clive's arms closed on empty air, and he found himself sprawled gracelessly across the paper-strewn desk.

"Odd sort of chap," said a familiar voice from behind him. "Probably be a big hit in the music halls back home, with that disappearing bit of his. I wonder if it's hard to learn. Are you all right, sah?"

Clive turned to see his old batman, Quartermaster Sergeant Horace Hamilton Smythe, standing in the doorway. The man crossed the room and extended a hand to help Clive to his feet.

"Except for my dignity, I'm just fine," said Clive. "Though I would have appreciated it if you could have arrived a few moments earlier."

"Sorry, sah," said Horace, completely deadpan. "We did our best. But you led us a merry chase."

Clive shook his head. "A rude end to my own coronation, I must confess," he said, referring to the impromptu ceremony that had been going on in the castle's courtroom. "But when I heard that villain N'wrbb behind me, I figured it was a safe bet he was up to no good."

A scream of dismay cut off Horace's answer. "The crown! You have lost the crown!"

It came from 'Nrrc'kth, who had followed Horace into the room, along with the other members of Clive's inner circle. She seemed to stagger. The muscular old woman called Gram reached out to steady her charge. Her ice-white skin more pale than ever, 'Nrrc'kth repeated dully, "Clive, you have lost the crown."

"You'd think she was the one who found it," said Annabelle Leigh. The dark-haired young woman stood at the door, leaning against the frame.

Clive was surprised to see the girl he had once known as User Annie. Above, in the castle courtroom, she had appeared exhausted—a situation he was relatively certain came about from the overuse of her Baalbec A-9, a computer device powered by her own body. He could not imagine that she would have had the strength to keep up with the breakneck race through the castle corridors that had led the group to this room. Then he realized that she must have been carried by Finnbogg, the powerful, mastiff-jawed dwarf who now crouched beside her, panting and looking up at her with adoration in his enormous brown eyes.

"This entire episode would have been avoided if you had killed N'wrbb when you had the chance."

Clive glanced to his right. Chang Guafe, the newest addition to their group, seemed to be radiating disapproval. It was all Clive could do to suppress a shudder. The creature—the *cyborg,* if he remembered Annie's term correctly—was a monstrous amalgamation of flesh and blood and mechanical parts. He was a superb fighter. But Clive had begun to suspect that neither pity nor compassion were to be found among Chang Guafe's many components.

"I think we'd better save this argument for later," said Horace. "From the sound of things, we're about to have company."

Clive looked past Chang Guafe. Horace was standing beside Annie, in the doorway where the group had entered. From beyond he could hear a babble of angry voices.

"Our people?" he asked hopefully.

Possible, said a voice in his head. *But more likely some of N'wrbb's remaining allies.*

Clive turned to the source of the voice and nodded.

Shriek nodded back. Her red eyes—spider's eyes—gleamed in the gaslight. She stood well over seven feet, towering above the small Portuguese sailor named Tomàs who stood beside her.

" 'Nrrc'kth," said Clive, "you were lady of the castle. Do you know another way out of here?"

Ripples of green hair shimmered over chalk-white shoulders as 'Nrrc'kth shook her head. "We are very deep in the catacombs," she said. "Very deep. I have never been here."

Clive looked around the room, marveling again at the Victorian study hidden here in the depths of this strange castle. Though the room contained two other doors, he had no idea where they led—and no interest in leading the group into a cul-de-sac where they could be cut down. "Horace, do you have any idea how many are out there?"

Horace Hamilton Smythe peered around the edge of the doorframe. "Can't see yet, gov'nor," he said. "But from the sound, I'd say it's a fair-sized mob."

"All right, we'll try the other doors," said Clive, at the same time wondering how long the group would follow him without questioning his leadership. He could be sure of Horace, of course. Some of the others, however, might present a problem. For an instant the idea that one of them might actually make a better leader for the group flashed through his mind. But the concept was so alien to his training as a British officer that it could find no purchase, and it rapidly faded away. Even so, Clive was painfully aware that if Neville were here, instead of himself, the question of leadership would never arise; Neville would be in charge, and that would be that.

"Shriek, Chang Guafe—try the doors."

The choice was natural, since with either creature it made no difference whether the door was locked. Chang Guafe's was not. Shriek's was, but the spider woman simply grabbed the frame with three arms—the fourth had been lost during the battle outside the castle—and pulled the door out of the wall.

"Closet," she said, clicking her mandibles. "No way out here."

Chang Guafe had had better luck. The cyborg's door opened into a small cloakroom, the cloakroom had another door at the back of it, which provided access to a narrow passage.

Clive was not surprised. He couldn't imagine his brother not leaving himself an escape route.

"Chang Guafe, you go first. Horace, you follow him. Then you, 'Nrrc'kth." He continued to deploy his people, with Finnbogg and Annabelle Leigh in the center and himself and Shriek covering the rear. Even in the midst of the confusion Clive had time to feel pleased with his arrangement. Chang Guafe's still unexplored mechanical abilities made him the logical one to lead the retreat; he knew, for instance, that if they were trapped in a dark tunnel the cyborg could provide artificial light. And Shriek's ability to alter her internal chemistry to make the spiky hairs covering her body poisonous, combined with her skill in throwing them, made her a lethal fighter. With Clive's own swordsmanship, the two of them could hold off the attackers longer than anyone else in the group. His only real worry was Tomàs. In watching the little sailor he had discovered that for all his bold talk, the man was not really a fighter. No time to worry about that now! The mob in the hallway was nearly on them, and there was nothing else he could do.

Pushing Tomàs ahead of him, Clive closed the door and threw the bolt. He doubted it would hold the crowd for more than four or five seconds.

But in a situation like this, four or five seconds could mean the difference between life and death.

CHAPTER TWO

Green Hell

On Midsummer's Eve of 1845, the year that Clive and Neville Folliot turned ten, their father took them to visit a country estate belonging to a friend of the family. Behind the ancient manor house sprawled an enormous hedge maze, planted nearly a century before. In the early hours of the evening Lord Tewkesbury walked his sons to the entrance of the maze and told them that, if they wished, they could go inside to play. Neville had been enthusiastic, Clive wary; it had not really surprised him when, less than five minutes after they entered the maze, Neville shot ahead of him and disappeared.

Even without Neville, or perhaps because of Neville's absence, Clive had found it pleasant to wander through the cool, dark green corridors created by the towering hedges. But as the hours that followed Neville's disappearance rolled on, Clive began a slow but certain emotional progression, from mild discomfort to anger to fear to terror to a sense that he had been chosen, for reasons he could not understand, to be given a foretaste of hell.

The discomfort was easy to deal with; life with Neville had made that feeling almost a daily experience. Anger was not much different. But as time went on, as he stumbled from cul-de-sac to blind alley, young Clive began to feel a kind of fear that was less familiar. He was not afraid he was going to die (an emotion that, even at ten, he had experienced more than once after loyally following his impetuous twin into some contretemps or another). Clive's fear now was more than he would live, and never be allowed out of this place. It was a fear that intensified every time he found himself passing the same small grotto—a grassy opening where a bubbling fountain in a moss-encrusted basin was watched over by a leering statue of Pan—without ever seeming to come at it from the same direction.

Some part of Clive knew his fear to be irrational. But that knowledge did not make the fear any less compelling. Nor did the fact that he *could* rationally believe his father would be willing to leave him in the maze until he found his own way out—willing to leave him overnight, if that was what it required.

Twice he heard his brother laughing somewhere ahead of him. Once Neville's voice came directly through the hedge. Then he seemed to disappear altogether.

As the evening wore on, Clive discovered some of the maze's more unpleasant secrets. Rounding an innocent-looking corner, he found himself face to face with a hideous statue. Its demonic features, made all the more terrifying by the lengthening shadows, seemed to carry a hint of something waiting, a dark promise of some terrifying change that would come with full night. Once he found a small door, only shoulder high. Seized with a sudden hope that it would free him from this green hell, Clive pulled the door open, then began to shriek when something made of fur and bones sprang out at him. The discovery that it was only a construct, mounted on a spring, did nothing to still the trembling that had overtaken him.

He heard laughter. Neville again? Or someone else? Given his experience so far, it was all too easy to believe that someone, or some*thing*, could sneak in here and stay for years without being detected, the only hint of its existence the sad fact that occasionally a small boy would go into the maze and never come out again.

He began to run. He heard laughter around the corners, and a faint voice calling his name. "Clive . . . Clive, we're waiting for you."

Who was waiting for him? Neville and his father? Or the creatures of the maze?

He ran faster. The shadows grew deeper. The leaves whispered and rustled around him, but he did not know if it was only the evening breeze or something else that passed among the branches. Reckless with fear, he careened from side to side, scratches blossoming like measles across his hands and face. He was gasping with exertion, each breath raw and rasping in his throat. Tears poured down his face, the salt stinging the scratches. The smells of roses and rot mingled oddly in the heavy evening air. He stumbled over a rock, and vomited as he hit the ground.

He lay there and wept.

It grew darker.

"Clive. Clive!"

The voice that whispered urgently to him from the other side of the hedge was not one he had ever heard before. He lifted his head from the ground. "Who are you?" he whispered.

"You'll find out someday. Right now we have to get you out of here. Stand up."

Clive did as he was told.

"Go straight ahead until you come to the second opening on your right. Go right, then left, then right. That will take you back to the Grotto of the Pan. Wait there for me."

Clive brushed himself off and began to walk. It was dark and hard to see. Winged insects battered against him, smaller ones sticking in the sweat on his neck and the vomit that still clung to his chin despite his attempts to wipe it away.

He came to the grotto. A gibbous moon had cleared the top of the hedge, creating pools of silver and shadows all its own. In the argent light Pan seemed to leer more wickedly than ever. When he saw the statue in the moonlight, Clive felt something lurch in the pit of his stomach; it was not until years later that he recognized it as the first stirring of his own adolescent sexuality.

He went to the mossy basin and used the bubbling water to lave his face and arms. It was cool and sweet against his scratched, sweaty skin. He took off his shirt, washed more completely, shook himself, then used the shirt as a towel for the water that remained.

Where was his unknown friend?

As if in answer to the thought, the voice came from behind the hedge: "It's good that I don't have to tell you everything. Cleaning up was the reason I brought you here. You should look as collected and casual as possible when you see your father."

Something about the voice made him feel safe, and Clive felt the trembling in his fingers lessen as he buttoned his shirt.

"Who are you?" he asked again.

"You may face the moon," said the voice, ignoring his question. "Or you can have it at your left shoulder."

"What do you mean?" asked Clive.

But there was no answer.

He faced the moon and began to walk. When a turn would place it at his left shoulder, he took it. When it did not, he moved on. Twice more the voice spoke to him, nothing of significance, simply an assurance that he was doing well.

After half an hour, he reached the end of the maze. As he was about to leave, the voice spoke to him for the last time.

"Clive!" He stopped to listen. "Two things. First, always remember to look for the pattern."

Clive nodded. When the voice didn't speak he said, "What else?"

"Learn to play chess!"

The comment was so unexpected that he snorted. "Who are you?" he asked for the third time.

There was no answer.

He stepped out of the maze. His father was sitting on a wrought-iron bench, legs crossed, cane over his lap, pipe clenched between his teeth. A line of smoke was curling around his head. Behind Lord Tewkesbury the close-cropped lawn rolled on like a sea of silver. Neville stood at the end of the bench, smiling contentedly. Beside him was a girl in a long white dress. When Clive stepped out of the maze they began to applaud.

It was in that moment that Clive finally accepted the

fact that, for whatever reason, he would always have to work harder than Neville. Whether it was a punishment for the sins of a past life, an accident of the stars at their birth, or simply the world asserting its orneriness, things would forever come more easily to his brother. For that one moment Clive hated his twin with a purity of feeling he was never able to achieve again.

The next day he began to learn to play chess.

That had been nearly twenty-three years ago. Clive had never learned who it was that led him out of the maze, though for years he had listened for that voice, hoping to thank his unknown benefactor. Later, when he entered the military, he had done his best to forget the entire incident. Terror was unbecoming to an officer. But now, barreling down the winding corridors that snaked beneath the castle of N'wrbb Crrd'f, pursued by a mob of that ice-white lord's angry supporters, Clive suddenly felt as he had in the maze that midsummer night. It seemed there was danger all around, that no turn was safe, no corridor without its perils.

And then it struck him that not only these catacombs but this entire world was much like that terrible maze.

Clive Folliot was not a timid man. But he had long ago learned that emotions never died. Like a disease that went into remission, they might fade from memory without ever truly disappearing. Somewhere in the heart or the head, in the blood or the bone, they lay waiting for the signal that would call them back to life. More resilient than Lazarus, they needed no master's call for resurrection—merely the trigger of a familiar sight, or sound, or smell.

So it was that as he ran through the twisting tunnel, Clive's childhood terror came lurching back to life, and he felt the strangling clutch of the old fear that he would be trapped in this terrible place forever. The feeling was as sudden and stark as a plunge into icy water, and for an instant he could not breathe.

Shriek, who was behind him, saw him stumble. She grabbed his elbow with her remaining lower arm, keeping him on his feet. It wasn't until days later that Clive recognized the irony in having a touch of kindness from a creature uglier than any his imagination had conjured up that night in the maze be the thing that helped him fight back his crippling terror.

They ran on.

The corridor they traveled through had dark blue walls formed from some glasslike substance. It was no more straight than a snake in motion, curving now to the left and now to the right in such a way that it made it impossible to tell how far they were ahead of their pursuers. In the center of the ceiling a thin strip of light blue material, about the width of a man's hand, glowed faintly. This was the only light.

Ahead, Clive could see a place where the corridor forked. He would leave it to Chang Guafe to choose the way.

The cyborg headed to the right.

That was fine with Clive. At this stage one direction seemed as good as another. Or at least it did until he reached the fork himself, glanced to the left, and saw a broad-shouldered man with thick, chestnut-colored hair dart around the corner.

Neville! He couldn't be positive it was his twin. But neither could he take the chance that it wasn't.

"Come back!" he yelled, trying to stop both Neville and the rest of his band with a single command.

"What is it?" clicked Shriek, who had stopped beside him.

"I think I saw Neville." Clive panted. "We have to go this way."

Shriek looked to the right. "The others are still running. I don't know if you can get them back."

Clive hesitated, then quickly realized that in doing so he might be lost. For the first of their pursuers had come into sight.

He sighed.

They were even bigger than he had expected.

CHAPTER THREE

He Who Sleeps

He began to whimper. It was an unusual sound for a man who had once been called "the bravest soul on two continents." He had laughed uproariously when he heard that comment. But the Belgian explorer who had made the statement was in a position to know, and when it was repeated at a gathering of the most noted adventurers of the day, they simply nodded their heads and smiled.

Of course that was a long time ago; long before the endless dream had begun.

He whimpered again, reliving, as he did on a regular basis, the battle that was his last memory of any connection with an assurance of being alive. The nightmare was vivid, and so horrifying that it always pushed him toward the edge of consciousness as he struggled to be free of it: to the edge, but never over.

It wasn't the nightmare that made him whimper, though; it was the endless pain that accompanied it.

He did have occasional lucid moments when he tried to wake. But his rebellious mind always refused to make the transition; indeed, the very thought of waking seemed to set off a mechanism that would plunge him back into the dream, some deep part of him deciding the dream was preferable to confronting the pain in a waking state.

It was not all bad. Occasionally the dreams were suffused with a warm pleasure that was almost orgasmic. But more often they were terrifying, more horrific than even the nightmares he had experienced as a child after seeing his father mauled, and killed, by a giant cat.

Again he whimpered, as he tried to escape from the strange sleep. For some reason it seemed more urgent than ever that he wake.

But to wake proved impossible—until at last the pain began in earnest, pain so intense that the escape of sleep was stripped away, like a scab being pulled off a wound. Now he wished that he could retreat back into the dreams, which he realized had been a refuge from a pain that had not ceased since he had been swallowed by the creature that had attacked them as they crossed the bridge over the great chasm of Q'oorna. But just as the pain had driven him into that state, its increased intensity now forced him back out of it.

Lightning seemed to sear through his brain as the terrible pressure on his head grew even stronger. He groaned, wondering if he was about to die, or indeed if he was dead already.

And still the slow grinding increased.

He tried to scream, but nothing happened.

No sound.

How long was it since he had heard anything?

God, the pain! It felt like his skull was being crushed. His body trembled and he tried to lash out, wrench himself free of whatever was causing this terrible agony.

Nothing happened. He had no sense of movement. In fact, other than the pain, he had no sense that he was even attached to a body.

Maybe the Christians were right, he thought, in one of the lucid moments that came between the crests of agony. It was an appalling thought. But once conceived, it would not go away. Was this Hell? Could this agony possibly be meant to go on forever?

He remembered the missionaries chanting, "The Lord thy God is a merciful God." It had always amused him that the words were usually a prelude to some graphic description of the horrors awaiting those who did not behave just exactly as the merciful god demanded.

He had been beaten once, for laughing at the missionaries' merciful god.

Mercy! he thought in desperation, just before the next wave of pain tore a soundless scream from a throat he was no longer sure existed.

If he was alive, he would have wished himself dead. But he wasn't sure that hadn't happened already.

Mercy, he pleaded again in his mind.

But the pain, indifferent to his plea, just kept getting worse.

· CHAPTER FOUR ·

Blue Battle

Clive dithered, and cursed himself for dithering. His friends had disappeared down one corridor. Someone who might well be Neville had disappeared down the other. And hurtling toward him was a band of N'wrbb's bloodthirsty gnomes.

"Run left, run right, or stand and fight!"

The memory of the childhood taunt, chanted by Neville whenever he could drive his twin to the edge of fisticuffs, rang in Clive's ears.

He gave up dithering and damned himself for a fool. How much of this dilemma came from the fact that he had abdicated his position as leader of the group by placing Chang Guafe at the front of their procession? It had seemed like a good idea at the time. But it left the cyborg making the decisions—exactly what Clive should be doing if he was to maintain any sense of leadership.

And he was determined to be the leader. He had let events push him forward as they would for far too long—both here in the Dungeon and out in the real world.

"Run left," he shouted to Shriek, heading in that direction himself.

The giant arachnid clicked her mandibles in concern, but followed Clive's lead.

The gnomes came pouring in behind them.

"Get ready to fight," gasped Clive, as they careened down the slick blue corridor.

It was a needless remark. Shriek was always ready to fight.

They reached one of the places where the corridor narrowed and at Clive's command turned to join battle. His heart sank as he saw the enemy's numbers. Worse, the gnomes were accompanied now by a group of tall, red-haired warriors, clad only in kilts and leather harnesses that crisscrossed their broad, hairy chests.

The numbers appeared overwhelming. But Clive knew they couldn't outrun their pursuers indefinitely, and he preferred to fight at this bottleneck, where no more than three or four of the enemy could face them at any one time, than to be caught in some larger space where they could be surrounded.

Shriek struck the first blow. It was not physical but auditory, and Clive smiled to see the dismay that overcame their enemies as his spidery comrade loosed her strange, ululating battle cry. Several of them stopped to clap their hands over their ears, trying to hold out the waves of piercing sound. Others, braver (or possibly more deaf) came surging forward.

Clive drew sword and entered battle. *Monsieur D'Artagnan would have loved this situation!* he thought to himself, as his blade plunged through the heart of an ax-wielding gnome. Alexandre Dumas's book about the legendary Frenchman had been among Clive's favorite reading material when he was younger, and as a boy he had often imagined himself facing such implacable odds. But never in such a bizarre place, against such an odd assortment of foes!

Another gnome scrambled over the body of his fallen comrade. Clive jumped back as the little man's ax made an arc that would have sliced him off at the knees had he remained standing still. He thrust forward with his sword, but the gnome was gone, plucked from the floor by the mighty Shriek, who had reached sideways with her lower arm. Clive felt a spatter of hot liquid as Shriek dashed the little man against the blue wall. At the same time another gnome had the misfortune to step into the continuing thrust of Clive's sword. He screamed as he died. Clive pulled the bloody blade out of the gnome's body and slashed at one of his comrades.

Beside him, Shriek fought on with her usual formidable efficiency. While her upper two arms were busy battling the gnomes at the front of the pack, she was using her single lower arm to pluck long, stiff hairs—spikes, almost—from her abdomen. She then flung the hairs at the foe. Filled with a quick-acting poison that could drop a man in a matter of seconds, the weapons seemed particularly effective against the gnomes, and their blackened, bloating bodies could be seen not only at her feet but scattered back through the crowd of yammering warriors.

And her strange battle cry warbled on.

Unfortunately, not all species have the same body chemistry, and the first time one of Shriek's projectiles embedded itself in the shoulder of one of the tall, red-haired warriors he simply grinned, plucked it out, and tossed it over his shoulder.

The action brought a cry of outrage from Shriek that threatened to crack the blue walls of the corridor where they were fighting. A few of the gnomes cowered. Others rushed forward to take their place. And the red-haired warriors began their own advance, striding over those gnomes who had fallen to Shriek's toxins, simply pushing others aside. Blue eyes and silvery swords seemed to shine with the same hungry light. Clive swallowed. The shortest of the redheads was easily a foot taller than himself, with a reach proportionate to his height. If his gambit didn't pay off soon, it looked like things would end right here.

Most of the gnomes had drawn back. Clive decapitated a last persistent battler, feeling a little sick as the gnome, whose ax had come within an inch of laying open his stomach, fell to the floor in two pieces. The face that stared up at him had become childlike in death. Suddenly it seemed a terrible thing to be battling people so much smaller than himself. Yet these men, if men they were, gave every indication that they would gladly have sliced him to ribbons if given the chance.

Now someone else was about to have a chance.

He felt a touch on his shoulder.

Courage, Clive Folliot, Shriek thought at him, using

her ability to communicate wordlessly—an ability she had created for every member of their group when physical contact was established. *Courage. I will try other toxins on these men. Battle bravely!* Then her battle cry rang out, and he not only heard it, he felt it—felt, but did not understand, for other than an increased sexuality, what Shriek experienced when she went into battle was so utterly alien to his English sensibilities that even communicated directly, without the baffle of words, he could not comprehend it.

Yet something seemed to infuse him, a rage and a passion that gave him both strength and a reckless disregard for his own life, the kind of disregard that allows a man to battle brilliantly—until the moment he is cut down.

A battle cry tore from somewhere deep within him. "God for Harry, England, and Saint George!" Swinging his blade back above his head, Clive rushed forward to strike the first blow, and felt a heady rush of satisfaction as a burly seven-footer toppled to his onslaught.

Now the narrowness of the corridor helped them even more than it had in battling the gnomes, for the redheads were too big to fight effectively two abreast. Even so, their numbers were so great—and their own battle haze so powerful—that Clive and Shriek found themselves being forced backward.

Again and again the arachnid's eerie cry echoed through the dim blue corridor. Again and again a warrior fell, only to have another take his place. Again and again they were forced slowly, inexorably back, back around a curve that opened, Clive suddenly realized, into a large round chamber.

Despair gripped him. Once they entered that space, the battle—and most assuredly his own life with it— would be ended. In the open the tall redheads would be able to encircle the two of them. Then they could chop them down from behind as easily as a child could pluck a pair of daisies.

"Forward!" he cried to Shriek, and as she picked up one of the warriors with her powerful upper arms and hurled him against his fellows they actually managed to regain a few feet. But the numbers were too overwhelming, and again they found themselves being forced back toward the chamber.

Clive tried to fight the impulse to keep glancing over his shoulder, knowing that every time he did he was open to attack. Even so, he stole a glance in the next momentary lull and almost threw down his sword in despair. They were inches from the chamber.

The redhead closest to him saw the glance, read Clive's reaction, and smiled coldly, revealing a mouthful of pointed teeth that would have seemed more appropriate in a hunting animal. He pressed his advantage. Clive stumbled, but before he hit the floor Shriek reached out to grab him. She pushed him to his feet, then screamed in rage and agony as a flash of silver went by her side, reopening the spot where her arm had been severed. Clive felt a moment of sickness as he saw the green ichor that oozed from her wound. At the same time he was filled with a renewed rage, and it gave him the strength to thrust forward and dispatch the warrior who had injured Shriek.

Now a new tone filled the spider creature's battle cry, a sharper edge, anger and pain mixed in one terrible sound that scraped and screeched along the edges of the corridor.

But Shriek was flagging. Clive got his sword caught in the leather harness of the next warrior, who drove forward even as the blood was spurting from his side. The chamber was inches behind them.

And then Clive's gambit finally paid off.

From behind the foe came a new sound, a basso profundo rumbling that with a little effort could be understood as Finnbogg's rendition of "God Save the Queen"—one of the songs the mastiff-jawed dwarf preferred to sing as he went plunging into battle.

And plunge he did, bursting into the rear flank with a ferocious assault of teeth and fists that sent gnomes sailing in all directions, whether they were actually running from this sudden nemesis or being flung upward as Finnbogg went rampaging through their midst.

Behind Finnbogg came the others: Horace and User

Annie, Chang Guafe and Tomàs, Gram and 'Nrrc'kth. Caught in the jaws of a late-springing trap, the dark-haired gnomes and the redheaded giants fought desperately. But the impact of Finnbogg's slavering attack had created a confusion that was only increased by the cold, methodical way in which Chang Guafe selected and dispatched his victims.

In the momentary respite he gained when his immediate opponents were distracted by the chaos behind them Clive realized that he had a new problem. The advantage of the narrow corridor, if not exactly turned against them, made it almost impossible to end this battle without the total destruction of one side or the other. Unless he could somehow get the enemy to surrender, they would have to fight on until there were none left standing. He was confident his group could win. He was less confident they could do so without serious casualties. Beyond that was the fact that he really had no wish to continue the carnage. Bloodshed for the sake of bloodshed was not his way.

"Lay down your swords," cried Clive. "Lay down your swords and we'll let you go!"

But his voice could not be heard above the chaos. The narrow confines of the hall echoed with Shriek's ululations, Finnbogg's gravelly singing, the moans of the wounded, and the clash of steel on steel. The blue walls were spattered with red, and the hot smell of blood filled the air.

Clive thought he was going to be sick.

"Lay down your swords!" he cried again, uncertain whether the redheads could even understand him. The battle raged on. Between Chang Guafe and Finnbogg the rear action had turned into a rout. The redheads were ready to retreat, but their path was blocked. They turned and pressed back toward Clive and Shriek. Shriek, mad with battle lust, grabbed the first of them and pulled him to her face. Her mandibles sliced his neck and blood spattered across her chest. Clive moved back beside her, creating an opening in the passage. The redheads took advantage of the opening and began to stream past them. Shriek, distracted by her current victim, did nothing to stop them at first. When she discarded the husk of the man she had just killed she screamed in rage. "Why do you let them escape?" she cried, grabbing another of the redheads. Clive heard a sickening snap that made him think she had probably broken one, or both, of the man's arms.

The enemy had nearly finished their flight. "Stay, Finnbogg," cried Clive as the last of the men ran past. Finnbogg, who had been snapping at their heels with his massive jaws, came to a halt beside Clive as if he had been pulled in by some invisible leash. He began baying like a hound, bouncing now on two feet, now on all fours, snapping and snarling but not moving forward another inch.

Chang Guafe, who had been fighting next to Finn-bogg, almost tripped over the raging dwarf. "Fool," he said to Clive. His voice was as cold as always, but it was the closest Clive had come to sensing anger from the cyborg. "Why do you let them go?"

"Our quarrel is not with them," said Clive. "It is with N'wrbb. There is nothing to be gained by killing them."

"There is nothing to be lost," said Chang Guafe, in such a matter-of-fact way that Clive knew he could never explain his feelings to the cyborg. He looked from Chang Guafe to Finnbogg. The dwarf was standing again, which placed his head a few inches below Clive's shoulder. A menacing growl still rumbled in his chest as he stared down the corridor where their enemies had fled. Clive glanced to his right. Shriek, trembling with rage, the unconscious red-haired warrior still dangling from her upper arms, was staring at him with anger and astonishment. He shook his head. How could he explain his feelings in such a way that they would not think him either totally mad or simply a spineless coward?

It was a relief to have the others join them. The sight of Horace, Annie, and Tomàs seemed to provide a sense of reality, a connection to a world he remembered as being more sensible than this mad Dungeon. Gram and 'Nrrc'kth were with them, their strange combination of human form with alabaster skin and emerald hair creating a kind of bridge from what the Englishman thought of as "real people" to the bizarre appearance of his other companions. He noticed that Gram's burly forearms were covered with blood, and realized with a start that she had been a full participant in the recently ended battle.

By consent they moved into the open area Clive had been so desperately trying to avoid a short time ago. The chamber was a nearly perfect circle, about twenty feet in diameter, formed of the same smooth blue material as the corridors. The strip of luminescent material that ran along the ceiling of the corridor extended to the center of the room, where it met four similar strips, each of which led to another corridor. Assuming they were not going to backtrack, they had four paths to choose from.

But they were not going to choose yet. It was clear that a confrontation was in the air. Clive would have insisted they press on in search of Neville. But whoever it was he had seen running down this corridor—Neville or simply someone who looked like him from behind—could have gone almost anywhere in the time they had lost fighting off the minions of N'wrbb.

"You are a sentimental fool, Folliot," said Chang Guafe. "There was nothing to be gained by sparing those men, and much to be lost."

Before Clive could answer, User Annie stepped into the argument. "Charge their blood to your own karma, 'borg. My ancestor has enough to answer for as it is."

"Karma?" asked the cyborg.

"Your cosmic checking account," said Annie. "The things you do this time around that you have to pay for in the next life."

Clive felt his stomach make a slight lurch as Guafe rearranged some of the metallic components running from his right eye to his shoulder. "Hope confused with fact creates folly and illusion," the cyborg said finally. "Those warriors were only people. They will not live again. Nor will you, or I, or Folliot."

"All the more reason to avoid unnecessary killing," said Clive.

A small, metallic tentacle emerged from the cyborg's neck and made an adjustment to a fold of metal covering his cheek. "People are only people," said Chang Guafe, while this work was in progress. "There will always be more where those came from. A few more or less will not make any difference in the long run. But it may in the short run. They may be regrouping even now, preparing to return and attack us. Or we may run into them on the way out. Sentiment and war do not go together. When you are attacked, it is war. You are sentimental, Folliot, which makes you a poor warrior."

Clive hesitated, uncertain of how to answer. The cyborg was correct, in a way. But he had never intended to be a warrior. He was a guardian of the empire. Which wasn't the same thing at all.

Or was it?

"Perhaps a poor warrior, but a better man," volunteered 'Nrrc'kth.

"Inferior by definition," responded Guafe. "Men are merely uncorrected products of natural forces. Any race of sufficient intelligence will take steps to improve itself."

"Is this how God has chosen to test me," wailed Tomàs, "by forcing me to listen to endless blasphemy?" He sat down, covered his ears, and began muttering a prayer in Portuguese.

"Poor little shit." Gram chuckled, running a blood-spattered hand through her white hair. "Wonder if he'll ever stop believing this God of his created all this to punish him for his wicked past. Seems like a lot of work for a pissant like him."

Clive realized it was time to assert himself. Past time, actually; if Neville had been here, the argument never would have progressed this far. "The point is," he said sharply, "as long as I am in charge of this party, I will be the one to make such decisions. Right now we have more important things to do than argue morality. To begin with—"

"Morality is an invention," interrupted Guafe. "Practicality is a fact, Leaders must be practical. You are not, and therefore should not lead."

Clive hesitated, trying to decide how to convince the cyborg that compassion and pragmatism could exist hand in hand. He briefly considered quoting Aesop's fable "The Lion and the Mouse," but quickly discarded the idea. Finally he was saved from himself by Horace, who jumped into the argument to inform Chang Guafe that nothing was less practical than an argument about leadership when things were still in peril.

Instantly, Clive understood what Horace was trying to do. If Chang Guafe had led him into a philosophical debate, he would have lost, no matter how brilliantly he argued. A real leader, someone like Neville, would not have been distracted by such issues at that time. *More than ten years,* thought Clive, *and Horace is still saving me from my own ineptitude.* For he was certain Smythe had seen the danger and stepped in to save him on purpose. Later, however, when he tried to thank the sergeant for the assistance, Smythe acted as if it had been entirely unintentional.

What bothered Clive was the nagging suspicion that Horace was trying to keep him in charge of the group for his own inscrutable reasons. Indeed, since he and the sergeant had first been reunited on board the *Empress Philippa,* Clive had never been entirely certain what sort of private intrigues enmeshed his old companion. Horace had been traveling in the guise of a Chinese mandarin at the time. The purpose behind that masquerade had remained an enigma—as had the motivation for every other persona Horace had assumed as their journey continued.

But whatever mysteries he was concealing, Horace Hamilton Smythe was a clever ally. When he turned his back on Chang Guafe, snapped off a smart salute to Clive, and said, "What next, sah?" in his finest soldier's manner, it ended decisively, if only momentarily, the conflict over leadership.

And left the bag firmly in Clive's hands. *What next, indeed?* he wondered, looking around the strange blue chamber. He had no idea where the man he had been pursuing might have gone. The material from which the corridors were formed was as hard as it was smooth, and retained no tracks of any kind.

On other occasions when they were stuck, they had turned to Neville's journal for assistance. Whether by science or by magic, his missing brother had continued to insert new messages in those pages, though generally they were so cryptic as to be of limited use at best. Anyway, when he had been taken into N'wrbb's castle, Clive had left the book with—

"Horace," he said, turning eagerly back to Smythe. "Do you still have my brother's journal?"

Horace's face seemed to sag. "I'm sorry, sah," he said morosely, "but I lost it during one of our battles. I tried to keep track of it. But it's hard to keep your mind on something like that when there's three or four blokes all trying to chop you into dog meat."

Clive nodded. Despite his disappointment, he clasped Horace on the shoulder. "I understand. And believe me, you're far more valuable to us this way than you would be as dog meat. Though I must say, I do wish we had a dog right now."

The thought struck both men simultaneously.

"Finnbogg," said Clive, turning to the still-growling dwarf. "How are you at tracking?"

"Good, good, very good," said Finnbogg eagerly. "Mighty Finnbogg has Mighty Nose. Can smell what no one else can smell, follow what no one else can follow— just like in the story of Snow White and Nose Red."

"You'll have to tell us that one soon," said Annie, who was constantly amused by the dwarf's version of familiar stories.

"But there were many men here," persisted Clive. "Can you sort out one scent from all these others?"

"Yes, yes," said Finnbogg. "Finnbogg's nose has mighty power!"

"One man came through here ahead of us," said Clive. "Not a dwarf. Not one of the giant redheads. He would have a different smell. See if you can find it."

Finnbogg moved back into the tunnel. Dropping to all fours, he began to sniff about. Occasionally he shook his head, causing his great jowls to flap and send slobber flying in all directions. In the dim blue light his enormous shoulders and upcurving fangs made the dwarf a truly imposing sight. Clive was reminded of the first time they had met the creature, at the base of the bridge of Q'oorna, and what a relief it had been to find that he was friendly. They never would have made it across the bridge without Finn's help. As it was, they had lost Sidi Bombay in the process—

Clive's thoughts were interrupted by a growl from Finnbogg. The dwarf came snuffling back out of the corridor and straight through their group, bowling over the desperately praying Tomàs—who happened to be kneeling in his path—as if he did not exist.

"Come on," said Clive, hauling Tomàs to his feet but addressing the group in general. "Let's move."

They followed Finnbogg into the corridor. Clive began to grow nervous as he realized the winding path was leading them deeper into the catacombs beneath N'wrbb's palace. He noticed the now familiar spiral of stars at several points along the way. The design seemed to pervade both the Great Dungeon, which was how he had come to think of this world—or worlds—and all the minor dungeons that they had managed to find along the way.

And still they traveled on. Clive felt his stomach gnawing at his backbone, announcing in no uncertain terms that it was time to eat.

He did his best to ignore it. The group was weary, most of them aching from the wounds they had received during their recent battles. Only Finnbogg, obsessed with following the scent of Clive's mysterious fugitive, seemed undaunted.

Yet, other than Tomàs's frequent supplications to his deity for release from this dream, there was little complaining. *They would have made good British soldiers,* thought Clive, as Finnbogg led them down another blue corridor. He wondered where they were in regard to N'wrbb's keep. Had they indeed managed to put some distance between it and themselves? Or were they simply traveling in circles underneath the castle? He was reminded again of the hedge maze of his youth, and wondered if they would ever find their way out.

He took consolation in the apparently logical idea that as long as they were following a trail they must, eventually, arrive somewhere else.

Finally even that consolation disappeared when the blue corridor they were following opened onto another chamber, where Finnbogg circled the floor with increasing distress until at last he sat down on his haunches and began to bay at the ceiling.

"Gone!" he cried. "Man-scent gone. Finnbogg failed. Mighty Finnbogg has let Clive down. Oh, dark, dark day for Finnbogg."

Clive looked around the chamber and reflected that suddenly the phrase "where in hell are we?" seemed a more accurate expression than he had ever imagined possible.

CHAPTER FIVE

Alone

"I am a man."

He repeated the phrase like a litany. It was, in fact, a prayer for sanity. Since he had awakened—how long ago?—the memory of his species was the only thing that seemed real to him.

What else was there? When he opened his eyes, he saw only a watery yellow light. Occasionally dark forms would move across the light, much like the specks that move across one's eyes when staring at the sky. The only difference was that these forms were larger and moved in a way that seemed more purposeful.

Those few forms were the extent of his perceptions. He could hear nothing, smell nothing, feel nothing.

So maybe he wasn't awake after all.

Maybe he wasn't even alive; just a disembodied consciousness floating in the ether. Would that make him a ghost? That didn't seem fair. Any ghost he had ever heard of could move about—if only to cause trouble.

But as near as he could make out, he had nothing to move. The unending pain seemed to indicate that he still had arms and legs, feet and hands. But if he did, he had no control over them at all.

He had long ago given up trying to scream. Nothing ever came out.

Solitude had never bothered him before. He had traveled for weeks, months sometimes, through some of the most remote regions of the world, places where it was a given that there would be no one to speak with.

But he had always known those times would end. Now he had no such assurance. For all he knew, he would be alone forever.

He would have wept, if he knew how.

He needed someone, anyone, to—to what? To talk to? He didn't seem able to talk anymore.

He needed to be in contact.

The next wave of pain came rolling over him.

But this time it didn't matter, at least not as much. Because just before it started, a voice began to whisper in his mind.

Hold fast, brave one. I am with you.

CHAPTER SIX

Ma-sand <Click>

As if being lost in a maze of catacombs beneath a medieval fortress on an alien world wasn't bad enough, Clive was rapidly becoming aware that they faced a new problem.

Shriek was in heat.

Actually, Clive thought he might even have been able to cope with a sexually aroused seven-foot-tall humanoid spider—or was it arachnoid human?—if it weren't for the fact that one of Shriek's particular talents was for empathic communication, and the related fact that she had already bound several members of the party into a web made not of silk but of spirit. This meant that they could often sense what the others were feeling, albeit in general terms—anger, joy, or fear being the most common things communicated. It also meant that when they chose, they could, by joining hands, experience a kind of mental communion that surpassed anything Clive had ever before experienced, or even heard of; a kind of telepathy that was leagues beyond the mysticism his friend George du Maurier had frequently described during midnight conversations around the fireplace at his club.

Yet they generally avoided this form of communication, for it was a link that allowed no secrets. Each one not only saw everything about the other, he shared everything—*everything!*—about himself. Since the first time it had happened Clive felt a twinge of embarrassment every time one of his more base thoughts floated to the surface of his mind. He had yearnings of which he was not proud, and fantasies that were surely not intended for his friends to share.

All that was bad enough. But now Shriek, the communicator, was broadcasting waves of sexual need that were creating new stirrings in his own blood, and presumably in the blood of everyone around him.

He first became aware of the problem while he was still trying to balance his need to maintain leadership with the reality that he had no idea which of the several available tunnels might lead them back to the surface. The suddenness of it reminded him of a day when he was thirteen. He and Neville had gone to a museum in London. As they wandered about, gazing at the paintings, he had been surprised to feel himself react to one picture not with his brain but with his groin. It was an experience both pleasant and mystifying, and not a little frightening. He felt as if a private part of his body had suddenly taken on a life of its own, independent of his control.

In time he had learned to identify, and to some extent control, his sexual urges. But now as he was standing, staring at the tunnels, he felt a warmth in his groin that was as unexpected, and inappropriate, as it had been that day in the museum. He had long ago accepted the fact that his rebellious body would intrude on his thoughts with little twitches of desire. But usually it was in idle moments—not when he was facing life-or-death decisions.

He tried to push the feeling away.

But it persisted. In fact, it was growing stronger. Clive was surprised. He knew the erotic was erratic, striking when and where it would. But he had been training himself to control it for nearly twenty years now. When he was a teenager, this kind of feeling had been overwhelming. Now he expected to be able to push it away, with the thought of savoring it more fully at some later time. But this feeling would not be pushed. He felt himself blush as the heat in his loins continued to grow.

"Ma-sand <click>," said Shriek, with a small moan.

"What?" asked Clive.

"Ma-sand <click>," she repeated. "It is a condition that occurs when our mating cycle coincides with a great battle. The lust we feel then is like no other. It is a condition to be desired, and feared."

She trembled as she spoke. The wound on her side had begun to ooze green again.

Clive glanced around. Only Chang Guafe seemed unaffected by Shriek's condition. Annie was pale and wide-eyed, a sheen of sweat glowing on her forehead. Tomàs was on his knees again, praying for deliverance from this new temptation. Finnbogg was running about in an agony of indecision, while Horace stood still, his eyes squeezed shut, as if wrestling with some internal devil. Unlike Horace, Gram's green eyes were wide open; she was staring at the sergeant with an obvious hunger.

Clive wondered if the older woman had the same ability as her niece. He glanced at 'Nrrc'kth, suddenly realizing that she represented the most pressing danger at this moment. He well remembered, from his first night in N'wrbb's keep, the power of her touch. It seemed to have an aphrodisiac quality all its own, as if her very body chemistry was designed to instill lust a man. The brush of her lips across his skin had been enough to lure him into an act of passion, never completed, that had resulted in the two of them being thrown into the prison beneath the palace. Now she was looking at him with an expression he remembered from that first encounter. He looked away nervously.

He had to get the group into motion. But how? Which way should they go?

The need emanating from Shriek, being re-created in his own body, made it impossible to think clearly.

"Shriek," he said desperately, "can you close it off?"

The spider woman shook her head miserably. "Ma-sand <click> has to run its course." A shudder rippled through her body, starting in the slender torso and moving in waves through the great abdomen. Her four powerful legs shook with the impact of her longing. A gout of green ichor spurted from the wound on her side.

With a wave of revulsion, Clive realized that in the intensity of her need, the arachnid was looking at him as a possible mate. He tried to hide the depth of his disgust, but it was clear from the hurt look that twisted her alien features she had absorbed his reaction. Damn creatures that could read your mind anyway. A man needed some privacy—especially in a situation like this!

On the other hand, a little telepathy could provide some useful information, as the horrified Folliot realized when the feedback from his link with Shriek filled his mind with pictures of her race in a mating frenzy. Caught in the grips of Ma-sand, Shriek was reliving her last great passion, which had ended, as Ma-sand always did, with the female consuming her mate. Suddenly the look of lust she had cast in Clive's direction took on new meaning, and he shuddered at the implications.

"Do not be disgusted, O Folliot," pleaded Shriek. "It is the way of our biology."

Another wave of longing moved through her body, causing the great abdomen to contract and then distend with her need.

"Biology," said Chang Guafe, his generally expressionless voice as close to expressing emotion—in this case, disgust—as Clive had yet heard it. "The ultimate in inefficiency. Folliot, are you going to lead us out of here, or must we stop for the orgy?"

The cyborg was right: the situation was degenerating rapidly. If Clive didn't do something to divert the erotic energy building up in the chamber, it was likely to culminate in a scene that would make some of the suppressed books he had read as a blushing youth seem tame.

But which way should they take? He couldn't think, couldn't concentrate. All he really wanted to do was take one of the women—Annie, 'Nrrc'kth, Gram, it really didn't matter at this point—back into one of the passages and perform wonderful, unspeakable acts until this unbearable longing was satisfied.

He grabbed his head between his hands, filled with self-loathing. For the love of heaven, what was he thinking of? Annie was his own great-great-granddaughter!

If only there were a pattern, a key, some kind of guide for him to follow.

The words whispered to him in the hedge maze so long ago seemed to ring in his ears: "Always remember to look for the pattern."

The pattern. What was the pattern? Was it the rule he had been given back in the maze? He whispered it to himself now:

"You may face the moon, or you can have it at your left shoulder."

That was all well and good, except there was no moon here. *Probably just as well, too,* he thought, taking a deep breath and trying to fight down the newest wave of lust sweeping through him. *It would likely just make things worse.* His mind, which, against his will, was replaying much of his own erotic history, threw up several memories of trysts made more thrilling by the presence of the moon and the stars. It was true. Bright lights in a dark sky had an undeniably arousing effect on him.

Bright lights in a dark sky!

No moon, no moon at all. But could not—ah, could not a spiral of stars be interpreted as a moon? Not literally, of course. But a circle of light in the sky. A circle of light in the sky!

You may face the moon, or you can have it at your left shoulder.

Clive began to run around the chamber like a madman, stopping before each corridor. "Not here, not here, not here," he muttered, his voice increasingly desperate. The others barely noticed him, so absorbed were they in their private needs.

He found the spiral of stars on the wall between the last two corridors. "You may face the moon, or you can have it at your left shoulder," he whispered. Then he turned and faced the others. "This way!" he commanded, in tones he would normally have reserved for dressing down the troops. Without waiting to see if they would follow, he started down the right-hand corridor, keeping the stars to his left.

CHAPTER SEVEN

The Ethics of Biology

As he trotted along one of the blue corridors, Clive reflected that he had no idea whether he had really discovered a key for escaping this underground maze. But he began to understand that there was a certain solace in having a tactic, even if it was the wrong one. He wondered (blasphemous thought) if the sense of security that came from having a plan, *any* plan, was a factor in some of the military idiocies he had witnessed over the last ten years.

Equally intriguing to him was the way in which the other members of the group had fallen in line once he began to march through the azure corridors with every indication that he knew what he was doing.

It hadn't happened instantly, of course. It was Horace, loyal as always, who first followed his lead. "Rum bit of business, that back there," he said to Clive when he had caught up with him.

Gram came next. While Clive would have preferred to believe that she was simply responding to his demonstration of leadership, he was honest enough to admit it was likely that her decision to follow him now was at least in part due to her current fixation on Sergeant Smythe. And even in their rather dire circumstances, Clive found some entertainment in observing his comrade's bemusement at having a broad-shouldered, emerald-haired woman of uncertain years eyeing him with amorous intent.

Annie and Tomàs had followed in short order, the latter now counting decades on his rosary, the former still pale and breathless. When Clive glanced back, the sight of Annie's dark eyes, slightly parted lips, and heaving bosom struck him as powerfully as had the painting that day in the museum. It took all his strength to turn away and continue walking.

Shortly afterward a melancholy howling told him that Finnbogg had joined the procession. *Poor fellow,* thought Clive. *If this kind of thing strikes him as powerfully as it did his ancestors he must be in misery—especially with no female Finnbogg in sight!*

A voice in his head whispered: *Only the tall woman and the cyborg are left, O Folliot. I will come last. Perhaps by hanging back I can keep from infecting the others with my need.*

It seems the best plan, Clive responded, even as he realized that this fleeting mental contact with the spider woman was restoking the fire in his loins. He closed his eyes and took several deep breaths. It helped, but not much.

In this way was Clive's small army reformed. The major change in the way they traveled was that where before they had been moving in close formation, they were now separated by wide intervals. *We're like mountain climbers on a horizontal slope,* thought Clive, *only instead of a rope, we're connected by strands of the mind.*

How his old friend du Maurier would have loved that!

The reason for the spacing was simple, of course. Each of them was trying both to give the others space, and at the same time to resist an urge that, once succumbed to, would leave them deeply humiliated, at the least.

Clive knew from previous conversations that Annie's views on such matters were far more liberal than his own. So it had come as somewhat of a relief to him that his great-great-granddaughter had not suggested that everyone just drop their inhibitions and have at it in the blue chamber. Maybe there was hope for her yet.

Actually it was Shriek he felt the most concern for, though it surprised him to find that he could feel compassion for anything so alien. It was hard to believe that the spider woman would not be intensely embarrassed over both her ordeal and the fact that she had broadcast her sexual longings—nay, *imposed* them—on the rest of the group. Even now, though he was trying not to, he could "see," through the strange connection she herself had created, how the impassioned creature was dragging her twitching abdomen around the chamber in an agony of longing.

Weep not for Shriek, O Folliot, the spider sent in her oddly archaic style. *My people learned long ago to accept their biology. We do not hate what we are, as your people seem to.*

Underlying this message was a sense of genuine bafflement that annoyed Clive. Who was this creature, to question the morality of his planet? To his chagrin, when he later tried to explain this to Annie, she snorted derisively and asked him who *he* was, to think that everyone on the planet felt the same way about sex that he did. Which was typical of the problems he had talking with his young descendant; she had a knack for making him feel vaguely guilty just for being alive.

Clive began to wonder how long Ma-sand generally lasted. Was it a brief flare of passion, or something more long term? He shuddered at the idea that the condition might be equivalent to that of a bitch in heat, lasting for another week or so. Then he realized that he was still thinking in terms of his own world. For all he knew, Ma-sand might last for months. What if arachnoid biology was such that once set in motion Ma-sand did not subside until the victim (for so he thought of Shriek in this circumstance) was able to satisfy her lust?

The question became moot when a feeling of delicious warmth washed through him and Clive understood, with some horror, that he was sharing Shriek's sexual satisfaction.

What had happened? It had seemed fairly clear from his last contacts with Shriek that she was unable to satisfy her own longing. From the gasps that sounded behind him in the corridor Clive knew that the others had felt it, too. He glanced over his shoulder, then quickly turned forward again, feeling like a peeping Tom intruding on a private moment.

But how had the creature consummated her lust? And what of the feeding frenzy that he knew must follow? The latter question was answered almost immediately, when Clive felt his belly contract with a pang of hunger that surpassed anything he had ever experienced. His body racked backward in a spasm of emptiness. He collapsed against the wall. If there had been anything organic within reach he would have shoved it into his mouth. To the horror of a detached portion of his mind that seemed to be observing all this from the outside, he actually considered turning back on his companions for the single purpose of finding something—anything!—to fulfill this unholy hunger.

He closed his eyes and pressed himself against the wall, trembling with need, and horror at the very existence of that need.

And then, almost miraculously, the hunger seemed to pass. *If only the memory would fade with it,* thought Clive.

But it did not, and would not, and he could not push aside the knowledge of how close he had come to doing something which, in the cool aftermath of that hunger, made him physically ill just to contemplate.

He could not turn to face the others. The fact that the need was not his own, that it had come from a creature in the grip of a biological imperative, did nothing to alleviate his shame. He should have been able to resist, and he knew that if the hunger had gone on he would not, could not, have done so. He was able to keep his rebellious mind from putting words to the act. But the picture, the image of what he was willing to do to assuage that savage hunger, would not go away.

He shook with self-loathing.

Your disgust is like a dagger in my heart, O Folliot, Shriek telepathed. *That which you despise is what I am. Yet I know that I am not evil. Can you not forgive yourself—and me?*

You are what you are, Clive answered silently. *I do not understand it. But I can try to forget it. I cannot do as much for myself. It was not—acceptable.*

What strange creatures you are, she replied. *The world is what it is. A tree is not morally superior to a volcano, any more than death to life.*

What we do with what we are is all that matters, countered Clive. *I believe I should have done better.*

Then I cannot help you, answered Shriek. *I can only offer my apologies. But I will tell you once again that it is only because of my respect for you, for other aspects of what you are, that I will not challenge you to a deathmatch as soon as we are face to face once more. In every moment you spend reviling yourself for what you just felt, you repudiate me and all my kind. I am not an evil creature, O Folliot. Yet you cover me with scorn.*

Clive paused. *You are what you are,* he thought at last. *Just so am I.*

Well thought, she answered, just before she broke the connection.

Clive considered trying to reach out and reconnect, for his curiosity about what had happened to resolve the Ma-sand was like another kind of hunger. But he restrained himself. It was enough for now to be free of the terrible hungers. He paused for a few moments to regain his bearings, then pressed on, trusting the others to follow. The corridor branched, and once more he used the starry spiral as his guide.

Without looking behind him, he sensed the others drawing closer together, an intuition that was eventually confirmed by the voice of Quartermaster Sergeant Horace Hamilton Smythe not far behind him.

"Well, sah," said the sergeant in carefully neutral tones, "that was what we call an interesting experience back where I come from."

Clive burst out in laughter. "Horace," he said, once he had caught his breath, "if that was merely interesting then either your life was far more exciting than I knew, or else you came from a family with a positive genius for understatement."

"I suppose it's a bit of both," said Smythe carefully.

Clive turned and clasped his old friend by the shoulders. "Sergeant Smythe, you are a rock. And a rock was just what I needed now."

Smythe smiled and inclined his head ever so slightly. "Glad to have been of service, sah."

He took his place beside Clive and they waited as the others drew closer. No one else spoke for the time being, but it was good to be reunited. Clive understood. They had been forced to share something intensely personal. Now they needed time to reestablish barriers.

He waited until he could see Shriek approaching, waited again until she was close enough to see him nod, then turned and began to walk once more, wondering, not for the first time, how long it would take them to find their way through this maze.

After a while he also began to wonder how long it would be before they could find food and drink again. The hunger he was beginning to feel now was but a pale echo of the appetite Shriek had broadcast a time ago. But Clive knew that unlike that short burst of need, this hunger would continue to grow. And if it could not be assuaged, then sooner or later it would do him—do all of them—in.

He called a halt for a rest and was astonished when Horace slumped back against one of the curving blue walls and then sat bolt upright with a shout of surprise.

"What is it?" asked Clive.

Though Clive's voice was lost in a babble of similar questions from the rest of the group, it was to him that Horace addressed his answer.

"It's Sidi Bombay, sah," he said in some astonishment. "He's alive!"

Horace closed his eyes and covered his face with his hands. When he looked up again his eyes were dark with despair. "He's alive, but he's in terrible, terrible trouble."

· CHAPTER EIGHT ·

Blood Bond

The idea that Sidi Bombay could be alive was preposterous on the face of it. With his own eyes Clive had seen the man disappear into the maw of the multi-tentacled horror that attacked them over the chasm of Q'oorna.

But then, he had seen Neville's body lying in its coffin, and Neville was not dead; of that much he was now convinced. So perhaps it was possible that Sidi too had survived what seemed like certain doom.

Indeed, Clive reflected, there were times when it seemed anything was possible in this mad world.

He recalled, with some chagrin, the first time he had met Sidi. Clive had been sitting outside the *boma* of their African encampment, smoking his pipe and contemplating both the evening sky and the strange adventure he had undertaken to please his father. Had he known then what the search for his missing twin would entail, would he have gone on? Or would he have turned back, tail between his legs, but still safely held within the world of his birth?

Clive didn't know the answer to that. But he did know that he could hardly have been more condescending to the gaunt, dark-skinned man who had startled him by appearing, as if by magic, out of the African night.

He had been almost as startled when Horace greeted the man in turban and white robes as if he were a long-lost brother. "We go back a long way, Sidi and I do," Horace had assured Clive on more than one occa-

sion. "You won't find many as can top Sidi Bombay."
And indeed, though much of Sidi's time with Clive had
been as mysterious as his first appearance, the old
Indian had served them faithfully on their journey into
the interior of Africa. Then, for reasons that remained
enigmatic, he had led them into the Dungeon. Actually,
it was never entirely clear that Sidi had known what he
was doing on that leg of the journey, any more than
had Horace. Yet Clive had never been able to shake the
feeling that his two aides had somehow taken control of
the expedition, and had purposefully steered him to
the strange gateway that led from Earth to the first
level of the Dungeon. Yet, once there, the two had
often seemed as mystified as he was by what was going
on. As it now stood, the true role of Sidi Bombay and
Horace Hamilton Smythe in this adventure was one of
the most tantalizing mysteries the Dungeon had presented Clive.

And for all of that, Sidi had gone to his death protecting Clive and his party. Or, if Horace was correct,
what had *seemed* like his death.

In the instant after Horace's startling announcement,
all these thoughts and more crowded into Clive's consciousness, giving way finally to a flood of images: Sidi
commanding the bearers with his natural combination
of ease and authority; Sidi tracking a gazelle with less
sound than a feather makes when riding the wind;
Sidi's face fixed in a grim battle smile as he wielded his
staff against seemingly insurmountable odds; Sidi delicately cupping a rare flower in his hand, his ugly face
split by a radiant grin; and, over and above them all,
Sidi using the cybroid claw to make his incredible climb
up the mad creature that had attacked them over the
chasm of Q'oorna.

Clive shook himself, trying to blot out the images so
he could concentrate on the moment. "Why do you say
this thing?" he demanded of Horace, who was sitting
on the floor of the tunnel, blinking in astonishment.

"Because he is," said Horace.

"Well, how do you know?" asked Clive, feeling not a
little exasperated.

"Go easy, Gramps," User Annie said sharply. "Maybe being in the Dungeon makes you weird."

"Finnbogg miss Sidi," cried Finnbogg, leaping about wildly. "Finnbogg Finnbogg from Finnbogg want Sidi back."

The rest of the group, who had never met the gaunt Indian, observed this scene with a variety of expressions, ranging from Chang Guafe's total detachment to Gram's mild amusement. Clive repeated his question, a trifle more gently.

"I dunno, sah," said Horace, shaking his head in astonishment. "I just leaned me head against the wall, and there it was, plain as day."

He leaned his head back to demonstrate, but this time nothing happened.

"Now ain't that funny," muttered Horace, tilting his head sideways. His eyes lit up. "There it is," he whispered in astonishment. "There it is!"

He jumped up and stared down at the wall as if he thought it might be bewitched. "I don't know what it is, sah," he whispered hoarsely. "But when I touch that wall the right way I can sense Sidi as sure as if he were right here in front of me. It's eerie, sah, that's what it is. Downright eerie. It's like something poking into my brain."

Clive looked at his usually unflappable right-hand man with dismay. He knelt and moved his hands over the section of wall where Horace had been sitting. He didn't know what he was looking for. A trapdoor, maybe? Anything to explain Smythe's strangely adamant pronouncement.

He found nothing unusual, save a slight smear of blood where Horace had pressed his head.

"You seem to have a wound, Sergeant," said Clive.

"So do we all, sah. The last day has been a bit rough."

"Heepers," said Annie, sounding mildly amused. "Same damn stiff upper lip you guys had in 1999."

Clive glanced around at his rag-taggle band and realized that what Smythe had said was true. Only the cyborg seemed relatively untouched. He chastised himself for not having stopped to deal with medical problems earlier. Remembering Shrick's wound, he moved his eyes back to the spider woman. The empty socket where her arm had been appeared to have sealed over with some kind of green chitinous material.

Do not berate yourself, O Folliot, she sent to Clive. *There has been no time for the catching of breath.*

He nodded his thanks to Shriek and returned his attention to Horace. "Let me take a look at that wound, Sergeant."

Horace stood up and turned around. Clive moved his fingers through the man's thick black hair until he found the gash that had left the bloodstain on the wall. It was at least three inches long. It had partially scabbed over, and there was a good deal of hair caught in the crusting; the rest of it was open.

"Could use some stitches," said Annie, who had moved next to him. "But the hair around it should be trimmed away first."

"Let me," said Chang Guafe, stepping away from the others and moving in their direction.

Before Clive could respond, the cyborg had reached out with a metallic tentacle.

"Christ!" yelled Horace, the suddenness of what followed drawing an unusual oath from his lips.

Clive blinked. Horace's scalp had been scraped clean of hair over an area extending an inch in all directions from the cut. The action left a patch of bare flesh at the back of his head about two inches wide and nearly five inches long. At the same time Chang Guafe had ripped away the scabbing, creating an open wound that ran like a crimson valley through the newly bald area.

"Now I will do my part," clicked Shriek. She closed her eyes for a moment, as if lost in thought. Then she plucked one of the spiky hairs from her abdomen. She ran the spike along the edges of the wound, then discarded it.

"That will disinfect the area," she said, in response to Clive's questioning look. "However, the wound must still be closed in order to heal properly."

She backed up to the wall and tapped it with her abdomen. Then, without moving the rest of her body, she twitched the abdomen about six inches to the right. She stepped away from the wall, turned, and bent to pick up the strand of thick silk she had created. "Hold still," she ordered as she returned to Horace, who had watched all this with some trepidation. Applying the silk to the back of his head, she covered the wound, pulling its edges together.

"The silk will hold for about six days," she said. "When it falls away, the cut should be nearly healed."

"Thank you very much, mum," said Horace in his best schoolboy tones. "And you, too, Master Guafe," he added, turning to the cyborg.

"You are welcome," Chang Guafe responded, "though I would urge you not to confuse pragmatism with sentiment."

"I'll work very hard to avoid it," Horace said seriously.

Pleased with what had just happened, Clive declared a general clinic. The group's wounds turned out to be more numerous, though (with the exception of Shriek's arm) less serious, than he had anticipated. In his own case the greatest problem was a severe soreness in the jaw, a souvenir from his battle with one of the tall redheads. Only Tomàs had escaped relatively unscathed, a situation Clive ascribed to the Iberian's favorite position in a battle: far at the rear. As for Shriek, she brushed aside his awkward attempt at condolences for the loss of her limb by pointing out that it was not as much of a disaster for her as it would have been for any of the others.

Out of the corner of his eye Clive noticed that Horace had resumed his position on the floor. The sergeant leaned his head back against the wall and closed his eyes as if trying to concentrate. This action was repeated over and over again, with what appeared to be increasingly frustrating results.

"I've lost it," said Horace bitterly when Clive came and knelt beside him. "Whatever the contact was, it's gone."

"That's good," said Clive.

Horace actually looked angry, an expression Clive

had rarely, if ever, seen the sergeant use in his direction. "You're a harder man than I thought, Major Folliot."

"Not hard," said Clive. "Pragmatic, as our friend Chang Guafe would say. Obviously Sidi is not here, so obviously you could not have contacted him. It seems clear that your feeling of connection came from a combination of intense longing and the fact that you had received a rather severe blow to the head. You and I have both seen this kind of battlefield delusion before, Horace."

"But this was different," said Horace slowly, somewhat less certain of himself.

"Now, Sergeant Smythe," said Clive jovially, "a short time ago I said you were as steady as a rock. Don't make me take back those words."

Horace blushed and turned away.

"Teddibly sure of yourself, aren't you?" said a feminine voice from behind. Clive turned to see User Annie staring down at them. "Did it ever occur to you that Horace might be right?"

Clive hesitated, then decided not to accept the challenge. "I suppose he might be," he said coldly. "Why don't you discuss it with him?"

He stood up and stalked off.

"Tight-ass Brit," he heard her say.

As Clive began to re-form the group he became aware of something to keep in mind for future reference. As much as they had needed the stop, it had cost him a great deal in terms of momentum. Once they had started following him, it had been easy enough just to keep on. Now it took a great deal of energy to coddle and cajole them all back into motion. 'Nrrc'kth, who had been pretty much silent until now, was particularly recalcitrant.

"I must eat before I can go on," she said imperiously.

Clive was deeply immersed in the thankless process of explaining that there was no food for anyone when he was interrupted by a shout from Horace.

"I've found him again!"

He turned around to see Sergeant Smythe standing with one hand pressed against the tunnel wall. Suddenly the sergeant's eyes rolled up into his head. His knees buckled and he slid to the floor. The passage of his hand down the wall was marked by a smear of blood.

Clive raced back to the fallen Horace. "What happened?" he demanded of Annie, who was standing nearby, her dark eyes wide with astonishment.

"He was muttering something about finding Sidi again," whispered Annie. "Then he cut himself; just grabbed a knife and slashed it across his hand. Then he slapped his hand against the wall. That's where you came in."

Clive knelt beside Horace and shook him gently. The sergeant's eyes fluttered open. "I found him, sah," he whispered.

"What do you mean, Horace? How did you find him?"

"Blood, sah. Blood calling to blood, somehow. We're blood brothers, Sidi and me. Didn't know that, did you? I suppose it shocks you, too. But it's the truth, and there's no man I'd rather have shared my blood with than Sidi Bombay. Blood is the key. I knew that when I realized the contact had come when I laid my wound against the wall. I had to get back in touch with him. So I made me a new wound."

Clive lifted Horace's arm and pulled open his fingers, which had clenched into a fist. An ugly gash stretched diagonally from the base of his index finger to the other edge of his palm.

"We'll get this closed up," Clive said gently.

"No, sah!" replied Horace ferociously, clamping his hand shut as he spoke. "If that's our only link to Sidi, then it has to stay open."

Clive hesitated. The look in Horace's eyes made it clear that to issue a direct order would be to risk insubordination. He was well aware that his position as leader of the group was founded on the unswerving loyalty of Sergeant Smythe. He could not afford to push the man too far. "Always try to avoid backing a man into a situation where his only way out is through you," an older officer had once told Clive, and it had proven to be useful advice. He changed course.

"Where is Sidi?"

"I dunno, sah. I found him, but he ain't here."

"Horace," Clive replied sternly, "I thought we got past this mystical nonsense once you told me the story of your encounter with the Ransomes and Philo Goode. It does us no good for you to hold things back."

"It hurts to have you say that, sah," said Horace mournfully. "Though I suppose you have good reason. But as I live, I'm being as straight with you as I can."

The others had gathered around to listen in on the conversation.

"Let me try," said Shriek.

She moved next to Horace and told him to place his hand against the wall once more. Then she reached out and took him by the other hand. Almost instantly she cried out in surprise and broke the contact.

There is no location for the man, O Folliot, she said in Clive's mind. *But the connection is true and clear, a direct tunnel into a kind of pain I have never before experienced. Smythe is a brave man, to reestablish it voluntarily.*

Clive nodded. He wondered if she had sent the message only to him or had included the others in her net of thought.

He knelt beside Horace. The man's eyes were squeezed shut, his face twisted into a mask of pain. "Enough," he said gently, pulling Horace's hand away from the wall. "Enough for now. There's nothing you can do for him."

"Oh, but there is, sah. I can find him and get him out of this mess. Old Sidi would do it for me. I can't do any less for him."

"And how do you intend to do this, Sergeant Smythe?"

"I don't know, sah. But by my mother's heart and bones, I swear that I'll find Sidi Bombay or die trying."

• CHAPTER NINE •

Double Bind

They were in motion again, which was good, though Clive was not sure how long he could maintain that condition. Food and water were becoming increasingly urgent issues, with 'Nrrc'kth occasionally announcing that she could not go another step without them.

He had no idea how long they had been walking through the blue tunnels—nor where they were in relation to their starting point. It was entirely possible (depressing thought!) that they had been making a spiral around the base of N'wrbb's castle and would come out not far from where they had begun.

If we ever get out at all, Clive thought gloomily to himself.

We will make it, O Folliot, Shriek sent cheerfully. *I have great faith in you.*

Don't do that! replied Clive angrily.

Do what?

Go digging around in my head without asking. It's nerve-racking.

Shriek signaled incomprehension, and Clive resigned himself to the fact that there were some things that simply could not be translated between species. But he decided to take advantage of the situation to satisfy his own curiosity.

As long as we're being overly personal, he sent, wondering as he did so if Shriek could translate nuance or simply broad meaning, *what happened back in the blue chamber? How were you able to end the Ma-sand?*

Shriek signaled surprise. *I assumed you knew. After all, there was only one possibility.*

It was Clive's turn to signal surprise.

Comprehension dawns, replied Shriek. *You remain trapped by your inhibitions, O Folliot—a problem you must shed if you are to survive the Dungeon. The cyborg took care of my problems with manual stimulation. He was the only one strong enough to protect himself from the feeding frenzy that follows the sexual climax.*

Clive tried desperately to hide his shock.

Do not dissemble, O Folliot, was her reply. *I understand now how crippled you were by your upbringing, so I try not to take your reactions personally.*

Now you are judging me, Clive answered.

True, though all I judge is your judgment. An interesting conundrum, is it not?

Before Clive could continue the argument, they were there. Or, he corrected himself, at least someplace different. After hours of the blue tunnels, to his right he saw not the typical branching, but a door made of wood. He reached for the handle. To his surprise, the door swung open easily.

"I thought nothing was allowed to be simple here," said Annie, who was standing behind him.

"Don't worry," said Clive, "there's probably a small army of two-headed monsters waiting around the next bend." He peered into the tunnel beyond the door. It seemed to be carved from rock rather than the strange blue material they had become so used to. "Besides, there's no light in this one. That ought to keep things interesting."

When he turned back he found that the others had clustered around him.

"At last!" cried 'Nrrc'kth, looking at the exit with an expression that bordered on lust. "Let us hurry, my love. 'Nrrc'kth hungers."

Clive ignored Annie's reaction to the term of endearment from 'Nrrc'kth. He had something far more worrisome to consider: there was no spiral of stars anywhere near the door.

Though he had not talked about it to anyone else

(did Shriek know anyway? he suddenly wondered), he had led them to this point entirely by use of the spirals and the clue he had been given as a child. It had been simply a hunch. But it seemed to have worked.

Or had it? For all he knew, they might have found their way out far sooner by some other route.

His head began to swim with questions. Was his tactic valid to begin with? If it was, had the stars led them to this place of escape—or was this simply a point to be passed as they followed the star-marked trail?

"What's the problem, Grampa?" asked Annie.

He chose to ignore the bait and simply answer her question: "I'm not sure this is the way we should go."

"We must!" cried 'Nrrc'kth. "Otherwise we will be in these tunnels forever. Or at least I shall, for you can leave my body behind when I perish, which I shall do if I do not soon eat."

"Tough it out, toots," Annie snapped. "The rest of us are coping. You can too."

"No, she can't," said Gram, a menacing look in her eye. "In our world the women of the palace are bred and raised differently than most. My niece is not being difficult. She is simply stating a fact."

"Great," Annie muttered. "A delicate blossom. Getting her through this alive is going to be like walking a tadpole through the desert on a leash."

"Shut up," snapped Clive, somewhat to his own surprise. "Horace, I want you to go on ahead a bit. See what you can find out. Move quietly, and try to come back without anyone on your tail."

"Yessah," Horace said quietly.

Clive looked at his old comrade in surprise, as he had expected Horace to greet the assignment with his usual vigor. But Horace gave him no time to question the subdued response; he had already begun moving up the new tunnel.

He was back almost instantly. "Two curves and then a door, sah. The door is unlocked. It leads to the outside."

Annie's whoop of jubilation was an indication of the reaction being shown by everyone except Chang Guafe and, to Clive's astonishment, Quartermaster Sergeant Horace Hamilton Smythe, who was looking very grim indeed.

"What is it, Sergeant?" he asked. "Something awful on the other side of the door you haven't told us about yet?"

"No, sah. Not at all. All those suns are shining to beat the band. Grass is green. Quite pretty, all in all."

"Where are we in relation to the castle?"

"Behind it. The tunnel comes out through kind of a cave, in a rocky patch about fifty yards from the moat."

"Is there anyone around?"

"Not that I could see, sah. Seems pretty quiet. I imagine they're all lying low, licking their wounds as it were."

"Is there food?" asked 'Nrrc'kth.

"Not that I could see, ma'am," said Horace. "But then I didn't look too long. I wanted to report back to the major here."

"It sounds about as good as we could have hoped for, Horace. My worst fear was that we would come up back inside the castle."

"Indeed, sah."

Clive looked at his friend impatiently. "Then why are you so glum?"

Horace hesitated before he spoke. "It's Sidi Bombay, sah. If we go out there I won't be able to get in touch with him again."

Clive started to speak, then paused. Here was a fine mess indeed. If he pressed the issue, Horace would have no choice but to follow him. *Or would he?* Clive suddenly wondered. Was it possible his friend and comrade would actually mutiny against his command and go searching for Sidi Bombay?

And what if he did not? One of Horace's greatest attributes was his loyalty. If Clive forced him to be disloyal to a comrade, what would that mean?

The problem with being the leader, O Folliot, is that you have no one else to make decisions for you.

Stop reading my mind! replied Clive, almost automatically.

The arachnid's response was like a chuckle inside his head. *I have not penetrated your precious privacy, O Folliot. I was simply observing your dilemma. Mind reading is not required when the situation is obvious.*

Sorry, Clive sent. *But unless you have any suggestions, I'd rather you left me alone so I can figure out what to do.*

Suggestions impose, questions lead.

Clive messaged puzzlement.

Do you mind if I speak to your sergeant, O Folliot?

Clive sent back the mental equivalent of a shrug.

Then ask me! she replied. The sending felt impatient, as if she were dealing with a rather slow child.

"Shriek," he said. "You are the only other one who has experienced this connection. Would you please speak to Horace?"

"Gladly," she said. She moved out of the group to stand next to Smythe. "Have you connected recently?" she asked, her fierce mandibles clicking with the effort of auditory speech.

"No, mum," said Horace. "But I suppose this is as good a time as any." He looked down at his right hand, which he had been holding closed. Suddenly he threw it open. Grabbing the fingers with his other hand, he pulled back on them, forcing the right hand back into an arc. The movement served its purpose; the gash across his palm was wrenched open. Gritting his teeth, he placed his hand against the wall. "God!" he cried, his body shaking with the impact of the connection.

At once Shriek reached out and took Smythe's other hand. She held on tenaciously, obviously fighting the urge to break the connection immediately.

"Enough!" she said at last. Clive had counted to seven in the interval.

Horace took his hand from the wall.

Shriek looked at him, and her puzzlement seemed genuine. "Does your friend seem any closer than he did before?" she asked.

Horace shook his head.

"Any further?"

He shook his head again.

"Then which way will you go to look for him?"

"I can't rightly say, mum."

"Is he in the blue tunnels?"

"I don't know."

"Can you reach him through the blue tunnels?"

Horace appeared increasingly distressed. "I don't know."

Shriek clicked her mandibles in an obvious display of sympathy. "Then what will you do? Will you go back, or will you go forward? At the next branching will you go left or right?"

"I don't know!" Horace cried in frustration.

"Then how shall you find your friend? There is no food or water here; how long can you search?"

"Not long," Horace admitted grudgingly.

"What would your friend have you do?"

Horace turned away and stared down the blue tunnel for a long time. He made no movement, except for a kind of rolling of his shoulders, which hunched up at regular intervals.

When he turned back, his face was calm. "Well, I guess the major was right. There's not much point in staying here, is there?"

Clive stepped forward. "I am bound by oath to find my brother, Horace. By your recent words you are bound to do the same for Sidi Bombay. Now I will take another oath myself: if we have not found your friend by the end of our quest for Neville, I will turn and help you as faithfully as you have aided me."

"Lord bless you, sah," Horace said quietly. "And let's be on our way. Sooner started sooner finished, as my mam used ter say. Though I think I'll bring up the rear for a bit, if you don't mind."

"Not at all, Sergeant Smythe, not at all." As Clive turned to lead his people out of the tunnel, Annie sidled up to him and said, "Very touching, Gramps—very loyal. Of course, I understand you made a vow like that to my great great grandmother once, too. Doesn't it make you nervous to keep promising things you may not be able to deliver?"

Before Clive could answer she had slipped away to stand with Finnbogg, who, as always, was ecstatic to have her attention.

CHAPTER TEN

Woman Times Three

"I don't much care for a world where the sun don't set, sah," said Horace.

They were sitting at the mouth of the cave, waiting for the revolving circle of starlike objects that lit this strange world to grow dim, a phenomenon that occurred on a schedule that provided a fair approximation of day and night.

"For one thing," Horace continued, "you can never tell what time it is—or how long it is till dark."

The latter was a particularly pressing issue because they had decided it would be too chancy to leave the cave during daylight hours. The turrets of N'wrbb's castle loomed ominously to their left, and it would be all too easy for a lookout—or even a casual observer—to spot their band if they tried to make for the forest about a quarter of a mile in the opposite direction.

"I can't wait until dark," wailed 'Nrrc'kth. "I have to eat now."

However, when Chang Guafe lashed out with a metallic tentacle and captured a small, furry thing that made the mistake of scuttling past the cave, 'Nrrc'kth declined to accept it.

"Must not be as hungry as she thought," said Horace dryly.

As far as Clive was concerned hunger was a minor issue compared to the parching thirst he now felt—a thirst made all the more maddening by the fact that N'wrbb's moat was within a minute's walk of their hiding place. Not that he would want to chance drinking

out of the moat; he had seen too many strange creatures rise to its surface when people were falling in
during the part of the battle that had taken place in
front of the castle. He had a feeling that a man who
stooped to drink from that water would lose his face
before he had enjoyed his first sip.

"Is there any way at all to judge the time?" he asked
of 'Nrrc'kth, who had been a free person at this level of
the Dungeon longer than anyone else in their group.

She shook her head dismally. "The circle of stars
waxes and wanes to a rhythm all its own," she said, as if
repeating a line of poetry she had learned long ago.

"No church bell to chime the hours?" asked Tomàs
from the corner where he sat fiddling with his rosary.

"You'll not find a church bell in N'wrbb's realm,
bucko," snorted Gram. "Nor a church, for that matter."

Tomàs crossed himself and muttered another prayer,
but it was drowned out by a growl from Finnbogg, who
was sleeping near Annie's feet. Clive shot her a warning glance and she reached down to comfort the dreaming dwarf.

Clive turned and looked out of the cave once more.
He was still stinging from the rebuke Annie had delivered as they were about to escape the blue maze.

Only Guafe seemed content. Clive wondered why,
until he finally realized that the cyborg had simply shut
down most of his functions.

I guess being mechanical has some advantages after all, he
thought morosely.

Shriek's voice came rustling into his mind: *You are
glum, O Folliot. Yet we have just managed a marvelous escape
under your leadership. You should be joyous!*

The inaction chafes me, responded Chive, *which is odd,
because I am usually a more quiet sort of man. Maybe constant adventure is addictive—like opium.*

Shriek signaled a question.

It's a drug on our world, responded Clive, *very hard to
stop taking, once you start.*

*Yes, we have things like that. But I sense there is something
else on your mind, my friend. I have not tried to discover it,
because I know that would distress you. Even so . . .*

Clive smiled. *There's no escaping you, is there? I am simply questioning my ability to lead the group. I would have lost Horace back in those tunnels, if you hadn't intervened.*

Do not berate yourself, O Folliot. It was no failure to have me solve the problem. Delegation of tasks is one of the keys of leadership. That was why I made you ask me aloud—so the others would know the decision was yours.

But it wasn't! Clive replied bitterly.

Of course it was. The suggestion was mine. But the decision to let me act was yours. If you had refused, I would not have interfered.

Why are you helping me in this way? Clive asked.

Ah, Shriek chuckled, *would you have all my secrets, O Folliot? Or am not I, too, entitled to some privacy?*

Just what I needed—another mystery!

All females are mysterious, O Folliot. Surely you have learned that much in your life.

Indeed. Indeed they are, friend Shriek. But if they were also all as supportive as you, then a man's lot would be much easier.

Her reply fairly twinkled with amusement: *And have you forgotten that I devour my mate under the proper circumstances?*

Another lesson, replied Clive, just before he broke the connection. *One should never argue ethics with a spider!*

Horace nudged him. "I think it's starting to get dark, sah!"

Clive looked up. It was hard to be certain, but it did seem possible that the circling stars had commenced their daily waning. In the period it took him to pace ten times from the front to the rear of the cave and back, the event had moved from possibility to certainty.

At full dark they left the cave and headed for the forest. The circle of lights overhead had dimmed to mere starpoints, leaving the level of illumination about that of a clear night with a quarter moon on Earth. Shortly after entering the woods they heard a stream. When they had slaked their thirst, 'Nrrc'kth found some bushes with berries she claimed were good to eat, and proceeded to consume so many that Clive was afraid she would be sick. Most of the others ate the same fruit, though somewhat more moderately. Shriek and Chang Guafe went off together. When they returned, about half an hour later, the spider woman let Clive know that they both had been able to find suitable food.

He decided not to pursue the details.

Despite their general state of exhaustion, Clive insisted they had to push on until they had put the castle at a greater distance. When it was finally clear that 'Nrrc'kth, at least, could go no further, they made camp in a small clearing that bordered another stream.

Then, and only then, did Clive allow himself to confront the fact that he had no idea what to do next. He had come all this way in pursuit of Neville—and now he had no idea where Neville was, or even which way he might have gone. According to N'wrbb, Neville had actually been staying in the castle. But if so, why had he made no move to try to free Clive after he had been imprisoned? Was it possible he hadn't known? That didn't seem likely. Neville always knew what was going on. That he didn't care? Maybe. Lord knew there had been little love lost between the two of them. But if that were the case, why all those mysterious messages in the journal, urging him onward?

Or had N'wrbb simply been lying?

Clive smiled. That was one explanation that was easy to believe.

He glanced at 'Nrrc'kth. Despite the time they had been imprisoned together, he had had little opportunity to talk with her. As protective as she was strong, Gram had kept her niece pretty well isolated while the younger woman was recovering from the abuse she had received at the hands of N'wrbb. During that interim Clive had busied himself with escape plans.

Well, no time like the present.

" 'Nrrc'kth," he said, sitting beside her, "was my brother really staying at the castle?"

"There was a man who looked much like you," said 'Nrrc'kth. "My consort always called him Brigadier Folliot. He did not live in the castle, but he was a frequent visitor."

"How long have you known him?"

'Nrrc'kth looked puzzled. Clive realized that whatever units she chose to answer in—days, months, years—it would not mean to him what it meant to her.

"For as long as I have been here," she said at last.

Clive considered that statement for some time, but couldn't make sense of it no matter how he approached it. From everything she had told him before, he was fairly confident that 'Nrrc'kth had been brought to the Dungeon quite some time before his twin had disappeared in Africa. Was "the Brigadier" really his brother, or was it someone masquerading as Neville? And if the latter were the case, what was the reason for such a bizarre charade?

"Do you have any idea where this man went when he wasn't staying with you?"

"All over," 'Nrrc'kth said with some certainty. "N'wrbb always greeted the Brigadier eagerly, because he carried much news. He was a great traveler."

She reached out and stroked Clive's arm. He shivered at the touch, which was unlike any other he had ever known. "I am frightened, Clive," she whispered. The light of the campfire danced in her green eyes, shimmered in her emerald hair. She looked like she belonged in the forest, though obviously she was not trained to survive under such circumstances. "N'wrbb will not let me go easily. He will be trying to track me down. Will you protect me?"

"With my life," replied Clive, wondering how many vows like this he could take before one of them finally caught up with him. From somewhere to his left he heard Annie snort in derision.

'Nrrc'kth nodded, causing her green hair to rustle provocatively around her alabaster shoulders. "There is a small city called Go-Mar on the other side of this wood," she said. "I know the Brigadier often passed through there, for when he came to stay he usually brought N'wrbb word of the mood of the populace."

Clive felt a wave of hope. Surely if they went to this city they could pick up Neville's trail again. "Tell me more of this place," he said to 'Nrrc'kth.

She frowned. "It is ruled by one of N'wrbb's men. My consort has many allies in Go-Mar. But he also has many enemies, which is why he was always eager for news of it. I believe it is the closest place where we can rest and get some real food. But we cannot stay there; it is infested with N'wrbb's spies. You do understand, Clive, that we will have to be fugitives now?" She shook her head remorsefully. "You should have killed N'wrbb when you had the chance. None of us will be safe until he is dead."

"It was not my way," said Clive.

She looked at him as if trying to fathom the workings of a mind entirely alien to her. "I still long for you," she whispered finally, and he knew she was referring to the interrupted tryst that had landed them in N'wrbb's catacombs to begin with.

"This is not the time for us," answered Clive, trying to be as diplomatic as possible. The chemistry of 'Nrrc'kth's touch still inflamed his passion. But the interim since their first encounter had given him plenty of time to question the wisdom of an intimate involvement with the slender alien woman.

He brushed her hair with his fingertips, then moved away to the spot where he had made his bed.

Chang Guafe, skeptical about anyone else's ability to stay awake, volunteered to take the first watch. Clive quickly fell into a deep sleep. But it did not last. Coming up from a strange dream of mazes and tunnels he was seized with a restlessness that finally woke him. When he opened his eyes and sat up he saw User Annie sitting opposite him. She was leaning against the trunk of a large tree. A silvery dagger dangled from her fingertips. Stray bits of starshine that found their way through the forest roof reflected off the edge of the blade.

"Why aren't you asleep?" he asked quietly, trying not to wake the others.

"I had a lot on my mind," she said, lifting the dagger and sighting along its edge.

"Such as?"

She shrugged. "It occurred to me that maybe I ought to kill you now, while I have the chance."

"I would prefer you didn't," he said, wondering how serious she was.

"So would I," she admitted. "But this time stuff is very confusing, you know. You've already got my great-great-grandmother knocked up. So you've done your bit as far as the family gene pool is concerned. The chain that leads to me is clear. But what if you get out of the Dungeon alive? Will you go back and marry her? That would change the whole family structure. If that happens, then what happens to me? Do I just vanish into thin air?"

"I don't know," said Clive.

"Of course, the fact that I exist now means you probably didn't get out of here—unless you're really the son of a bitch that family legend claims, and just never went back to her. So let's say you didn't get out. Why didn't you make it, Grampa Clive? Is it because I killed you tonight, so that you wouldn't mess up the family chain?"

She tossed the knife from hand to hand, and Clive felt a tightening at the back of his throat. Annie had told him enough during their travels to let him know that the world she came from was scored with violence. Was it violent enough to prepare her to kill her own ancestor?

"The thing is, as long as you're alive, you're a threat to me. The minute you're dead, I don't have to worry about it anymore." She tightened her grip on the knife and smiled. "I wonder if this would be the world's first case of great-great-grampicide. I think the Greeks would have liked that. How about you?"

"Are you serious?" he asked, trying to keep his voice even.

She shrugged. "You asked what I had on my mind. That's the answer."

He eyed the blade. "Have you thought about this a lot?"

"When I have time," she said. "Usually I'm too busy trying to stay alive to have time to think. Of course, I wonder how much of that is your fault, too—you and that apeshit brother of yours."

He would have raised an eyebrow, but the light was too dim for her to see it.

"Do go on," he said softly, settling for words.

"Yes, do," she replied mockingly. "God, Clive, I've been trying to figure out what to call you. Great-great-grandpa was too long. Gramps was better, but it didn't really seem to fit. Now I think I've got it. You're more like a maiden aunt than anything else I can think of. How about Auntie Clive? What do you think of that?"

"I'd rather you kept trying."

She laughed. "Proper British reserve. You're so predictable, Clive. I suppose it makes you comfortable, in a boring sort of way."

He was glad it was dark enough so that she couldn't see him blush—and even more glad that, unlike Shriek, she couldn't read his mind without actually touching his hand. His feelings about Annie were an ungodly jumble of paternal pride, sexual attraction, anger, and, for the moment at least, fear. He had no wish to share them with his young descendant.

"You were talking about how much of the danger you've faced is my fault," he said. "But my recollection is that the prison where we first met you wasn't the safest place on Earth."

"You're so terrestrial, Clive. We're not *on* Earth anymore! Or hasn't that sunk into your thick British skull yet? Besides, who saved whose ass when it was time to get out of that prison? Or should it be *whoms*? Anyway, that's not what I'm talking about. We're all in this together, I suppose. But the question is, *why?* I mean, doesn't it strike you as kind of odd that out of all the people who have been brought here, I should end up rambling around with my auntie Clive? I surely can't figure out why the people in charge of this place could give a rat's dick about little Annabelle Leigh—except that my uncle Neville seems to be about the busiest person in town. So every once in a while I ask myself, 'Annie, why are you here?' I usually get one of two answers: A., 'Why is there air?' or B., 'Bad bloodlines.'

To tell you the truth, the latter makes a little more sense."

Clive fingered his jaw, which was still aching from a blow he had taken during their last battle. "I, too, wonder what strange twist of fortune brought us here. But being Neville's brother has been hard enough. I'm not willing to shoulder the guilt for every wrong connected with him."

Annie laughed. "Why, Aunt Clive, I think that may be the most human thing I ever heard you say. And all this time I had been wondering if you weren't another cyborg in disguise."

"Alas, little Annie, merely flesh and blood—all too given to sins of the flesh, and lately all too bloody."

"Listen, Unk, I'll make you a deal. You don't call me 'little Annie' and I'll drop the 'Aunt Clive' bit. Okay?"

"An excellent compromise," said Clive.

Annie put down the knife. "You planning to start boinking 'Nrrc'kth?" she asked.

Clive hesitated, once again struggling to interpret Annie's strange twists on their mutual language. "If that means what I think it means, then no, I'm not. And furthermore, I don't think that's the kind of thing a young lady should discuss with her great-great-grandfather."

Annie laughed. "Well, if you're sleeping alone, Grampa, you mind if I cuddle up like we used to before we figured this out? It's kind of cold and dark in the woods tonight."

Clive patted the ground next to him. Annie stretched out beside him and laid her head on his chest. "God, I hate this place," she whispered.

He put his arm around her shoulder and fought back an impulse to promise that he would get her out of here. He had made too many promises already. And this was one he really didn't think he could keep. He pulled her a little closer. "I hate it too," he said huskily. "Even so, I will always be grateful that I was allowed to meet Miss Annabelle Leigh of San Francisco."

"You're such a twit, Clive," she whispered. Then her

head seemed to grow heavier on his shoulder, and her regular breathing told him that she was asleep.

Rest did not come so easily to Clive Folliot, who lay awake for a long time, staring up at the circle of stars and trying not to be too aware of the warmth of the woman next to him.

· CHAPTER ELEVEN ·

L'Claar

She entered his mind softly, and her touch was like ice on a burn, like water on a parched tongue, like a candle in a dark room, like the smell of salt water to a sailor who has been too long inland.

I am here, brave one, she whispered, as she had so many times now. *You are not alone.*

He was getting stronger. When she first came to him he could make no response. It was only her intuition that had convinced her he was still alive, still—as she put it—salvageable.

O venerable one, will you not speak to me?

He had been trying to speak to her for a long time now, but his mind had been driven past words by the unending pain. He spent the intervals between her contacts trying to gather words, remember how to use them, find some way to respond.

His greatest fear was that she would give up and not come back. Every time she ended the contact he experienced a panic that overwhelmed even the tides of pain that he had been suffering for what seemed like several thousand eternities.

Frantically he tried to recall the words he had so laboriously assembled after the last contact. Intimately familiar with dreams, he recognized the fear and frustration he now felt as a common dream motif: needing desperately to run, yet being unable to move at a pace any faster than a crawl. The thought was expressed in images and feelings rather than words.

Words. One word. *Who.* That was it, the beginning of

the thought he had worked so hard to form. Where was the rest? Why couldn't he find the words?

But the first word proved to be a lure, drawing others to it. They swam up from the darkness of what had once been his mind, strung themselves together, and formed the message: *Who are you?*

The delight that greeted this achievement almost pushed away the pain.

She answered his question.

I am L'Claar. And you?

And as if finding those first words had unlocked some prison where the rest of his words had been held captive, the answer came to him quickly, and like a sudden burst of sunlight. He would have shouted it, had he been able. As it was, he thought it with every fiber of what was left of his being.

My name is Sidi Bombay!

CHAPTER TWELVE

Tankards Away

"The wrath of N'wrbb is a terrible thing."

'Nrrc'kth was standing beneath a tree that looked vaguely like a larch, addressing the entire group. "I can assure you, my former consort will neither forgive nor forget the fact that we escaped him. We must be constantly wary, for he will be searching for us, hoping to bring us back, to punish us."

"How far does his influence extend?" asked Clive. "Surely once we have traveled far enough we will be free of his grasp."

"I fear not," replied 'Nrrc'kth. "His reach goes far indeed, for he is a power in the Dungeon and has many friends."

Clive frowned. As if they didn't have enough troubles already! After consulting with Horace, he finally decided they would spend the daylight hours in the forest, then strike out for the city once they had darkness to hide them. In order to shorten that final leg of the journey, they erased all traces of their first camp and moved to the far edge of the wood.

Shortly after they began walking, Finnbogg sniffed out a narrow road, little more than a path, really, that meandered through the forest in the general direction they were heading. This generated a short debate about whether or not they could count on the road leading them out of the wood, and even if it did whether they should take the chance of meeting other travelers. Finally Clive decreed that since there was no other way for them to take a bearing in the woods, they would follow the road but move parallel to its course, hoping that in this way they could avoid being seen by anyone else.

The forest was well populated with small animals. Shriek and Chang Guafe soon proved themselves excellent, if unorthodox, hunters, and by midday they had provided enough small game to make a very satisfactory meal.

By Clive's reckoning it was less than an hour after they had eaten that they spotted the edge of the forest. They backtracked a bit, and made a new camp, far enough from both the road and the open lands that no casual traveler could see it. The rest of the day passed slowly. Some of them napped. Others wandered restlessly around the perimeter of the camp. Annie and 'Nrrc'kth seemed to circle each other like a pair of cats, somehow managing, to Clive's relief, to avoid actually speaking to each other. Gram straddled a log and amused herself by using her dagger to carve a large replica of Tomàs's crucifix.

Clive wandered away from the group. The trees fascinated him, for while the forest itself felt much like the ones he had known as a youth in England, there were subtle differences in the formation of its individual elements. He found a small stand of something that seemed close to oak, and another that was much like ash. But the most dominant species was one totally unfamiliar to him. Covered with yellow-green leaves that were almost perfectly round, the trees bore a small, sweet nut that 'Nrrc'kth had told him was used extensively in cooking by the peasant class at this level of the Dungeon.

He was gathering a handful of the nuts when he happened to notice Horace leaning against a nearby tree and gazing at the ground with a morose expression. He debated briefly about whether to intrude on the man's privacy. Finally he called a soft "hallo." Horace blinked and looked around as if coming out of a trance.

"Hullo, sah," said Horace. "Just having myself a bit of a think."

"So I see," said Clive. "And unless I miss my guess, it had to do with Sidi Bombay."

Horace smiled ruefully. "Ah, there's no keeping anything from you, sah."

Clive considered pointing out that there was a great deal that Horace had managed to keep from him in the past, but decided to let the point slide. Instead he took a seat underneath another of the nut trees and said, "Is it worth a chat, Horace, or would you rather keep it to yourself?"

Smythe spread his hands. "Not much to say that you don't know, sah. I'm sure Shriek was right when she persuaded me to leave those blue tunnels. But I can't help feeling wrong about it anyway. And of course the mystery of it all is eating away at me, too. I want to know what those tunnels are. They're not the kind of thing you'd expect to find under that sort of castle. So who made them? And why? And what do they have to do with Sidi Bombay?"

Clive shook his head. "I don't know, Sergeant. But it's not for lack of thought, because I've been asking myself the same questions since we found our way out of that maze. I don't know how it is possible to survive what happened to Sidi over the chasm of Q'oorna. But as you assure me that he is alive, I believe it. And I believe something else, too." He paused, and poured the nuts he had gathered from one hand into the other. "As vast and strange as the Dungeon is, there seems to be some thread tying our group together. Not only tying us together, but pulling us on." He shook his head. "I know that sounds awfully mystical. But you've known me long enough to know that I don't have much truck with that sort of thing. I don't think we're in the realm of the gods here, Horace. But there is something strange at work in the Dungeon, some power, possibly some great mind, possibly a group of men, or things that pass for men; in any event something far more powerful than anything we have ever known. I don't pretend to begin to understand what it's all about. But as sure as I am sitting here, I believe there is some rational explanation for it all."

He leaned back against the tree and looked off into the distance for a while before continuing. "I can't help also believing that this power has some sort of plan for us. I'm not talking about fate, or kismet, or any of that nonsense. For all I know, whoever is behind all this is simply playing with us, the same way that we would play with an infant. The point is, I believe that if Sidi *is* alive we're going to find him sooner or later; perhaps even before we find Neville. Because for whatever reason, Sidi Bombay is bound to us, and we to him. I believe that whoever, or whatever, brought us here wants us together. I do fear that once we find your old friend we may have to turn ourselves inside out to rescue him. But find him we will."

He stood up and brushed off the leather trousers he had been given by N'wrbb Crrd'f before he had earned that man's hatred. "And one more thing, Sergeant Smythe. When we started all this, I was only looking for my brother. But it's moved far beyond that now. I'm tired of being pushed and pulled every which way without any thought of what I want. I don't know why I was brought here, and I don't know who's behind it, but by God I am going to find out or die in the process."

The expression on Horace's face had altered completely. The corners of his mouth were compressed as if he were trying to keep from breaking into a grin. His eyes were fairly twinkling. "Major Folliot, I've been waiting ten years to hear you talk like that. I told you before, a soldier knows when an officer has what it takes. But sometimes you can't figure out what it's going to take to get it out of him. I feel like—well, sah, I don't know what I feel like, except a fair genius for seeing what you had inside you when you kept it so well hidden from even yourself. I tell you, I hope we make it back home, if for no other reason than so I can collect my five pounds from that fool McGinty."

Clive raised an eyebrow and Horace actually looked as if he were going to blush. "Private bet, sah," he said. "I'd rather not discuss it, other than to let you know I was on your side."

Clive didn't know whether to laugh or be insulted. Finally he clapped Horace on the shoulder and said, "I hope you get to collect that five pounds, Sergeant Smythe. For both our sakes."

But even as he said it, he recalled the questions Annie had asked him the night before, and wondered what it would mean for his young descendant if he did indeed find his way out of the Dungeon.

It was beginning to grow dark as Clive and Horace made their way back to where the others were waiting. Shrick was sitting at the edge of the circle, sucking the blood out of the decapitated body of one of the small, rabbitlike creatures she and Chang Guafe had been capturing throughout the day. *Is all well, O Folliot?* she telepathed when she saw him.

As well as can be expected, replied Clive. *And things here?*

Shriek's reply carried overtones of amusement. *The cyborg has spent most of the day with his circuits off. The unspoken tension between the two younger women has been increasing; I think 'Nrrc'kth was less than amused to find User Annie sleeping by your side this morning. Tomàs and Gram have had a discussion of religion that ended with her threatening to drive the cross she was making through his heart. Finnbogg has been melancholy; like you, he seems to find inaction very difficult. As for myself, I have missed your company, but have managed to fill the time by filling my belly. I would have preferred to be done before you arrived, as I realize you find my eating habits as shocking as my sexual traits. But one does what one can.*

Clive, who had indeed been revolted at the sight of the spider woman clutching the still-kicking body of the lepine creature, tried to wave away his reaction, but immediately realized it was pointless. Shriek automatically knew when he was faking. *Is there any privacy on your world?* he asked rather plaintively.

Not really.

It must make things difficult.

She sent him the mental equivalent of a shrug. *We're simply far more honest with each other. The thought of living your way fills me with overwhelming loneliness. Everyone so far apart, so ignorant of everyone else.*

He could feel her shudder as if it were his own. *Yet, if I could read your mind as you do mine, you could not tantalize me with questions about why you are so helpful to me,* he teased.

If you could read my mind as I do yours, I would not need to have my little secrets, Shriek replied almost gleefully.

The long-distance tête-à-tête was interrupted by Horace tugging at Clive's sleeve. "Are you all right, sah?" he asked.

"I'm fine, Sergeant Smythe. I was just having a little conversation with Shriek."

"I see, sah. Well, it's just about time for us to get moving. I thought you might want to do the honors, so to speak."

"Thank you, Sergeant Smythe. I shall."

And so they set out, as oddly assorted a group as Clive could ever have imagined, walking along a starlit road to a strange city where he hoped to pick up once more the trail of his elusive twin.

Several hours later they trudged into Go-Mar, foot-sore and famished. 'Nrrc'kth was on her feet again, though she had been carried for much of the second half of the journey by Chang Guafe. Shriek had volunteered to share the job, but 'Nrrc'kth had shrunk away in fear. Finnbogg, who was possibly the strongest of all of them, had also tried to do his part. Unfortunately, he was so short, and 'Nrrc'kth so tall, that no matter how he held her, some part of her body was dragging along the ground. So the task had fallen mostly to the cyborg, who made no comments about it, to Clive's combined relief and astonishment.

Unlike the village they had found on the other side of N'wrbb's castle—a village—which looked as though it had been plucked right out of rural England, Go-Mar seemed a dreamlike jumble of styles and forms. Tudor-style houses, so familiar they filled Clive with a nostalgia that was almost an ache, stood chock-a-block with shops and dwellings that had an obviously Moorish influence and pagodalike structures that reflected the pictures he had seen of the uttermost East. But the majority of the buildings were not even that familiar. They wandered past a handful of tall, slender spires that seemed to shimmer in the starlight, as if they had been made from mother-of-pearl. Not far past these towers was a cluster of perfect spheres, so dead black in coloring that they reminded Clive at once of Q'oorna, the first world they had encountered on their journey. Not far away stood a very tiny structure that puzzled him greatly, until he decided that it was no more than an entrance to a dwelling built completely underground.

The only theme connecting all these buildings was that of fortification. The few windows they saw were small and covered with shutters. Most doors were reinforced with thick, crossed planks, the only exceptions to this rule being those made of a material Clive had never seen before.

The city was neither walled nor guarded. At first it was more quiet than Clive had anticipated. He decided that their trip had taken longer than he thought and the entire place was asleep. But before long they came to a tavern where the lights were blazing, the laughter was loud, and something that sounded vaguely like music was tinkling through the only open windows they had so far seen.

"Food!" cried 'Nrrc'kth.

"Beer," muttered Horace, almost worshipfully.

Tomàs started counting rosary beads.

Clive started to say something but was interrupted when the door of the tavern opened and a whimpering bundle of arms and legs came hurtling out to crash against the cobblestones.

The door was filled by the outline of a burly, blue-skinned man who was shouting angrily in a language that had not the vaguest similarity to anything Clive had ever heard before. Thus it struck him particularly hard when in the middle of the string of invective he heard three distinctly English words. The first was *pounds*, which made him suspect that the wretch on the cobblestones had failed to pay his bar bill. The second and third were *the Brigadier*.

The words almost took his breath away. Had Neville

been here recently? Certainly there could not be very many men in the Dungeon who went by that title!

He was about to go barreling into the bar to ask what they knew of Neville when he realized they had a small problem.

" 'Nrrc'kth, what do they use for money in this city?" he asked.

The woman's green eyes went wide. "I have not an idea," she said. "As the consort of N'wrbb, I never had to buy anything."

Clive looked around at the group. "Does anyone have anything that might pass for cash here?"

After a moment of silence that was somewhat uncomfortable, Gram nudged Tomàs. "Out with it," she ordered. Tomàs scowled, but as she outsized him by twelve inches and a hundred pounds, he finally succumbed to her glare. Reaching inside his shirt, he pulled out a small leather bag and tossed it to Clive.

When Clive caught it he heard the distinct jingle of coins.

Before he could ask where Tomàs had obtained the purse, Gram spoke again. "Now the rest of it," she said softly.

Tomàs grimaced, then reached inside his shirt and pulled out two more purses. Gram stared at him. He looked back defiantly. Moving so quickly that Clive missed the details of the action, Gram stepped behind the little Portuguese sailor and pinned back his arms with one of her own well-muscled limbs. She thrust her right hand down the front of his pants. While Tomàs howled in anger and embarrassment she fished around a bit, then finally withdrew her hand, clutching yet another purse.

"I thought you had one tucked away down there," she said triumphantly. Pushing Tomàs aside, she added the purse to the other two and handed them to Clive.

Tomàs stood away from the group, glaring at Gram and muttering in a way that gave Clive the distinct impression the white-skinned woman had grabbed more than the purse while her hand was inside Tomàs's trousers.

"Where did these come from?" he asked, holding the four purses cupped in his hands.

"They're mine," said Tomàs.

"He cut them off N'wrbb's men during the battle in front of the moat," said Gram. "You should have seen the little devil. He kept himself out of the action for the most part, though occasionally he'd jump in and get one of the enemy in the back when he could. Well, I don't mind that. War is war. But he always had an ear cocked for the sound of a falling purse. Amazing how brave he was whenever money hit the ground."

"A love of money doesn't seem to fit your theory that the Dungeon is a place where you are being tested by God," said Clive, trying to hide his amusement.

"An old habit," Tomàs said bleakly. "And one of the many reasons the Lord has sent me here, I am sure. May I have them back?"

"It would seem a crime to lead you into temptation," said Clive, tossing one of the purses to Horace and another to Annie. He tucked the third into his jerkin, weighed the fourth in his hand, and finally tossed it back to Tomàs, who looked at it with intense longing before crossing himself and handing it on to 'Nrrc'kth. From the look on his face, Clive decided that the lust for money was not the only earthly sin to which Tomàs was still prey.

He turned back toward the tavern. The thought of strong beer and hot food in a cheerful pub was almost overwhelming after the last several weeks of prison fare. He was about to head for the doors when he realized with some dismay that if N'wrbb was indeed looking for them they were far too conspicuous to enter a public place together. Even in the Dungeon it would be hard not to notice a group that included a cyborg, a seven-foot-tall spider, a four-foot-tall dwarf with a face like a bulldog, and a towering green-haired woman of ethereal beauty.

"I know what you're thinking, sah," said Horace, who stood at his right side. "Taken together we stand out like brass balls on a baboon."

"That was the general thought, Sergeant, though the

phrasing was a little less vulgar. What shall we do about it?"

"I will be glad to remain outside," said Chang Guafe. "I find little to entice me in such a place."

"Thank you," said Clive.

"I, too, will remain outside," said Shriek.

Clive hesitated. He had been counting on the spider woman's gift for wordless communication to help him out if they couldn't find anyone whom they could speak to directly. But there was no question that Shriek was the single most noticeable member of the band. He accepted her offer, and decided he would have to count on Annie's gift for languages to carry them through. Gram was torn; it was clear she was eager to enter the tavern and toss back a flagon of ale, but she was equally set on keeping her niece out of the place. For her part, 'Nrrc'kth was adamant that she was not going to stay outside with Shriek and Chang Guafe unless she was accompanied by someone else she was more comfortable with. In the end Gram's protective streak won out, and she stayed with 'Nrcc'kth. The four of them stationed themselves in the alley. With a promise to bring back food and ale, Clive, Horace, User Annie, Finnbogg, and Tomàs entered the tavern.

"Whoa," whispered Annie, tucking her arm through Clive's as they walked through the door. "It's the *Star Wars* cantina all over again."

"Comlink failure," replied Clive, surprising her with some of the jargon she had used to keep him distant when they first met.

She laughed. "Sorry, Grampa. That was a scene in one of my favorite old movies when I was a kid. The heroes went into a bar that was filled with every kind of nearly human creature you could imagine."

Clive nodded. That was certainly a good description of the sight that met their eyes now. The room was low and filled with smoke. Rough-cut beams as thick as his waist ran across the ceiling. Other beams, nearly as big, ran diagonally from ceiling to walls, acting as braces. And everywhere there were beings that didn't qualify as people by any definition Clive would have used but that were, according to Annie, "close enough for government work."

They elbowed their way to the bar, where a yellow-haired man was dispensing drinks. He had pointed ears and two holes where Clive normally expected to find a nose, but otherwise looked very human. Clive held up his hand, fingers extended, to indicate five drinks. The man held out his own hand, palm up.

"Payment in advance?" asked Clive.

The man shrugged and tapped his hand. Clive extracted a coin from the purse he now carried and placed it in the bartender's hand. He shook his head, touched the coin with an extraordinarily long finger, then tapped his palm in two spots next to it. Clive debated trying to haggle with him, decided it wasn't worth it, and laid down two more coins.

Less than sixty seconds later they had five mugs filled with a hearty ale that was, according to Horace, possibly the single most satisfying thing he had ever drunk. "Not that it's all that good, mind yer," he told Clive. "But I think this is the longest I've ever gone without."

But while the rest of them began to quaff the brew almost immediately, Tomàs stood and stared at his for a long time. Finally he raised it to his lips, the expression on his face as reverent as if he were praying, and began to drink. He did not stop until he had drained the tankard. With a gesture to the bartender he indicated that he wanted another. Presumably satisfied that Clive had a satisfactory medium of exchange, the noseless man brought it without advance payment. Again, Thomàs stared at it for a long time, then downed it in a single, long pull.

Clive, who was busy looking around the room for someone who might speak English, missed it when Tomàs ordered himself a third drink. Horace and Annie did not, but became distracted when Clive indicated that he thought someone was staring at them in a suspicious way. Was it one of N'wrbb's men? Or possibly, as had already happened more than once, someone who had known Neville and wasn't quite sure if Clive was the same man? The latter possibility meant they might get some information out of the man. However, it also carried the danger that it was someone Neville had wronged. Clive rubbed his jaw, which was still bothering him.

The man, a hulking brute with an ax strapped to his thigh, rose from his seat. He was just starting in their direction when a fracas broke out on the other side of them. To Clive's distress, it seemed to center around Finnbogg and Tomàs.

As he sorted things out later, someone at the bar had made a gesture that Tomàs found offensive. Tomàs, having finished a fourth tankard of the potent ale, had responded with a torrent of abuse, the meaning of which was clear in any language. Seconds later the first punch was thrown, and it was all downhill from there.

But all Clive saw now was Tomàs on the floor in front of the bar, locked in a wrestling match with a much larger man. The semicircle of half-drunk men surrounding them was held at bay by a ferociously growling Finnbogg. Distracted by the battle in front of him, Clive lost track of what was going on behind him, and it was only a last-minute shove from Horace that saved him from having his skull split in two by the ax that came whistling through the air to bury itself in the bar.

Clive's instincts had been sharpened during his time in the Dungeon. Without an instant of hesitation he rolled over and drove his foot up into his attacker's genitals. The burly man cried out in pain and doubled over. Clive, who was already up on his knees, grabbed the back of the man's head in both his hands and drove it into the floor. The noises around him indicated that the trouble was spreading, but Clive was momentarily stunned by the words he had heard his assailant utter just before he lost consciousness: "Damn you, Folliot."

He rolled the man over and slapped his face, trying to rouse him.

"No time for that, sah," said Horace, tugging at his arm. "We'd best get out of here. We don't need to attract any more attention than necessary."

Clive looked up, and ducked as a three legged stool went shooting by his head.

Horace was right, as usual. The entire tavern seemed to have become a single massive brawl.

"Where's Annie?" he asked, knocking aside an oncoming man who had scales instead of skin.

Horace pointed behind them. Clive turned in time to see Annie hurl a stoneware pitcher, which broke over the head of someone who was about to throw a knife into the melee. Finnbogg was leaping about in front of her, growling ferociously at anyone who dared get too close. Two man lay on the floor in front of the incensed dwarf. Clive could see a jagged edge of bone sticking out of one man's sleeve, indicating that he had tangled with the dwarf's massive jaws. Everyone else was keeping his distance.

"Let's get them, and get out of here," said Clive.

Horace nodded. Without waiting for Clive, he waded into the brawl in the direction of Tomàs. Clive turned and headed for Annie. The floor was slippery with ale, the air thick with shouts and curses. He realized as he worked his way through the tangle of men and women that his greatest advantage in the whole situation was that he had had time for only one drink. Smashing together the heads of the last two men who stood in his way, both of whom were deep in their cups and mumbling about the "big dog", Clive called to Finnbogg to let him pass.

The dwarf was almost blind with rage at the thought that anyone would dare to threaten his beloved Annie, and it took a moment before he recognized Clive. When he did he moved aside with a throaty growl, then resumed his guard stance.

"Get on my back!" yelled Clive. Annie jumped on, wrapping her legs around his waist and her arms around his neck. Then he called Finnbogg. With the mastiff-jawed dwarf to clear a path, the brawling drunks parted before them like the waters of the Red Sea rolling back at Moses's command. Even so, Annie had to use Clive's sword to lash out behind them once or twice.

Horace met them at the door. He had Tomàs tucked

under one arm and a bloody sword in his other hand. They nodded to each other and made a hasty exit.

But not hasty enough. Recognizing that the instigator of the entire brawl was escaping, several men detached themselves from the mob inside the tavern and came hurtling through the door, howling for Tomàs's head.

It's more than we can possibly handle, Clive thought in despair, just before Shriek came bursting out of the alley, wailing her heart-stopping battle cry and leaping to the front of the mob. The sight of the giant spider slowed them down enough for Gram and Chang Guafe to launch a counterattack from the side. Clive took advantage of the confusion to contact Shriek.

There's an almost endless supply of bloodthirsty drunks inside. We can't fight all of them. Have everyone follow me.

It shall be as you wish, O Folliot, she responded, *though I would rather stay and fight.*

Shriek!

I was merely expressing a preference. You start. I will contact the others immediately.

Clive grabbed Horace and Annie and pointed down a nearby street. Then he threw Tomàs over his back and started to run, trusting Shriek to gather the rest of the group.

Fifteen minutes later they were still dodging through alleys and around corners. Unfortunately, the mob had almost doubled in size because two of the streets they ran down had taken them past other taverns, whose late-night customers had been more than willing to join a chase, no matter what the quarry.

Clive, who had handed Tomàs over to Chang Guafe, was not sure how much longer they could keep ahead of the mob. Then, as if to demonstrate that there was no situation so bad it could not be made worse, they ran past a pair of mounted horsemen who must have recognized them, for they began to shout, "Stop, in the name of N'wrbb Crrd'f!"

The horsemen started after them, but got tangled in the mob that was on foot. The confusion gave Clive and his people enough time to round a corner and get halfway down a block, where they were stopped by the sight of a door swinging open and the sound of a voice crying out, "Neville! Quick! You can hide in here!"

CHAPTER THIRTEEN

Emmy Storm

Clive was used to being attacked when he was mistaken for Neville. So it was surprise enough that someone thinking he was his brother was actually offering them shelter. But when the voice that called to them turned out to belong to a short, slightly stocky woman with flaming red hair who threw her arms around him crying, "Oh Lawks, I've missed yer, my old sweetie," Clive's relief at finding shelter quickly gave way to nervous embarrassment. What would happen when she found out he *wasn't* Neville? Would she scream? Call for help? Throw them back to the mob?

Actually, Clive realized that unless she had a lot of friends, it would be hard for her to manage the latter. He didn't want to stay where they were not welcome. But welcome or not, they were going to take advantage of this hiding place until the mob was gone.

"Ah, Neville, Neville," purred the woman, "what have you gotten yerself into this time?" She was rubbing her hands up and down Clive's back, her face still buried against his chest.

Clive hesitated. The foyer where they stood was but dimly lit by a pair of oil lamps. While he and Neville were not identical, they could easily pass for each other under such circumstances. Should he simply go along with the mistake?

He decided against it. Such a deception went against his nature. Besides, if Neville really did have a relationship of some kind with this woman, there would be too many places where she might catch him out.

Yet the mob was howling in the street at this very moment. Perhaps now was not the time to enlighten her after all. He put his arms around her and squeezed her tightly to him.

"Oh, Neville," she cooed.

He counted seconds. The sound of the mob began to diminish. Good. Drunk and in the dark, they were continuing the chase, unaware that their quarry had gone to shelter.

He waited another few beats, then reached down to try to disentangle the woman's arms from around his waist. "I fear there has been some mistake, madam," he whispered.

"Oh, Neville, don't tease like that. Yer always so full of nonsense when you come to visit me. Why don't you just give yer poor Emmy a kiss and stop fooling like that?"

"Look at me," Clive said gently. At the same time he sent a message to Shriek: *Have Horace stand ready to help me quiet her if she screams.*

It shall be done, O Folliot. As usual, her communication carried layers of meaning; the undermessage that rustled in his mind this time seemed tinged with amusement.

"Look at me," Clive said sternly.

The woman pulled back and looked up into his face. She was not exceptionally beautiful. But her snub nose and the dusting of freckles that ran across her cheeks filled him with a sudden longing for the Scottish highlands where he had spent his summers as a youth.

The distress that filled the blue eyes scanning his face was replaced by sudden comprehension. "You're Clive!" she announced with some delight.

Clive was pleased that his brother had bothered to mention him to this woman, and annoyed with himself for being pleased.

"That's right," he said gently. "Neville is my brother."

"Oh, I know that," the woman said cheerfully. "He's mentioned you to me on several occasions. Well, don't just stand there. Come on into the parlor."

She took his hand and began tugging him forward. Still astonished by her reaction, he followed willingly.

The rest of the group came with them, led by Finnbogg, who was the current proprietor of the now-unconscious Tomàs.

Emmy led them through a pair of thick red curtains. Clive looked around in astonishment. Except for a certain crudity in the work, the decor of her parlor looked like it could have been transplanted directly from his homeland. The large room was filled with overstuffed chairs and settees, upholstered in dark fabrics that had a velvetlike texture. Embroidered cloths covered the small tables that stood next to most of the chairs. Each table had a lamp, its wick turned low, flanked by two or three short glasses and a bottle of dark amber liquid.

As homey as the familiar furnishings made it seem, it was clearly not a home. It took a moment for Clive to recall where he had last seen a room like this. When he did, he began to blush.

"Are you thinking what I'm thinking, sah?" asked Horace, who had stationed himself at Clive's right hand.

"Ain't it lovely?" Emmy asked cheerfully. "A little bit o' England in this awful Dungeon. Now, why don't you introduce me to your friends, Clive. Are any of you hungry?" she asked, scanning the group with sudden concern.

"I am," 'Nrrc'kth said emphatically.

Emmy crossed to the wall and pulled on a thick red rope. Clive heard a bell tinkle somewhere in the distance. Within seconds a tall, green man wearing nothing but a loincloth entered the room through another set of curtains.

Emmy addressed him by a name that started with "Mar" and ended with a kind of fizzing sound made by lifting her upper lip and blowing through her front teeth. When she had finished her instructions he nodded and disappeared. He reappeared, pushing a cart laden with fruit and cheese, just about the time Clive had finished introducing the rest of his friends.

With Mar/fsssh's help Emmy arranged several of the chairs into a large circle. Those of the group who had a basically human design were grateful for the accommodations. The others—Shriek, Chang Guafe, and even

Finnbogg—chose their own ways to relax: Shriek positioned herself behind a settee and leaned over it, resting her arms on the back; Chang Guafe straddled an ottoman and began rearranging his face; and Finnbogg crouched on the floor at Annie's feet.

"Well, now," said Emmy. "Ain't this nice?"

Clive admitted to himself that, given the fact that she was feeding them excellent food in an atmosphere of extreme peace and quiet, it was very nice indeed.

"The girls have pretty much turned in for the night," said Emmy. "I was just getting ready to lock up when I heard the ruckus outside. Lucky for you that I did!"

"Lucky indeed," said Clive, spearing a chunk of pink fruit that had the texture of a melon but a taste that was more like spiced pears. "And your hospitality is greatly appreciated."

"This and more for Neville Folliot's brother," Emmy said with a smile. "And more than that, if you're half as good in the sack as he was."

The reactions to Emmy's statement were varied but distinct: Clive blanched, Horace coughed discreetly, Annie chuckled, and 'Nrrc'kth made a noise in her throat that was close to a growl.

Is this part of the human mating ritual? Shriek asked privately.

Not usually! replied Clive.

Emmy looked around the room. "Did I say something wrong?" Almost immediately her cheeks began to color. "Damme if I didn't," she said. "You'll have to excuse me, Clive. I've been working in this fucking Dungeon so long I've forgot how things are at home. Well, we'll put that on hold for a bit. Why don't you tell me what you've been up to?"

"Searching for my brother, mostly," said Clive, "though that quest has landed us in trouble more often than not."

"I don't envy you that job," said Emmy. "Old Neville, he moves faster than any man I ever met. I'd swear there was someone after him."

Clive hesitated. Could that be the cause of his brother's peregrinations? Was someone trying to capture him? That would explain why he never stopped to wait for them. But if that was the case, then who was it? And why?

"Did he ever mention anything like that?" asked Clive.

"Not hardly!" said Emmy. "He'd come swooping in here, sweep me off my feet, and be gone again before I ever had a chance to talk to him."

As she spoke her eyes traveled over Clive's frame. It was obvious she was comparing him to his brother.

"When was the last time you saw Neville?" asked Clive.

Emmy closed her eyes and began counting on her fingers. "About six months ago, I'd say, though it's hard to tell about the passing of time in this place."

"How did you get here?" asked User Annie.

Emmy closed her eyes. "The Ripper done it," she said, after a moment.

"Do you mean Jack the Ripper?" asked Annie, stirring uncomfortably in her chair.

Emmy nodded.

Clive turned to Annie. "Is this Jack Ripper someone you know?"

"Of course not!" Then she looked at him. "But you ought to. Or at least I think you should. Shit. I never was good with dates. What year did you say you came from?"

"Eighteen hundred and sixty-eight," replied Clive.

Annie turned to Emmy. "And what year was it when you came here?"

"Eighteen hundred and eighty-eight," said Emmy.

"Well, that explains it, Grampa: right era, wrong decade. Jack the Ripper was this homicidal maniac who started chopping up London hookers about twenty years after you took off for the Dungeon."

Clive's first instinct was to protest that he had been in the Dungeon for only a month or two at the most. He knew that Annie had come from the future, of course, as had that strange band of Nipponese soldiers they had encountered. But somehow he had considered them anomalies, people plucked out of time and brought back to his own era. Until now he had managed to convince himself that it was still 1868 in the real world. But now there was Emmy, the first person he had met here who had come from a time that was so close to his own—so close, and yet so far. Suddenly he was struck by a baffling vision of time as an endless ribbon, stretching forward into the future, back into the past. Were the Lords of the Dungeon truly able to range up and down that ribbon, snatching people from any part of it, willy-nilly? And what did that mean for him and his band? If they ever *did* manage to escape, what time would it be in the real world?

He realized that Emmy was speaking.

". . . married for a short time. My husband was a lousy bum, but he gave me a lovely name, don't you think? It was good for business, too. The sailors always used to say that their idea of heaven was 'a port in Emmy Storm.' Course, that wasn't until after my old man left me. Once you get hungry enough, you'll do whatever you need to survive, don't you know. I had me a fair career, too, until the house where I was working offended some pollytician and I ended up back on the streets right about the time old Jack was starting *his* career. It was right scary for a time then, I can tell you. I mean, it clearly wasn't safe to be out on the streets at night, at least not plying your trade, if you know what I mean. But a girl's got to eat, don't she?"

Emmy adjusted her pink robe and looked around for some sort of confirmation. "Anyway, I'm out walkin' one night when this gennaman starts to chat me up. I talked with him a bit, but he was kind of funny about it; I couldn't tell if we had a deal or not. Course it was like that sometimes, with the shy ones. Well suddenly I realize we've walked down a side street, and there ain't no one in sight. The fog was good and thick that night—couldn't see your feet without bending over. All of a sudden he grabs my arms and says, 'I've had my eye on you, Miss Storm.' "

Emmy Storm's eyes were wide with the horror of what had happened next.

"Well, I knew that was the end of me. 'You're Jack!' I

screamed. I pulled my arm away from him and started to run. But he had me in a blind alley. I reached the end of it and turned around. Jack was walking toward me, kind of slow, just a shape in the mist. His black cape was billowing out behind him, the fog swirling around in front. I could see the knife in his hands; he was holding it way out ahead of him. It was a long one, believe me. But that wasn't the worst thing. The worst thing was that he was laughing. Not a big laugh; just kind of a quiet chuckle, like he knew some private joke."

She shivered and rubbed her hands over her arms. "He got closer and closer. His breath smelled of coffee. He put his knife to my throat. I screamed and pressed back against the wall—and there wasn't any wall there!" She chuckled, but it was a feeble sound, undercut by memory. "Jack the Ripper's face was the last thing I ever saw of home—which I suppose is one reason it don't bother me as much to be here as it does some." This time her laugh was more genuine. "You never saw such a surprised expression in your life as Jack had when I slipped out of his grasp. Of course I guess my own face must have looked pretty good when I looked around and found myself in this place. Didn't take me long to get used to it, though. I always did land on my feet. That's what Will Storm said, just before he left me. 'I'm not worried about you, Em. You always land on your feet.' I guess my feet are pretty well sunk in here now. Seems like I've been here forever. The only thing that still puzzles me is why they brought me here."

Clive shrugged. "Why have they brought any of us?"

"I'm sure I don't know," said Emmy. "But according to Neville, no one comes to the Dungeon by accident."

"Do you mean people are chosen for specific reasons?" asked Clive, sitting up and staring at her.

Emmy shrugged. "Well, that's what Neville made it sound like."

"What else has Neville told you of the Dungeon?" asked Clive.

"Not an awful lot. I mean, there are the things that most people know, like about there being nine levels to the place." She looked at Clive. "You did know that, didn't you?"

Clive shook his head, feeling unaccountably foolish.

"Well there," Emmy said cheerfully. "You learn something new every day, don't you, ducks?"

"Then what level are we on?" asked Annie.

"I would think this is the second level," said Horace, "that is, assuming Q'oorna was the first."

"Oh, it is," said Emmy. "At least, that's what Neville told me. I've never been there myself. This is where I landed, and this is where I'm staying."

"Smart move," said Annie. "Q'oorna is not what you would call the vacation paradise of the cosmos."

" 'Nrrc'kth," said Clive, "do you know any of this?"

The slender woman looked up from the melon she had been systematically consuming and shook her head. "N'wrbb did not discuss matters of state with me."

"I knew," said Finnbogg.

"Yes, I'm sure you did, Finn," replied Clive, declining to mention that he had learned some time ago that it was impossible to separate what Finnbogg knew from what he made up.

He turned back to Emmy. "Assume we're ignorant," he said. "Which, unfortunately, is not that far from the truth. Most of us landed in the first level. And with the exception of Finnbogg, most of us haven't been here that long."

Actually, he wasn't sure Finnbogg had been in the Dungeon very long either; it was hard to tell, since the last time the matter had come up the dwarf had claimed he was brought here ten thousand years ago. *And how about Shriek,* he wondered. *How long was she here before we met her?*

Too long for my tastes, O Folliot, she sent. *But not long enough to learn the answers I need.*

I asked you not to do that! he shot back.

She sent him one of her peculiar mental shrugs. *I heard you call my name.*

Unaware of the private dialogue, Emmy started to

answer his question. "What else can I tell you? You want to watch out for the Chaffri, of course. Getting involved with them is bad business."

"What are the Chaffri?" asked Clive.

"Haven't the foggiest idea, ducks," Emmy replied. "But you asked me to tell you the kind of thing that everyone knows. Well, that's one of them. 'Watch out for the Chaffri.' It's just something you learn early on around here. Of course, the Ren run the place. Oh, this is hard, Clive. I don't know what to tell you."

"Start with the Ren. Who are they?"

"Just what I said. The people who run the place. Well, I don't know that they're people, exactly. I've never actually seen one of them. Don't know anyone who has, for that matter. But that's just something else everyone knows: the Ren are in charge of the Dungeon."

"I thought the Q'oornans were," said Clive.

Emmy snorted. "That's like saying the Irish run England. Q'oorna's just the place the Ren picked to use as an anchor when they built the Dungeon."

"What was their reason for building it?" Clive asked eagerly.

"Oh, I don't know, love. Why does a bird build a nest? Why are there stars in the sky—not that there are in this lousy city, not what you'd call real ones, at least. But you get the idea. I mean, it's just something they did."

"Well, who are they?"

"Now I just told you that. They're the ones who built the Dungeon."

Clive conceded defeat.

"Coo, what's the matter with me brain?" cried Emmy, slapping herself on the forehead. "I've got something that'll help you with all this."

"What is it?" asked Clive eagerly.

"Your brother's journal. He left it with me, told me to give it to you if I ever see you."

Clive caught his breath. Annie started to say something, but he motioned her to silence.

"Where is it?" he asked.

She giggled. "It's upstairs, in my room."

"Would you please get it for me?" said Clive, trying to hold his temper.

The coy look became downright lascivious. "Why don't you come on up and look at it in private, ducks?"

Annie could barely contain her mirth. 'Nrrc'kth, however, was making an unpleasant noise in her throat again.

"I'd rather look at it down here," Clive said uncomfortably.

Emmy shook her head. "Neville said I was to give it to you and you only. I think you better come up." She turned to the others. "Mar/fsssh will find places for you to sleep. We'll see you in the morning."

Then she took Clive by the arm and led him out of the room.

· CHAPTER FOURTEEN ·

The Cave of Cerberus

Emmy Storm closed the door of her room. "Ain't it nice?" she said, turning to Clive and pushing herself against him.

"It's remarkable," he responded.

And indeed it was. The room was dominated by an elegant four-poster bed, complete with ruffled canopy. The bed was on a dais, two steps up from the rest of the floor. To the right of the dais stood a tall wardrobe, carefully carved with symbols that had no meaning Clive could decipher, yet seemed somehow to be filled with hidden messages. A chest of drawers with the same motifs stood at the right. Both were polished to a rich, deep finish. Near the dresser stood a washstand, which held an elegant marble pitcher and basin. The coverlet on the bed appeared to be made of silk; the wallpaper was not unlike some he had seen in Paris about five years earlier.

"Where did you obtain all this, Mrs. Storm? I mean, the Dungeon does not strike me as being the sort of place where one looks for this style of decoration."

"Do you have to call me Mrs. Storm?" Emmy asked with a little pout. She played with the laces on Clive's jerkin, then combed her fingers through the thick, chestnut-colored hair that lay behind them. "It's so formal."

He cleared his throat. "I'm sorry . . . Emmy."

"That's better, ducks," she said, kissing him on the curve of his jaw. "As for your question—let's just say that I have a very good class of customer. Powerful sorts, if you know what I mean. Some of them are fond enough of me that they bring me little presents now and then."

"But do they actually travel in and out of the Dungeon to do so?" asked Clive, filled with a sudden hope that there might be some way to escape after all.

"Shhhh!" hissed Emmy. "That's not the kind of thing we talk about here."

"Surely no one can hear us," said Clive.

Emmy looked around fearfully. "Who knows what can happen in the Dungeon? Anyway, I didn't bring you up here to talk about that kind of business." She loosened the belt of her robe. "Men come from great distances for me, Clive, and they pay very well. But for Neville Folliot's brother—it's on the house, and well worth it if you're even half as good as he was."

Until this moment Clive had experienced a growing hunger for Mrs. Storm; he had recognized the possibility of this kind of liaison when he followed her up the stairs to her room. But the invitation to compete with Neville in still one more area of endeavor had the same effect on his libido as a quick dip in an icy mountain stream. His desire disappeared, replaced by an anger he was barely able to contain.

"My brother and I are very different men, Mrs. Storm. My quest to find him has far more to do with a promise to our mutual father than with any kind of filial devotion. I'll thank you to fetch me that journal."

Emmy Storm drew back from him. Her blue eyes registered a succession of emotions that started with shock, worked their way through sorrow, and climaxed in anger.

"Neville told me you were a prig," she hissed. "He didn't tell me you were pompous to boot."

"The journal, Mrs. Storm."

As Clive watched her cross to the dresser he found himself hoping that Shriek had not been listening in on this particular conversation.

What conversation? asked the familiar voice inside his head.

Never mind, he replied. *Go away. I'll tell you later.*

The now familiar mental shrug was followed by a momentary feeling of emptiness that let him know she was gone. He returned his attention to Emmy, who had opened the bottom drawer of the dresser. Moving aside a stack of lacy underthings, she drew out a familiar-looking volume. It was bound in black leather. Clive held his breath, hardly able to believe it was possible. Three times already they had lost and mysteriously recovered Neville's journal. It hardly seemed possible that the miracle could happen again. But then, reflected Clive, considering the past history of the little book, maybe it was inevitable.

Emmy Storm placed the book in his hands. When she looked up at him he saw tears shining in the lashes of her wide blue eyes. Had he really hurt her so much? Or was she merely acting for his benefit? He reached out to brush them away. She turned her head and kissed him gently on the wrist, then moved in closer and laid her head softly against his chest.

An hour later, lying beside her and watching her breathe, it took all the reserve Clive could muster not to ask if he had lived up to her expectations. She brushed his cheek with her fingertips. He placed his hand on her stomach, and slept.

He was awakened by a pounding on the door and the sound of Horace Hamilton Smythe's voice.

"Sah! Do wake up, sah! We've got trouble."

Clive rolled out of bed and pulled on the vaguely medieval costume he had been given in N'wrbb Crrd'f's castle. While the soft leather boots were still intact, the rest of the outfit had suffered considerable damage during their recent adventures. The maroon trousers, also of leather, were torn out at one knee. The scarlet jerkin was now discolored by numerous patches of dried blood. Some of the blood was his; most of it belonged to others. He grabbed Neville's journal, then opened the door. "What is it, Horace?"

Smythe looked even more agitated than he had sounded. "We've got company, sah. The house is pretty well fortified, and Mar/fsssh is trying to stall him. But the doors won't hold long if he really wants to come through them."

"For heaven's sake, Sergeant Smythe, who are you talking about?"

"Why don't you look for yourself, sah," said Horace, pointing to a window at the end of the hallway.

Clive began to stride along the corridor.

"Try not to be seen!" called Horace.

He drew aside a curtain made of damask and peered down into the street below. N'wrbb Crrd'f was pounding on the door with the hilt of his sword. Standing behind the tall, almost grotesquely slender man was an army of nearly a hundred.

Clive sighed, and wondered briefly if heaven were sending him an instant punishment for indulging in the sins of the flesh with Emmy Storm. "Are the others up, Sergeant?"

"Been up, sah. Already eaten."

He headed back for the bedroom. Emmy was already out of bed, slipping into her pink robe.

"Is there a back way out of here?" asked Clive.

She looked startled. "Of course there is, ducks. Not that anyone much minds what other folk do around here. But I was so used to needing a way for customers to slip out unseen that I had it built in when I bought the place."

"You're an angel, Emmy Storm," said Clive, kissing her on the forehead.

"That's what they all say. Come on, I'll show you the way, if you'll tell me what this is all about."

"Sergeant Smythe," said Clive. "Where are the others?"

"In the kitchen," replied Smythe. "Mar/fsssh sent us there when the ruckus started."

"That's good," said Emmy, as she started down the stairs. "It puts us close to the back way out. I'll lead you."

As they passed through the hallway Clive could hear Mar/fsssh explaining patiently that he could not possibly open the door without permission of the lady of the house, and, yes, of course he had sent someone to fetch her, but as she was very testy when awakened unexpectedly, it was likely the poor unfortunate chosen for that task would come back with several bruises, and possibly some broken bones as well. Clive almost wished they could stay for the rest of the green-skinned man's recitation, which was clearly going to go on for several more minutes, despite the angry shouts from the other side of the door.

"He's very good at what he does," said Emmy, leading them into the kitchen. Clive's people were there, as well as a number of females of varying species, most of whom were chittering with excitement. Something smelled delicious, and Clive found himself lamenting the fact that he was about to miss breakfast.

"This way," said Emmy, stepping from the kitchen into a room that appeared to function as a pantry. She reached inside one of the cupboards. Clive heard a click, and a section of the wall pivoted inward on invisible hinges to reveal a corridor paneled with dark wood.

"This opens onto an alley behind the house. On the other side of the alley is an abandoned building. You can hide in there until dark—it won't be safe for you to travel through the city anytime before that. I'll send Mar/fsssh with some food for you later in the day. Go!"

"Bless you, Emmy Storm," said Clive. He pulled her close and kissed her, aware even as he did so that Chang Guafe would be judging this as inefficient behavior. He started down the corridor, and didn't look back, even when he heard the entrance snap back into place behind him.

Clive held Neville's journal in his hands for several minutes before he actually had the heart to open it. Though he appeared to be staring at the gold lettering that decorated the otherwise plain black leather of the cover, he barely saw it. His mind was too busy repeating the memory of the first time he had held the mysterious book.

He had been standing atop a cliff in Q'oorna, Horace Hamilton Smythe and Sidi Bombay at his side. They did not yet know that they were in Q'oorna—only that they had somehow stumbled out of their own world into someplace terrifyingly new. As if that had not been frightening enough, they had found a coffin at the top of the cliff, which Horace had opened to reveal Neville's body. Clive's fingers trembled at the memory. This very journal had been clutched in the cold hands that lay crossed on his dead twin's chest. Opening it, he had found a message from his brother. That had been strange enough. But sometime later, opening it again, he had found a new message, written *after* he had begun to carry the journal.

To date, there had been four messages in all. Twice, and now a third time, the journal itself had been mysteriously returned to him after he thought it lost. That Neville was not dead he was now certain. But by what legerdemain he continually managed to insert new material into the journal Clive had no idea.

He ran his fingers over the black leather cover. What kind of message would he find this time? Something helpful—or one of the maddeningly cryptic messages that reflected so well the way Neville had always dealt with him, any assistance hidden beneath a mask of teasing that occasionally rose to the level of torment?

He sighed and opened the book, which he knew from experience would be blank up to the page where the new message had been recorded.

In the past the color of the ink had sometimes been related to the message—as the green ink that had been used just before he met emerald-haired N'wrbb and 'Nrrc'kth.

This time the ink was blue.

Little brother, you astonish me. Like our father, I had no idea how resourceful you truly are— resourceful enough, perhaps, to penetrate still deeper into the mysteries of the Dungeon. Follow me as far as you can, for every level deeper is one level closer to the heart of all this madness. Catch me if you can, and I will be forever grateful.

The next level waits. But you have missed the easy way and, alas, I have small hope for your arrival, for the remaining route is the very definition of suicide. Even to survive is dangerous, for if you should somehow manage the passage through the Cave of Cerberus, you will almost inevitably rise in the consciousness of Ren and Chaffri alike.

All is danger here, Clive. All is danger.

Clive stared at the message for some time before he closed the book.

"Well," asked Annie. "What does big brother have to say this time?"

"Nothing very encouraging," Clive replied. "It would appear that if we are to find Neville we have to try to penetrate the next level of the Dungeon."

Chang Guafe had been sitting in a corner, shortening one of his arms. "Then we can continue to travel together," he said.

Clive, who was well aware of Guafe's desire to find those who were responsible for his arrival here in the Dungeon, had mixed reactions to this statement. The cyborg was a continuing challenge to his leadership. Yet he brought considerable strength to their party, strength they would undoubtedly need many times on the road that lay ahead.

"Is vengeance really pragmatic?" he asked, wondering if he could actually annoy the mechanistic creature.

"It is pragmatic to have a goal," said Guafe. "It keeps one moving."

Clive sighed and wished he had never brought up the question. He wasn't in the mood to argue semantics with someone from another planet. He was grateful when Horace deflected the matter by returning attention to the journal.

"Just what does your brother say, sah?" he asked.

Clive quoted Neville's comments as exactly as he could, knowing without looking that when he opened the book again the message would be gone.

'Nrrc'kth looked up in shock. "The Cave of Cerberus?" she asked.

Clive nodded.

"Even my consort spoke of that place in cautious tones," said the white-skinned woman.

"Neville does, too," said Clive. "But unless anyone has a better idea, that's where we're heading next."

Tomàs, still bleary-eyed from his bender the night before, proposed that they simply stay in Go-Mar. Clive invited him to do so if he wished. The little sailor considered it, but it was clear that the prospect of remaining in the hostile city by himself was even more intimidating than following the band into whatever lay ahead.

To Clive's astonishment, when Emmy arrived with food later that afternoon, coming herself instead of sending Mar/fsssh, she was able to give them clear directions to their next destination. "Heard all about it from a couple of my customers, ducks," she said cheerfully. But her tone changed as she began to remember what she had heard. "It's no place for the likes of you, love. Nor anyone else who wants to stay alive very long," she added, her voice serious.

"Why?" asked Clive. "What will we find there?"

"Can't rightly say." Emmy shrugged. "They were pretty vague on that account. Just said it was an awful place. Why don't you just stay here with me for a bit, instead of rushing off into more trouble?"

"Do you really want the nine of us cluttering up your place of business?" asked Clive.

Emmy looked around the room. "It was more you I had in mind, ducks," she whispered.

Clive shook his head. "We arrived on your doorstep as a group, Emmy Storm, and we'll leave the same way. Even if I were alone, I could not stay, much as I might enjoy it. I have too many promises to keep."

"That's the problem with men," Emmy said without rancor. "The good ones are all so busy running around keeping their word they don't have any time for you. Well, I hate to see you go, Clive Folliot, but if go you must, then I'll tell you the road to take."

After she had explained the safest way out of the city, and told them all she remembered of the road they would follow thereafter, Clive pressed one of the bags of coins into her hand.

"This is not for services rendered," he said with a

smile, "but to help cover the damage N'wrbb and his men caused when they searched your house."

"Well, since you put it that way, ducks, I'll be glad to accept," said Emmy, tucking the bag into her generous bosom. She kissed him on the cheek. "Take care of yourself, Clive Folliot. The world is short enough on gennamen as it is."

Clive didn't even have to turn around to know that the snort he heard came from his great-great-grand-daughter.

When darkness came they followed Emmy's directions and escaped Go-Mar without incident.

Clive glanced around nervously. The forest through which they wandered seemed the very definition of menacing. Strange shapes flitted among the trees. Cries and howls sounded in the distance. The light of the faded stars cast grotesque shadows through the twisted branches of the gnarled old trees. Yet it was not the eerie forest that bothered him, as much as the worry that N'wrbb would somehow discover where they had gone, and continue his hunt for them.

Yet it was three days since they had left Go-Mar, and they had seen or heard no sign of the man.

Even so, they had resumed their old pattern of traveling by night and sleeping by day. The primary difference was that they now had a definite goal in mind: the entrance to the third level of the Dungeon.

Fingering his jaw, which was still bothering him, Clive stole a glance at Shriek. The green chitinous material that covered the place where she had lost an arm appeared somewhat swollen. He wondered if she was developing an infection. The thought bothered him. He knew too many soldiers who had survived a battle only to succumb to the aftereffects of a wound. It eased his mind some that he did not detect the sweet-rotting smell that often accompanied the condition.

But then, who knew what a spider with gangrene would smell like?

Do not worry about me, O Folliot, she whispered in his

mind. *I will be fine. I am more concerned about what we will face when we reach the Cave of Cerberus.*

Clive nodded. *The thought concerns me, too.*

I am picking up an image, she replied. *Does this name have meaning for you?*

Knowing Finnbogg's penchant for collecting legends and folklore, and thinking he might feel a special affinity for this material, Clive called to the dwarf to join them. Finnbogg trotted over. Even in the dim starlight Clive could see that he was smiling hugely, as he usually did whenever someone paid him any attention.

"Here's a bit of information I thought you might fancy, old chap. This cave we're heading for has a name that seems to have been taken from an old legend back on my world. Some of our people believed that the entrance to Hell was through a cave guarded by Cerberus, who was a huge, three-headed dog."

Finnbogg shivered, and suddenly Clive realized that in the Dungeon it was never wise to take such a connection lightly. Back home he could reasonably expect a cave with such a fanciful name to be fronted by a rock formation that resembled a dog, or something equally innocuous. Here—well, here it could mean almost anything. Maybe the cave really was guarded by some monstrous, caninelike creature. Given all they had been through, he would hardly be surprised to discover that it was the entrance to Hell itself.

While Emmy's directions had been clear as to the how of finding the cave, she had been a little vague on distance. Clive began to wonder how long it would be before they actually reached their destination. He was still contemplating the mystery of what they would find when they got there when the sky began to grow light again, and they stopped to rest.

Clive asked Horace to distribute some food. With his long experience as a quartermaster, it had made sense to put Smythe in charge of the extra provisions Emmy had provided for their journey. By supplementing her contributions with large quantities of the small sweet nuts they were now so used to, plus such game as Shriek and Chang Guafe captured along the way, they expected to be able to spread the food out over at least three more marches.

Clive was slicing himself a piece of cheese when Gram came and plopped down next to him. To his surprise, the muscular woman reached out and took his hand, invoking Shriek's neural web of communication. She looked into his eyes, and the message was delivered without the use of spoken words:

I am worried about 'Nrrc'kth. I know that she often seems a burden to the band. I would be the first to admit that she is nervous, high-strung, oversensitive. But it was not her choice to come here, any more than it was mine, or yours. She did not join this expedition to make things more difficult.

The point is, I don't know how much longer she can stand this.

What do you want me to do? asked Clive.

Gram shrugged. *Try not to push her too hard. Don't make her feel like she is a terrible person for not being as strong as the rest of us. Maybe defend her a little from the others.*

Here the intimacy of the connection betrayed Gram. While she tried to couch her thoughts in generalities, Clive understood at once that the sniping between Annie and 'Nrrc'kth was one of the woman's major concerns. On the heels of that knowledge came a wealth of related thoughts and images—pictures of Annie and himself as seen through Gram's eyes, a sense of combined amusement and disapproval, a desire that he pay more attention to 'Nrrc'kth.

Gram pulled her hand away.

"Damn that spider woman anyway," she said. "I should have known better than to try this fancy shit. Talk's good enough for the likes of me."

Clive fought down an impulse to defend himself against what he saw as the older woman's charges. He was trying desperately to keep things together as it was. The implication that he was letting 'Nrrc'kth down annoyed him. Holding his tongue for a moment gave him a chance to realize that, regardless of the reality, the *idea* that he was failing her had to be dealt with.

He remembered Shriek's dictum: "Suggestions impose, questions lead." It had been effective with Horace. Maybe it would work again.

"What do you want me to do?" he asked.

"Not much you can do," Gram said. "Oh, maybe you can try to keep Annie off her back a bit. But the real problem is that it's a rough world out here and she's not meant to be part of it. But here she is." Gram sighed. "Maybe I just needed to talk to someone about it. You seemed like the right one."

"I'll do what I can," Clive said softly.

"I know that, ducks." Gram patted his cheek and gave him a wicked imitation of Emmy Storm. "You do what you can for all us gals." Then she let her face grow serious again. "You're a good man, Clive Folliot. You're doing all right."

With a grunt she got to her feet and walked away. Clive looked after her, trying to sort through what seemed a dozen conflicting emotions that the short conversation had stirred up in him.

Later, when Annie asked if she could sleep beside him, he spoke to her about 'Nrrc'kth.

"I know," she sighed. "I suppose I really should take it easy. But honestly, Grampa, the woman drives me out of my mind." She smiled. "I hate to admit it, but you're not the only one hauling your cultural prejudices around behind you. I was raised to stand on my own two feet. Those Sunbonnet Sue types give me the pip."

While Clive didn't understand the exact reference, her meaning was clear.

"Anyway," she continued, "I'll try to be a little less rough on Sue in the future."

The next march didn't provide much opportunity for Annie to test her new resolve. Before they had gone far enough for 'Nrrc'kth to begin complaining, they had reached the boulder that Emmy had told them would indicate the place where they were to leave the road.

Clive wondered if the formation was natural, or if the Ren—or whoever had created the Dungeon—actually had a sense of humor.

The boulder, which was twice his height, looked remarkably like the head of a giant dog.

They loosened their weapons and started down the path. Finnbogg grew nervous. When Clive asked him why, he claimed it had to do with the smells along the trail.

Their way led across a wide stream, which they crossed with the help of stepping stones. Not much farther on the trees thinned out, as the terrain became ever more rocky.

Clive thought he heard the baying of a hound somewhere ahead.

"Stay close together," he cautioned. "Chang Guafe and Shriek, come up and walk with me. The three of us will be the first to face this thing, whatever it is."

The path led them into a rocky ravine, the sides of which grew increasingly steep as they went on. They came to a spot nearly blocked by a rocky spill. Rounding it, they found that the ravine opened into a large cul-de-sac that was almost pastoral in appearance. The area was nearly fifty yards in diameter. Lush green grass that reached to just below Clive's knees was speckled by an astonishing variety of wildflowers; some were pale, but most were extremely vivid in color. To their right, a clear brook splashed over the upper edge of the ravine, creating a waterfall nearly a hundred feet in height. The water collected in a small pool at the base of the falls, which emptied into a brook that ran across the meadow and then disappeared into the rocks on the other side.

The back wall of the cul-de-sac was a sheer face of rock, slightly higher than the rest of the ravine. At the bottom of that cliff, approached by a winding gravel path, Clive could see a large wooden door.

· CHAPTER FIFTEEN ·

The Finnboggi

Clive stood in front of the wooden door, Shriek at his right side, Chang Guafe at his left. The cliff towered above them. He hesitated. What was the protocol in a situation like this? Here they stood at the entrance to the Cave of Cerberus, and the door was closed. Did you knock, and wait for someone to answer? Or did you just open the door and take your chances?

Proper British education won out; Clive knocked.

Immediately a tremendous howling began on the other side of the door. Clive jumped back involuntarily, wondering what kind of creature they would face when the door finally opened.

Shriek was there at once, reassuring him. *Courage, O Folliot,* she sent. *You are not alone.*

His response was almost snappish: *I was startled, not frightened.*

Shriek replied with wordless amusement, then focused her attention on the door, which was beginning to open.

Clive held his breath. The howling was joined by a low, growling sound. A moment later a third voice began to bark. He shuddered. Three voices. Were they indeed about to face the three heads of Cerberus?

He stepped back as the door swung in his direction. The voices grew louder.

Clive prepared himself for the worst—and was barely able to contain his laughter when he was confronted by the reality. Cerberus indeed! While he was, in truth, faced by three doglike heads, they were attached to three very separate but very familiar-seeming bodies.

Clive's incredulous stare was broken when he was almost knocked to the ground by Finnbogg, who went barreling past him shouting, "Finnboggs! Finnboggs from Finnbogg!"

And indeed, that was what he was seeing: a trio of dwarfs who were almost certainly of the same race, and possibly even members of the same family, as the faithful canoid companion of Clive's group.

He stepped back as what appeared to be a joyful reunion came spilling out of the mouth of the cave. All four dwarfs were shouting, laughing, and barking. Seconds later they were rolling around on the ground in a mock battle that was punctuated with occasional growls, but more frequently with shouts of glee.

Annie came to stand beside him. "Three dog heads is not the same thing as a three-headed dog," she said, taking his arm.

"What was that phrase you taught me a few days ago?" asked Clive. "Something about 'Close enough for government work . . .' "

Annie laughed and squeezed his arm. Finnbogg continued to roll around on the greensward with his new companions.

Clive felt Shriek sigh. Without trying, he tapped into her thoughts, which were filled with an intense longing for others of her kind. With some embarrassment, he realized that he was inadvertently guilty of the same kind of mental eavesdropping that he had so frequently chided her about. He began trying to justify it to himself in terms of his concern for her, and then realized that was exactly why she had wanted to listen in on him: she cared. Delicately, he withdrew from the contact, feeling somewhat chastened. If she realized what had happened, she was kind enough to let it pass unmentioned.

The laughing dwarfs were on their feet once more, each slapping the others on the back, all of them sniffing around in what Clive took to be a canoid form of greeting.

"Are you going to introduce us to your friends, Finn?"

asked Clive, after what he deemed a properly diplomatic interval.

"Sure sure," Finnbogg panted happily.

He made some guttural noises, and the three other dwarfs lined up in some semblance of standing at attention. Once they were still, Clive realized it was easier to tell them apart than he had thought. Their resemblance to Finnbogg, in fact, was not much greater than that of one human being to another. His eyes were simply not used to sorting out the kind of features that distinguished these creatures one from another. He looked at them more carefully. The dwarf standing at the left of the row had a somewhat broader nose than the others. The one in the center was shorter and a trifle more slender than his friends, though in the case of this particular species "slender" was definitely a relative term; Clive realized with some amusement that this fellow could probably be described as the runt of the litter. The third dwarf had a very pronounced forehead, accentuated by bristling eyebrows that sprang away from his head almost like the spray at the bottom of a waterfall.

"Finnboggs must meet friends," said Finnbogg to the dwarfs. He then proceeded to introduce the eight remaining members of Clive's party. To Clive's amazement, Finnbogg concluded by introducing the three dwarfs as Finnbogg, Finnbogg, and Finnbogg.

"But what are their names?" he asked.

"Finnbogg," said Finnbogg.

"All of them?"' asked Clive, becoming annoyed.

Now Finnbogg looked puzzled. "All Finnboggs," he affirmed.

"But what do you call each other?" Clive persisted. "Surely you don't all call each other by the same name."

Finnbogg looked unhappy. "Finnboggs," he said dismally. He cowered away as though he expected Clive to hit him.

"Here, here, old fellow," said Clive. "I'm not going to hurt you. I just want to get this straightened out. You're Finnbogg. If I call this fellow Finnbogg too, it will get rather confusing—but not so bad that we can't deal with it. But if I call both of you Finnbogg—and then him—and him—well then how will you know whom I'm talking to?"

"Finnboggs will know," moaned Finnbogg.

"Do you call each other Finnbogg?" asked Clive.

Finnbogg shook his head.

"Well, what *do* you call each other?"

Finnbogg looked at the other three dwarfs for help. They stood with their hands behind their backs, their jaws clamped shut.

"Let me try, sah," said Horace, stepping up beside Clive.

"Be my guest, Sergeant Smythe."

Horace turned to Finnbogg. Taking him by the arm, he led the dwarf a little way apart from the rest of the party. The other three dwarfs stood stolidly in front of their door. Clearly their display of exuberance on discovering a fellow Finnbogg had been a momentary lapse of duty. Now that they had settled down, no one was going to enter the cave without their permission.

"It's magic, sah," said Horace a few moments later, walking back with Finnbogg in tow. "Or perhaps I should say 'fear of magic.' See, Finnbogg and his chums believe that if someone knows your true name, then they have magical power over you. I've heard that one myself here and there over the last few years. To tell you the truth, I wouldn't be surprised if the reason Brother Finn likes to gather up stories and legends and stuff is that he thinks they're real. I get the feeling a lot of 'em match what they believe back where he comes from."

Clive glanced at the burly dwarf, who was standing about five yards away. His hands were clasped behind his back and he wore a look of aggrieved sincerity.

"Are you telling me, Sergeant Smythe, that his name isn't really Finnbogg?"

"Not exactly, sah. It's just not his truest name."

"Well, what is?"

Horace looked astonished. "I couldn't say, sah, not even if he had told me—which he hasn't."

"Do you mean to tell me, Sergeant Smythe, that if

you knew Finnbogg's real name, you'd feel bound by this superstitious claptrap to keep it to yourself?"

"No, sah, I'd feel bound by my word. If a man trusts me with a secret—and I consider Finnbogg a man for all that—I don't see that it's my place to be judging his reasons for wanting it kept a secret. Learn a lot more secrets that way in the long run, sah."

Clive hesitated, uncertain whether he was being reprimanded or lectured—or both. "Well, what are we to call him then?"

"I think 'Finnbogg' will do fine," said Horace. "It has so far. Might be a bit of a problem if the others were going to come with us, but I don't think they've got that in mind."

Clive crossed to where Finnbogg stood. "Look here, old chap," he said, "I need to know a bit more about this name business. Why do you all call yourselves by the same name?"

Having a conversation with Finnbogg was not an easy task, even under the best of circumstances. When Clive was finished with this one his head was swimming with stories about the planet Finnbogg being invaded by men from other worlds who captured the Finnboggi and spirited them off to different planets. It was hard to tell whether Finnbogg's people covered the entire world of Finnbogg or occupied only a restricted corner of it. It was hard to tell anything for certain when one talked to Finnbogg. Clive did make out that the natives had closed ranks against the outsiders, and at that time—which Finnbogg again stated as being ten thousand years ago—they had developed the tactic of referring to themselves as Finnbogg.

When Clive asked the dwarf if he would share his real name, he was rewarded with a look that indicated Finnbogg considered the question almost perverted.

He changed the topic. "Your brothers seem set to guard the cave. Are they going to let us through?"

Finnbogg seemed relieved to have the conversation brought back to current matters.

"Not sure," he said. "Better check."

He went off to speak to the trio at the cave. Clive

looked around and was pleased to see that the others had taken advantage of the momentary respite to enjoy the almost pastoral surroundings. 'Nrrc'kth and Gram were sitting on the grass, talking with Tomàs, who was, as usual, fondling his rosary. Shriek had climbed about fifteen feet up the cliff, which Clive would have considered unscalable. She was perched there now with serene equanimity, apparently enjoying the midday warmth. Chang Guafe was fiddling with his components, seemingly oblivious to the attractions of the countryside. Horace and Annie had wandered back to the stream, where Annie was now wading with obvious delight. She slipped and recovered herself, laughing merrily as she splashed about. The sight filled Clive with vague longings that he chose not to examine.

His reverie was interrupted by a howl of dismay from the cave. He turned and was astonished to see the three guardians encircling Finnbogg. Thinking that they had attacked the poor fellow, he began sprinting to his comrade's defense. But he had not gone far before he realized that the weeping and moaning was on Finnbogg's behalf, and that what had looked like an attack was really just the others embracing their friend.

Shriek, who was looking down on the scene from her rocky perch, contacted Clive. *They seem to consider him a lost soul.*

That's an encouraging reaction, responded Clive.

Not all fear is rational, O Folliot. She was scuttling down the cliff face, her movements hampered slightly by the missing arm.

Clive continued walking toward the group of dwarfs. "What's the trouble, Finnbogg?" he called. As he did he found himself wondering how many of them would respond.

Finnbogg the First, as Clive currently thought of him, struggled his way out of the dogpile.

"They say the cave is very bad," replied Finnbogg. He paused, listening to the commotion behind him. "No—not the cave. The gateway. The other Finnboggs live in the cave. The cave is good. The cave is home.

But the gate is bad. Very bad. We should go back, should forget this bad idea."

"Why is the gate so bad?" asked Clive.

Finnbogg made some throaty noises, then paused to listen.

"The gate is bad. Finnboggs don't know why. Only know it is. The Chaffri told them. 'Guard cave,' they said. 'Guard cave. Let no one through. Gate is very, very bad.' "

"Sounds to me like the Chaffri just don't want anyone going through there, sah," said Horace.

"I was just thinking the same thing, Sergeant Smythe. Finnbogg—tell your friends that we must pass, and that we would like to do so as friends."

Finnbogg looked worried. "Will be hard," he said. "Finnboggs hate having choices. Finnboggs like to know duty, then do it. Where is duty? To Chaffri? Or to friends?"

"Why do they have any allegiance to the Chaffri?" asked Clive.

Finnbogg turned to the squat trio standing behind him and conducted another brief conversation. "Finnboggs don't give a fig for Chaffri," he replied, using an expression he had picked up from Horace. "Finnboggs mostly want us not to get hurt."

"Tell them we'll take our chances," replied Clive.

Another long parley between Finnbogg and his brethren ended with the three mournful-looking dwarfs pushing open the great wooden door to the cave and standing aside as the nine adventurers stepped through.

The Cave of the Finnboggi was about the same size as Emmy Storm's parlor. It was comfortably appointed, with three beds, three chairs, and three washstands. In fact, with the exception of the large wooden table that dominated the center of the room, there were three of every item that was of any importance. Clive could see a few spots where the walls had obviously been hewn by hand, but for the most part they appeared to have been naturally formed. The stone was ruddy, with streaks of black. The whole was lit by numerous candles that gave the room a curiously welcoming appearance.

Clive looked around admiringly. Before he could speak he heard 'Nrrc'kth's voice: "Ask them if they have any food."

Finnbogg translated, and the three dwarfs responded as if they had been given a royal command. In what seemed no more than a matter of seconds, the larders had been raided and baskets of food fairly covered the table. Cheese, fruit, and bread were there in abundance. But most of all there was sausage, glorious sausage, the finest, Clive thought, that he had ever tasted.

"Finnbogg food," said Finnbogg proudly, taking a hearty bite from one of the sausages. "Real food!"

"Real food," agreed Clive, placing a cordial hand on Finnbogg's back. "Real food indeed."

Later, when he had taken the edge off his appetite, Clive leaned over to Finnbogg and said, "I don't see anything so awful in here. Ask them where the gate is, would you, Finn?"

Finnbogg's translation of the question was greeted with unhappy looks and a burst of guttural sounds.

"Back there," said Finnbogg, pointing toward the rear of the cave.

A blanket hung on the wall in the direction in which he had gestured. Clive walked over and lifted the corner, expecting to find another barrier, perhaps a heavily barred door.

All he saw was an opening to another cave.

"Whatever is back here, it can't be very aggressive," he said. He started to step through the opening, but a shout from Horace drew him up short. "I wouldn't do that if I were you, sah," said the quartermaster sergeant. "Never know about doors around here. Let's have Brother Finnbogg find out a bit more for us."

However, according to the Finnboggi, there was no danger in entering the next chamber. The danger was in the gateway itself.

Clive could feel the tension in the group as the others gathered to peer into the next chamber. One of the Finnboggs brought a handful of candles and a burning taper. Then, with their own Finnbogg holding aside the blanket, they stepped into the chamber.

The stone walls that had seemed warm and inviting when softened by homey furniture, a multitude of candles, and abundant good cheer now became foreboding, almost eerie. The cave narrowed to a tunnel where darkness ruled, giving way only briefly to the passage of their candles. The light itself seemed entrapped, unable to stretch more than a few inches in front of the candles.

This I do not like, commented Shriek.

The nervousness of the usually implacable arachnid did more than anything else to set Clive's nerves on edge. She caught his reaction at once, of course.

I pray your pardon, O Folliot. My intent was not to alarm you.

It's all right, responded Clive. *If I can have the benefit of your reassurance, then surely I should be willing to listen when you are feeling frightened.*

Her reply—*I wouldn't go so far as to say I was frightened*—had a touch of offended dignity that would have amused Clive in less intimidating circumstances.

After a short time the passage widened, bringing them to a third cave. As the group entered, one by one, the accumulation of candles provided enough light that Clive could examine their surroundings.

The cave was smaller than the first two—an almost spherical chamber about fifteen feet in diameter. In the center of the smooth stone floor was a wooden door. It was square, about five feet to the side, and sturdily constructed. A massive handle was implanted in the side closest to where they had entered. Thick hinges made of some bronzelike material joined the door to the rock on the opposite side. The group gathered around the opening. Clive set down his candle, looked around at the expectant faces, then grabbed the wooden handle. Bracing his legs, he pulled upward. At first the door refused to move. He tried a second time with no better luck. Deciding that if one more pull didn't do the trick he would turn the task over to Chang Guafe, he crouched down and thrust upward with all the power of his thighs. The wooden door came free so suddenly that it popped up, and it was only by leaning against it that Clive managed to keep from falling through.

"Good God," he muttered, staring down in utter astonishment at what he had uncovered.

CHAPTER SIXTEEN

One Down

Clive had been expecting a stairwell of some sort, or perhaps only a tunnel—something, anyway, that would lead them farther toward the next level of the Dungeon. So it was a matter of some astonishment to him that what he actually saw when he pulled open the trapdoor in the cave floor was the next level of the Dungeon itself.

What made the sight particularly appalling was the fact that the next level was several thousand feet straight down from where he stood.

Clive, who had climbed mountains in Switzerland as a youth, had never seen a drop of such magnitude. His stomach seemed to press up against one side of his ribcage in protest at the sight. His knees buckled. And his brain simply rejected the idea that what he was seeing was real.

He let the door fall back into place and squatted on his haunches. He stared straight ahead. He did not, however, see anything in the cave. His mind was filled with the appalling sight that lay beyond the door.

He was brought around by the voices of the others insisting that he tell them what he had seen.

He stood up, puzzled. How could he explain what lay beneath the door without sounding as though he were mad?

"It's like a hole in the world," he said at last. "As though the ground here was the sky of the level that came next."

"What do you mean?" asked Annie. She sounded

nervous; more nervous, thought Clive, than he had ever heard her sound before.

Still squatting, he tapped the door. "On the other side of that wood is another world. But it is not one that we can just step into."

He closed his eyes, remembering what he had seen. "I keep wanting to call it an abyss. But that's not what it is. There's an entire world beneath our feet. It's just—very far away." He grimaced in frustration. "I can't explain. You'll have to see for yourselves."

At Clive's direction, Chang Guafe stationed himself at the left side of the door, Shriek at the right. Once he had lifted the door out of its socket, they were to open it the rest of the way. Again Clive warned the others that what they were about to see would shock them. He told them he feared that it would keep them from going any farther. But he didn't know any better way to explain it than to show them.

He heaved at the door. Chang Guafe and Shriek grabbed the edges of the door and hauled upward.

They looked down at twenty-five square feet of sky.

What came next happened too fast for Clive to really understand it. He heard Annie scream. Glancing over, he saw that she had swooned. Her knees crumpled, and she began to fall toward the hole.

'Nrrc'kth, who was standing next to her, reached out to catch her. Annie's weight threw the tall, slender woman off balance. Arching her back, she managed to throw Annie back away from the hole.

And then she was gone.

Clive's impulse to reach out for her would have taken him over the edge, too. In fact he started forward, almost lost his balance, and only at the last instant caught himself from following 'Nrrc'kth through the doorway. He knelt on the rocky lip of the opening, staring hopelessly and helplessly at 'Nrrc'kth's body, falling, falling, falling toward the ocean that rolled so far beneath them. Gradually her screams diminished. After a while he realized that they had been replaced by the sound of Gram's sobbing.

He turned to find the white-skinned woman dragging User Annie toward the hole. Annie, conscious but obviously confused and disoriented, was making only token resistance.

"You bitch!" screamed Gram. "You flaming, self-righteous bitch!"

Clive jumped to his feet. Horace reached the women before he did, but Finnbogg, growling and snapping was there before either of them. It took all three of them to subdue the half-mad Gram.

"She killed my girl!" Gram moaned dully once they had wrestled her to the floor. "She killed my girl."

Annie sat nearby, her face hidden in her hands. Finnbogg crouched at her feet, growling protectively.

"What happened?" she whispered—though the tone in her voice made Clive think she already knew. The look in her eyes as he told her what had just occurred confirmed that feeling: she knew what had happened, but had been hoping she was wrong.

"I've never been able to deal with heights," she said softly. "They terrify me. And that—" she glanced in the direction of the hole where 'Nrrc'kth had disappeared, "that thing shouldn't even be there."

She turned her head away. Clive watched her shoulders working and ached to take her in his arms, hold her, comfort her. He realized he was held back at least in part by his fear of what Chang Guafe would say. Beyond that was the fact that he simply had to cope with how the whole group was going to face this new situation.

He put his hands on Annie's shoulders. "It's not your fault," he whispered, wondering, as he did, if that were really true. He kept his hands there for a moment, appalled at how fragile she suddenly seemed, then rose and walked back to the hole.

Gram was slumped against the far wall of the cave, Horace and Shriek standing guard on either side of her.

"Gram," said Clive softly, "I'm sorry."

She made no response at all. Clive bent and touched her shoulder. But the older woman was too deep in her grief to respond. She sat as if frozen, staring straight ahead.

Clive hesitated, then stood and stepped away from her. Grief, whether his own or Gram's, was not a luxury he could indulge right now.

Tomàs squatted about four feet from the lip of the hole, praying intensely. Chang Guafe was right at the edge, seemingly untouched by the tragedy that had just occurred, or even by fear of what they now faced. "I have examined the hole," said the cyborg. "The construction is fascinating. Here, try this." Gripping the rocky edge of the hole, Chang Guafe extended one tentacle around the edge.

Clive, not as certain of his stability as that of the half-mechanical creature, lay on his belly before extending his head and shoulders across the rocky lip.

He was glad he had taken the precaution, as the sense of vertigo produced by staring straight down at the ocean that rolled thousands of feet below might have been enough to send him plummeting after 'Nrrc'kth. He scanned the water for any sign of the woman, knowing even as he did so that it was a hopeless action. No one could survive such a fall. And even if her corpse was floating somewhere below, it would be too small to locate from this distance.

The only thing he saw breaking the seemingly endless stretch of water was a pair of islands, far off to the right.

"Reach through," said Chang Guafe. "Feel the underside."

Clive brought one arm forward, lifting his head as he did so. The vertigo returned. Until now he had been so absorbed by what lay beyond the opening, he had not really examined the passage itself. The rock on which he was lying seemed far less solid as he realized that it was only about two inches thick.

At the cyborg's direction he put one arm through the hole, reaching back to feel the underside of the area where he was lying.

He cried out in astonishment as he discovered that there was no underside. With his hand directly under his chest, he had expected to feel the cool, smooth rock on which he lay. It was not there. Even more shocking was the fact that he himself was not there. Hooking his arm around the edge of the hole and reaching upward far enough so that he should have had his hand pressed against his own breast, Clive felt nothing but thin air.

Cautiously, he pulled himself forward and leaned over the edge.

The opening he was leaning through appeared as a hole in the sky. Turning to the right and the left, he saw blue extending in all directions, marked by an occasional cloud.

Placing his hands against the edge of the opening, he pushed himself back and sat up, his head reeling.

Horace came over to stand next to him.

"Well, sah, what do we do next?"

"I don't know, Horace. It would seem that we've finally come to a dead end. I don't see any way that we can get from here down to the next level."

He felt a tug in his mind from Shriek. But before he could understand the message she was trying to send him, he was distracted by a scratching and a howling in the stony passage that led to the chamber.

"Trouble!" cried one of the Finnboggs, bursting into the chamber. "Big trouble."

The dwarf tried to explain the matter, but his mastery of the common language of the Dungeon was insufficient to the task. Finnbogg the First stepped in, and after a conversation of brief, growling noises turned to Clive and said, "Trouble indeed. Bad N'wrbb has come. He has many men. He wants his woman back."

A heaviness seemed to settle over the chamber as everyone looked toward the hole where 'Nrrc'kth had disappeared.

CHAPTER SEVENTEEN

I Will Always Return

Where am I?

It was not the first time Sidi Bombay had asked that question of his unknown friend. Actually, it was not quite proper to say "unknown." He knew the friend was female, and that her name was L'Claar.

Beyond that she remained an enigma—and enigmatic.

You are here, she replied, as she always did when he thought the question intensely enough to force her to respond.

He had pursued that circle before:

Where is here?

Where we are.

It was like reasoning with a child. It frustrated him, but he held his anger, for fear of alienating his only contact with—what? Reality? The outside world? Sufficient to say "his only contact." For there was no one else. Just Sidi and L'Claar.

She retreated as a wave of pain rolled over him.

That makes me sad, she whispered in his mind, when the pain had gone and it was safe for her to return. *I should stay with you. But I'm not strong enough. So I draw away and cry instead.*

It's all right, he replied. *As long as you come back.*

Always! I will always return!

The thought was so fierce it startled him.

Have you ever been left? he asked.

Sudden sorrow flooded through him, and a sense of loss so intense that he would have been hard pressed to say whether he would trade his own recurring physical pain, which until now had seemed so excruciating, for the burden L'Claar carried.

What happened? he asked.

But she was gone.

Sidi was sorry. But he was no longer worried.

He knew she would return.

CHAPTER EIGHTEEN

Over the Edge

Clive looked at Finnbogg. "Will the Finnboggi try to hold N'wrbb off, or will they let him in?"

The jowly dwarf looked aggrieved. "Finnboggs loyal. Finnboggs die before they let bad men in home."

"I hope it won't come to that," said Clive. "But if they will seal the door against N'wrbb—or better yet, if they can convince him we never came here . . ."

Finnbogg growled. "Finnboggs don't tell tales."

This was so patently untrue that Clive didn't know how to respond. He needed the Finnboggi to help. But he didn't have time to work his way through the tangles of Finnboggian reasoning. Before he could say anything, he was contacted by Shriek.

Have them seal the door, and let it go at that.

By this time Clive trusted the spider woman completely. He issued the command. As Finnbogg went trotting down the corridor he turned to ask Shriek what she had in mind.

He held back that thought. Shriek was hunched down against one wall of the cave. Her multifaceted eyes were closed, and she was so obviously deep in concentration that Clive hesitated to interrupt her.

Suddenly she leaped forward. Clive cried out in horror as he watched her drop cleanly through the hole in the floor.

Her words tickled in his mind with a trace of amusement. *Worry not, O Folliot. Just relax and follow me.*

Even as he received her words, he saw the thick cable of silk with which she had attached herself to the cave wall. Lying stomach down on the floor, he peered over the edge of the hole. His friend dangled about twenty feet away, dropping slowly toward the distant sea as she released more silk from her spinnerets.

Clive turned to Horace. "Get Finnbogg," he said. "We have to move fast. There's no telling how long the Finnboggi can hold off N'wrbb and his men. We've got to get down before they can force their way in here and cut that silk."

Horace nodded and vanished down the corridor. Clive looked around the room. "You first, Tomàs," he said.

The Portuguese sailor looked at him in astonishment. "Down there?" he squeaked. "Along the web of an *arachna*?"

"You can do that, or you can stay here and have N'wrbb slit your gullet," Clive said coldly. "With the time you've spent climbing ship's rigging this should be easier for you than for anyone else. Now move! The rest of you, watch him to see how he does it."

Tomàs grabbed the line and scrambled over the edge. When Clive saw the cord in Tomàs's hand he realized that while it was enormously thick for spider webbing, the lifeline on which they were about to depend was actually less than half the thickness of his little finger. Suddenly it seemed frighteningly slender.

Annie looked up dully. "Clive, I can't," she whispered.

"You have to."

But he knew even as he said it that she could never make the descent. The image of 'Nrrc'kth falling endlessly through the sky flashed into his mind. He couldn't stand to lose another one of the party that way.

Especially not Annie.

He looked around. There were only three among them he felt might be strong enough to carry her that far safely. But Shriek was already gone. And Finnbogg, powerful as he was, would hardly be able both to hold Annie and to manage the descent; his arms were simply too short.

That left only one choice. Clive began to phrase the question as carefully as he could.

This is not the time for diplomacy, O Folliot, sent Shriek. *Take command, or lose it!* He felt the impatience underneath her words and his cheeks grew warm. But he took the message to heart.

"Chang Guafe," he said crisply, "you will carry Annie. Follow Tomàs down the cord."

Without a word the cyborg walked to Annie and wrapped a pair of metallic tentacles around her waist.

"Clive!" she cried, as the cyborg picked her up and started toward the hole. "I can't do this!"

"You don't have to," said Clive. "Chang Guafe is going to do it for you. Just close your eyes and hold still."

But her terror was too great. She struggled to break free of Guafe's hold. The cyborg stopped. "I will carry her," he said. "But I will not fight her. Shall I render her unconscious, or leave her?"

Clive hesitated only a beat. "Do whatever is necessary," he said coldly, trying to cover the wild swings of emotion he felt as he watched his descendant's terrified struggles.

Annie shook her head. Her eyes were wide, and wild. "Clive, you son of a—"

Suddenly she went limp in the cyborg's grasp. Tightening the two tentacles that held her, Chang Guafe extended a third tentacle and formed it into a loop around Shriek's cord of silk. To Clive's astonishment, the cyborg paused before sliding over the edge.

"I hope to see you below," he clicked.

Clive nodded, and Chang Guafe vanished through the opening.

Horace had not yet come back with Finnbogg. Aside from Clive, only Gram remained in the chamber. She sat slumped against the wall, staring dully at the floor.

Clive was about to bark an order at her, then hesitated. He wasn't sure why, until he realized that he was expecting some advice from Shriek. But the spider woman had plenty to deal with on her own right now.

What was the best tactic to take with the mourning Gram? Should he command, or cajole? There was little time for the latter, but even less for taking a tactic that wouldn't work at all.

He knelt beside the sturdy, green-haired woman. "Come along, then, Gram," he said cheerfully. "Your turn to go over the edge."

She didn't move.

He took her hand and pulled her to her feet.

She stood in one place.

"Gram," he said urgently, "we don't have that much time!"

Finnbogg and Horace came back as he was leading her to the opening.

"The Finnboggi are negotiating with them, sah," said Horace. "Depending on how N'wrbb's patience holds out, that ought to chew up quite a bit of time."

"Very good, Sergeant Smythe. Why don't you and Finnbogg go over next?"

Smythe glanced at the clearly reluctant Gram. "Sure you won't be needin' a bit of assistance here, sah?" Without waiting for Clive's answer, he took Gram's other arm and helped tug her toward the hole. "Over you go, old gel," he said cheerfully.

Clive bent to help Gram and felt a shock of dizziness as he looked down at his comrades descending into the sky below. Gram took the cord in her hands, slipped over the edge, and started to follow the others down the silken trail.

"I'm worried about her, Horace," he said softly, as soon as she was a few feet away.

"I wouldn't be, sah," said Horace. "She may be acting awful glum, but her type don't let go easy. First time she makes a little slip she'll grab on to that cord of Shriek's like a baby on a tit. She won't be able to help herself. She's too full of life to let go of it just because she's lost something. Now then, who's next, sah?"

In rapid order Finnbogg, then Horace, then Clive took their places in the line of descent. When he was a few feet below the hole Clive looked up. The sight was absolutely eerie: clear blue sky stretched in every direction as far as he could see. The only exception was the twenty-five square feet of cave floating directly above him like a hole in the heavens.

He tightened his grip on the cord and looked straight ahead. A gust of cold wind started him swiveling. Save for an occasional cloud, all he could see, no matter which way the wind turned him, was a blue that seemed to go on forever.

He let his eyes travel down the long white cord.

Finnbogg and Horace were directly beneath him. Next was Gram. She was moving more slowly than he would have liked, but already she seemed more alert. He hoped her attitude would continue to improve. Dangling from a piece of spider silk in the middle of the sky was hardly an ideal situation in which to deal with the problems that would come up if she decided she was too depressed to carry on!

While the others were moving hand over hand, Chang Guafe was actually sliding down the cord. The cyborg appeared to have extended something from what Clive considered to be his knee area, in order to keep from moving too fast. The sight of Annie's still form dangling at Guafe's side closed like a fist over Clive's heart.

A few yards below them was Tomàs. Despite his protestations of fear, the wiry sailor scuttled so confidently along the cord that he looked almost at home here in the sky.

At the bottom of the long white trail, over a hundred feet away, dangled Shriek. She continued to drop away as she released more silk from her bloated abdomen.

How long will it last? he wondered, looking past her to the sea. He could not begin to estimate the distance they had yet to cover.

He leaned his forehead against the cord, feeling thankful for the tacky coating that made it relatively easy to cling to. In fact, the greater part of his efforts seemed to be directed not so much toward holding on to the cord as toward letting go, so that he could continue the downward climb.

Is all well, O Folliot? asked Shriek.

As well as can be expected, replied Clive. It struck him how useful it was to be able to communicate with her even though she was at the other end of their chain. What a tool this mind linking would have been for the military! *And how are you doing?*

As well as can be expected.

She could not conceal her concern. Without actually framing it in words, he sent a question.

It is a very great distance, she replied. *I am not sure how far my silk will extend.*

Clive looked down and swallowed. He thought of 'Nrrc'kth, whose body had disappeared into those distant waters. He looked down at the others and realized that all of them, even Tomàs and Guafe, had become very dear to him.

Do what you can, he replied.

Her response was almost snappish: *I am!*

They continued the descent.

Clive had no idea how long it went on. Occasionally he would look up to gauge their distance from the opening. He wondered how the Finnboggi were making out with N'wrbb. Had they somehow managed to talk him into going away? Or were they even now risking their lives to hold the door against his army? How long did they have before someone came and cut the cord, sending them all plummeting to the sea so far below?

Later he looked up and saw that someone had closed the door. A shiver rippled through him. It had been strange enough to have that hole in the sky. Now he was descending a thin silken cord that stretched above him and then suddenly just disappeared, like the rope in the Indian trick.

A stiff wind began to blow. It came in gusts, turning the cord into a pendulum. Clive himself was the anchor. Shriek formed the bob, and as he looked down he was appalled at the sweep her rounded form was making through the sky.

A cry from Gram nearly stopped his heart. He looked down and saw her burly form virtually wrapped around the cord.

"She started to slip, sah," yelled Horace. "Caught herself just in time. Don't think it'll happen again. Gave the old gel just the scare she needed."

"Quite right," said Clive, who was beginning to feel quite queasy from the back-and-forth motion of the cord. He put his cheek against the silk and wished that his jaw would stop hurting. This long, silent descent gave him too much time to think about it!

The only consolation was that he could finally sense they were making progress, as his vision of the sea changed from that of a vast, nearly smooth plain of bluish green to a choppy, rippled, multitoned surface.

His arms and shoulders ached. He wanted desperately to be allowed a respite of some sort. With some chagrin he realized that though he was a strong man by nature, and had recently been considerably toughened by his experiences in the Dungeon, he was probably having more physical trouble with the climb than anyone else along the cord.

He studied the islands he had seen when he first peered down from the hole in the Cave of the Finnboggi. How far away were they? He began to wonder if he—or any of them—would have the strength to swim that far, even if they managed to reach the sea in safety.

"All right, sah?" asked Horace.

Clive realized with a start that he had let himself drift into reverie, and in doing so stopped moving. Horace was several yards below him.

"Quite all right, Sergeant Smythe," he yelled down.

He began to move once more. His hands were abraded and sore from constant contact with the sticky silk. Fortunately, the leather breeches and boots he had been given in the castle of N'wrbb protected his feet and legs, which he had to keep wound in the silk in order to hold on. Clive silently thanked his enemy for this one friendly gesture—though he noted that he would have been even happier if a pair of gloves had been included with the outfit.

I am flagging, O Folliot.

As always when they were mentally linked, he picked up not only Shriek's message but a host of undermessages about her condition and perceptions. Usually they were little more than background noise. Now, however, he was appalled at the arachnid's exhaustion, and a little ashamed at his concern for himself when she was in such bad shape.

He looked down. They had made significant progress. But they were still hundreds of feet above the water.

How much farther can you go on? he asked.

I do not know. I can feel my reservoirs running low. But it is hard to say whether I can spin another fifty feet of silk, or another five hundred. If I rest a bit it will help.

Then rest, he replied.

I shall tell the others, she sent.

So there they stopped, and there they stayed, an oddly assorted octet, collected from across time and space only to find themselves dangling from a slender silken cord that started at a hole in the sky and stretched achingly down toward the seemingly endless sea of the Dungeon's third level.

It began to get dark. Clive heard a cry and realized that Annie had wakened. She shrieked twice and then was silent. He closed his eyes and leaned his forehead against the silk.

Darkness fell swiftly. After what seemed an eternity of hanging in the blackness, Clive finally received a message from Shriek: *I can go on now, O Folliot.*

Can we make it to the bottom? he asked.

I do not know; I will go as far as I can.

You can do no more, replied Clive, though he was sure that she also caught his emotional reaction, which was far less philosophical than his words.

And so they began again, moving slowly down that slender cord. He realized that Shriek had sent the same message to each of the others. To his surprise, the idea made him slightly jealous. He had been thinking of her as his private friend. How many conversations did she have with the others that he was not aware of?

It chastened him a bit to realize that at one time she would have been aware of that question and answered it almost instantly. Now that he had been so adamant about not wanting her to read his mind unless they were actually communicating with each other, she would not be aware of his question and therefore could not answer it. And it was not something that he wanted to ask her; it sounded too insecure, too childish, too much like—what? A jealous lover? The idea was so ridiculous he actually laughed out loud. The sound disappeared into the night around him.

But it was soon replaced by another sound, one that had been growing slowly louder as they moved down, so gradually he could never mark the instant when he actually began to hear it.

It was the sound of the ocean, moving beneath them.

And still they continued their descent, until the moment when Shriek once more reached out to touch his mind.

It is done, O Folliot. I have no more silk in my belly.

CHAPTER NINETEEN

A Dark and Trackless Sea

Trying to ignore the chill that had rippled through him, Clive began to make his plans. *How far are we from the water?* he asked Shriek.

I do not know. It has long been too dark for me to see. I can hear the waves clearly, and Tomàs says that he can smell the sea so strongly that it has made him homesick. But whether the water itself is no farther away than the length of my body, or several times that distance, I cannot say.

Shall we drop, or try to hold on until morning?

Her response carried with it an unspoken despair. *We have no idea how long it will be until morning. Nor do we know how long my silk will hold. It was not really meant to support eight people for hours on end. It could come loose at the top—or even be cut, if somehow N'wrbb and his men make it back to the cave from which we made our exit. If that should happen, you would be in the gravest danger, for you are at least a hundred feet farther from the water than I. Your fall would likely be fatal. This is probably also true for those nearest you on the cord.*

Clive shivered. Even if Shriek were only ten feet above the surface of the sea, it meant he was at least a hundred and ten feet up. He looked down. Horace had to be somewhere close below, but he could see not a single trace of the man. Was there no moon of any kind at this level of the Dungeon?

Finally he made his decision. *We drop!* he sent to Shriek.

I will tell the others, she sent back.

He hung in the darkness in silence, awaiting the next

message from his seven-limbed ally. He was not sure how long it was before her words rustled into his mind.

I shall drop now, O Folliot.

Good fortune! he replied.

And to you, she answered.

Then she let go. Clive was struck with a wave of vertigo, and realized that she had not broken the mental connection. He was sharing her fall. God, how could it take so long?

Then suddenly the connection was gone, with only a blackness to take its place. Dark within, dark without, Clive realized that Shriek had lost consciousness.

If so, they had to get down to her. She could be drowning even now!

But what if the drop were so great that they all lost consciousness?

What if? Was there any other choice, hanging here in a dark sky where they had no real connection above or below?

"Move down!" he bellowed. "Move down as fast as you can. Someone has to help Shriek."

Horace picked up the cry and shouted it to Finnbogg, who passed the message to Gram, though it was likely she had heard Clive's shout anyway. From Gram to Guafe, from Guafe to Tomàs the message passed.

And there it stopped.

"I cannot," whined Tomàs. "It is dark, and I am afraid. I do not want to let go."

The message was carried back to Clive, who began to seethe with rage and helplessness. He had no time for cajoling now. Shriek was in trouble.

"Tell Chang Guafe to slide down and push Tomàs off the end of the silk if necessary," he snapped.

The message passed from Horace to Finnbogg and down the chain.

Tomàs heard it before Guafe actually started to move.

"No!" he cried in desperation. "No, you cannot do this! No! *Nooo!*"

The last cry lengthened into a scream that was followed at length by a splash.

"Move!" bellowed Clive. "Everyone, down the silk and into the water. We'll have to stick together!"

He began to move himself, once more descending hand over hand along the sticky silk.

He heard another splash. That would be Chang Guafe and Annie.

Before long he heard Gram and then Finnbogg hit the water. Now there was an ongoing confusion of shouting and splashing. The sounds were desperate, and Clive cursed the darkness that kept him from seeing how his people were faring.

"See you below, sah!" said Horace.

Instants later Clive himself came to the point where his feet lost contact with the silk. As he dangled alone in the darkness, with only his hands wrapped in the cord and no idea how far it was to the water and the confusion below, he had a sudden sympathy for the fear that had immobilized Tomàs.

It made little difference that he could actually hear the others below. It was the fact that he could not see what he was dropping into that made the idea of letting go of the silk so appalling.

He wished that, like the others, he had someone coming along behind him, someone to push him into letting go.

But there was no one.

He closed his eyes—ridiculous in the dark, but somehow comforting—and let go.

Now there was nothing, only darkness all around as he fell endlessly toward the water. His body reacted as it had been bred to over countless millennia, with a surge of panic that seemed to heighten every sense and to slow the passage of time.

Despite his best efforts to strike feet first, Clive landed on his back. The impact seemed to push every bit of air from his lungs. He had just time enough to note that it was not that different from running into a brick wall when the water closed over him and he realized that he was sinking fast.

Lungs empty, he was desperate to draw breath, but knew it would be fatal.

He began to stroke upward, then realized that he

wasn't sure which way was up. The darkness, the sudden drop, the pain of the impact had left him wildly disoriented. He had to breathe!

He forced himself to stop moving. It felt as if someone were tightening a band around his chest.

But he waited. His lungs were empty. He should sink.

When he was finally sure of the direction he was moving, he began to stroke the opposite way. His head felt as though someone had managed to get inside of it and was trying to pry open his mouth and nose.

Breathe! commanded his body. And still he resisted, because to obey that command would be fatal. Resisted, and resisted, and resisted yet again until suddenly his head broke through the surface and he began to suck air in great wheezing gasps.

Air. But still no light. Where were the others? He heard a splashing to his left. "Horace?" he called. "Shriek?"

A great wave lifted him up. Dizzy with motion, he cried out again.

No answer.

Where had they all gone? Another wave picked him up, seeming to lift him toward the sky. Had the sea been this rough all along? Or were these great waves something that had come with the darkness?

Treading water, he turned in a circle. "Finnbogg! Annie! Where are you? Any of you?"

No answer.

He turned again, riding a wave that soon sent him hurtling into a watery trench.

Where were the islands he had seen before? If he could find the islands he could at least try to swim in that direction. But he was totally disoriented. If he began to swim he was as likely to head into the trackless ocean as to strike land.

Another wave picked him up. But even as it did, a despair more terrifying than mere waves washed over him. It seemed too much to bear. After the tortuous descent, the terrifying plummet, to find himself alone in this dark, tumultuous sea—

And then even that thought disappeared, as he was grabbed by unseen hands and pulled below the surface.

CHAPTER TWENTY

The People of the Sea

Clive woke to the sound of waves lapping softly against sand. He lay for a minute without opening his eyes, trying to remember what had happened, where he was.

He remembered the descent, his panic at finding himself alone in the dark sea, the sudden terror of being pulled beneath the waves by unseen hands. But that was all. What had happened next?

He could not remember.

He felt stiff and sore. His cheek was pressed against a coarse surface. The smell of surf was mingled with a rich, fruity odor that he could not identify.

He opened his eyes.

In the dim light—morning light, or had he been out longer than he thought?—he could see that the sand on which he lay was blue. He was parallel to the shore, facing the ocean. The waves rolling in now were far smaller than the monstrous ones into which he had fallen the night before. Long-legged birds, their gray plumage shot through with pink, strode through the curl of the waves. Now and then one of them would peck into the sand with its long, rounded bill. The birds were at least six feet tall.

He moved his arms. His leather clothes were nearly dry. They had become uncomfortably stiff.

Where were the others?

As if in answer, he heard a moan nearby. Pushing himself up from the blue sand, he turned his head and saw Horace lying on the sand not more than five feet away. Beyond the quartermaster sergeant lay other bodies.

All of them? Clive pushed himself to his knees and began to count. All of them—even Shriek. He suddenly realized that he had been most concerned about how she would survive the plunge into the sea, as she did not seem built for swimming. Or could she walk on water?

He staggered to his feet to check on the others. A voice from the waves stopped him.

"They are all alive."

He turned and tried to choke back a cry of surprise. A strange figure, manlike yet totally inhuman, had risen from the waves. The speaker was tall, taller even than the giant shore birds. It was hard to tell the color of his skin, for it had a metallic sheen and seemed to shift from blue to green to gray in the dim light. The stranger had no hair. However, a small crest seemed to run along the center of his skull.

Though he was clearly of the sea, the newcomer was not what Clive would have called a "mer-man," for he had legs rather than a tail. Though he was nude, he seemed to have no genitals; at least none that were visible. Clive assumed he was male only because the muscular chest was broad and flat, with no hint of breasts.

The man sank back into the sea for a moment, then rose again.

"You will have to forgive me," he said. "I cannot breathe well in your air."

He spoke a variant of the *lingua franca* that seemed to hold wherever they went in the Dungeon. Though the accent was strange, Clive was able to understand him with little trouble. His voice had a strange rasp. Clive wondered if that was because it was meant to be used underwater, not in the open air.

"Who are you?" he asked, taking a step closer to the man. As he did, he noticed that the blue sand was much the same color as the water, so that the line where they met was indistinct.

"My name is . . ." Here the man made a grinding sound in his throat that Clive found impossible to reproduce. The sea-man smiled. "You may call me Ka. It will be simpler, and not insulting."

The way he said "not insulting" indicated that honor was a serious notion for his kind. Clive made a mental note to try to avoid insulting the man.

He heard some of the others stirring behind him.

"Your friends are awakening," said the sea-man. "Good. That is why I remained behind—to make sure that everyone was not merely alive but well."

"But who are you?" asked Clive. "I mean, I know your name is Ka. But who are your people? What have you to do with us?" He looked around. "How did we get here?"

"The People of the Sea brought you, of course," said Ka. "We watched you most of yesterday, climbing down from the sky. It was an astonishing sight. We have seen others come through that hole on wings, or with small machines that let them fly. But no one has ever *climbed* down—not in the most distant memory of our ancestors, according to the Way Speaker."

"The Way Speaker?" Clive questioned.

Ka ducked down for a moment, then stood again. Water rolled off his broad shoulders, down his metallic-looking skin. The surf beat against his sturdy thighs. The ocean stretched unbroken behind him. "The Way Speaker provides guidance for the People of the Sea by consulting our ancestors on what was, what is, and what shall be. You and your friends created a great deal of confusion for the Way Speaker yesterday."

Ka seemed almost amused by the idea of the Way Speaker being confused.

Clive felt a hand on his shoulder. Turning, he saw Annie standing beside him. Her black hair, still damp, clung to her head like a skull cap. Her large, dark eyes were wide with wonder at the sight of Ka. Horace stood beside her. Most of the others were on their feet now, too.

Clive turned back to Ka, uncertain how long he had before the man disappeared beneath the waves for good.

"How did we confuse your Way Speaker?" he asked.

"By falling into our home!" said Ka, as though it were a stupid question. "Eight of you thrashing about over our heads, ready to die right in our living area. Some of us were insulted, for it seemed very rude. But the Way Speaker determined that there was neither fault nor intent to insult on your part. Only desperation. After long consultation we decided to rescue you."

"Decided?" asked Clive. Ka ducked back into the water. Clive waited for the sea-man to rise before finishing his question. "Why would you have to decide whether to rescue someone who was drowning? Would you not do so automatically?"

Ka shook his head and frowned. "We have little to do with the people of the land," he said. "For the most part they fear us, though for no good reason, as we have never intentionally harmed one of them. But if one of us becomes tangled in their nets, they are as apt to kill us, or take us to shore, which is the same thing, as they are to free us. Of course, it is very rare for one of us to get caught in such a way." He said this last very fiercely, as if the idea of being caught was a great insult.

"We do not like the people of the land," he continued. "But the ancestors pointed out that you were of a different place, and had done us no harm." He paused. "They also indicated that someone among you had a role to play in the struggle that has overtaken the Dungeon."

"What struggle?" Clive asked eagerly. "Which of us?"

But Ka shook his head. "I have said too much," he rasped. "We do not involve ourselves. The islanders come. I must leave!"

"Wait!" cried Clive.

But it was too late. Instead of merely ducking beneath the waves, Ka turned and leaped, arcing over a wave and then disappearing into the blue-green water.

When he resurfaced, about fifty feet away, only his head and shoulders showed above the waves.

"Good luck, Folliot," he shouted.

"Wait!" Clive cried again. "How do you know my name?"

But Ka was gone.

Clive turned to Annie. "I didn't even have time to thank him," he said bleakly.

She took his arm and began to speak. But before she had uttered two words she was interrupted by an uproar from behind.

They turned and saw several hundred people standing at the place where the beach ended and the grass began.

· CHAPTER TWENTY-ONE ·

Lightning Rod

The main group of people was small, even the tallest of them barely reaching five feet. But they were beautifully formed, as if the Greek ideals of body proportion had been re-created in miniature. They had dark hair, dark eyes, and glossy skin the color of old pine cones. They were wearing loincloths and nothing else—even, Clive noted with interest, the women.

Scattered here and there among the islanders were the kind of anomalies Clive had come to expect in the Dungeon: a tall, blue-skinned woman with three breasts, a towering creature who looked more like a praying mantis than a human, and a short, round something covered almost entirely with lavender fur. Most striking of all to Clive's eyes, primarily because he was so abnormally normal-looking, was a rather distinguished man of middle years. He had ruddy skin, thick, silvery hair, and a bushy mustache. Dressed in the proper fashion he would not have looked out-of-place in the House of Lords. As it was, he gave a certain elegance even to the simple, one-piece white linen suit he was currently wearing.

The distinguished-looking man nodded at Clive but said nothing. The diminutive majority beat their fists against their breasts and cried "Hail, sky warriors!" several times. Suddenly, as if on a signal, they began to surge forward.

Clive braced himself for a battle. But the people were smiling. Laughing merrily, they lifted Clive and his friends to their shoulders and began to carry them away from the beach.

He felt Shriek tickle at his mind. *This is an unexpected reception, O Folliot.*

Unexpected indeed! replied Clive. *But then, being alive is a surprise at this point.* He hesitated, then added, *I was very worried about you. I was afraid you would not survive the fall, or the waters.*

Her answer was emotional rather than telepathically verbal.

The group was carried along a path that wound upward between walls of lush vegetation, primarily enormous ferns. To Clive's eyes the contrast between the tiny tribesmen and the ferns made the plants seem even bigger than they actually were. The foliage was wet, either from dew or a nighttime rain, and droplets of cool water fell onto Clive's face as the triumphant procession wound on. Beyond the ferns he saw tall, slender trees and a profusion of vines. The vines carried large, oddly shaped clusters of flowers that created great spatters of color throughout the jungle. The air was redolent with the fruity smell he had noticed on the beach. He looked up and saw something with wings, neither bird nor insect, drift by overhead.

They arrived, at length, in a village consisting of a circular cluster of thatch-roofed huts. The villagers set them down, formed a big circle, and shouted "Sky warriors!" once again. Then one of the women stepped forward. Like the others, she was small and exquisitely formed. Long, dark hair flowed like black water over her shoulders. Her only ornamentation was a band of scarlet feathers circling her upper right arm.

She began to speak. As with the sea creatures, her language was a variant of "Dungeon Standard." However, this branch of the language seemed to be farther out on the tree than most, and Clive understood not more than one word in three. The words he did catch, however, were of great interest, for woven through a speech of considerable length and enthusiasm he heard *Ren, Chaffri,* and *the Great Lord* several times each.

Clive turned to Annie. Unlike Shriek, who needed an initial physical contact to establish her unique brand of unspoken communication, Annie had an innate linguistic ability—an ability enhanced by her connection to the Baalbec A-9.

"Could you make head or tail of that?" he asked.

Annie laughed. "Not completely. But I think I got most of it. It seems they consider us gods from the sky. Like Ka and his people, they watched us climbing down Shriek's thread yesterday, until darkness finally closed their vision." She lowered her voice. "It's probably just as well that they didn't see us when we made our final drop into the water. They would probably be somewhat less impressed. A few of them were near the beach and saw you talking with Ka. That cemented things. They think you're pretty damn fine to be friends with one of the Sea People. They seem to think of Ka and his kin as ferocious monsters. From their point of view, you had to be incredibly brave or powerful to be talking with one of them like that."

Clive glanced at the woman who had spoken. The top of her head was barely higher than his waist. Remembering the towering Ka, he realized why these little people might fear the Sea Folk so deeply.

"What was all that about the Ren and the Chaffri and the Great Lord?" he asked, tearing his eyes from the tiny woman's beautifully formed breasts.

Annie shook her head. "I had a hard time making all that out."

"Perhaps I can help," said the tall, silver-haired man. He had been standing near the rear of the crowd, leaning against one of the huts. At the sound of his voice the little people moved aside respectfully.

"My name is Green," said the man, reaching forward to shake Clive's hand. Clive felt the older man's deep, clear eyes boring into his own. "I have a home near here," he continued. "It is somewhat different from these huts. I think you might like it."

He paused, then added, "I have a rather interesting chess set. Perhaps you would care to join me in a game?"

Clive smiled. The idea was wildly enticing. It seemed so basic. So homelike.

He turned to the others. "What do you say? Shall we take Mr. Green up on his invitation?"

"You misunderstand me," Green said quickly. His voice was pleasant but firm. "This invitation is for you only, Major Folliot."

Clive hesitated. Shriek sent him a mental nudge: *I think it would be wise to accept, dear heart.*

Clive was too preoccupied with the question at hand to pay much attention to the affectionate term by which Shriek addressed him. *Perhaps,* he responded. *Yet I hesitate to divide the group. The last time I did such a thing I ended up in N'wrbb's catacombs, and you all had to rescue me.*

That seems to be your function in much of this, replied Shriek.

To be rescued? Clive asked somewhat indignantly.

No. To function as—as— The message faltered, and he had a sense of her searching for the right word. Finally it came in the form of a picture, a picture clearly dredged up from his own subconscious mind.

It was a picture of a lightning rod.

Anyway, she continued, *this invitation seems far more cordial than did N'wrbb's.*

Clive signaled agreement, and added that, if nothing else, his curiosity would probably drive him to accept Green's offer.

"Is something wrong?" asked the older man.

Clive blushed, and wondered how long he had been ignoring everyone while he communicated with Shriek. He had gotten so used to holding private conversations with the spider woman while they walked that he had forgotten others were not aware of what he was doing.

"Excuse me," he said hastily. "I was considering your invitation." He paused. "I think I would like to accept."

Horace Hamilton Smythe raised an eyebrow but said nothing.

"Good," Green replied jovially. "I believe you will not regret it."

Placing Horace in charge of the group, Clive followed the mysterious Mr. Green out of the village and into the jungle.

· CHAPTER TWENTY-TWO ·

Green Haven

For a time neither Clive nor Green spoke as they walked through the jungle. The path continued to lead upward, skirting basalt–like outcroppings. They passed occasional pools, and once a tall, thin waterfall that struck with such force Clive could feel its spray some thirty feet away.

"This is a very beautiful place, Mr. Green," Clive said at last.

"It's just Green," said the other man, with a hint of amusement in his voice.

"I beg your pardon?"

"My name is Green. Not Mr. Green. Just—*Green*."

"I don't understand."

"You don't have to. I don't have to understand why you're called Clive Folliot to know that's your name and do you the courtesy of calling you by it. Just so with me. My name is Green, and I'll thank you to use it properly."

"Just so," said Clive, a trifle stiffly. "Anyway, this island is quite lovely . . . Green."

"I'm glad you think so. That is why I chose to retire here. I do hope it will last. Tondano is one of the few places left untouched by the war."

"The war?" asked Clive.

"Ah, here we are," said Green, ignoring Clive's question as completely as if it had never been asked. "Home. Green Haven, as I like to call it."

Clive looked, and looking, saw that it was good. He had seen many astonishing things since he had entered the Dungeon, but most of them unpleasant. Women excepted, he had seen nothing here anywhere near as lovely as Green Haven.

The house was built on many levels. Much of it was stone, and much was glass. Water ran through it, and out over one rocky ledge, creating a waterfall that rivaled the one he had seen on the path. It seemed as sturdy as a solid English home, as ethereal as an elfin castle. In places it seemed to disappear into the ground, almost as if it were part of the earth itself.

"Do you like it?" asked Green, the pride in his voice quite evident.

"Yes," said Clive. "It's wonderful."

They followed a secondary path to a door made of some dark wood carved in intricate geometric patterns. The door had no handle, and for a moment Clive wondered how they were going to get in. Then Green reached out and placed his hand on the jamb. The door slid sideways into the wall. Clive was still glancing over his shoulder at this wonder as Green led him into the house proper.

"The first thing I want to do is get you some clothes," said Green. "I think you've gotten about all the use you're going to out of those wretched things."

Clive looked down at the leather togs he had received in N'wrbb's castle. They had been torn and filthy when he had entered the Cave of the Finnboggi. Now they were stiff and salt-stained as well.

"That would be much appreciated," he said.

Green touched a panel, and another door slid open, revealing a small room. "You'll find several outfits like the one I am wearing inside. They may seem small, but they will stretch to fit your frame. When you leave, I'll send outfits with you for the rest of your group." He leaned through the doorframe. "The opening there— the one to your right—leads to a room where you can bathe if you wish. When you're ready, touch this panel and the door will open again."

He stepped aside and Clive entered the room. The door slid shut behind him, causing him to feel a momentary burst of panic.

"A bad sign, Folliot," he said to himself. "Anyone who gets that upset when a door closes has been in prison more often than a gentleman ought."

Looking around the room, he found a stack of the white suits. Between the shrinking and the stiffening of the leather he had some difficulty in stripping off his clothes. It was only after he had removed them and stood nude in the center of the room that he realized how terribly uncomfortable they had become.

He stepped through the other door Green had indicated and found a small, rock-lined pool, fed by a stream that flowed down one wall. He could not see where the water drained. Soap and towels lay beside the pool. Gratefully, he immersed himself in the warm, bubbling water.

When Clive emerged from the little room half an hour later, totally clean for the first time in several weeks and dressed in a white suit that was more comfortable than anything he had ever worn, Green was nowhere to be seen.

Clive started down the little hall. He found the man in the first room he came to, sitting on a cushion and staring at a large glass tank filled with colorful fish.

"Ah, you're ready! Come on, I'll show you some of the house while we head for the game room."

Green Haven's rooms were open, sprawling, and gracious. Great stretches of glass gave some of them an airy feeling that reminded Clive of the Crystal Palace. Other rooms seemed to have no walls at all. The second room like this that they came to opened onto a small pond where large yellow blossoms floated on clear, still water.

"This is very beautiful," said Clive. "But what is the point in having a sturdy door at the front of the house, when rooms like this are left wide open?"

In response, Green touched a hand-sized panel on the wall beside the door. Instantly a gray curtain obscured the pond.

"The house is well fortified," said Green. "Yet life here on Tondano is so peaceful I sometimes forget to

keep my defenses up." He shook his head. "Very foolish of me."

All the rooms were decorated with strange artifacts
which were clearly drawn from many cultures. As they
continued through the wonderful house Clive began to
suspect that perhaps the objets d'art so liberally distri-
buted on walls and shelves came from many *worlds* as
well. In one room he picked up a cube of crystal, about
six inches on a side, and was astonished to see that it
held a perfect three-dimensional image of himself. He
was so startled that he dropped it. He blushed, feeling
like a fool. But his embarrassment quickly turned to
suspicion.

"Where did you get this?" he demanded of Green.

"I made it."

"Why does it have my image in it?"

"Because you're the one holding it," replied Green.
"It's nothing more than a very fancy mirror. It does
have one nice trick, though. Once someone has held it,
the image continues to reflect his actions for at least a
quarter of an hour after he puts it down."

Clive looked at the crystal cube. His reflection looked
back at him, its face showing the kind of wonder and
confusion that he was feeling.

"What makes this a particularly clever bit," Green
said cheerfully, "is that you don't even have to be in the
room for it to show what you are doing. Handy thing
to have around if you're raising kids."

"Where are you from?" asked Clive, placing the block
back in its resting place.

Green shrugged. "Here and there. I've moved around
a bit in my life."

"From Earth?" persisted Clive.

"Now see here, young fellow," Green said sternly. "I
brought you here for a game of chess, not an interrogation. I'll thank you to mind your manners."

He turned on his heel and continued walking, obviously expecting Clive to follow. But Clive's attention
had been drawn by another artifact, something as simple and homey as the cube was exotic.

It was a black-and-white photograph held in a silver

frame that sat propped on a piece of polished black stone. The details were different—the hair was a little fuller, and the thick spectacles were missing. But there was no mistaking that cheerful, round face and the kindly eyes that held such hints of mischief. It was Father Timothy F. X. O'Hara, the beer-soaked old priest who had helped nurse Clive back to health after his misadventures on the coast of East Africa.

He snatched the picture from its resting place and hurried after Green. "Where did you get this?" he demanded.

"It was a gift," Green said smoothly. "From an old friend."

"But I know this man!"

"I don't doubt that you do," replied Green. "However, that does not give you call to make so free with my possessions. I'll thank you to put that back where you found it."

"But he lied to me," said Clive.

"I don't find that any more surprising than the idea that you know him," said Green. "Now please put the photo back where you found it."

Clive locked eyes with the older man. The gaze that met his was solid, unwavering, yet not without a hint of compassion.

Finally he shrugged and returned the photograph to the place where he had found it.

"Father O'Hara took care of me when I was suffering from exhaustion in Africa," Clive said quietly as he walked back to where Green stood waiting for him. "He was very good to me. But when I told him about some of the things I had seen—the circle of stars, the waterspout—he tried to convince me that I was mistaken. Why did he do that?"

"I do not speak for others," said Green. "It may have been simple kindness. It may have been something far more complex. I would suggest that you ask him yourself."

"And how am I to do that?"

Green shrugged. "He stops by here every once in a while. You may have a chance to see him before you go. That is, assuming you are planning to leave this island."

He raised a bushy eyebrow, indicating that he meant it as a question.

"Indeed, we intend to leave as soon as possible," said Clive, still struggling with the idea that Father O'Hara had access to the Dungeon.

"And why is that? Can you possibly think there is anyplace else in this hellhole that can be half as pleasant as the island of Tondano?"

"We're looking for—" Clive caught himself. "Why do you wish to know?" Despite his sudden wave of suspicion, he tried to keep his voice courteous.

Green laughed. "I really did wonder how long you were going to go on like that. You are a trusting thing, Clive Folliot. Sometimes you seem far younger than your three and thirty years."

"How do you know my age?"

"I know a great deal about you," Green said sternly, "and about a number of things that concern you. For example, there is this—which I suspect you might be glad to have returned to you."

Reaching into a pocket of his one-piece suit, Green withdrew a familiar-looking black book.

"Neville's journal!" exclaimed Clive. He felt a rush of embarrassment as he realized that he had not even known he had lost it. Most likely it had fallen from his pocket when he dropped from Shriek's thread last night. Or perhaps while he was thrashing about in the water. "How did this come into your hands?" he asked suspiciously.

Green shrugged again. "Not everyone on the island is afraid of Ka and his people. They gave it to me. I give it to you as a sign of good faith—something I would suggest you require of anyone in the Dungeon who begins asking you too many questions."

Clive felt himself blush. "Are you going to tell me what this is all about?" he asked.

"Are we going to play chess?" replied Green.

"At your pleasure," Clive said tersely.

Green led him to another room, clearly designed for

leisure purposes. They walked down three wooden steps to enter it. Large cushions were scattered about the floor. In the center of the room was a sunken circular area, reached by another three steps. In the center of this area was a large, circular table, with the pattern of a chessboard imprinted on the top of it.

"You live like a sultan!" said Clive.

Green laughed. "A little more sedately, I am afraid. All those wives would tire me out. But I do like a bit of comfort in my life. Are you such a Spartan that it offends you?"

"Not at all," said Clive. "Not at all."

Clive discovered that the game area was carpeted with a material he had never experienced before. What he first took to be an Oriental rug—thick, soft, and smooth as silk—was decorated with a pattern that he slowly began to realize was actually changing in a gradual but constant fashion. The design remained Oriental. But the motifs and embellishments shifted as he stood upon them, so slowly that he could not actually see the process happen, but so surely that if he looked carefully, looked away for a few seconds, then looked back, he could detect the difference. Sometimes it was an alteration of color, sometimes of scale. Yet despite the continually shifting elements, the whole was never out of balance; the design never seemed to lose its integrity.

He was fascinated, and might have become totally absorbed in watching the shifting pattern if the discreet sound of Green clearing his throat had not brought him back to the present moment.

The man was holding a pair of wooden boxes. He held out his hands, allowing Clive to choose one of them.

Almost like choosing weapons for a duel, thought Clive, recalling the strange story Horace had told of his duel along the Mississippi River.

He studied the boxes, but they appeared identical. He looked at Green's face, but there was no clue to be found there. He decided to leave it to chance, and reached for the box closest to his right hand.

Green smiled. "I think you will like this set," he said, sliding back the cover on his own box and gazing at the chess pieces inside. Moving to the far side of the circular table, he sat cross-legged on the floor in front of it, propping himself up with several cushions that lay within arm's reach.

Clive took his place opposite Green and began to set out his pieces.

The pawns were an odd lot, yet somehow seemed appropriate for a game of chess here in the Dungeon. They reflected a variety of physical types, half vaguely human, half no more resembling a man than a bat resembles an elephant.

It was when he started unpacking the major pieces that Clive's fingers began to tremble.

First came the castles. As he lifted one out of the box he realized with a start that it was clearly meant to represent the Black Tower of Q'oorna. Clive closed his fist around the piece, then closed his eyes as he was seized by memories of the day he had first stood in that astonishing structure, which was carved from a single piece of black basalt that provided a wide, almost sprawling base and then stretched slowly upward in an ever-narrowing spire, the height of which still made him dizzy to remember. He recalled standing side by side with Horace Hamilton Smythe and Sidi Bombay in the great hall of the Tower, where they had faced nearly certain death at the hands of a mongrel horde of warriors. Most of all, he remembered their imprisonment beneath the Tower, where he had found his many times great-granddaughter, Annabelle Leigh.

Clive opened his fist and stared at the Tower cupped in his palm. After a moment he raised his eyes to look at Green, a question on his lips. But the silver-haired man was busy arranging his own pawns and clearly gave the impression that he was not to be interrupted.

Clive turned his attention back to his pieces. He placed the castles on the playing surface, then caught his breath as he unpacked the knights and found two perfect replicas of Horace Hamilton Smythe, carved from a green stone that resembled jade.

The bishops, carved from onyx, represented Sidi Bombay. Unlike the knights, they were not identical. One showed Sidi as the old man whom Clive knew. The other figure was taller, smoother, more muscular—Sidi as he must have been thirty years earlier.

"Ah," said Green. "Now *there* is a figure well known to certain circles in the Dungeon."

Clive looked up. The older man was staring at him, eyes intent, challenging.

Clive accepted the challenge. Without a word, he reached into the box and drew out one of the two remaining pieces.

King or queen? he wondered as he unwrapped it. It was the queen. She lay face down in his hand. When he rolled her over to examine her, he cried out in astonishment and nearly dropped the piece.

The queen, carved from some unknown white stone, was a perfect replica of his mother.

He placed her on the chessboard and looked at the remaining piece with mingled fear and curiosity.

Who would be the king?

But when he unwrapped the last piece, he found nothing more than a simple column, smooth and white, its only ornamentation a five-pointed crown carved on the top.

"What does this mean?" demanded Clive, setting the piece on the playing surface with the others.

Green smiled at him. "Chessmen have always been symbolic. They are open to many interpretations."

"Why did you bring me here?" asked Clive. "To torment me with unanswered questions?"

Green frowned. "Don't be so self-aggrandizing. I have more important things to do with my time than think of ways to torment you. The point of all this is to get you to *think*. You haven't been doing much of it lately, and if you don't start, Clive, you're not going to survive this adventure!"

Clive's first reaction was anger. Who was this man to criticize what he had done over the last dangerous weeks? He had survived, hadn't he? Wasn't that a miracle in and of itself? What did he want of him?

But before he could say any of that Green had leaned toward him. His voice low and intense, he whispered, "Think, Clive. *Think!* You learned to play chess when you were a boy. You learned it well. Use what you know."

And suddenly Clive's anger boiled over. "But I don't know the goddamn rules anymore!" he cried, pounding his fist on the table so hard that several of the chessmen fell over. "How can I play the game if I don't know the rules?"

"Rule one," said Green, and his voice seemed to carry a hint of compassion. "Figure out the rules."

"Who are the Ren and the Chaffri?" Clive replied almost instantly, seizing on the question that over the last days had come to seem almost central to the mystery of the Dungeon.

Green paused. "They are a pair of ancient races," he said at last. "Very old, very powerful, very—sad." On the last word the pitch of his voice dropped, so that it came out almost as a sob.

"Why sad?" asked Clive, leaning forward intently.

"The loss of wisdom is always sad."

"Are you of the Ren?"

Green shook his head.

"Of the Chaffri?"

Again he shook his head.

"Then what are you?"

"A bystander," Green said almost wistfully. "Just an innocent—"

So intent had the two men been on their conversation that neither of them had realized when Horace Hamilton Smythe came slinking into the room. So it was a complete shock to both of them when he hurled himself into the game pit and plunged a long, thick knife through Green's immaculate white linen suit and into his heart.

CHAPTER TWENTY-THREE

The Harvest Is Coming

He floated, wrapped in pain, waiting for her to come. But when she arrived, when her mind reached out to touch his, it was timid, as if she were afraid he would be angry. The idea astonished him. How could he be angry with her? Without her he would be lost beyond redemption.

What is it, dear one? he responded, struggling to keep his thoughts gentle in spite of the searing pain.

She tried to hide her distress. It was pointless. He knew her thought patterns, her feelings, too well for that kind of dissembling. When she quivered, as now she did, it was as if he could feel the tremor through his own skin. Strange, considering that he was so out of touch with his own body that he could not even locate his arms and legs; they were simply part of the total experience labeled PAIN, which aside from thoughts of L'Claar was all that existed inside his skin.

Suddenly he was frightened. She was his comfort and his solace. Yet, when her mind had reached out to him this time, her turmoil had struck him as a thing that was almost physical.

It is nothing, she lied, and he was hurt by it, because until now there had been no lies between them.

Don't! he thought, almost desperately. *Never lie to me. We are too close. It hurts me too much.*

All is pain, she responded.

Then let us not give each other any more than is necessary.

But it will pain me to tell you this, she said.

Any more than it pains you to hold it in?

He could feel her sigh as though it were his own. *The Harvest is coming,* she finally replied, *and I fear for you.*

What Harvest?

The Harvest of Souls.

What do you mean? he asked.

But the answer to that question was locked away so deeply that, as close as they were, he could not begin to find it.

And Sidi Bombay, who had thought for an eternity that he had nothing left to lose but L'Claar, found that he was frightened for himself.

I will be back, she whispered in his mind as she pulled away, leaving him to writhe in the agonies of whatever hell it was he had fallen into.

CHAPTER TWENTY-FOUR

The Mind of Horace Smythe

Clive leaped across the gaming table. It collapsed beneath his weight, scattering the mysterious chess pieces in all directions. Locking his arms around Horace's waist, he pulled him away from Green's writhing body.

Horace offered no resistance. When Clive wrenched the knife from his hands and threw it across the room, he simply blinked in astonishment and said, "Sah?" in a plaintive voice that Clive found somehow more frightening than the violent act that had preceded it.

Not bothering to answer, he turned his attention to Green. The silver-haired man lay sprawled across the stack of pillows, gasping for breath, his hand clasped over the spot on his breast where Horace's knife had struck.

Clive knelt tenderly by the older man's side. Pulling aside the protecting hand, he received his third surprise in less than that many minutes. Rather than the sticky mess of hot blood he had expected, he found a spot of red no bigger than a tuppence. If the knife had actually penetrated the suit, and he was sure it had, there was no sign of it now. The fibers had somehow closed together again, completely sealing whatever damage had been done to the fabric.

If only human beings could be fixed so easily, he thought. Holding Green's hand in his, he placed his other hand on the older man's cheek.

"Listen to me," gasped Green. "I don't have long."

"You're not going to die," Clive said foolishly.

"I know I'm not going to die!" said Green, his tone

sharp despite the weakness in his voice. "I don't wear this stupid suit for nothing. But despite its protection, I am badly wounded. I will have to go for help soon."

"I'll go," said Clive. He glanced over his shoulder at Horace, who was now staring down at his own trembling hands with an expression of deep horror.

"Shut up and listen!" said Green in exasperation. He closed his eyes and winced in pain, his hand tightening on Clive's. "The suit will take me. In fact, it's trying to take me now. I can only hold on for another moment or two. There was a great deal I wanted to tell you. There will not be time. Now the first thing you must know is this: your friend is not to blame for what just happened. He is subject to control from outside, through certain devices that have been implanted in his brain. No doubt they helped him get through the house defenses."

Green's voice was growing weaker. He motioned to Horace. "Come here," he said weakly.

Horace crossed to where Clive knelt beside Green. Glancing up at his old friend, Clive saw someone who seemed very much a stranger. His face was the color of ashes. His eyes were deep pits of guilt.

"I will absolve you," Green said crossly, "if you will remove that stupid expression from your face." His hand tightened on Clive's once more. "*Listen*. The implants can be beaten. You must be alert, always alert to strange impulses that seem to come from nowhere. When this happens you will feel a slight headache, and perhaps a tingling in your scalp. Concentrate. Block the sendings. It is not that hard, once you know what is happening. Your main vulnerability lay in your ignorance. But you must stay alert. Otherwise—"

He spasmed, and his hand tightened around Clive's like a vise.

"I have no more time," he whispered.

Clive watched helplessly as he faded out of sight. It reminded him of the man beneath N'wrbb's castle, the man in what was supposed to be Neville's office, who had vanished in almost exactly the same fashion.

His hand closed around empty air.

He stared at the place on the cushions where the imprint of Green's body could still be seen, and his ears rang with the very last words the man had managed to choke out, words that seemed to hang in the air even after he was gone: *You learned to play chess for a reason.*

After a moment he turned to look at Horace.

His old friend looked back bleakly. "I dunno what happened, sah," he said, his voice low, quaking. "Last I remember I was standing down on the beach with Miss Annie, talking about whether we could use a raft to move on. Then I'm lying on the floor here with a knife in my hand, you crouched over me looking like blood and thunder, and that poor chap workin' on what seemed to be his last breath."

Clive sighed and got to his feet. The world seemed to be swirling around him. He felt as if he had been standing on what seemed to be rock, and suddenly discovered that it was quicksand.

He had had warnings, of course. Horace's behavior from the time he had rejoined Clive on the *Empress Philippa* had occasionally been most mysterious. But in the Dungeon he had been so solid that it had been all too easy for Clive to slip into the long-established habit of relying on Smythe completely. Even those occasional moments when he seemed lost in himself, staring into space, Clive had chalked off as having to do with his concern for Sidi Bombay. Now he wondered if during those moments Horace had been receiving instructions from the mysterious force that had driven him to this calamitous act.

Horace stood at attention, waiting for whatever punishment Clive should choose to mete out.

But how could punishment be appropriate? The victim himself had absolved Horace from blame.

"New Orleans?" he said softly.

Horace understood the question. "I don't think so, sah. I think it happened before that."

"Another adventure you've not told me about?" asked Clive.

Horace sighed. "During those times I was on leave I did a number of things I was asked not to talk about, sah. But I suppose that doesn't matter much now. I mean, I don't think anyone will be too worried if I talk about them here."

"Why don't we restrict it to this particular situation for now, Sergeant Smythe." He glanced at the cushions. "I have no immediate appointments. Why don't you tell me whatever you know about what's going on."

He piled some cushions against the wall of the game pit and motioned for Horace to do the same.

"Unfortunately, there ain't that much to tell, sah," said Horace, settling in. "I mean, there's a story around it all, but only a small part of it seems to have anything to do with what just happened."

"Why not just tell the story and let me be the judge of that?"

Horace nodded. Voice subdued, still shaking, he began to tell his tale:

"It was the winter of 1858—ten years ago, back in our world—when a certain person in the government, someone I had done some work for previously, asked me to make a trip to Tibet to gather some information. Seems the Crown had gotten word of a rebellion brewing in India, and one of our sources indicated that the push behind it all was coming from up north.

"Well, as the major knows, I have some ability with disguise. Started when I used to hang about the music halls as a lad. Did a bit of work for some of the folks, and they used to teach me some turns for a bit of a lark. Good people, them theater folk. Taught me a great deal in their own way—a little music, a little language, some acrobatics and all. Surprising how much some of that can come in handy later on in life.

"Anyway, between the acting and the fact that I had picked up a bit of Tibetan while I was assigned in India earlier on, I guess I seemed a natural one to find out what was really going on up there.

"So they shipped me out to India.

"A few days after I got there I went native and started making my way toward Tibet. No need to go into all the details of that right now, sah, though it was quite an adventure, I can tell you. Most people 'know' that not many white men have made it into Tibet so far. But a few of us have been there more often than people think.

"I can tell you, Major Folliot, it's a strange country. Strange people, strange language, strange ideas. And those mountains! Ain't nothing else like 'em on Earth. They just rear up to the sky as if they were scratching at heaven's underbelly. I'm not much of a mystic, sah. But I'll tell you: if there's any of the old gods still hanging about, that's where they'd be hidin'. At least, that's what I think.

"Now when you're trying to track down something like this the main rule is simple: follow the money. Usually that's a little easier to say than it is to do. But still and all, it seems to work, and that's what I was trying to do. Worked pretty well, too, until I got to that monastery.

"I knew there was something odd about the place from the time we got there. But that's no surprise in Tibet; you expect things to be sort of strange.

"But this wasn't just Tibet-strange. It was something weirder. I'd seen enough of Tibet by then to know that the way this place was decorated, the statues, the carvings on the walls—well, they didn't quite seem to fit.

"I never would have gone there if the fellow I was traveling with hadn't suggested it. We had been out in the cold an awful long time, and we were running short of food. When he told me he knew of a place where we could rest and get some stores, it seemed a good idea. I had a lot of faith in that fellow, too. A little Sherpa he was, worth a dozen ordinary men. At least, that's what I thought at the time. Now I'm not so sure.

"Anyway, we hadn't been there long when I took sick. Too much cold and yak butter, I thought. Now I wonder if it's not something else, something those monks fed me. I fell into a fever. Almost like a trance it was, sah. Lord, I never had such dreams as I did then. All sorts of stuff about weird creatures cutting me up. Kind of nightmares a man could die from, if you know what I mean.

"When I finally came to, I had the most bejeezus headache in history.

"Well, things get a little funny after that. Me and the Sherpa stayed in the monastery for another two weeks or so, while I got completely better. But after that, every once in a while I'd have times when I just sort of lost track of things. I'd be going along all sort of normal, and then next thing I knew some time would have gone by that I couldn't remember nothing about. Sometimes it was only ten minutes. Once it was a month and a half, and didn't that scare me, I want to tell you.

"The thing is, it never happened when I was on duty. I used to be terrified of that—figured if it ever happened, I'd be all washed up. For a long time I just thought I was lucky. But that never really made sense. It was *too* lucky, if you know what I mean.

"Funny how you can hide stuff from yourself. If I'd thought about it, I probably would have known that was the case. But I didn't want to think about it, if you know what I mean. Besides, I was kind of better after it happened. I mean, I could do things I couldn't do before—like piano playing. Oh, I could play the piano all along. But Mendelssohn and stuff—I learned it like it was nothing.

"Anyway, I think that's when it happened. That time I told you about in New Orleans, when I had that duel—I wonder if that wasn't the first time they activated whatever these things are. That circle of stars in the handle of Philo Goode's gun—well, maybe it was some kind of a signal or something."

Horace sat with his head clenched between his hands. His fingers twitched over his scalp, as if seeking the mysterious implants.

He looked up at Clive with haunted eyes.

"I dunno, sah," he said. "With what I got in my head right now, maybe you should just cut my throat and get it over with."

CHAPTER TWENTY-FIVE

A Snake in the Grass

Clive snorted. "That kind of self-pity is so unlike the Horace Smythe I know that I almost wonder if it's coming from those implants. Get rid of me now while you can, indeed! Buck up, Horace. Green said you can control this, and control it you will, now that you're aware of it.

"Besides, you and I have things to do. I made a promise to help you find Sidi Bombay, and I have no intention of backing out of it. So let us make some plans and then get moving once again."

Despite his hearty words, Clive knew he could never again be entirely sure of his old friend. It was a very lonely thought.

They decided to search the house for anything that might be of use on their travels. But aside from some foodstuffs, the artifacts filling Green Haven were simply too arcane to be of much use.

However, the real reason for not taking anything became clear to Clive only when he returned to the gaming pit and picked up the white queen that looked so much like his mother. He wanted it very much. When he hesitated, then carefully put it back on the chessboard, he realized it was because he was expecting Green to return.

He turned to Horace. "We should go now. We'd better see how the others are making out."

Horace looked somewhat nervous. "Are we going to tell them what happened, sah?"

Clive hesitated. His first impulse was to hide the

incident, pretend it had never happened. But the hand was too tightly knit for that kind of secrecy. It would only prove divisive in the long run. And they had a right to know. Unpleasant as it was, from here on in traveling with Horace was going to present a degree of risk. The man might indeed be able to control any directives sent to him through the implants in his skull. But what if he slipped? What if even once the Ren, or the Chaffri, or whoever had placed those infernal devices in his head, managed to send him a message he could not ignore? Whose life might be forfeit then?

And what of the islanders? How would they react to Green's disappearance? Would he and Horace now be charged with murder, be thrown into some kind of prison again?

When he thought about it, Tondano hardly seemed the kind of place to have a prison. How did they punish wrongdoers?

He looked at Horace. "We will not tell the islanders," he said. "At least not for now. However, we must tell our people."

Horace blushed, but raised no objection.

As they were leaving Green Haven, Clive stopped to gather several more of the white suits from the room where he had cleaned up. He felt this was acceptable, since Green himself had said he intended to send clothes for the rest of the group.

"Here, Horace," he said. "Wash up in there and then try on one of these."

The quartermaster sergeant was quicker about his ablutions than Clive had been, and within a quarter of an hour the two men were heading down the path from Green Haven, scrubbed clean and dressed in white linen.

The village was empty when they arrived. However, they could hear people shouting and laughing off to their left. Following the sounds, they made their way through the several yards of giant ferns to a scene that seemed derived from Eden.

About three dozen of the islanders were bathing in what was essentially an enlarged version of the pool where Clive and Horace had washed. This communal pool was fed by a waterfall twice the height of the one he and Green had passed on the hike to Green Haven. It was divided into two parts. First came a long, trembling drop that ended in a wide basin formed from rock. From there the water poured over the lip of the basin and rushed down a slope into the main pool. The little people were gathered on this rocky slope, sliding with the water into the pool to the accompaniment of a great deal of shouting and laughter.

The falls were eight or ten yards to the right of where Clive and Horace stood. The pool itself was some thirty or forty feet in diameter. Pink and yellow flowers dotted its clear surface. The jungle grew right down to its banks on the opposite edge. On the side where Clive and Horace stood the trees were separated from the pool by a grassy slope about fifteen feet wide.

Flowers grew in thick profusion around the edge of the grass. Small animals wandered in and out of the jungle, seemingly oblivious to the human activity. Clive noted a handful of beautiful deer built in proportion to the tiny islanders, and several other creatures that, aside from the fact that they had four legs and fur, were unlike any animals he had ever seen before.

The beauty of the scene was enhanced by the fact that the islanders were swimming in the nude, a sight Clive quite enjoyed until he realized that Annie was swimming with them, and in the same condition.

"Annie!" he shouted. "You come away from there!"

At the sound of his voice she looked up and waved. "Ho, Clive! Isn't it wonderful? Come on in!"

"I most certainly will not!" he yelled. "You come out!"

"Don't be such an old fart," she replied. "I'm having a good time."

With that she ducked her head under the water and swam to the opposite side of the pool. He could see her nude body moving through the clear water. The sight was deliciously erotic. Clive swallowed, torn again by the conflicting emotions that struck him whenever he was aware of Annie's sensuality. Sometimes he wished he had never discovered that she was his descendant.

He shook his head. That kind of ignorance was what had gotten old Oedipus in so much trouble!

He hesitated for a moment, uncertain whether to try to force her out of the pool or to simply walk away. A vision of trying to wrestle a wet, slippery Annie into one of the white jumpsuits leaped unbidden into his mind. He squeezed his eyes shut and tried to force away the image.

His unsuccessful effort was interrupted by a scream.

Opening his eyes, he saw that an enormous snake had slithered into the pool. It had coiled its body twice around Annie and was trying to drag her out of the water and into the jungle.

The little people were scrambling out of the water, screaming and shouting. Annie struggled in the serpent's coils. Her thrashing legs sent arcs of crystalline droplets flying in all directions.

Without an instant of hesitation Clive went bounding down the bank. The place where the islanders had shucked their loincloths was a few paces in front of him, and he had noticed some knives and machetes among the discarded fabric. He grabbed a blade in each hand and started around the bank, knocking over two of the frightened islanders as he did so.

"Help me, you fools!" he snarled. But he didn't have time to look back to see if any of them were going to do anything but run.

He would have preferred to approach the monster from its head. To do so he would have to make his way across the slippery rock surface and through several yards of jungle. He decided to go left instead.

About halfway around the edge of the pond the forest met the bank, and he had to splash into the water to continue. Time seemed to slow down. His senses were extraordinarily alert—every sight, every sound registered more clearly and distinctly than usual. He was aware of the individual drops flung past him by Annie's struggle with the snake. He noticed every variation in the sound of the reptile's body thrashing in the pond. Even the scent of the flowers seemed stronger now.

In the few seconds it took him to circle the pond he gained a clearer picture of the serpent. Its body was as thick as his waist, with a head as broad as his own chest. The scales were red, green, and brown, the largest of them almost as big as the palm of his hand. The actual length of the creature was impossible to determine, as the end of its tail was hidden somewhere in the jungle to his left. The body extended from the foliage across a segment of the pond. Still in the water, it looped twice around Annie, then stretched past her to girdle a tree where the great malevolent head drooped over a branch. The snake was gazing back at Annie almost impassively as it waited for her struggles, which were already getting weaker, to cease.

With a shout, Clive launched himself through the air. He landed on the snake's body. Wrapping his legs around it, he began to hack at the monster with the knives he had grabbed from the shore. The serpent rippled, spasmed, arced through the air, and almost threw him off.

He held on, though he nearly lost his grip when the great length of the tail came smashing back against the pool. It dragged him beneath the water, then pulled him back to the surface. He lost one knife. Gritting his teeth, he stretched his arm forward and plunged the remaining knife into the writhing body. Using the knife as a handhold, he began to pull himself forward. The action created a dual motion; as Clive moved forward the knife slid back. Thick red blood began to well out from the numerous small trenches he was carving in the serpent's flesh.

The tail whipped back and forth, dragging Clive over the surface of the pool. He continued to pull himself forward.

At some point he noticed that Horace had joined the fray.

He was within arm's length of Annie now. She was still conscious, but her struggles were feeble, almost over. The sight filled Clive with a new rage. He pulled

himself forward just a little farther, then let go of the
snake and splashed his way to the edge of the pool. He
moved forward, positioning himself between Annie and
the creature's head. He wondered whether it was poisonous, vaguely remembered that the great snakes killed
by constriction, and went right for its eyes.

It was perhaps the single most frightening moment
of his life. The snake saw him coming. Its eyes seemed
to be made of fire and ice. It opened its jaws, and Clive
realized that they could easily encompass his head and
shoulders.

The great head lunged forward—faster, he thought,
than it should have been able to. He leaped sideways
and barely avoided being caught in the enormous jaws.

Now the head wove back and forth in front of him,
supported in midair by the thick, powerful body that
looped back around the tree, then trailed down to the
water where it held Annie in its coils.

The unthinking rage that had propelled him forward when he first saw Annie trapped in those scaly
loops had subsided. Suddenly Clive felt his heart beating its way up his chest, as though it were trying to
escape.

The snake seemed to be waiting for the right moment to strike. A terrible cold came over Clive. He
remembered outrageous tales of snakes hypnotizing
their prey. He had dismissed them out of hand. But
that had been in another time, on another world. Who
knew what this monstrous creature could do?

He shook his head to clear it. Instantly, the snake
struck. If it had caught him head-on it would have
been the end; it would simply have engulfed his head
and shoulders, clamped down for the time it took to
cut off his breath, and then either dropped him or
swallowed him whole.

But he moved sideways just enough that the snake
missed its mark. The lower jaw struck his right shoulder. It was like being hit by a battering ram. He went
staggering back into the water.

"Just a bit more, sah," said a voice behind him. "Keep
it busy a little longer and we'll have her out."

He glanced to his left and saw Horace and several of the islanders struggling with the coils that held Annie.

The momentary distraction was nearly fatal. The serpent lunged forward again. Clive moved sideways at the last possible instant and the head struck the water like a cannonball. He threw himself back onto the neck. The snake reared out of the water. It began to thrash back and forth, trying to throw him off. Clive felt himself being whipped through the air, several feet above the surface of the pool. With both legs and one arm wrapped around the writhing, looping body, he reached forward with his right arm and sliced open the snake's neck. A freshet of blood shot out from the wound, seeming to rival the waterfall itself as it stained the pool's clear water a deep crimson.

The snake plunged forward, striking the water with a loud *crack!*

Clive was thrown from its back. He felt himself being pushed sideways by the reflexive writhing of the great body.

"That's done it, sah! We've got her now!" he heard Horace yell.

And then he lost consciousness.

When Clive came to, he was lying in one of the huts they had seen in the village. Annie lay on a bed of leaves opposite him. She was still nude. He looked down and realized that he was, also.

He grabbed a leaf and pulled it over his groin.

His body ached in a dozen places.

He heard a noise. Glancing up, he saw about a dozen of the islanders gathered around the doorway.

When they saw him look in their direction they began to laugh and cheer.

One of them, an older woman, stepped forward. "You better?" she asked.

Clive nodded. "Where are my clothes?"

She looked puzzled.

"My clothes!" he repeated, reaching out to tug at the end of her loincloth.

"Mufti?" she asked.

Clive felt a surge of excitement. That word, so familiar in his own past, was hardly a part of the Dungeon's
lingua franca. It could have come from many places, of
course. But still . . .

"Do you know Neville?" he asked.

The woman smiled. "Neville!" she said happily. "Clive.
Neville. Great Lords from the sky!"

"He's been here!" Clive cried triumphantly. "We're
on the right track after all."

"What a remarkable family I come from!" Annie said
sardonically.

Clive glanced to his side and saw his young descendant
supporting herself on one elbow. She was smiling, as if
she found his interview with the island woman highly
amusing. He turned away quickly.

"Mufti," he replied. "For me, and for her. Please."

"Mufti!" said the woman. "Will bring Great Lord and
his woman mufti!"

Annie burst out laughing.

Clive lay back and fixed his eyes on the thatched
ceiling.

A few minutes later the woman came back into the
room, carrying two sets of the white linen suits he and
Horace had taken from Green Haven.

"Great Lord Folliot's other mufti deep in blood," she
said, handing him one set. She gave the other set to
Annie, then turned back to him. "You mufti. Then we
talk."

"Would you please turn around?" he said.

The woman looked puzzled.

"Turn around!" Clive repeated, making a circling
motion with his hand.

Annie giggled and stood up. Clive turned his face to
the wall.

"I'll get dressed in just a minute, Grampa," she said.
"Then I'll take the lady here outside while you put on
your clothes."

"Thank you," Clive said crisply. He stared at the wall.

"Okay!" said Annie, after what seemed several days.
"We're leaving."

He waited a moment, then turned back. He glanced

at the door. To his relief, the crowd was gone. He wondered if Annie had asked them to go. The girl did seem capable of understanding his feelings sometimes, no matter how much they amused her.

As he fingered the strange devices that closed the suit, Clive reflected that the first order of business would be to find out what the islanders knew of Neville. Ducking to step through the door, he found the rest of his group, as well as several dozen islanders, waiting for him. The islanders began to cheer wildly, beating the ground with poles and stamping their feet in approval.

Clive looked puzzled.

Shriek came to his rescue. *You have done a great deed, O Mighty Folliot,* she sent. *The people of Tondano greet you as a hero. They will make legends about you.*

Not if they find out what else has happened today, Clive thought before he could stop himself. It was all the opening she needed; he had cracked the door, and she gathered the details of the episode at Green Haven in an instant.

This is bad, she sent. *But perhaps not as bad as you fear. We have learned that the islanders do not have much contact with Green. They know him as one who comes and goes, comes and goes. They are used to him disappearing for weeks on end. Perhaps by the time they start to miss him, he will be back from wherever he has gone to heal. We will discuss the trouble with Horace later. For now, worry not, O Folliot. Relax and enjoy your celebration!*

Clive decided this was good advice and sent her a vow to do exactly as she suggested. The group clustered around him, grinning and clapping his shoulders. Even Chang Guafe seemed impressed at what he had done, though he did pronounce the deed "unpragmatic," at which point Annie told him to "stuff it."

All of them, save Shriek and the cyborg, were wearing the white suits that Green had provided. It was so strange to see the entire group clean, groomed, and wearing clothes not filled with holes that Clive found himself continually staring at the others, trying to get their new images clear in his head. Tomàs had even found a way to scrape off most of his beard. Clive ran his fingers through his own chestnut-colored beard and decided that he would keep it for a while longer.

"Come along, sah," said Horace, taking him by the arm. "There's something stirring on the beach I think you'll be interested in."

Gram positioned herself at his right. She looked strange in her new clothing, the chalk white of her skin blending almost invisibly into the white of the fabric, the green of her hair standing out more strongly than ever. She seemed tremendously impressed with what Clive had done, and it was from her that he learned what had happened after he lost consciousness.

"Horace and the Tondanans carried you and the girl back to the village," she explained. "Then Mai-lo—that's the local healer, the old woman who was in the hut with you—did what she could. Lucky for you that suit the old man gave you was made of pretty strong stuff. When Mai-lo came out she told us you were badly bruised but hardly had a cut on you. The girl wasn't so lucky. Even though that snake's skin was smooth as a baby's ass, it dragged her over enough rocks and branches that she got some pretty bad cuts. Mai-lo spent a lot of time smearing her with stuff so she wouldn't get infected."

Clive could not help but notice the way Gram refused to refer to Annie by name. He wondered if the older woman would ever come to terms with Annie's role in the death of 'Nrrc'kth.

Horace, who was walking on the other side of him, picked up the story.

"Once you and Miss Annie were seen to, I found Shriek and asked her to contact the others. Then I passed out the suits we got from Green. Mai-lo gave the two of you something she said would make you heal faster, but that would keep you sleeping for a while. Even so, once we all got cleaned up we just sort of gathered at the village, waiting to see how you were going to make out."

Clive was touched by their loyalty, a feeling that turned to astonishment when they reached the blue sand beach and he discovered that the villagers had spent the afternoon preparing an enormous feast in his honor—the main course of which was to be the great serpent. As darkness fell the cooking began over huge open fires the Tondanans had prepared at the edge of the sea.

At first Clive chafed at the situation, for he was eager to pursue the matter of what the islanders knew of Neville. But it seemed ungracious to force the matter while they were so busy preparing to celebrate his victory. Finally he decided it could wait until morning. The decision seemed to drain some tension from his body. His single-minded pursuit of his brother had consumed all his attention for so long that the idea of spending an evening relaxing with his friends seemed almost decadent.

The sky grew black. Some of the fires blazed and settled into coals, while others were continually fed for the light they would provide. The meat of the snake emitted an amazingly savory aroma as it sizzled over the coals. The smell mingled with that of the ocean. Clive sat down and listened to the surf as it rolled in, pulled at the sand, and rolled back out, its sound a low susurrus behind the laughter and chatter of the Tondanans.

After their recent battles and travails it was almost too pleasant to bear.

Some time later Annie came to speak to him.

"I wanted to thank you," she said, settling into the sand beside him.

"It's all right," he said. "I'd do it for any descendant."

He tried to keep his voice light. But he was uneasy, uncertain how to respond to this woman who was so tightly connected to him and yet so wildly different in the way she saw the world. It would have been easier if he could have freed himself of the vision of her naked body shining in the island sunshine, sparkling with crystalline droplets of water. But the picture seemed burned into his skull.

"Clive?"

He turned to look at her. The firelight seemed to catch in her dark eyes. Such beauty!

She put her hand on his arm, lightly. "We're different, that's all," she whispered.

He nodded.

The feasting went on. Later Clive watched as Annie joined some of the Tondanans as they danced around one of the fires. She looked joyful, free, sensuous.

He wished that he could do it too. But when the little people came and tugged at his hands, begging him to take part in their dance, he laughed and told them he could not.

Finnbogg came and sat beside him, looking oddly civilized in his white linen suit.

"Mighty Folliot is unhappy?" he asked.

Clive shook his head. "Not unhappy, Finn. Just confused."

The dwarf nodded vigorously, causing his jowls to wobble up and down. "Finnbogg knows what that's like. Finnbogg usually confused too, you bet."

Clive laughed. "What's bothering you, old chum?"

"Other Finnboggs. Don't know what happened. Don't know if Finnboggs safe, or dead."

Clive sobered. As comical as Finnbogg was, the dwarf's concerns for his people were as deep and real as anything that he was feeling himself.

"I understand," he said, putting a hand on Finnbogg's shoulder. "I, too, left someone at home whom I am worried about."

Finnbogg sighed and stared out at the ocean.

Clive followed the canoid's gaze and found himself speculating about Ka and his people. What was the sea-man doing now, he wondered. What was it like to live underwater?

Shriek walked by on the sand, clutching a piece of hot snake meat in one of her claws. She did not reach out to contact him, but he felt a pleasant wave of contentment as she passed.

A while later she came back to join Clive and Finnbogg where they sat. Slowly the others grouped around them. It felt good.

The islanders continued to sing and dance on the beach, which was lit by torches and bonfires.

Clive wondered if this level of the Dungeon had a moon or stars.

It was later in the evening, when most of the torches were out and the fires were only coals, that Clive was struck by a memory of the morning's events in Green Haven.

"The journal!" he cried. "Neville's journal. Green gave it back to me and it was in the pocket of that suit. Horace, do you know what happened to it?"

"Not to worry, sah," Horace said with a chuckle. "I have it right here."

He reached into one of the pockets of his suit and extracted the familiar black volume.

He passed it to Clive, who stared at it for a moment before opening it. The mystery of Neville had gotten lost in the day's celebrations.

He leafed through the pages eagerly.

There was indeed a new message!

The others followed him as he walked to the nearest torch. The light was so dim that he still had to squint to make out the writing.

"Well, what does it say?" asked Gram, who seemed to have attached herself to Horace for the evening.

Clive hesitated, then read the message aloud:

"Brother,
    The resourcefulness of you and your group continues to astonish me. We may make our way out of this whole mess yet.
    I have found the way to the next level. It is called the 'Gateway of the West.'
    If you can make your way there, perhaps we will meet in the Dungeon's fourth level.
    Remember, Clive, nothing is certain here. All is danger and treachery. Learn from everyone. Trust no one.
    Find me, and you will learn astonishing things."

"Is that all?" asked Tomàs.

"It's enough," said Clive. "We know our next destination. We're heading for the Gateway of the West."

"That is deep far," said an unfamiliar voice.

Clive looked to his left. Mai-lo, the old woman who had brought him his "mufti," stood at the edge of the group, barely within the perimeter of the torchlight. Her face was grim.

"I beg your pardon?" said Clive.

"Gateway of the West is deep far. Deep far, deep danger. Stay on Tondano, Folliot Serpent Slayer. Stay with clear water. Stay with good food. Stay with sweet people. Sweet people be happy. Folliot be happy. Do not go, like other Sky Lord. Do not leave the people."

Clive closed his eyes for a moment.

"Where is the Gateway of the West?" he asked.

The old woman pointed out across the water. "Deep far."

He turned to the others. "Tomorrow we shall begin to build a raft."

He raised his eyes and looked at the dark shape of the island looming behind him in the night. The perfume of its flowers filled his lungs. He closed his eyes and shook his head.

"And may God have mercy on us all," he whispered.

"A-men to that, sah," said Horace Hamilton Smythe, his voice thick with the memory of the terrible thing he had done that morning. "A-men to that indeed."

• CHAPTER TWENTY-SIX •

Bold Endeavor

Early the next morning Clive sought out Mai-lo to find what she knew of Neville. Because he was not yet fluent in the islanders' version of the Dungeon's *lingua franca*, he asked Annie to accompany him.

"Neville!" said Mai-lo reverently when Clive mentioned his brother's name. "Great Lord from the sky, like Clive."

"Did he climb down from the sky as we did?" asked Clive.

The tiny woman shook her head. "In the great flying machine came Neville. With wings like kleetah, it skimmed across the sea."

"Wings like what?" asked Clive, turning to Annie for help.

"You've got me on that one, Grampa," she said. "What are *kleetah*, Mai-lo?"

"Kleetah come from north, go to south. Never stop to visit."

"Well, there," said Annie. "Now you know what kleetah are."

"Never mind," said Clive. "The important thing is Neville."

"Neville," said Mai-lo reverently.

"How long ago was he here?" asked Clive.

"Long before Mai-lo was born," said the woman.

"Would you try that one?" he said, turning to Annie. "I'm not having much luck."

Annie plunged into conversation with the woman, hauling up fragments of linguistic variants Clive had heard but not really absorbed along the way. Occasionally she reached within her bodice to adjust the Baalbec A-9, murmuring little incantations like "input" and "analyze" as she did.

But when she was finished she turned to Clive and said, "I can't make much more sense of it than you did. According to what she says, the visit of Neville is an old legend among her people. He came from the sky, he did some good works—"

"That doesn't sound like Neville," muttered Clive.

"Now, Grampa, don't be bitter. As I was saying, he did some good works, and then he vamoosed."

"Well, there you have it," said Clive. "One more little mystery. Just what I was hoping for when I got up this morning. Come on. Let's go build a raft."

"I'm right behind you," she said.

Tomàs, as things turned out, was not.

"I have done this once before," he said, when Clive had gathered all of them on the beach to begin making plans. "When that fool Christoforo Colombo said we were going to sail across the ocean to the Indies, I thought, 'This man is crazy.' But at that time I had nothing to live for. For pay, I was willing to gamble on his craziness.

"But here—here we have much to live for. This island is good and sweet.

"You others, you do not know what it is like to head out on an ocean that maybe has no end. To sail and sail when you do not know where you are going, or if you will come to an end. You do not know how frightening it can be."

"No one is going to force you to go," said Clive, his voice sharp. Tomàs's speech had disturbed him, primarily because it reinforced his own questions about the plan to continue the journey.

Why did the alternative idea of staying peacefully on this beautiful island instead of risking their lives on a probably hopeless quest seem so impossible?

"Why not force him to go?" asked Gram. "The little pissant would still be locked up underneath—" she shuddered, and could not bring herself to say the name of the man who had desired 'Nrrc'kth for his consort, "—would still be locked up, if it wasn't for us. We need someone who knows the sea. Tomàs is the only one here who fits that description. So what is there to discuss? He comes whether he wants to or not."

Tomàs stepped behind Chang Guafe.

"No one is going to force him to go," Clive repeated firmly. "But I will tell you, Tomàs, that I want you along and will be sorely disappointed if you do not come. Gram is right, you know. You would still be imprisoned if not for us. There are many places along the way where you might have died if not for us."

"If not for you, people might have left me alone!" exclaimed Tomàs. "We have not been chased across the Dungeon because of a little Portuguese sailor, Folliot. It is you they are after."

"Are you so sure?" Clive asked shrewdly. "I have come to believe that no one is here by accident. If I am right, then perhaps they are after you, too, Tomàs. Perhaps they have been after you all along. Who knows why anything happens in this crazy world?"

He paused, then added, "Besides, if this is all a religious experience, as you keep telling me, then why stay here? Should you not continue with us on our pilgrimage? Would not remaining here be a breach of faith?"

"*Sua muito stupido,*" muttered Tomàs. He walked away, fiddling with his rosary.

Clive was well aware that Tomàs found it almost impossible to change his mind in front of others. So he let the matter drop temporarily, figuring that if Tomàs was going to come around, he would do it on his own or not at all.

Later that morning the rest of them began to build their raft. They were helped in this endeavor by the islanders. But it was a reluctant assistance, and the little people made frequent pleas for "The Great Snake Slayer" to stay and bless their tribe with his presence. Eventually the project generated enough interest to draw in the other outsiders, and they found themselves working side by side with the three-breasted woman and the round lavender creature, whose name was so unpronounceable that Clive referred to him only as Fuzz.

As Clive had hoped, once they actually began working on the project Tomàs was unable to resist telling them what they were doing wrong. He came edging in as they began to lay out the design for the raft and was soon deeply involved in the plans. He said nothing further about abandoning the party.

Clive was relieved. As annoying as Tomàs could be, it was going to be important to have someone with nautical experience on the next step of their journey.

They decided to fashion the bulk of the vessel from the trunks of the tall, slender trees Clive had noticed when the islanders had first carried them up the hill to the village. At first he thought they might bind these together with some of Shriek's webbing. But the spider woman feared that long periods of immersion in salt water would probably dissolve anything she could manufacture. In the end, they settled on using vines from the jungle, which they soaked in an infusion Mai-lo taught them to make. She claimed this process would render the vines less subject to wear and decay, and as proof she pointed to a fish-drying rack that she said had stood since she was a little girl.

Shriek proved invaluable in gathering the vines themselves, since even with one arm missing she could scuttle up the trees twice as fast as all but the most agile of the islanders. Once in the treetops she was able to make her way along branches no human could have negotiated. With her pincers she would clip the vines neatly and precisely at their source. Then, if the next vine they wanted was nearby, she would simply cast out a bit of web and swing between the trees. It was a fascinating sight, and Clive never tired of watching the enormous arachnid soar from tree to tree.

Once the vines were clipped, they would fall to the forest floor, where Annie and Finnbogg gathered them for the soaking process. The fact that he was working side by side with Annie for most of each day gave the jowly dwarf shivers of ecstasy. But after the third day

Annie complained to Clive that he was beginning to get on her nerves.

"It's not that I don't like him," she said rather plaintively. "It's just that he's so damn eager to please me he's always underfoot. He reminds me of a golden retriever my friend Marj had back in San Francisco." She shivered. "I can't stand having someone slobber over me like that."

Clive laughed. "Try to put up with it for a bit longer, if you can. I think it would break the poor fellow's heart if I split the two of you up right now."

She rolled her eyes, but didn't mention the matter again for the next several days.

The weather was so uniformly pleasant that they slept on the beach most nights, retreating to the pair of huts the villagers offered them only on the few occasions when a heavy rain came up. The first of these downpours came without wind, the water seeming to pour straight down from the heavens. The second major rain, however, was accompanied by such heavy winds and high seas that Clive began to wonder if the venture they were planning was truly mad after all.

He was relieved to find that the Dungeon's third level was not without moon or stars, as he had initially feared. In fact it was blessed with an abundance of the former; on some nights there were actually three moons to be seen drifting overhead. The eerie beauty of that sight made him feel farther from home than ever.

He checked the journal every day, but there were no new messages from Neville.

As the days went on, the pleasure of shared work seemed to draw the eight travelers closer together. Only Gram seemed outside of what they were doing. She worked well enough, lending her great strength to help them move the logs they were using for the body of the raft. Occasionally she roused to the point of snapping at Tomàs. Two or three times she even sat next to Horace during a meal. But for the most part she seemed wrapped in a world of her own, a world painfully separate from the rest of them. During this time she never spoke to Annie at all, and if she did happen to look at the younger woman, it was as though she were looking right through her.

After giving the matter some thought, and discussing it with Shriek, Clive finally suggested that they have a small memorial service for 'Nrrc'kth. Gram agreed, though without enthusiasm. Annie seemed frightened by the idea.

The next night everyone but Chang Guafe, who pronounced the whole idea "sentimental mush," gathered by the sea to bid formal farewell to 'Nrrc'kth. Annie was silent. Gram stared out at the water. Finnbogg howled and snuffled throughout the entire service. It was a subdued and unhappy group that made its way back to the place where they slept on the sand.

Clive slept uneasily that night, and woke quickly when he felt water dripping on his legs. He sat up. The night was dark, but the embers of their fire showed a tall form looming near his feet.

Before he could cry out, a familiar voice said, "I have something for you."

He relaxed; it was Ka, of the Sea People.

"Greetings, Ka," said Clive. He sat up. "What is it that you have brought?"

Ka bent down. Clive heard the clink of metal as he placed something on the ground.

"These are ornaments we preserved from the body of she who fell from the sky," said Ka. "When I heard you speak her memory by the water tonight, I decided that you might want to have them."

"You heard us?" asked Clive, feeling slightly embarrassed. He had not been entirely comfortable with being spokesman for the group as it was. The idea of an outsider listening in on his eulogy for 'Nrrc'kth made him even more self-conscious.

"My people have been watching you," said Ka. "No one has ever attempted to cross these waters on such a vessel as you are building. We are interested to see what will happen."

"And these ornaments?" asked Clive.

"One of my people found the woman's body a few days after your arrival."

"What happened to the body?"

"We ate it, as is proper."

Horrified, Clive reached out and grabbed the sea-man's arm. "You did *what*?" he hissed.

"We ate her," said Ka, snatching his hand out of Clive's grasp. "It was a very great honor! Normally we only do that for our own people."

Clive could think of no response to this remarkable statement, which for some reason brought to mind 'Nrrc'kth's ethereal beauty far more clearly than had the service he had conducted earlier that evening. He felt tears welling in his eyes.

"Do you want these or not?" asked Ka. His voice was harsh, offended.

"Yes," Clive said softly. "It was good of you to bring them."

"You are welcome," said Ka.

From the sound of his voice Clive guessed that the sea-man's breath was nearly gone, so he was not surprised when Ka turned and ran past the dying fire. The darkness swallowed him, and it was only the sound of his splashing that assured Clive he had returned to the sea.

Clive held the ornaments and stared into the blackness, trying to sort through his feelings. What Ka had said still sent waves of revulsion rippling through him.

But he had only done what his people did. And he had brought the ornaments.

The next morning Clive gave them to Gram and told her that they had come from the Sea People. He did not tell her what had happened to 'Nrrc'kth's body, though he later reflected that perhaps in the culture they came from it would have made no difference. He longed for a world where things made sense again.

Gram stood holding the ornaments for several minutes. Then, without a word, she turned and ran from him. He didn't see her for the rest of the day, though at one point he passed a clump of bushes and heard a deep, heavy sobbing from inside. He paused, uncertain whether he should offer the gift of companionship or the gift of privacy.

In the end, he decided to walk on.

When Gram rejoined them for dinner that night she was very quiet. But the next morning she made a suggestion about the construction of the raft, the first she had offered since they began the job, and Clive began to feel easier about her.

After supper Clive and Annie went for a walk along the beach.

"I think she just needed to know for sure that 'Nrrc'kth was dead," said Annie, climbing up onto a rock where they often sat.

Clive climbed up to join her. A flock of the giant seabirds waded through the water nearby. They watched them for a while in silence, though Clive found his gaze continually drifting toward the distant horizon.

"Funny thing is," said Annie, "knowing that 'Nrrc'kth is dead makes it easier on Gram, but harder on me."

"I don't understand."

"Well, the way I figure it, Gram was never convinced that 'Nrrc'kth was really gone. But now that we know someone found the body, she has to accept it. She can stop waiting for her to reappear and get back to the business of living herself." Annie paused. "The thing is, I think I was hoping she was alive, too. Sometimes at night, when I was trying to get to sleep, I would say to myself, 'Hey, look, Annie, maybe you didn't really kill her after all. Maybe you just sort of made it so that she got, you know, mislaid for a while.' "

She sighed and turned away from Clive.

"As long as I could tell myself that, I didn't have to deal with what really happened." She laughed, a short, bitter sound. "I never said anything. But I had this stupid fantasy that we might find her while we were floating around on this damn raft. Stupid. Stupid Annie."

Suddenly she began to shake. He put a tentative hand on her shoulder and she twisted toward him. Laying her head on his shoulder, she surrendered to the tears.

In addition to Annie and Gram, Clive had another worry during this period: what to do about Horace

Hamilton Smythe. Finally he decided to discuss the matter with Shriek.

The others must know, she sent, concurring with his original decision. *If anything happens later on and you have not told them, it will destroy your credibility.*

That's what I thought, replied Clive, shooing away one of the giant seabirds.

He had asked Shriek to walk along the beach with him so that they could talk in private. He had thought that once they were alone, they would speak aloud. But somehow the mental communication seemed easier.

My chief worries are Tomàs and Chang Guafe, he thought to her.

I agree. The others will accept the problem fairly well. But the sailor is suspicious, either by nature or by experience, and will not like this news. And the cyborg will consider the risk of keeping Smythe along impractical.

Perhaps I should tell everyone except Guafe, suggested Clive.

Secrets have a way of coming out, dear heart. If you don't tell him, one of the others is bound to let it slip. She hesitated. *On the other hand, it is not inconceivable that the cyborg might feel compelled to take some 'pragmatic' action to protect himself from this potential threat.*

Clive hesitated, then put her implication into thought-words. *You mean he might kill Horace rather than take the chance of his giving in to the implants?*

It is not a prediction. But such an event would not surprise me.

Clive had a vision of the cyborg rolling Horace over the edge of the raft while everyone else was sleeping.

He shivered.

I will not tell Guafe, he decreed.

As you wish, O Folliot.

Clive stood on the beach and examined their handiwork. *This raft,* he thought, *is a masterpiece.*

It was early morning. He had awakened, as he often did, before the others. But today instead of lying on the beach and reviewing his plans, he had arisen and come here to think.

The raft was nearly finished. Thirty feet long, twenty feet wide, with a ten foot by ten foot cabin in the center, it was an impressive sight. A mast rose from the center of the cabin, stretching upward some thirty-five feet. From it hung a pole around which was wound a sail the Tondanan women had woven from the thin, tough grass that grew on the far side of the island. The sail was fifteen feet wide and nearly twenty feet high, and Clive could hardly wait to see it filled with wind. At one end of the raft was a large rudder mounted on a pivot. It was tipped up onto the deck, where it would remain until they were in water deep enough to accommodate it.

This morning they would provision the raft with fresh fruit and dried fish. They would check the barrels they had made from the trunks of tapa trees for leakage one last time, then fill them with fresh water and bind them to the sides of the cabin.

And then they would launch the *Bold Endeavor* in her quest for the Gateway of the West.

He shivered in anticipation.

"You are eager to go?" asked a metallic-sounding voice behind him.

Clive turned to see Chang Guafe standing at the edge of the beach. Since the cyborg rarely slept, it was not unusual to find him wandering about at odd hours of the day.

"Yes, I am ready to leave," said Clive.

"I share that goal," said Guafe. "This island is satisfactory. We could be safe here, if we assume that no one is actively seeking us at this level. But there are things to be learned. I will be glad to be moving once again."

Clive felt a twinge of affection for the cyborg that he knew Guafe would find ridiculous. He wondered if he was making the right decision in withholding the information about Horace's implants, then decided that yes, the choice had been "pragmatic."

It was not long before the others joined them at the raft. Several of them, Tomàs in particular, had headaches from the farewell party the Tondanans had thrown the night before, an extended cycle of feasting, drinking, and dancing that had gone on longer than Clive would have wished.

Now they seemed bound together by a kind of nervous energy. With barely a word being spoken they began the final tasks. They worked swiftly and efficiently, and long before noon, far earlier than Clive had expected, they were finished.

The islanders, both villagers and "others," gathered on the beach to watch the final preparations. They helped with the filling of the water barrels, which was done at the pond where Clive had killed the great snake.

When it was finally clear that there was nothing left to be done, both groups fell silent.

After a moment Mai-lo stepped forward and walked toward Clive. He squatted to face her, and she kissed him on both cheeks.

"May you voyage safely, Great Slayer of Snakes," she said.

"May Tondano remain ever peaceful," he replied.

He rose and walked to the raft. The others joined him. Working silently, they removed the blocks that held the raft in place and began to roll it along the logs that led to the ocean. The great wooden platform moved slowly at first, but soon it picked up momentum. A triumphant cry went up as it struck the water. The voyagers scrambled onto the raft. The islanders surged forward, helping to push them out through the surf. They stayed with the raft until the water was nearly up to their necks.

At a signal from Tomàs, Clive and Horace unfurled the sail. It hung slack for a second, then it caught the wind and bellied out, tan and tight against the cloudless blue sky. The raft picked up speed and began to scud across the water. The islanders yelled and cheered. Clive felt his heart leap with exhilaration.

The voyage of the *Bold Endeavor* had begun.

CHAPTER TWENTY-SEVEN

Wrecked Fred

Clive sat with his feet dangling in the water, enjoying the play of the sea breezes through his hair and beard. Between the light wind and the current, the raft was scudding over the water at a fair pace. Behind him he heard the sizzle of fish being grilled over the fire pit they had constructed from a large, porous rock provided by the islanders. He leaned back on his elbows and stared up at the wide expanse of blue. It felt good to be in motion again.

Annie came and sat next to him.

"If you weren't such a prude I'd shuck this damn thing and go naked," she said, plucking at the one-piece white outfit provided by Green.

"Would you not talk like that?" said Clive, almost reflexively. He was feeling too content to want to spar with his descendant right now.

"I'm serious," said Annie. "I've spent the last hour trying to cut the legs off this thing so I can get a little sun on my skin. It just won't cut. It's tough as blazes to begin with, and when I do manage to get the knife through it, the fabric closes up behind the blade like it had a zipper in it."

"A what?"

"A zipper." She hesitated, uncertain of how to explain a device that was so thoroughly familiar to her. "It's a sliding thing we use to hold pieces of cloth together. Like buttons, only better." She sighed. "God, sometimes it's hard to remember we're from the same planet, Clive. Anyway, the stuff won't cut."

Since Clive was well aware of this, he didn't feel a need to comment on it. The remarkable properties of the white linen suits—their ability to withstand almost any kind of abuse from blades to blazes; their impermeability to any kind of stain; and most surprising, their adjustment to outside temperatures so that those wearing them never felt either too warm or too cold—had been amply demonstrated during the period when they were building the raft.

"It looks good on you," he said. Which was true; without being too tight, the suit clung to her body in a way that accentuated her willowy frame and rather pleasant curves. Her tan skin and jet-black hair, considerably longer now than when he had first met her under the Black Tower of Q'oorna, were both enhanced by the contrast of the white fabric.

Annie snorted. "You're so male," she said. But her tone was more pleasantly teasing than antagonistic.

They sat together, scanning the horizon and enjoying the salty smell of the water. After a while Clive went to the cabin. When he returned, he was carrying Neville's journal and a piece of charcoal from their fire pit.

"I figured I might as well use all these empty pages in the front of the book for something," he said, when Annie raised a questioning eyebrow. "Hold still. I'm going to draw your picture."

Annie giggled. "I didn't know you were an artist."

"In my day," replied Clive with mock severity, "*everyone* learned to draw."

As he sketched, Clive found himself reviewing events since they had left Tondano. In those eight days they had stopped at three islands. Two had been small, pleasant, and unpopulated. On the third island, larger than the first two combined, they had been greeted by a group of tall, fair-skinned people as friendly as the Tondanans. Their leader, a man named Caral, had listened to the voyagers' story with interest. He had advised them to stay on the island. When Clive told him that this was impossible, he simply shrugged and ordered

his people to give them some provisions and help in
the refilling of the water barrels.

"There are many islands between here and the Gateway of the West," said Caral, as he stood on the beach
with Clive. "Most are good. Some have dangerous places,
or people. We have heard tales from other travelers of
great perils between here and the Gateway. Whether
they are true—who knows? None of us have been there.
We are happy on our island."

Clive nodded. He had heard nearly the same speech
from Mai-lo. And like Mai-lo, Caral assured him that
the prevailing current would continue to carry them
westward. But he could provide no additional guidance
on how to find the Gate. Clive's greatest fear now was
that they would sail right past the transition point. That
was the main reason they were stopping at every island,
whether they needed provisions or not. He was hoping
that as they traveled farther west they would find people who could give them more specific directions for
finding the Gate.

"Do you ever think we should have just stayed on
Tondano?" asked Annie, breaking into his reverie.

"Sometimes," said Clive. "Briefly." He hesitated, uncertain how to explain his almost inexplicable need to
connect with the brother who had filled his life with
such turmoil. And as for his father—Clive shook his
head. The idea that he would ever get out of the
Dungeon alive, that he would ever see the man again,
seemed preposterous. But if he did, Clive knew he
couldn't go back without feeling he had done everything he could to find Neville.

In fact, he just couldn't go back without Neville. He
couldn't face the cold stare, the angry silence, the pain-
ful knowledge that his father considered him an utter
failure, a knowledge that seemed to lurk in every corner of his father's house, every moment he spent in the
presence of the bitter old man.

Clive was recalling his last interview with Lord Tewkesbury when Annie yelled and knocked him backward.

"What are you—" he cried. Then he saw it himself, a
great black shape gliding toward them just under the

surface of the water. As it reached the front edge of the raft, the creature dove and swam beneath them. Clive revised upward his first estimate of its length. The thing was at least fifteen feet long.

" 'Ware all!" he cried, worried about what would happen if the thing should try to surface under the raft.

But a startled shout from Horace a moment later let him know that the beast had passed underneath them without incident.

"Sorry for the surprise, Grampa," said Annie. "That thing was coming so fast I wasn't sure I could convince you to get your feet out of the water in time. I had a feeling it was looking at your toes as a midday snack."

"Many thanks," said Clive. He glanced down at his feet and decided that in the future he would keep them on the raft.

Though they kept watch, they saw no more of the large creatures that day. Late in the afternoon, however, they saw an island looming on the horizon. Tomàs took the rudder and directed a course that would take them into the bay they spotted as they drew nearer.

Darkness was falling as they pulled the *Bold Endeavor* onto the beach. Leaving Gram, Tomàs, and Finnbogg to guard the raft, Clive led the others onto the island to search for anyone who might give them information about the Gateway of the West.

Shortly after they entered the jungle it became dark enough that Clive asked Chang Guafe to provide some artificial light. But before the cyborg could rearrange his components, they were startled by a noise, and suddenly there were torches all around them. When Clive's eyes adjusted to the harsh glare he saw that they were encircled by at least fifty men. They were a dour-looking lot, clad in heavy black outfits that must have been very unpleasant in the hot, bright light of this level's days. An odor of stale clothing and long-unwashed flesh hovered over the group.

Clive raised his hand in a gesture of peace. "Hoy," he said, using the variant of the Dungeon's universal greeting that seemed most prevalent at this level.

"Drop your weapons," replied a tall, lean man. He spoke in a variant of Basic Dungeon.

They didn't have many weapons to drop. Shriek and Chang Guafe traveled unarmed. Clive, Horace, and Annie had lost the weapons they were using in the third level when they fell from Shriek's webbing into the sea; all they carried now were some wooden daggers given to them by the Tondanans. Of course there was the Baalbec A-9 hidden beneath Annie's suit. But their would-be captors didn't have to know about that.

Horace and Annie looked to Clive for their cue. He hesitated. The odds were ten to one. On the other hand, Shriek and Chang Guafe were spectacular fighters. Yet, even if they managed to overcome the black-clad men, his group would surely suffer some serious wounds, if not worse. Better, he decided, to wait until the odds might be more in their favor.

He threw down his weapon and raised his arms. Annie and Horace did likewise. The arachnid and the cyborg lifted three arms and a variety of tentacles skyward.

"You will come with us to the city," said the leader of the islanders. The group of men then closed around Clive and the others, holding a variety of swords, knives, and pikestaffs so that they were readily visible. Without another word, they began herding their captives along the trail.

Clive was puzzled. He had expected an interrogation: where are you from? why are you here?—anything along that line. This silent treatment was unnerving. Once again he found himself in a situation where the only rule he could be sure of was that they had to be ready to do whatever was necessary to survive. But that wasn't enough to base a strategy on. He clenched his jaw in frustration, then winced at the lightning stab of pain that shot into his head.

Almost instantly he felt a question from Shriek.

I have a sore tooth, he responded. *I think it was injured back in the battle under N'wrbb's castle.*

Why do you not simply get rid of it?

It's not that easy! he sent, amused in spite of his pain

and their situation. *Anyway,* he continued, *we have more urgent matters to contend with. What do you think we should do about all this?* He suddenly realized he had not consulted her while he was deciding how to respond to the demand that they drop their weapons. Well, maybe that was good. He didn't want to become too reliant on her. On the other hand, he valued her advice.

Just what we are doing, she replied, smoothly and calmly. *Watch and wait.*

Can you contact the others at the raft? he asked.

She signaled a negative, explaining that she needed more of a connection, either having the object of a message within eyesight or a tangible link such as her web, which had let her communicate with him during their descent from the preceding level even after darkness fell.

They marched along in silence, coming at length to a torchlit city consisting of low buildings fashioned from sunbaked mud. Despite the torches, the streets were empty. This struck Clive as strange, since it was not more than an hour since darkness had fallen. He studied the buildings as they walked; most were fairly small and seemed residential in nature. The style for all of them was very much alike—none of the variety they had found in Go-Mar. Finally they came to a central plaza, which was surrounded by much larger structures than they had seen anywhere else in the city. One of these sported a set of three towers. The central tower was topped with a large wooden X, which made it look vaguely churchlike.

They came to a halt in the center of the plaza.

"Now what?" asked Clive, addressing the tall, sour-faced man who appeared to be the leader of the group.

"Silence!" he hissed angrily.

While they waited, Clive and Shriek had a mental conversation, in which they tried to decipher the nature of the city where they now found themselves. They had no real success, but it kept them occupied.

After a time a deep-toned bell began to toll in one of the towers. The doors of the churchlike building swung open slowly and a great number of men and women—

all dressed exactly as their captors—began slowly filing down the steps. All wore the same dour expression, until they spotted the prisoners in the center of the plaza. Suddenly a low murmur began to run among the crowd. Smiles began to show. The same eager, hungry light seemed to gleam in a multitude of eyes.

Clive shivered, and nodded in acknowledgment of Shriek's silent message: *I like this not.*

The crowd gathered around them, murmuring and smiling. Clive noticed many children in the group, something he had not often seen in the Dungeon.

Finally an imposing figure appeared on the steps of the "church." He was dressed in black, like all the others, though his robes were much more voluminous. He wore a large, three-cornered hat. Around his neck was draped a length of scarlet fabric, the ends of which were decorated with long white beads. He held a black staff, half again as tall as he was himself, in his right hand.

He paused when he saw the prisoners. A cruel smile crept slowly over his face as he began to descend the steps. Clive watched uncomfortably as the man approached.

He stopped in front of the group and raised his staff.

"Who is the Lord?" he asked. His voice was deep and harsh.

Clive hesitated. On Tondano they had spoken of the Great Lord Neville. Could that be what the man wanted him to say?

Somehow, he thought not.

"What is the Law?" asked the man.

One of us should answer, Shriek whispered in his mind.

Answer what? replied Clive. Before he could think of anything to say, the man spoke again.

"When is the Last Supper?" he demanded.

"I don't know what you're talking about," said Clive. "Perhaps if you could—"

"They fail," said the man with the staff. "They will be suitable for the Festival."

The men who had originally surrounded them now closed around them and began to hustle them off.

"Wait!" cried Clive. "You have to give us a chance. We don't understand your questions."

But the priest, if so he was, had turned away. The crowd was murmuring happily to itself over his performance.

Clive and his friends were marched across the square to the large building that stood opposite the church-style structure. They were forced to climb a flight of broad steps leading to a pair of huge wooden doors.

Once inside the doors they were herded across a large foyer to a smaller door, which opened onto a staircase that spiraled down so far that Clive lost count of the steps. The stairs finally ended in a short corridor with floor and walls made of stone. A pair of torches held in wire baskets hung on either wall.

At the end of the corridor was an iron door. One of the men moved ahead of them to open it. Speaking harshly, he directed them to enter the cell.

Clive hesitated. They were still outnumbered, though not by as many. But they had no weapons and, again, it seemed unlikely that they could escape without serious injuries. Better still to wait, he thought, though he began to question that decision when the guards didn't simply tell them to enter the cell but herded them toward the door with their spears and pikestaffs.

Clive was the last in line. The guard behind him jabbed him in the kidneys with the blunt end of a spear. As Clive grunted and staggered into the cell, the door closed behind him with a clang.

The cell was dark, the only light coming from a small window, not much larger than a man's fist, centered in the upper part of the door. At Clive's request Chang Guafe finished the adjustment he had begun in the forest; a moment later a glow emanating from the end of one of the cyborg's ever-changing array of tentacles filled the cell with a dim light.

Clive looked around. Their cell was about twelve feet square, devoid of any furniture. The floor was covered with dried leaves. He recognized them—they had been stripped from the same trees from which they had built the *Bold Endeavor*. But the faintly spicy smell that usually made them so pleasant was overlaid with a reek of urine and fecal matter. It was all Clive could do to keep himself from gagging.

One other being shared their prison, a man who lay sprawled in a corner gazing up at the ceiling. Although he had ignored their entrance, once Chang Guafe began to provide some light he sat up and looked around, rubbing his eyes in surprise. His long, dark hair was bound with a red cloth, and he wore a vest decorated with various colorful insignia that were mostly unfamiliar to Clive's eyes. When he spoke, his voice was hoarse and low, as if he had not used it for some time.

"Hey, man," he said. "You guys got any grass?"

"Grass?" asked Clive.

"You know, like, some good shit?"

"Sir," said Clive, his voice firm, "may I remind you that there are ladies present." He closed his eyes briefly when he heard Annie, who was standing behind him, snort.

The bearded man sat up and looked at them more closely. "Shit," he said, scratching his head. "White suits. I knew it. This is an institute, right? Damn. I knew that stuff Turko sold me was going to fry my brain."

"What is your name?" asked Clive, trying to turn the conversation back to comprehensible grounds. "How long have you been here?"

"Well, back home they called me Wrecked Fred," he said, pushing himself to his feet. The man then wiped his palms on his faded blue pants and extended a hand to Clive.

After a brief hesitation, Clive accepted the gesture. "Clive," he said. "Major Clive Folliot."

"Oh shit, the military! Is this some kind of experiment? You guys kidnapped me to see how we react to stress or something like that, right? I'd write a letter to my fucking congressman—if I knew who he was."

Struggling to find some kind of sense in the man's ramblings, Clive focused on the one word that jumped out at him.

"I will thank you to watch your language!" he said sternly.

"Will you stop protecting me, Grampa?" said Annie.

Her voice seemed to hold equal parts anger and amusement.

She turned to the stranger. Her voice was gentler than Clive's. "How long you been here, anthro?" she asked.

Wrecked Fred dug his fingers into his hair and scratched, as if the answer were hidden someplace atop his scalp. "Three days," he said. "At least, I think."

He looked at her piteously. "Are you here to help me?" he asked. "I know I must have gotten into some bad shit. I've had bad trips before, but nothing like this. I can't make it stop."

Annie looked at him sadly. "The Dungeon's not a trip," she said. "You're really here—wherever here is—just like the rest of us. It sucks. But it's real."

Fred squeezed his eyes shut, as if he could make them all go away. "The last thing I remember was getting stoned and falling asleep in the park. When I woke up, I was still in a park. At least, there were trees all around me. But they were different, somehow. None of them looked right. I must have spent a whole day wandering around, trying to figure out where I was, looking for something to eat. Swore at least fifteen times I'd never drop acid again. I was sure I'd come out of it sooner or later. But damn"—he looked around the room—"you guys don't look right for a trip. You're weird enough, that's for sure," he said, his eyes lingering on Shriek. "But you're too solid around the edges or something. I don't get it."

"What city was it?" asked Annie.

"San Francisco."

"Heepers! Left my heart there myself. What year?"

"What do you mean, what year?"

Annie looked at him crossly. "Undense, airhead. What year was it when you left?"

"The same year it is now. I've only been gone three days."

She sighed and pointed at Clive. "He's from 1868," she said. "I bussed here from 1999. When are you from?"

Fred groaned. "Are you sure this isn't an experiment?"

Deciding that Fred was not dangerous, Clive stepped aside and let Annie continue her conversation, from which he concluded that Fred's long beard, faded pants, embroidered vest, and headband were standard uniform where he came from.

Clive went to stand beside Shriek, who was broadcasting a sensation that seemed vaguely like amusement.

How do you understand what he says? asked Clive. *He's not speaking the common tongue, and you haven't pulled him into your web of communication.*

I am reading him through you, she replied. *Since we do not communicate by words, as soon as you understand what the man says, I can understand it.*

A troubled thought flittered across Clive's mind.

One can listen to a mind in many ways, she sent, in response to his distress. *Just because I am in union with you at the moment, it does not mean that I am delving into your innermost secrets, my sweet.*

Clive started. It was the third time she had used a term of endearment when communicating with him. She caught his reaction and responded, formally, *We have shared a great deal, O Folliot.* Then she broke the connection.

Clive returned his attention to the dialogue between Annie and Fred, though between Fred's rambling and a lingering concern over the conversation with Shriek, he found it hard to concentrate on what they were saying—until Fred began to tell what he knew of their captors.

"Yeah, they asked me the same questions," he was saying to Annie. "Shit, I didn't know what the fuck they wanted me to say. When they asked me 'What is the Law?' I said it was a pig. I think that was the wrong answer."

Annie laughed. "What did they do?"

"The head man announced I was a failure; made me think of my father. Then he said I was suitable for the Festival, and they hustled me across the street and down the longest fucking stairway I ever saw and threw me in this cell."

"Do you know anything more about them?" asked Annie.

Fred shook his head. "Only one thing. Something the man who brings the food told me yesterday. I thought he was only kidding. But from what you're telling me he might have been serious."

"Well, what did he say?" asked Annie in an exasperated tone that Clive recognized very well.

"He said they were missionaries from the Church of the Holy Cannibal."

CHAPTER TWENTY-EIGHT

Dental Hygiene

Clive sat straight up out of a sound sleep. What had happened to his jaw? He wondered if someone had been hitting it with a hammer while he was sleeping. Unwanted tears came to his eyes. They were not from sorrow or self-pity but rather a simple physical reaction to a pain so intense it seemed to be peeling off the side of his face.

He looked for the others. But though his eyes were wide open, he could see nothing; the cell was as dark as the inside of a coffin.

Moaning softly, Clive pulled himself across the floor until he came to a wall. He hunched himself up and sat there with his jaw cradled in his hand. He moaned again, torn between wanting companionship and not wanting anyone to see him in this condition.

He was not surprised when Shriek tickled at his mind, seeking to find out what was wrong. He did not have to answer the question. As soon as he opened himself to her probing she was aware of the sizzling pain in his jaw.

That tooth is in bad shape, my friend, she commented.

That is the most unnecessary message you have ever sent me, he thought crankily. Immediately he regretted the tone of his response. But there was no time to retrieve it. No sooner thought than sent.

Ah, replied Shriek. *But the regret was received just as quickly. My people are used to sharp responses and quick apologies.*

That may not be a bad system, mused Clive, knowing

that she would read the thought. *Among my people the sharp words seem to come out far easier than the regrets. We seem to have a tendency to keep our apologies to ourselves.*

A puzzling system, responded Shriek.

Clive didn't answer. He was distracted by a stab of fiery pain that went lancing through his jaw.

Shriek's next message was firm but gentle: *I think it is time for that tooth to come out.*

Clive's wordless response seemed to amuse her. *Such a fuss from so brave a man!* she chided. *Worry not, my proud warrior. I can help you through this crisis. I will prepare a spike that will mask your pain while the deed is performed.*

Clive's misery was too intense for him to argue with her. He moaned an agreement. Then he moved his jaw the wrong way and cried out as a shaft of pain seemed to push at his eyeball, trying to drive it out of his head.

Almost instantly Shriek was at his side. *You will feel a brief prick of pain,* she thought to him. *Then warmth, then nothing. Relax now and try not to move.*

She placed two of her spindly arms behind his shoulders to maneuver him into position.

Relax, she murmured in his mind again. *Pride that does not allow necessary help is foolish. Lean on me.*

He was in too much pain to resist. He relaxed against her body and with her third arm she maneuvered the spine she had plucked from her abdomen into the soft flesh just beneath the curve of his jaw. He flinched at the additional assault on his screaming nerves, then felt a rewarding flood of warmth, and then a growing detachment. He closed his eyes and began murmuring in gratitude.

He experienced the next several minutes as though they were a dream. He was awake yet not awake, connected to his body yet apart from it.

He heard Shriek scuttle across the floor to where the Chang Guafe stood, lost in whatever passed for sleep when he turned off most of his circuits. Next came a clicking noise as Shriek tapped on the cyborg's armor with one of her chitinous claws.

"Cyborg, activate your circuits," she said softly. "I have need of you."

Clive was vaguely aware that Shriek was the best choice among their party to intercede on his behalf with the cyborg. She seemed to get along with Guafe better than anyone else in the party, though whether that was because they were both so different from the others or because of her abilities as a communicator or simply because they had formed a bond while they were hunting together Clive had never been certain. In any event, the cyborg would be less apt to grumble in response to a summons from Shriek than from any of the rest of them.

Clive realized he didn't care if the cyborg grumbled. He didn't care about much of anything right now, as long as he could drift in this hazy respite from the pain.

A low light began to filter into his consciousness; Guafe must have returned to awareness.

He could hear the others begin to stir, muttering drowsy questions.

His mind began to wander. He seemed to be growing more and more disconnected from everything around him.

He remembered that there was something he was supposed to be worried about. What was it?

Ah—the things that Fred had told them about the church that controlled the island. Their Festival was coming. Fred had said something that made him think this was a bad thing. What was it?

He saw the cyborg staring down at him. The strange face was devoid of emotion. Clive wondered what Guafe was thinking, tried to ask, found that he no longer had the power of speech.

A pair of tentacles grasped the corners of his mouth and pulled it open.

Clive watched as though from a distance, fascinated by the process. He knew it was actually happening to him, but couldn't quite make the connection.

He saw Annie standing nearby, looking at him with a worried expression on her face.

It's all right, he thought. *I'm fine.*

She gave him no response.

Oh, Clive thought dreamily. *I forgot. That only works with Shriek. Oh well. Fiddle-dee-dee.*

He was vaguely interested to see a small door slide open at the side of Guafe's neck and a long, narrow tentacle with a glowing spot at the end extended toward his mouth.

"You should have waited to anesthetize him," the cyborg said to Shriek. "I am not absolutely certain which tooth it is."

Clive couldn't pick up Shriek's nonverbal answer. He wanted to be annoyed, but couldn't find the energy.

It's all right, he thought, trying to placate the cyborg. *Take two. I've got a mouthful.*

"What an inefficient piece of work," muttered Guafe, as he manipulated both Clive's jaw and the glow light that he had inserted into his mouth. "Why don't they use interchangeable parts?"

"They hadn't figured them out back then," Annie said defensively.

Suddenly Horace's face loomed into view. "What's going on?" he demanded.

"Quiet," said Guafe. "I prefer not to be distracted. I have to find the correct configuration of my own parts to do this properly."

Annie whispered in Horace's ear. A respectful silence descended over the cell.

A door on the cyborg's chest opened and a long, sturdy tentacle ending in a pair of pincers began to emerge.

Clive felt himself drifting further from reality. The wrenching he felt in his head as the cyborg twisted out the ruined tooth seemed to be happening to someone else altogether.

Don't feel bad, Annie, he thought, as he watched her face twist in sympathy.

"The area beneath the tooth is deeply infected," commented Guafe. "I want to make sure it is all cleaned out before we close the opening."

Sounds good to me, thought Clive.

His equanimity was almost disturbed by Horace's shout: "What's happening? What's going on?"

"Shriek!" yelled Annie. "What's happening to him?"

What's going on? Clive wondered vaguely. *What are they all so upset about?*

"Grab him!" yelled Horace. "Hold on to him!"

"I'm holding him as tightly as I can," Guafe said sharply. "It's not doing any good."

"He's going!" cried Annie. "What is it? What's happening?"

What's happening? wondered Clive, as the world began to swirl around him. It was the last thought he had before everything went black.

▪ CHAPTER TWENTY-NINE ▪

Another Mind

Sidi Bombay was jarred out of the twilight regions of his mind by a sudden, ferocious connection with a consciousness that clearly was not L'Claar's.

He stirred in fright.

Since the last great wave of pain had passed he had been drifting in a state between awareness and sleep, wondering vaguely when L'Claar would return. He had longed for the gentleness of her presence.

But unlike L'Claar, whom he sometimes envisioned as a clean, silvery flame, this new consciousness was dim, rumbling, harsh. He sensed a mind that was shrouded and unclear, like a moon seen through a deep fog. And he sensed other things: a great, almost never-ending hunger; a deep, simmering anger; and then a sudden burst of power that seemed to sear its way through his mind with a burning clarity that belied the muddiness of his original perceptions.

Who are you? he thought nervously.

At first there was no answer. Then his mind began to fill with sendings. The first was that of a smooth blue corridor, twisting and winding through infinity. Next he saw again the chasm of Q'oorna, and the battle that was his last memory of the world outside the haze of pain where he now existed; the image caused him to shudder, though it was strictly a mental effect. The third and final sending was not an image at all, only an impression of massive and terrible betrayal.

If he had had eyes, he would have wept.

As it was, he wondered long at what all these things

meant, and felt strangely empty when the mysterious intelligence that he had been sharing with left him.

He drifted back into pain and dreams while he waited for L'Claar.

▪ CHAPTER THIRTY ▪

Evening Services

Clive opened his eyes. The world was black around him. The drifting feeling persisted.

He closed his eyes and waited.

Drifting.

After a time he opened his eyes again. He seemed to be in some kind of room. It was smaller than the cell, which was the last place he remembered with any clarity. The wall in front of him was white. He turned his head to the side, a movement that seemed to take several hours. At first he thought the wall to his right had been painted black. Then he realized that it was made of glass, and whatever was behind it was in darkness. He took a day or so to turn his head the other way. The wall to his left was covered with switches, dials, and buttons.

A dim yellow light shining down from the domed ceiling provided enough illumination for him to see that he was lying in the center of a circular table.

After a while a light began to shine in the area behind the glass. It came up slowly, giving his eyes time to adjust.

He saw four or five people, or near people, standing on the other side of the glass. He could hear the low susurrus of their voices as they murmured among themselves. The noise held a vague tone of concern.

Everyone behind the glass wore white suits similar to the one in which Clive himself was still clad. One of the people was Father Timothy F. X. O'Hara. Another was the man known as Green.

Clive knew that this should have been interesting to him but couldn't summon up the feeling. He tried to call out to them but found that his voice didn't work. Even worse, he didn't care that it didn't work. He wanted to care. But caring seemed like too much effort.

He let his head roll back so that he was staring up at the light again.

He closed his eyes.

After a while he sensed that the others had entered the room and were gathered around him.

"I still can't believe you did this," said an unfamiliar voice.

"It really was unwise of you," said a second voice. After a moment Clive recognized it as belonging to Father O'Hara.

Were they talking to him? What had he done that was unwise?

"I did as I thought best," said a voice that Clive recognized instantly. It was Green. That was good. Green was his friend.

He thought for a moment. It must be that they were talking about something Green had done.

What had he done?

"But giving him one of these suits?" persisted the first voice.

Green hesitated, then said firmly, "I provided suits for all of them."

"You did what?" cried a fourth voice.

"I provided suits for all of them," Green repeated defiantly.

Everyone seemed to break out talking at once. In his hazy condition, Clive found it impossible to follow the conversation. Only the conclusion was clear. "This is your fault," the first voice said angrily. "You deal with it."

Then there was silence.

When Clive opened his eyes again he was alone. He wondered how much time had gone by. He was so disconnected from everything that he would not have been surprised to learn it was five minutes—or five days.

"Ah, I thought you'd come around fairly soon," said a friendly voice.

Green!

Clive tried to speak. All that came out was a kind of clicking sound.

"That's all right, old chap," Green said comfortingly. "Don't expect to talk now. I'm going to send you back well before you come out of this. The question is, will I send you back with memory intact?"

Clive's eyes must have indicated his reaction to this pronouncement.

"Don't be so alarmed!" Green said cheerfully. "I have no intention of tampering with your memory as a whole. I'm just not sure you should be allowed to hold on to this particular incident. It could be very dangerous for the rest of us, you know. If Philo Goode, as you think of him, got word of this he could raise hell. Just a few words in the right place and—" He sighed. "Well, I don't even want to think about what would happen in that situation. But what to do about this one? Of course, I can arrange things so that you don't consciously remember today's experience. But if anyone *really* wants to know what you've been up to, that won't make any difference. They'll just root around in your head until they find out. The other alternative is to excise this memory altogether. But that's considerably more dangerous, as you can well imagine."

Clive blinked nervously.

"Oh, do cheer up!" said Green. "Hasn't it come clear to you yet that we're on your side? We just have to be careful, is all. The others aren't at all pleased with me for letting this happen. But I only gave you these suits to cover the most dire emergencies. It took us quite a while to figure out why it brought you here now."

Green chuckled. "That spider woman who travels with you is quite resourceful. The altered venom she used to anesthetize you lowered your metabolism so much the suit thought you were dying. Pulled you back here, the same as mine did the day your friend nearly put his knife through my heart. First time anyone's ever come to this place for a toothache! We gave you a new molar, by the way—just to show that there's no hard feelings."

He paused for a moment. Clive, who had been holding his eyes open for ten or fifteen years now, let them close.

He felt Green's hand on his shoulder. "If it were up to me, I'd have you stay," he said softly. "But the others already feel that I'm playing a bit fast and loose with the rules. They wanted to send you back before you even woke up, although that was silly, since it would likely either have killed you or destroyed the suit. Now, however, it is time for you to go. But don't worry; unless one or the other of us comes to an untimely end, we will most certainly meet again."

The firm hand squeezed his shoulder. "Goodbye, Clive. Be careful. And for the sake of all of us, start to *think!*"

When Clive opened his eyes again, everything was black.

"Green?" he asked nervously. "Are you here?"

No answer.

Had he been sent back, or not? He slid his hand over the surface on which he lay. The rustling of leaves made him think that he was back in the cell. He took a moment to consult his other senses. The unpleasant odors of stale excreta confirmed his guess.

But where were the others? He called them by name, one after the other. No one answered. He cast out with his mind, hoping to contact Shriek.

She was nowhere to be found.

He closed his eyes and dropped his head back against the floor. He lay that way for a long time, limp and unmoving.

Finally he began to feel hungry. He pushed himself to his knees, tried to stand, and promptly fell over.

He took several deep breaths and pushed himself back to his knees. Crawling across the floor, he bumped into the bucket that had contained their drinking water. He put his hand in and felt a few inches of warm water on the bottom. He took a sip, then another, then poured the rest of it over his head.

How long would this dizziness last? How long had he been gone?

Where had he gone?

His mind throbbed with dim memories of meeting Green in—what was it? A hospital room? That didn't seem right.

He clutched his head, trying to will away the dizziness and confusion.

The dizziness went, though it took longer than he would have wished. The confusion insisted on staying.

After a while he tried to stand again, and was pleased to find that his feet were willing to stay underneath him. Stretching his hands before him like a blind man, he shuffled forward until he found the wall. He leaned against it. His head was swimming from the exertion. To his relief, the feeling passed fairly quickly. He stood away from the wall and tried to assess the state of his body. He nodded gratefully when he realized that his strength was coming back more quickly now.

But where were the others?

He felt his way along the wall. The cell door was open—not surprising, since until his unexpected return there had been nothing to keep in. He felt his way around the door, then placed one hand on the wall of the corridor that led back to the stairs. The wall felt gratifyingly real, warm and rough beneath his fingertips. He needed that sense of solidity here in the darkness, where it was easy to imagine that somehow the world had disappeared.

Clive walked slowly along the corridor until he reached the base of the stairs. He stood for a moment, listening. A small animal scuttled through the darkness somewhere ahead of him. He heard no other sounds.

He began to climb. Even though he moved slowly and cautiously, he slipped more than once on slick spots on the stairs. Despite the silence, he feared he would be apprehended at any moment. But no one arrived to stop him.

When he reached the top of the stairs he hesitated, uncertain of what to do. It was difficult to believe there would be no one on the other side of the door. Or was it? He had no idea what time it was. Perhaps it was the middle of the night.

He held his breath and listened.

Nothing.

Opening the door a crack, Clive peered around the edge. The room on the other side of the door was as black as the stairwell. He felt a sudden sense of panic, as he began to wonder if he was blind after all.

Should he call out? No, that was insane. But this vast darkness was terrifying. In the cell, in the corridor, on the stairs, the darkness had made sense. The walls had given him a feeling of perspective. Now all that was gone. The darkness was all that remained.

He began to walk forward, moving slowly, fearful of tripping over something he could not see. Part of him wondered if this were all some cruel joke, if soon the lights would blaze on and the islanders would leap out and capture him all over again.

The only sound was that of his own footsteps, which echoed back to him from walls he could not see. He kept his arms stretched out in front of him, until finally his probing fingers met a smooth wall.

Right or left? he wondered, trying to recall from his one brief passage through the room how it was constructed, and where his blind journey would have landed him. Finally he decided that whether he had to go a few feet or ended up circling the entire room, either way he would reach the main doors sooner or later.

He went to the right, and in a matter of seconds found the door.

Pressing his ear to the wood, he listened.

He could hear voices, but they seemed to be shouting from somewhere far away.

Moving stealthily, he pulled on the door. He was relieved to find that it was not locked, and even more relieved to find that he was not really blind.

The sky was dark, as was so often the case at this level of the Dungeon. But in the distance he could see the blaze of what appeared to be several hundred torches.

Still moving carefully, he pushed the door open another few inches. He put his head through the opening and peered in all directions. The plaza was deserted.

Quickly Clive slipped through the door. He pressed it gently shut behind him, fearing there might be some unseen guard sleeping in a nearby corner.

By the time he had reached the perimeter of the torchlit area his strength and reflexes felt close to normal. Positioning himself behind a broad tree trunk, Clive looked out on a scene that resembled the nightmares he had suffered as a youth after hearing an ignorant country minister preach on the "sinful rites of the heathen."

The population of the city, including women and children, was gathered in an enormous clearing lit by three bonfires. The fires were so large that Clive felt their heat even from where he stood.

A stone table, a yard wide and at least three yards long, was positioned between the fires. Six enormous men stood behind the table, their arms crossed over their chests. Behind them, on a broad platform about five feet high, stood the priestlike character who had questioned Clive in the village square.

He was preaching hellfire and brimstone. The flowing sleeves of his long black robe slid down his sinewy arms as his enormous hands stretched toward the congregation, exhorting them to be true to the revealed word of their faith, the gospel according to the Holy Cannibal of God.

Clive's stomach wrenched as he realized where the ceremony was heading.

Behind the platform, Clive saw two large cages. They appeared to be made from saplings lashed together. A pair of priests stood guard before each cage. In the flickering light of the torches and the bonfires, Clive could just make out the silhouettes of the people in the second cage. It was the towering form of Shriek that let him know his friends were imprisoned there.

He began to circle the outer edge of the ceremonial ring. As he did so a loud wail rose from the crowd. In unison, the supplicants threw themselves to the ground and began to pour dirt over their heads. At the same time, two of the burly priests who stood behind the stone altar went to one of the wooden cages. They opened the door and brought forth a man who appeared to be one of their own. His arms were bound behind him. Even from where he stood, Clive could see that the man's eyes were wide with fear.

The acolytes, as Clive thought of them, knocked the man down, then picked him up by his head and feet. He struggled as they carried him to the table. His terrified cries made the flesh on Clive's shoulders creep.

The priest raised his staff before him, holding it parallel to the ground. "Who is the Lord?" he cried.

"Whoever is strong!" replied the flock.

"What is the Law?"

The dreadful answer came in tone of quiet reverence. "Eat or be eaten!"

Now the priest extended his staff, moving it in an arc over the heads of those closest to him as he asked the final question:

"When is the Last Supper?"

"When we grow too weak to do what must be done!"

"The Law is of the Lord, given to us that we might live," intoned the leader. "Tonight is the Festival of Those Who Survive—those who are not too weak to do what must be done. Tonight we feast, and in feasting celebrate our strength. Tonight is not the night of the weak. Tonight is not the night of the outsider. The weak are but fodder for the strong. Those who do not consume the weak will one day be consumed. Strike— strike in the name of the Lord who gave us the courage that has led us to this day!"

Horrified, Clive watched as the priest at the head of the stone table wrapped his fingers in the hair of the screaming man who lay bound before him. Wrenching back the man's head, the priest slashed downward with a long knife. To Clive's surprise, a cry of horror went up as the man's blood spurted forward onto the altar.

"We do what must be done," the priest said solemnly.

"We do what must be done," moaned the flock.

Clive shivered. He had been distracted, first by the power of the priest's voice, then by the horror of the ceremony. Now he began moving again. Let these madmen consume one another. He had to get his friends out of here.

But as he circled the ceremonial ring Clive realized that the most appalling aspect of the entire spectacle was that aside from the actual sacrifice, the participants did not seem at all mad. This was not a scene of orgiastic rites. The intonations were solemn. Heard, but not seen, the service might almost have been taking place in that country church he had been taken to as a child.

Clive was not much worried about being seen now. The attention of the congregation was riveted on the gory scene taking place at the stone altar, as the butcher-priests began to flay and fillet the man whose throat they had just cut. Clive felt his stomach begin to heave. He knelt and vomited forth the water he had drunk back in the cell. Wiping his mouth, he stood and moved on.

He stopped behind a tree, about ten feet from the cages, afraid that when his group spotted him one of them might make a sound that would attract the attention of their captors.

In the flickering light, Clive was able to discern the silhouettes of Horace, Annie, Shriek, and Wrecked Fred.

Where was Chang Guafe?

He ducked back behind the tree as a pair of priests came for another victim. Clive studied the cages; the doors were held in place by nothing more than a sturdy crossbar—all that was needed, he realized, since everyone inside the enclosures had been carefully bound.

From what he could make out, the far cage held people who were actually members of the strange island sect, including women and children. When the priests opened the door of the cage, most of the group within huddled back in terror. Two or three, however, stood their ground. The priests took one of these, an old man with a pronounced limp.

All attention, including that of the guards in front of the cages, returned to the center of the circle. Clive dropped to his belly and began to creep across the soil, cursing the conspicuous whiteness of the suit Green had given him. He would have taken it off, but the skin underneath was nearly as white.

As he moved slowly over the ground, Clive heard a cry from the congregation. He swallowed thickly as his treacherous mind pictured the splash of blood that must have called forth the reaction.

He reached the cage and felt a surge of despair. The bars, made of wrist-thick saplings, were so closely spaced that when he tried to thrust his hands through they stuck at about the point where his thumb joined his palm, leaving his fingers wriggling helplessly on the other side. He could never untie his friends this way. With no blade of any kind to slice their bonds, how could he free them?

For that matter, what good would it do if he could? Under the best of circumstances he might be able to eliminate one of the guards at the front of the cage without attracting attention. To eliminate both of them without an uproar was beyond the limits of possibility.

He ran his hands down one of the uprights to the point where it sank into the soil. He tried to shake it loose. It was rock solid. He tried digging around it, but the dry earth felt like mortar.

He was staring at the cage, sick with desperation, when Shriek contacted him: *Welcome back!* she whispered in his head. *Ignore the bars,* she added. *I have another way.*

Before he could respond she sent a warning that the priests were coming again. At her command, the others shifted their bodies to hide him. Clive stared between their legs, and trembled with anger as he watched the priests drag away a screaming child.

Annie slid down the wall and pressed her face to the bars. "Glad to see you, Grampa!" she whispered.

He began to answer, but a message from Shriek cautioned them both to silence.

Moving awkwardly, the spider woman joined Annie beside the wall. Suddenly Clive realized that while the others had only their arms bound, Shriek had also been hobbled, with each of her front legs tied to the corresponding rear leg. Her upper arms were bound behind her back, and her single lower arm was lashed against her side by several loops of tough, fibrous cord. The cords looped above and below the spot where she had lost her other arm. In the dim light the wounded area appeared even worse than it had the last time Clive had noticed it. Certainly the swelling had increased.

Reach through the bars and try to remove my scab, she instructed, half in words, half in the kind of images she sometimes utilized to transmit her messages.

He began to question her, but she sent a message of urgency: *No time for discussion!*

He stood up, and Shriek turned sideways so that he could reach the scab. The others, responding, no doubt, to her silent instructions, moved to give them the greatest coverage. He touched the wounded area gingerly, wondering if she thought the green, chitinous material would be strong and sharp enough for him to slash their bonds.

Placing his hands three bars apart, Clive pushed his fingers into the cage and grabbed the edges of the scab, which was slightly larger than a saucer. Shriek flinched, then pressed herself closer to the side of the cage to give him a better purchase on the scab. He pulled at it, trying to be gentle. Her angry reaction came not from pain but impatience.

We have no time to make this easy, she thought to him. *Hold it as firmly as you can!*

He pressed his fingers against her flesh. The skin was rough but yielding, and he was able to work the tips of his fingers a little farther under the scab.

Hold fast! she sent, and as he tightened his grip she lurched away from the bars. It was all he could do to keep from crying out as her pain lashed into his brain. He looked down at his shoulder, half-expecting to find his own arm missing.

He recovered himself, then caught his breath in astonishment. The scab had come off in a single, shieldlike piece, which he now held between his fingertips. But he had misunderstood the point. It had not been to use the scab. It had been to free the new arm coiled beneath that scab, an arm that Shriek now began to stretch and flex in a tentative way.

It was not quite ready, she told Clive. *But there's no helping that. It will do for now.*

The arm seemed to stiffen and grow thicker before his very eyes.

It's taking in what you would call blood, she explained, reading his question. *Another moment and I will be able to manipulate it. It will be awkward. But it should do what we need.*

He shifted the piece of chitinous material so that he was able to grip it between the fingers of one hand, then withdrew his hands from the cage. A familiar cry went up from the group surrounding the altar. The appalling sound drew Clive's attention. As he looked up he caught a savory aroma drifting through the air. His stomach lurched, but he had nothing left to vomit.

Shriek was tugging at his attention. *I am going to begin freeing the others. When all of us are loose, circle the cage. As the priests come for their next victim, I will prepare two spikes. When all attention is on the priests, Horace and I will eliminate the guards. When you see them fall, open the door.*

Clive signaled his agreement and Shriek went to work on Horace's bonds. As Clive watched he fingered the edge of the scab, which he still held in his right hand. The green disk was brittle but exceedingly sharp. Perhaps his original guess as to Shriek's intention was not altogether worthless. He gestured to Annie, and when she backed over to him he began to saw at the ropes holding her hands. More than once the edge of the chitinous disk crumbled. But more than once a strand of the tough rope separated beneath his attack.

You are very ingenious, sent Shriek, when she realized what he was doing.

And you are very brave, replied Clive, as he continued to saw at Annie's bonds.

Annie cleared her throat in warning and Clive ducked as one of the guards turned to look in the cage. Wrecked Fred had positioned himself to hide Shriek's free arm behind him. She continued to work, even as the guard glared into the cage. Clive sensed her frustration, which she was broadcasting in waves almost as strong as the sexual need she had expressed when she was in Ma-sand. The rope was tough, and the pincers at the end of her new arm were still tender. She was having a hard time cutting through the fibers.

Clive returned his attention to his own work. But suddenly the chitinous disk broke into several pieces; the shards fell to the ground, leaving him clutching a tiny segment between his fingers.

"Damn," he whispered. But even as he lost his tool, Shriek sent him a message of triumph. She had cut the rope binding Horace.

Horace wriggled his hands and shrugged free of his bonds. He immediately bent down to work on the hobbles around Shriek's legs.

Clive knew that these were the most dangerous moments. If one of the guards should turn now, all would be lost. But their full attention was directed to the gory spectacle in front of them. And they had little need to keep watch on what happened inside the cage—with the prisoners bound, they were present only to keep order when the priests came to choose their victims.

Clive crept around the edge of the cage. *Should we act now?* he asked.

Wait, responded Shriek. *Their attention is diverted. But the priests might return at any moment. We don't want to be caught in the act.*

Clive signaled agreement. The wait was excruciating. The immediate task of freeing his friends from their bonds accomplished, he became increasingly aware of the unholy events inside the circle. Suddenly another question struck him.

What happened to Chang Guafe?

Shriek's response carried a twinge of regret. *From what I can gather, the cyborg is dead. The priests considered him inedible, and separated him from the rest of us shortly after your disappearance—a matter I am most eager to learn more about, by the way. Anyway, from the gossip of the priests and guards, I have the impression that our friend put up a remarkable fight, but was finally overpowered. They buried him earlier this evening.*

Clive felt a pang of sorrow. For all their conflicts, he had developed a certain attachment to the cyborg, if only because they had shared so many dangers.

At least one of those wounded by Chang Guafe is on tonight's menu, commented Shriek.

Clive signaled his incomprehension. He would have thought that from the islanders' point of view, someone who had fought the enemy would be a hero.

Do you not understand the nature of the ceremony? asked Shriek. *Those selected are—* The transmission was interrupted by the return of the priests. *Stand ready,* she warned.

Peeking around the corner of the cage, Clive felt his heart begin to pound as he watched the priests open the door of the first cage to make their selection. How long would the carnage go on? Could they really be planning to kill everyone in both cages tonight? The dark thought that it seemed like more meat than the crowd could consume was interrupted by Shriek's command: *Now!*

He watched with grim pleasure as two of the spider woman's spikes came thrusting through the bars of the cage. Without a sound the two guards crumpled to the ground. He wondered if she had killed them or merely immobilized them.

Don't be sentimental! commanded Shriek. *Move!*

But he was already slipping around the edge of the cage. It was quick work to lift the crossbar and let the others out. Horace, Fred, and Annie came first, pressing against the wall of the cage. Shriek waited till last, as they had to open the door wider to make room for her bulging abdomen. Clive saw that a woman in the other cage had noticed their escape. Would she sound the alarm—out of spite, or some strange loyalty to her kind?

But the woman remained silent. A cry went up from the congregation even as Shriek disappeared around the corner of the cage.

Clive started to follow her into the woods, then hesitated.

He looked back at the other cage.

Could he really leave those people there to die?

He turned again to follow his friends, then turned back. He knelt and removed the slender daggers strapped to the guards' sides.

Shriek's signal came as a combination of exasperation and urgency: *Come!*

A moment!

You endanger us all!

She was right. But the others—

He seemed balanced on the edge of a razor, death on one hand, moral despair on the other.

The agony of indecision was brief; it ended when Shriek took matters into her own hands.

CHAPTER THIRTY-ONE

Island Hopping

Clive awoke to the smell of sea breezes, the touch of ocean spray, and the wrath of Shriek.

The first two were immediately evident; the latter took a bit longer to make itself known.

"Well, there you are," said Annie, when he first opened his eyes. "I was wondering when you would be coming around."

"Where?" Clive asked vaguely, trying to fight off the return of the disorientation he had experienced earlier.

"Here," said Annie. "The raft. You Clive, me Annie." She paused, then added, "Oh, screw it, you wouldn't know that reference."

"How did I get here?" asked Clive.

"Shriek carried you. I think she's pissed, but I'm not sure. She's not communicating much right now."

Clive sat up.

"Ah, there you are, sah," said Horace, coming around the side of the cabin. "Breakfast in a minute. Tomàs is helping me cook it now."

"How long have I been asleep, Sergeant Smythe?"

Horace rolled back his eyes, as if consulting some sort of internal clock. "Five or six hours, I'd say."

Clive looked around. "What happened?" he asked at last.

I put you out, so that your foolish compassion would not result in all of us being recaptured.

The voice that sounded in his head was harsh, angry. *Who is the leader of this group?* Clive replied sharply. *You are, for now. But there are many ways to lose leader-*

ship. One way is for those who are led to decide you are not worthy. An even worse way is for you to foolishly throw away the lives of those you are leading.

Get out of my head! Clive said angrily. He slammed down the mental barriers he had been trying to learn to erect between himself and Shriek's telepathy.

He needed time to think; it was impossible to have an argument with someone when they could watch you form your ideas. He knew that in one way Shriek was right: his actions *had* endangered them all. But he couldn't bring himself to feel that it was acceptable simply to desert the other victims. He shook his head. It was all too confusing.

Annie looked at him curiously. "What's going on?"

He hesitated. "Shriek and I were having an argument about last night. What happened after she put me out?"

"We snuck off through the jungle." Annie looked unhappy.

"What's wrong?" he asked, touching her arm.

It was her turn to hesitate. She shrugged. "I don't know. I guess I was thinking about—the others."

He nodded, pleased to know he wasn't the only one with second thoughts.

"I wonder how a religion can become so perverted," he said softly.

"Shriek played touchie-feelie with one of the guards," replied Annie. "She dug out a lot of weird stuff. Maybe you can get her to explain it to you."

"I don't know," said Clive. "She's not very happy with me at the moment."

"I know. It's sort of floating in the air." She paused, then said, "Horace explained about the suit after you disappeared. It was so weird, watching you just fade out like that! I thought we'd never see you again. What a surprise it was when you came creeping up behind that cage. Talk about arriving in the nick of time. What happened to you, anyway? Where did the suit take you? Did you learn anything?"

Before Clive could answer, Horace poked his head

around the side of the cabin again. "Breakfast, sah," he said.

Clive stood up somewhat tentatively. He was pleased to discover he was not experiencing the weakness he had felt while recovering from Shriek's anesthetic.

He was even more pleased when he walked around the cabin and discovered Chang Guafe leaning against the cabin wall, reorganizing his tentacles.

"I thought you were dead!" exclaimed Clive.

"I was buried," said Guafe. "It's not the same thing."

"Comlink failure," replied Clive, resorting to one of Annie's old phrases.

The cyborg detached a pair of tentacles and deposited them in a little door that suddenly opened in the area of his body roughly analogous to an abdomen. "When I realized that the islanders were going to try to kill me, I simply shut down my systems. They decided I was dead, and buried me. I waited several hours, then dug myself out. I had just made my way back to the beach when I saw Shriek come running out of the jungle with you slung over her shoulder."

"It was a bit of a mad scramble after that, sah," interjected Horace. "Turned out Gram and Tomàs and Finnbogg had nearly been captured themselves. They'd holed up in a spot near the beach, and when they saw us come running out of the woods, they dashed out to join us. It was all we could do to get the raft back in the water; them cannibals had dragged it up the beach almost to the edge of the woods. We were barely away when they came bursting out onto the beach themselves." He chuckled. "You should have heard the ruckus they raised when they saw that we'd slipped their grasp."

The cabin door opened and Finnbogg emerged. Wrecked Fred was close at his heels.

"Mighty Folliot has recovered!" the dwarf cried happily.

Clive felt himself blush. Shriek, who had come around the corner of the cabin during Horace's speech, took the liberty of sending him a message: *The others do not know exactly what happened last night. I told them that you were suffering from temporary insanity, and that it was a rare*

*but not unprecedented aftereffect of the anesthetic I had given
you.*

That was most presumptuous of you, Clive shot back.

*If you want them to know what was really going on, feel
free to correct their understanding of the situation,* Shriek
replied fiercely.

Clive felt as though his scalp were starting to sizzle.
But he kept his peace. As they ate he told the others
what he remembered of his second encounter with the
mysterious Green.

"What I can't figure out is whose side he's on," said
Horace, when Clive had finished his story.

"Ours," said Clive.

"I know that, sah. But whose side are we on? I get the
feeling there's some kind of war going on between
the Ren and the Chaffri. But I don't know which one
is the enemy."

"Both," Chang Guafe said simply.

"That's quite possible," said Clive.

"Shit," said Fred. "It's just like home."

As the day wore on the tension between Clive and
Shriek began to affect the rest of the crew. "I wish you
two would kiss and make up," said Annie, late that
afternoon. "You're getting on my nerves."

She was cutting the buds off some of the small, bitter
tubers the Tondanans had given them. Along with fish,
the brown, egg-shaped vegetables had become the main
staple of their diet during the voyage. Clive sat down
beside her and picked up a wooden knife. He began
working on one of the tubers. Tomàs was at the rudder. A light wind filled the sail. Most of the others were
dozing, some in the cabin, some stretched out on the
deck to soak up the afternoon sun.

While Clive was still thinking about Annie's complaint, Wrecked Fred came stumbling out of the cabin.
He blinked in the sunshine, stretching and yawning.
"Sunshine and fresh air!" he said amiably. "Far fucking
out!"

"*Help* fucking out," said Annie, before Clive could
register a complaint about Fred's language. She pointed
to the pile of tubers.

Fred smiled and sat down to join them.

"Tomàs and this one make a great pair," said Annie, motioning toward Fred with her knife, but speaking as though he weren't there. "One of them thinks he's caught in a religious experience, the other can't convince himself the whole situation isn't a result of whatever he was smoking last."

"I'm convinced," said Fred. "Even my worst trips never lasted this long."

"Nothing ever lasts long for your type," said Annie. The words could have been harsh, but they were softened by her voice, which held a kind of tweaking good humor.

Clive looked up from the tuber he was working on. Was it possible that his descendant was flirting with this scruffy character? He glanced over at Fred. Seeing him in the light, Clive realized that behind his long hair and unkempt beard the newcomer was actually rather handsome.

Annie used her knife to indicate a slogan written on the man's vest. "You a Deadhead?" she asked.

"Went to a concert just three weeks before I came here," he replied.

Her smile was radiant. "Tell me," she commanded, in that abbreviated way in which she sometimes spoke.

That launched the two of them into a conversation about music—at least it seemed to be about music—that Clive found totally baffling. After a while he put down his knife and wandered away.

Suddenly the deck of the *Bold Endeavor* seemed terribly lonely. With the discovery of the alien implants, he was no longer completely comfortable with Horace. Annie seemed wrapped up in the newcomer. Shriek was still angry with him.

He stared morosely at the seemingly endless sea. He didn't blame Shriek for being angry. He was angry himself. His behavior had been foolish. Unpragmatic, as Chang Guafe would have said. And yet—and yet what? What good could he have done those lost souls in that other cage?

Longing for someone of unquestioned loyalty, he

finally sat down next to Finnbogg, who was dozing fitfully in the sunshine. When the dwarf began to kick, as if he were dreaming, Clive laid a hand on his shoulder and spoke to him soothingly. Ahead and to the right a flock of flying fish came soaring out of the water. Clive watched them for a moment, then turned his attention elsewhere. They seemed to belong here. He was painfully aware that he did not.

He noticed Gram sitting against a wall of the cabin. She was staring out at the water, a morose expression on her face. He knew what she was thinking about, and found himself blinking back tears as he remembered 'Nrrc'kth's fall to her watery grave. He remembered Ka telling him what the People of the Sea had done with the emerald-haired woman's remains, and wondered if cannibalism was endemic to this level of the Dungeon.

Late that afternoon they passed another island. They decided not to stop on its shores. They would have to land again before long, but for now they were just as happy to sail on while they could.

However, the next few days found the crew of the *Bold Endeavor* increasingly restless and uneasy. They had pushed themselves so hard for so long that it was difficult to accept the fact that their progress was now determined by nature. No matter how they worked, they could not make the wind blow harder or the current flow faster. Even so, their sense of urgency was hard to escape. But as the days continued to pass in a kind of dreamy haze they finally began to relax and adjust to the pace imposed on them by the sea.

The only time they were on the alert was when they came to an island. Then they would argue about whether to land. After the first time this happened Clive realized that it reflected a change in his position within the group. Before the adventure with the cannibals, he knew they would have deferred to his opinion. They might have questioned him, but he would have felt comfortable that he was going to prevail. Now that was no longer a given. He felt a kind of desperation as he realized his leadership of the group was slipping through his fingers.

Shriek was of no help in this matter. While she never stood against him, she no longer offered him her silent counsel. She did not seem actively angry, but she remained disapproving and distant.

Her withdrawal pained him, but he realized that he was also angry at her. Despite the odds, he was not convinced that they could not have rescued the other prisoners. They had managed the impossible before. Why not this time, too?

After about a week every island they spotted gave the voyagers cause for a new debate. Some of the crew, particularly Horace and Finnbogg, saw maintaining their supply of fresh water as their foremost concern. They were always in favor of landing, even if the water casks were down only by a quarter. Clive, too, was determined to land, for he felt that they should ask everywhere they could for information about the Gateway of the West. The others, particularly Annie and Shriek, were opposed to what they considered unnecessary risk, and argued against landing whenever their stores were relatively full. Wrecked Fred and Gram simply didn't care.

It was on one of these stops that they first gained the somewhat disconcerting information that to enter the Gateway of the West they would have to pass through the "Jaws of Hell."

"I don't much like the sound of that, sah," said Horace, when the tall, slender octopod they met on the beach of a small atoll delivered the information.

Using Annie as an interpreter, Clive tried to pump the creature for more information. But this tidbit was all it had to offer. They thanked it, and before leaving traded some of the small tubers, of which they were thoroughly tired, for a good supply of a tart, juicy fruit—something of which the octopod claimed to be equally tired.

That night, when most of the others were asleep, Clive took out the journal. He flipped idly through its blank pages, remembering the substance of some of the strange messages they had carried.

It had been so long since he had last received a new

message that he was quite surprised when he turned a leaf of the book and discovered a brief note in Neville's distinctive handwriting. His surprise turned to horror as he read the words by the light of the nearly full moon.

Brother: All has changed. The mission you are on can lead only to death. Turn back! I adjure you, as you love your life, turn back!

With trembling fingers Clive closed the book and stared out at the moonlit sea.

CHAPTER THIRTY-TWO

Gur-nann

The next morning, when Clive repeated Neville's latest message it set off a round of debate more fractious than any the travelers had yet indulged in.

"Turn back to where?" demanded Chang Guafe. "Shall we sail against the winds and the currents back to Tondano and live a life of quiet ease? Somehow I don't think it is possible."

"The winds might change later in the year," Tomàs said meekly. "I would not mind trying to go back."

"I think Chang Guafe means it is unlikely we would be allowed to live in peace," said Horace.

"Why not?" asked Fred. "If we don't bother anyone, they ought to leave us alone."

"Are you still stoned?" asked Annie. "Were you bothering anyone when they brought you here? Were you bothering the missionaries when they decided to eat you? Get real, Fred."

"We might as well stop here as anywhere," said Gram, and Clive ached to hear the quiet resignation in a voice that had once been so feisty.

"No," said Shriek, resorting to actual speech for emphasis. "We must forge ahead. Whatever Neville Folliot says, the answer to all this lies in front of us."

And so it went, round and round among them. The argument was still raging when a large island appeared slightly to their north, immediately creating by its mere presence a subargument about whether they should land on it.

When Clive finally proposed that it would make a

good place for them to rest and think through what they would do next, the others agreed, some of them more reluctantly than others, and Tomàs steered them to the shore.

Made wary by their experience with the Church of the Holy Cannibal, they moved slowly up the blue beach, armed and ready for battle. Though he understood the necessity of such an approach, Clive was always afraid they would appear so warlike that they would drive anyone they met into attacking just for the sake of defending themselves.

In this case, however, their approach was met with laughter. An enormous man stood at the edge of the sand, sheltered by the overhanging jungle fronds. His flesh was as blue as the beach itself, his hair as white as Gram's flesh. He was nearly as tall as Shriek. His body was rounded, his arms and legs massive. At first glance he seemed fat. On closer examination, Clive decided that the flesh was solid and strong.

He hesitated. If the man were alone, he would be no problem. If the island held many more like him, and if they were hostile, the little band of voyagers would be in big trouble.

"Be them weapons for defense, or for to conquer?" asked the man, pointing to the blade Clive carried thrust through the belt of his suit.

"For defense," said Clive, grasping the opportunity to act as spokesman for the group. He hoped it might help reestablish his claim to being their leader.

"Don't need 'em," said the man. "The island of Gurnann be's friendly to strangers who be's friendly to it."

Clive had experienced enough treachery since his arrival in the Dungeon not to be placated by such a simple statement.

"Are you alone here?" he asked.

The blue skinned man laughed. "Think I be dumben 'nuff to say?"

Clive couldn't help but smile. "What is your name?" he asked.

"I be Gur-nann. This be my island. Them be your

womens?" He glanced around Clive to admire Annie and Gram.

A ripple of laughter cascaded out from the jungle behind him. Gur-nann's mouth rumpled in disgust. But the expression softened to a smile as he made a gesture with one massive arm and several dozen small people who looked much like the Tondanans came creeping out from among the trees. "These be my people. You want to be my people, you can stay. I be boss. Got it?"

"Got it," said Clive. He nearly told Gur-nann that some of them might indeed wish to stay, but decided that it was foolish to display the rift in their ranks. He decided to fall back on the words he had used on several other islands: "We have no wish to stay. We ask only to restock our food and water, and to learn whatever you may tell us about the Gateway of the West."

Gur-nann scowled. "Why Gateway?"

"We travel there in search of my brother."

"You be great fools. Gateway lies behind Jaws of Hell. You be wanting to go to Hell?" He chuckled at his witticism. Clive noticed that despite his girth, Gur-nann's flesh did not wobble as he shook with amusement.

"I sometimes feel we're already there," he replied quietly.

"Not here!" Gur-nann said adamantly. "Island of Gur-nann be good place. Foolish travelers put down weapons. Come, see. Maybe even be staying."

Shriek, who carried no weapons, stepped forward and took Gur-nann by the hand. He looked at her in surprise. Clive realized she was establishing a new link of communication. She dropped his hand and turned to the others.

It is all right, she sent, and Clive felt a pang to realize it was a general message, that she was not speaking to him alone. *He is so sure of his power he has no thought of treachery. We can travel safely in his domain.*

Gur-nann's expression had changed to one of amazement. Clive understood; he would never forget how he had felt when Shriek first wrapped him in the webs of her mind. He knew that in their moments of contact she had probably made the islander aware of most of what had happened to the group over the last few weeks.

"You be mighty warriors," he said, addressing the group. "You face the wrath of Ren and Chaffri alike, but you be welcome on the island of Gur-nann."

The sky was shading into tones of rose and purple. For Clive, the day on the island had been pleasant, though somewhat frustrating. After showing them around, Gur-nann had urged them in the strongest possible terms to take the time to fortify their raft with side rails, in order to provide some protection from the various creatures he claimed were lurking in the ocean ahead of them. After some debate, the group had decided it was a good idea. Even those not sure about continuing the journey were willing to help—partially, Clive suspected, because it would put off the day of decision.

The islanders had prepared a large meal of fruit and fish, which they served to the travelers with a great deal of ceremony. Gur-nann got roaring drunk and began telling salacious stories. Feeling restless, Clive had separated from the others and decided to take a walk along the beach. When he saw Annie sitting at the edge of the group and staring into the distance, he invited her to come with him.

They walked for a while in silence, Annie playing tag with the waves. Finally he decided to broach a subject that had been on his mind for the last several days.

"You seem to be very partial to young Fred," he said awkwardly.

She laughed. "Jealous, Grampa?" she asked, in that direct way of hers that he found so utterly disconcerting.

He decided to hide behind formality.

"Am I not allowed to be concerned about the company my many-times great-granddaughter keeps?"

"You can be as concerned as you want," Annie said cheerfully. "It won't change things."

When Clive scowled she laughed and tweaked his nose. "Listen, Grampa. Wrecked Fred is the first person I've met here who comes from anywhere near my time, I can talk to him about things no one else would understand. And God, the things I can learn from him! Don't forget I was a musician back home. A lot of songs I used to play had their roots in things that were happening when Fred was around. He's not a musician. But he was into that stuff. He can tell me about the people. I mean, he used to read *Rolling Stone* back when it was still about music."

"So you have no romantic interest in him?" persisted Clive. He wished he could retract the words the instant he had uttered them.

Annie laughed. "He might be good for a roll in the hay. But he's not husband material."

The comment made Clive so angry that he didn't speak to her for the next fifteen minutes.

Later that night, when the group had gathered on the beach to sleep, she strolled over to where he had stretched out on the sand.

"Hey, Grampa," she said. "You still mad at me?"

Clive grunted noncommittally.

"Well, at least you're not sure," she said, folding her legs and dropping to the sand with a graceful movement.

"Stars are nice tonight, aren't they?" she said after a while.

"They remind me of the night we tried to send that message to George du Maurier," he replied.

"Did you ever get an answer?" Annie asked mischievously.

He smiled. "Since the whole idea was to use the Baalbec A-9 to enhance our combined mental powers, it would as likely have come back to you as to me."

"Well, I haven't heard from anyone named George lately. What do you say we try it again?"

Clive looked at the stars. What was this Dungeon, that one of its lower levels could have such a sparkling firmament? Surely it was something more complex than one level overlaid upon another. Was it perhaps a series of worlds, linked in some scientific or even some mystical fashion?

The idea seemed incomprehensible. But then, he reminded himself, this entire experience was beyond rational comprehension. If he accepted what had happened so far as real—well, the only logical extension was that *anything* was possible. Including, he supposed, the ludicrous idea that he could reach back across space and time and contact his friend du Maurier.

"Why not?" he said at last, in response to Annie's question.

She took his hand, and they lay back and stared at the stars. He wondered for a moment if she was merely seeking the closeness they had shared the last time they had tried this experiment.

Don't flatter yourself, Folliot, he thought sharply.

"Let me adjust the Baalbec," said Annie, reaching inside the top of her white suit with her free hand.

He waited, enjoying the smell of the breeze that swept in from the sea.

"Okay," she said. "Let's give it a shot. Same drill as before?"

He nodded, and the two lay back in the sand and stared at the sky.

Du Maurier, are you out there? he thought. *Can you hear me?* He found himself seized with a sudden desperation to connect with his old life as he tried to pour all that he had seen, all he had experienced, into the communication. He started to urge du Maurier to contact Annabella Leighton, to tell her what had happened. Quickly he quashed the thought. What would happen if du Maurier did indeed receive the message and told Annabella to wait for Clive? Would she put off her trip to America, and thereby *not* found the line that would lead to Annie? He glanced nervously at his young descendant, as if he expected her suddenly to wink out of existence.

To his tormented relief, she was as solid, and delicious-looking, as ever.

"Well," said Annie. "If he heard us, he sure didn't say anything to me."

"Nor to me," said Clive.

They continued to gaze at the stars. After a while
they slept.

As the travelers threw themselves into improving the
raft, the impact of Neville's message seemed to wear
off. Listening to their conversations, Clive could sense
the group consensus shifting toward continuing the
journey. As he explained to Annie one evening after
dinner, he had made the same decision for himself
shortly after he first read the message, partly because
he had come too far to be turned back now, partly
because he was just tired of having Neville call the tune
to which he would dance.

Somewhat to his surprise, the work on the raft was
finished in less than three days. The cheerful help of
the islanders had actually made the job enjoyable. Even
more pleasing, from Clive's point of view, was the fact
that he saw Gram smile again. She seemed to have
taken a shine to the outrageous Gur-nann, and by the
afternoon of the third day his ribald comments about
everyone and everything actually made her laugh.

So Clive was surprised, but not astonished, when the
older woman announced that she was not going to
continue the journey.

"Gur-nann has asked me to stay here and be his
bride," she told the assembled group on the morning
of their departure. "Think not ill of Gram that she
should leave you in this way. But I have nothing left to
travel for. You others, you have things to do—promises
to keep, vengeance to seek, questions to answer. For
me, there is nothing ahead of us. Who can I take
revenge on? Only N'wrbb, and he is far behind us. Let
me stay here without regrets."

"I can only wish you well," replied Clive, placing his
hands on the broad shoulders of the emerald-haired
woman. But he wondered to himself if even on this
isolated island she would be safe from the war that
seemed to be brewing all around them.

He embraced Gram, then turned away, surprised at
how attached he had become to the gruff old woman.

One by one the others said their farewells. Annie was

last, and though Clive could not hear what passed between the two women, it seemed to be conciliatory. When Annie came away she went to stand by herself.

Clive could not be sure, but he thought she was weeping.

CHAPTER THIRTY-THREE

Kraken Up

After a time there were no more islands. The raft continued to move westward with the current, but day after day the surface of the sea remained unbroken by anything save an occasional leaping fish.

With the kind of curiosity that makes one pick a scab, Clive checked Neville's journal every morning, though what he would do if he actually found another message within those mysterious pages he was not certain.

On the morning of the sixth day after they had last seen land he was sitting at the front of the raft, leaning against one of the newly constructed rails. Holding the little book in his hands, he gazed out at the water and wondered how they would ever find the Gateway of the West in this vast ocean.

He sighed and looked down at the journal, wishing that if Neville did write something it would be more useful than his usual exhortations and dire warnings. He ran his fingertips over the black leather cover, then opened the book and began to flip through its pages. To his surprise and initial delight, he discovered a new entry.

But as his eyes scanned the page his fingers began to tremble.

"What is it, sah?" asked Horace, who had observed Clive's reaction.

Clive hesitated. Finally he decided to read the message aloud. "Listen to this," he said. "I don't know quite what to make of it, though it may explain why some of the messages we have received were so strange and contradictory."

He turned his eyes back to the book and read aloud:

"Brother, beware; the journal is tainted. That you have survived until now is a miracle. You have my deepest apologies for all this. I have only now discovered that the enemy has gained access to this tool, and has sent you false messages in my name.

Beware the journal. Beware of everyone! I can write no more, for—"

Clive looked up. "The message ends there," he said grimly. "That's all there is."

"Doesn't sound good, does it, sah?"

"No, Horace. It does not."

He turned his attention back to the sea, wondering what had happened to his brother.

The wind and the currents were stronger now, and though they saw no real islands, occasionally they passed great rocks thrusting their craggy heads through the waters. These made Tomàs nervous, and he began to insist that they use the rocks to tie up at night, for fear they would run aground in the darkness and damage the raft. This sometimes required a great deal of maneuvering, which Clive found tiresome in the extreme. It made him glad he had joined the army rather than the navy.

One morning, shortly after they set sail for the day, the crew of the *Bold Endeavor* was sitting on the deck, sharing a sparse meal of fish and tubers, when a school of the flying fish appeared off the starboard side of the raft. However, instead of leaping away from them, as they usually did, the creatures began heading toward the raft.

At first Clive found it amusing. He had often wanted to see the creatures up close. But when Fred yelped in pain as the first soared over the deck, his amusement turned to worry. Suddenly he felt a fiery sting on his own cheek. Astonished shouts began to erupt around him as more of the fish came sailing above the deck.

"Poison!" he cried. "They're spitting poison! Into the cabin!"

They scrambled for the small shelter. Soon all save Shriek and Chang Guafe were inside. From the other side of the wooden walls Clive could hear the *wheek, wheek!* of the fish as they went flying overhead. He also heard an occasional cry of a higher pitch, usually accompanied by a shout of satisfaction from either the cyborg or the arachnid.

"You can come out now," said Chang Guafe after several minutes had gone by. "The creatures are gone."

Opening the door, Clive was surprised to see the deck littered with the bodies of the menacing fish. Many of them bore wounds that he suspected were a result of one or another of Chang Guafe's specialized tentacles. Others were wound in lengths of Shriek's silk.

"It was good hunting," clicked the spider woman, "though the cyborg fared better than I, as he did not have to protect his eyes."

Clive noticed smears of yellow on her chitinous exoskeleton, which he assumed were remnants of the projectile poison.

A half-dozen or so of the fish were still flopping listlessly on the deck. A few others gasped and flapped their wings. Most were stone still, their orange eyes filming over with death.

Clive bent to examine one.

"I would not pick it up," said Chang Guafe. "The flesh might well be irritating to your skin."

Clive nodded and drew back his hand.

The fish was about the length of his forearm. Its body was mostly white, though it darkened to greenish yellow around the belly. It had long, stiff fins which it used like wings to propel itself through the air. Poking at its mouth with his knife, Clive saw a double row of needle-sharp teeth.

He thought of Mr. Darwin's controversial theory and

wondered what kind of conditions would cause such a creature to evolve.

In the end they decided against trying to eat the fish, and Shriek and Chang Guafe simply shoved the multiplicity of bodies off the deck and back into the sea, except for about a dozen, which the cyborg saved for what he called experimental purposes. When Clive asked Chang Guafe why he had killed so many of the animals, the cyborg seemed astonished by the question, and pointed out that he would try to kill anything that attacked him.

As the days rolled on the perils of the sea continued to grow. Twice one of the great, dark creatures they had seen early on in the voyage went gliding under the raft. Though they made no menacing gestures, their sheer bulk was frightening—especially as the second actually scraped the raft with its back, lifting one side about a foot higher than the other. For a terrifying moment it seemed they were going to capsize. Everyone not in the cabin went staggering to the port side, and Annie was able to save herself from slipping over the edge only because of the rails Gur-nann's people had helped them install.

Clive found himself wishing he had some better writing implement than his bit of charcoal, so he could inscribe some of their own adventures in Neville's journal. The long stretches of quiet sailing were conducive to daydreaming, and he often fantasized about escaping from the Dungeon, writing the book that he had originally thought would detail his adventures in Africa—how tame that all seemed now!—and finally marrying Miss Annabella Leighton. But whenever his mental wanderings reached this point he would become uneasy, as the question of what that would mean to User Annie intruded on his pleasant speculations.

Still, he would have liked to record his impressions of the various perils they faced: the sharklike creatures that threw themselves out of the water but were turned back by Gur-nann's rails; the tempest, brief but ferocious, that nearly swept them all overboard; the long, many-suckered tentacle that came creeping across the deck to wrap itself around Finnbogg's leg one afternoon when most of them were napping. He knew they would make good stories, and he wished he could save more details than he could record in a charcoal sketch.

He wondered idly how Maurice Carstairs, the newspaperman who had helped finance his trip to Africa, would view such outrageous dispatches. How long had it been since he had sent a dispatch to Carstairs, anyway? How long had they been wandering in this accursed world?

They were drifting aimlessly now, arguing among themselves about whether they had already passed the Jaws of Hell and the Gateway of the West. Their supplies of food and water were running low. The food was not so bad, as it seemed they could always catch fish. But water was becoming a real problem. Sometimes at night, when they tied up to one of the isolated tors, they could find rainwater that had collected in indentations in the rock. Checking first to be sure the water had not been made salty by the spray from the waves, they would use Fred's shirt—the white suits did not absorb water—to soak up the puddles and transfer them to their water casks.

Toward the end of one of these seemingly endless days Clive was lying on his stomach, staring out at the horizon and composing an imaginary release for Maurice Carstairs, when he noticed a disturbance in the water behind them. At first it was minor, the kind of rippling that might be caused by a stray gust of wind. But then the water began to roil more vigorously. Suddenly he saw a scaly coil lift above the waves.

To his surprise, one of the Sea People was wrapped in the coil, struggling silently, desperately for his life.

"Battle behind us!" cried Clive. Without waiting for the others to join him, he leaped overboard and began swimming toward the fight.

As Clive stroked toward the surging water where the sea-man struggled, he wondered, momentarily, what he was doing. Before he really had time to consider the question, he felt a sinuous tentacle wrap around his leg. He yelled as he felt it try to pull him under the water.

As the pressure on his leg increased he began to thrash in a desperate attempt to stay above the surface. When it became clear that staying on the surface was going to be impossible, he drew in as much air as he could and actually dived toward the tentacle.

He opened his eyes. The world around him was blue and green, dim, mysterious. His heart jumped as he saw the long tentacle which stretched down from his leg to disappear in the darker waters below. The fact that he could not actually see the foe somehow made it worse.

He drew his knife from his belt. Though the blade seemed woefully inadequate to the task, he gripped the tentacle about a foot beneath where it wound around his leg and began to slash at the sinuous, slimy flesh.

At first the creature tightened its grip on his leg. But as he continued his assault he could feel its hold begin to loosen. If only he could keep his breath long enough to finish the job! Tightening his own grip, he began to saw at the tentacle. Blood began to seep into the water, curling away from the tentacle like strange, dark blossoms. Suddenly the tentacle unwrapped itself from his leg and slithered between his hands, snaking down until it was lost from sight.

Clive stroked upward, burst through the surface, and sucked in air hungrily, choking on the water that streamed down his face into his nose and mouth. He saw Horace swimming in his direction. Finnbogg was paddling along awkwardly behind him. Looking beyond them, he was horrified to see that the raft was sailing away from them at a rapid clip. *Why don't they stop?* he thought, before he remembered how difficult it was to maneuver the craft. He saw the sail drop, and realized that Tomàs was doing the best he could to slow the craft's progress. Even so, it seemed entirely possible that the raft would be out of sight before this fight was over.

He turned and started for the site of the battle again. His heart was thudding against his ribs as he realized that any second one of those tentacles might come coiling up from below and draw him back under the surface. Even as the thought crossed his mind he saw one of them burst through the water about thirty feet ahead of him. It was followed by another, and then a third. They swayed above the waves like the gigantic tendrils of some strange seaweed. Suddenly a fourth tentacle erupted skyward, spraying water in all directions. The struggling sea-man was clutched in its grip, shouting angrily in that strange, guttural language that Clive remembered from his first conversation with Ka back on the beach at Tondano.

Well, hero, thought Clive, *now that you're here, what do you do?*

He didn't have long to consider the question. Horace's shout of warning was drowned out by the splash of another tentacle bursting up through the water behind him. Before he could maneuver away, it had wrapped itself around his shoulders and was drawing him below the waves again.

The tentacle was thicker, stronger than the first had been, and it drew him swiftly into the dark water below. Clive's knife arm was pinned to his side. He struggled to transfer the blade to his other hand, all the time traveling deeper beneath the surface.

His eyes widened as he saw the great, dark shape toward which he was being drawn. It was a tapering cylinder, half again the size of a railway car. The end facing him seemed to consist of little more than a great maw, surrounded by a ring of writhing tentacles, some of them enormous, dozens of others relatively small—no more than six or eight feet long. Hidden behind the fringe of the tentacles he could see one great eye staring coldly at him through the darkness.

A kraken! he thought, remembering the legendary sea monster of which he had read so much as a child.

With a sudden burst of strength he managed the transfer of the knife. But now several other tentacles had wrapped around his body. He was being pulled toward the gaping maw at an ever-faster rate.

He struggled desperately to free himself. But the

kraken was in control now. More tentacles joined the others. One of them, slimy and lined with suckers, crept across his face. It burned, and he was grateful for the white suit, which covered most of his skin. Suddenly he wondered if the suit would draw him away from the creature if he neared death. His mind, working at an incredible rate, promptly presented him with several images of ways in which he could die too quickly for the suit to save him, beginning with decapitation.

Both his arms were pinned now. He struggled, but it seemed to have no effect.

Suddenly Finnbogg was beside him, tearing at the tentacles with his mighty jaws. Blood gushed into the water, creating a dark cloud around the ferocious dwarf. Clive could feel a shudder ripple through the tentacles that held him. Something that might have been a scream came ripping up from the monster below.

His arm free again, he stabbed at the remaining tentacles. As the last fell away he reached for Finnbogg, and the two of them swam for the surface.

They came up into a bubbling hell. Torn, ripped tentacles were shooting up on every side of them, spattering blood in all directions, whipping the water into a crimson foam. He tried to shout a warning to Finnbogg, but his voice was lost in the sound of the water splashing and crashing around them.

He swam forward, maneuvering his way through the forest of tentacles, and began to stab at one of the writhing appendages that held the sea-man. He realized that the kraken's victim faced a danger distinctly different from his own: if the monster managed to hold the man out of the water too long he would suffocate in the air.

Clive dug his knife through the muscular flesh and dragged it down, tearing open a bloody canal. The tentacle spasmed, loosed its hold on the sea-man, and withdrew into the water. Another smashed upward to take its place, knocking him sideways with the force of its passage. Momentarily stunned, he choked on a mouthful of water and thrashed to push himself back above the surface.

Horace and Finnbogg were in the thick of the battle now, Horace slashing about with his knife, Finnbogg rending and tearing with his mighty jaws. They succeeded in causing the creature to drop the sea-man, who disappeared beneath the surface.

Clive heard a voice call his name, barely audible above the crash and splash of the battle. He turned, and shouted in rage as he saw Annie swimming in his direction. She was carrying a shaft of wood. Wrecked Fred was not far behind her.

"Go back!" he shouted, before a tentacle wound around his leg and he had to turn his attention to cutting it loose. He couldn't hear her response, but it sounded like "asshole."

Now the man from the sea was on the surface again, stabbing at the tentacles with a knife of his own. *We might just win this yet!* Clive thought exuberantly.

An instant later, as he saw a great form begin to rise toward the surface, he realized that their success might be their downfall. Rather than driving the monster to retreat, their efforts had only driven it to attack harder. Behind the ring of tentacles the huge orange eye shone through the water like lamps through the London fog. Suddenly the creature broke through the surface. Water streamed down over the vast stretch of its back. The tentacles stretched before it, flagellating the water until it seemed as though it were boiling with blood.

Escape was out of the question. There was nothing to do but fight on. Clive felt himself lifted into the air. He tried to grasp the tentacle that held him but it was thick with slime and his hand slid off. He slashed at it with his knife. It dropped him, and he landed back in the water with an impact that forced the breath out of him.

The world seemed to be made of blood and water. His ears were filled with the curses of his friends, the roaring of the kraken, the thunderous splash of the water.

To his horror, he saw Annie still swimming through the turbulence, heading straight for the body of the kraken. He tried to shout a warning, but was stopped by a tentacle that wrapped around his neck. He kept an eye on the slender form of his descendant as he began to slash at the sinuous length of flesh that was beginning to choke the life out of him.

She still had the shaft of wood. But now the creature had grabbed her. It lifted her and carried her toward the great maw, huge enough to swallow all of them in a single gulp. Clive severed the tentacle holding him, gasped in air, and cried out in horror as he saw how close Annie was to the creature's mouth.

Suddenly she wrenched herself around and plunged forward with the shaft of wood she carried.

A piercing cry seemed to shake the very sea as the wood lanced through the orange lamp of the creature's eye.

The tentacles began to spasm. They thrashed through the water, sending geysers shooting into the air. Another great cry tore from the creature's throat.

And then everything was still. The tentacles twitched, feebly, on the surface of the roiling water.

The battle was over.

CHAPTER THIRTY-FOUR

The Jaws of Hell

Of all the surprises the Dungeon had dealt them, thought Clive, none seemed more unlikely than the idea that Wrecked Fred would be of some use. But the fact was, they would have been lost without him. Watching the others leap into the water, and realizing that the raft could not be turned around, Fred had remembered the stories they had told him about the descent from the sky along Shriek's silk. After a quick conference, she had spun a loop of silk that he slipped around his waist, and he had started after the others, with the arachnid playing out silk as he went. Once he reached the site of the battle, he had stayed out of the action for fear of severing their only connection to the raft.

But Shriek was not the only one still on board the raft who had played a part in the events. The reason Annie had been able to kill the kraken with her slender lance was that the end of the wood had been smeared with a powerful poison, which Chang Guafe had been extracting from the dozen or so flying fish he had saved for "experimental purposes."

Clive learned all this as the weary warriors slowly made their way back along the strand of silk that connected them to the raft. They pulled the sea-man with them, for he had lost consciousness about the time the battle ended, and while they could not keep him aboard the raft, it seemed wrong simply to leave him floating in the water.

The sea-man represented the final surprise in all these events, for it was none other than their old friend Ka.

In a way Clive was glad, for it helped justify what he knew Chang Guafe would describe as his "unpragmatic" behavior in leaping into the sea to save a stranger. Even so, he felt somewhat abashed, wondering if things might have been easier if he had waited to consult with the others, as Fred and Annie had done.

Yet, if he had, might not Ka have died in the interval?

He shook his head as a wave washed over him. Sometimes making sense of life seemed about as likely as finding a perfect cup of tea—something he would have considered trading several of his teeth for at the moment.

Ah, an old friend, signaled Shriek, when they neared the raft and she saw whom they were bringing with them.

Yes, and a rather battered one, replied Clive. *We cannot keep him on board the raft, nor can we simply leave him to drift away. Can you weave some kind of net, or sling, so that we can pull him with us as we travel?*

It can be done.

He noticed, sadly, that she did not end with the fondly respectful "O Folliot" with which she had once closed most of her communiques.

On board the raft they exchanged stories, congratulations, hugs. Clive made a special point to compliment Chang Guafe on his foresight in preparing the lethal extract that had finished the kraken.

"It was an interesting experiment," replied the cyborg.

Clive also thanked Finnbogg for saving him when the kraken had dragged him under.

Later, Tomàs and Horace used the last of their fruit to prepare a special dinner to celebrate the victory over the kraken.

Darkness came quickly, but not completely, as the triple moons were particularly bright this night. The winds were down, and the sea ahead seemed clear and open, with few of the rocky crags in sight. After a short debate they decided not to tie up, but rather to drift with the current through the still night, trailing Ka behind them.

Chang Guafe volunteered to keep the watch, which he could do quite efficiently at quarter-power. Clive envied the cyborg his ability to rest without fear of falling asleep. Another thing that would have been useful for the military!

He was not sure how long he had been asleep when he was roused by a cry of rage and fear. His reflexes honed by the constant perils of the Dungeon, he moved from sleep to full awareness almost instantly, leaping to his feet at the first indication of trouble.

The cry had come from Ka, who, on coming back to consciousness and finding himself held in a net, had begun to bellow in a voice that quite literally raised the rafters.

As the others woke they came running to join Clive at the back of the *Bold Endeavor*.

"Ka!" he shouted. "Ka, it's me—Folliot. You're safe. You're among friends!"

The sea-man thrashed and howled, tangling himself in the sling that Shriek had created to keep him safe. Clive remembered what Ka had told him about what happened when one of his people was trapped in a net belonging to the islanders.

"I'm going out to him," he said to the others.

Slipping over the side of the raft, he immersed himself in the moonlit sea.

The water was pleasantly warm. Clive spoke soothingly to Ka as he followed the line of silk connecting the sea-man to the raft. At the same time he found himself hoping that the motion of his feet would not prove particularly enticing to anything large and toothy that might be lurking in the waters below.

"Ka," he said, over and over. "It's me—Folliot. You are not trapped. We will not harm you. Be at ease."

Suddenly the sea-man was still.

"I am sorry," he said. His voice was hoarse, scratchy. "I did not realize. When I woke and found myself in this net, I panicked. I am embarrassed."

This last was spoken with such a profound note of shame that Clive ached for the man.

"There is no shame," he said softly, treading water. "You were disoriented by your battle with the kraken."

"You saved me," said Ka.

"We returned a favor," replied Clive. "Though truth to tell, I did not know it was you at the time. But your people did us a kindness. We could do no less when we saw one of you in trouble."

"Nonetheless, I am deeply grateful. I would be even more grateful if you would help me disentangle myself from this net. The touch of it makes my heart pound."

"Gladly will I free you," said Clive. He swam toward Ka with a leisurely breast stroke, telling himself that the fear he now felt himself was irrational. Ka was large and strong. He looked strange and frightening in the moonlight. But he was a friend.

"I am surprised to find you here, so far from the waters of your people," said Clive, as he used his knife to cut through Shriek's silken cradle.

"I told you we were curious about your voyage," said Ka. "My people assigned me to follow you without interfering, to see what you would do."

Together they began to stroke back toward the raft. Eager hands reached down to pull them onto the deck. Ka hesitated, then accepted the gesture.

"I can sit with you briefly," he said. "Then I must return to the water."

His moist skin gleamed gray-green in the moonlight. The muscles that moved and shifted beneath that skin were thick and powerful.

"The creature from which you freed me is very rare," continued Ka, speaking now to the group as a whole. "Yet it seems there are more of them every year. According to the Way Speaker, they come from either the Ren or the Chaffri."

"What do you mean, *from* them?" asked Clive. "Did they bring these monsters with them from someplace else?"

"No. We fear it is something even worse. We think they have created these creatures from other things that were already living here on the third level. Both Ren and Chaffri have great powers, and they seem to have no qualms in how they use them. They breed things—new things never seen before. Some of them are very bad, like the thing you call the kraken."

Clive nodded. "What do you know about the Gateway of the West?"

"Why do you ask?" replied Ka.

"That is where we are attempting to go, though we are not quite sure how to find it. We've been told that to reach it we must pass through the Jaws of Hell."

"This is terrible," cried Ka. "You must turn back!"

"Why?"

"The Jaws and the Gateway are spoken of in whispers among my people. They are most perilous. You must turn back."

"But what are they?" asked Clive.

"The Jaws are a pair of rocky walls, very sheer, very high. They are nearly at the end of the ocean. The water pours through them at a great rate. What is beyond the Jaws no one knows, for no one who has gone through them has ever come back."

"Do you know where they are?"

Ka hesitated before answering, "All the People of the Sea know how to find the Jaws."

"Will you lead us there?"

"Should a friend show a friend to his doom?"

"Not to his doom, but to his destiny," said Clive.

"Oh, very good, Grampa," whispered Annie. "Very poetic."

He glared at her but refused to dignify the comment with an answer. "Will you take us there?" he repeated.

Ka stared out at the sea. "I owe you my life," he said somewhat bitterly.

"No," said Clive. "Say rather that we no longer owe you ours. We have made a fair exchange. I ask you this as friend to friend, not in payment of a debt."

Suddenly the sea-man slipped over the edge of the raft. For a moment Clive thought he was leaving them on their own. But he was only returning to the water, where he belonged.

His head thrust out of the waves, into the moonlight. "All right," he said. "I will guide you."

Two days later Annie was the first to spot the Jaws, though when she initially saw the vertical line they created on the horizon, a line extending from the sea straight into the sky, she thought it was a flaw in her vision. After a while, still not certain what it was she was seeing, she called the others to look.

"That is your destination," said Ka, swimming to the front of the raft. "That is the Jaws of Hell."

For the rest of the day it seemed that no matter what else they were doing, the rafters found themselves glancing ahead to marvel at the pillar cleaving the sky ahead of them.

"It's incredible," Annie whispered to Clive that evening. They were sitting at the front of the raft, watching the sun set. As the glowing orange ball settled into the sea it appeared to be perfectly bisected by the Jaws.

Finnbogg, who was standing behind them, seemed nervous. "Finnbogg only see one jaw," he growled. "Where's the other?"

"I don't know, Finn," said Clive. "But I suppose we'll find out soon enough."

Yet, despite the fact that they had moved along at a good pace through most of the afternoon, it was clear they were still a great distance from the rocky column, the top of which was lost in a bank of clouds that seemed to hover perpetually around its peak. At least, they presumed the peak was hidden in the clouds. As Horace pointed out, for all they knew the rock simply went straight up forever.

Before coming to the Dungeon, Clive would have scoffed at such a statement. Now he simply looked at the pillar of stone and wondered.

It was three days before they finally reached their destination. Ka had long since bidden them a regretful farewell.

"Friendship has brought me this far," he had said. "Now that your destination is clear, only foolishness would take me farther."

Clive had understood, though he deeply missed his friend. Ka had told him many interesting things about the ways of underwater life while swimming alongside the raft. Clive, in turn, had spoken to the sea-man of his own home. They shared the bond of men who are far from where they belong, and want to return. The difference was that while Clive still traveled an unknown path, Ka was now on his way back home.

And so they approached the way out of the third level the same way they had entered: alone.

But in other ways things are much different, thought Clive as he looked over the raft and considered the changes that had occurred in the group—Gram and 'Nrrc'kth gone, Wrecked Fred slowly but certainly taking his place among their number. Clive wondered if he would ever truly feel like their leader again. At the same time, he found himself overwhelmed with an almost unbearable fondness for all of them.

Tomàs prayed almost incessantly. Other than that, no one but Fred, who was new to this kind of adventure, spoke much of the peril ahead.

The current was stronger now, pulling them ever more swiftly toward their goal.

On the morning of the final day Clive could see that the rocky face of the Jaws seemed to curve away from them. Though they had considered it a pillar all along, he realized they had no reason for that belief. Was it really a column, with the rocks forming a complete circle? Or did it stretch away behind the face in a long, narrow passage? Just what was on the other side of the Jaws?

"We'd better drop the sail," Tomàs said a few hours later. "We're traveling so fast I can barely control the raft."

Clive joined the others in rolling up the woven sail. When he stood up after lashing the sail into place, he saw for the first time why their destination was called the *Jaws* of Hell.

The rocky column, which had appeared so solid, was actually split up the front, forming an opening through which the ocean waters poured at an appalling rate, creating the current that was now carrying the raft forward at a breathtaking pace.

After their long, slow approach, the Jaws now appeared to loom larger with every passing instant.

The roar of falling water filled the air, making it almost impossible to talk.

The gap between the two walls of rock was nearly thirty yards wide. To steer through it would have been easy, had it not been for the row of sharp, fanglike rocks spaced across the opening.

"These Jaws have sharp teeth," yelled Horace, leaning against Clive's ear.

He nodded and looked forward again.

In the soaring column beyond the cleft he could make out an open space, and then more rock, indicating that the formation was actually an enormous cylinder.

Now the opening was only a few hundred feet ahead. The great stone pillar seemed to fill their vision. Somewhere to the right and the left, the ocean rolled around it. Bending back his neck, Clive looked up. The Jaws stretched straight up until they disappeared into the clouds, as if they thrust through the underbelly of the sky.

"All to starboard!" bellowed Tomàs, leaning against the rudder as they careened forward on the breast of the surging water. His voice was barely audible above the crash and roar of the waves. "All to starboard!"

Even as he shouted the words, the raft lurched sickeningly sideways. With the others, Clive scrambled up the sloping deck to try to keep the craft from capsizing. Shriek scuttled forward, clutching the rail to keep from slipping over. Working quickly and efficiently, she bound each of them to the railing with her webbing, checking to be sure all had knives with which to free themselves if necessary.

Buffeted by the waves, the raft headed toward one of the three great fangs, which reared some forty or fifty feet straight out of the water. Tomàs leaned on the rudder again. The raft glanced against the stony formation, jarring them unmercifully, but shot sideways and ahead.

Clive felt a surge of triumph. They had survived the Jaws of Hell!

Then he looked ahead and realized the ordeal was just beginning. Some hundred feet ahead of them the water poured over a cliff. The area between was strewn with more of the deadly rocks.

He heard a cry of despair behind him. Turning, he saw Tomàs clinging to the rear rail. He was moving the rudder desperately from side to side. But it was clear from the easy play that it had snapped. Out of control, the *Bold Endeavor* began to spin as it rushed along on the crest of the water.

Clive was completely soaked from the crashing waves. Annie tried to shout something to him, but her voice was lost in the roar of the water. He heard the timbers of the raft groan as some of the bindings snapped with a crack that could be heard even above the tumult of the water.

They sideswiped one of the giant rocks with a crash that shook his teeth. The merciless waters pulled them on, and they shot over the crest of the falls.

The raft tipped forward until it was almost vertical. Only Shriek's webbing kept them all from being thrown off into the water as they plunged down the face of the monstrous falls.

The world exploded in white as the raft split in two and the adventurers disappeared into the spume at the base of the cataract.

Clive felt himself pounded down, lifted up, then heartbreakingly pushed down again before he could catch a breath. The roiling water tumbled them end over end. Suddenly, when it seemed he could hold his breath no longer, the piece of raft to which he was still bound erupted through the surface.

We did it! he thought, sucking air triumphantly. *We survived the Jaws!*

The moment of triumph was shortlived as he shook the spray from his eyes and saw, at last, the Gateway of the West.

▪ CHAPTER THIRTY-FIVE ▪

The Worm

Sidi Bombay was burrowing his way through time and space when he felt L'Claar tugging him back to the drifting world of pain that was his own.

Why did you do that? he asked angrily.

She drew away. *Why are you angry?* she asked.

The feeling behind the question was unbearably intense.

Another mind has touched mine, he thought, feeling as though he had somehow been unfaithful. *It is dim. It confuses me. But I cannot resist it. It takes me places, and the pain goes away, a little. But I cannot see the places that we go. I sense the difference, but cannot understand it. Yet I feel that someday I might. What is it, L'Claar? Who touches me this way? Is it a way out?*

Her answer held a strange mixture of fear and pride. *It is a worm,* she answered. *Only the strong become connected this way. Only the brave survive. But the priests will want you more than ever now. The Harvest is coming, and I don't know what to do.*

Will the Harvest change things? he asked.

She signaled an affirmation.

Then how can it possibly be worse? he asked.

I do not know, she answered. *I only know that I will lose you if it happens. I do not want that to be.*

He tried to answer, but the presence of the second mind, the mind that was not L'Claar's, intruded.

Don't go! she pleaded.

He struggled to maintain the connection. But when

she left, reluctantly, the other returned, and over whelmed him.

Time rolled on. After a while the connection was almost constant. He was able to continue communicating with L'Claar only because the other mind seemed dulled much of the time, and her communication was still clear and direct, slicing through the other like a sturdy wire being driven through a thick pudding.

I am losing you, she mourned. He would try to comfort her, but it was hard, for what she said was true. He felt himself merging more and more with the other, becoming less and less himself.

But then one day she came to him in great excitement. *Hold fast, hold fast,* she whispered in his mind. *I have had a vision. Those who would help you are on their way. Hold fast.*

But Sidi Bombay was deep in the grips of that other mind, and could not answer.

▪ CHAPTER THIRTY-SIX ▪

"My Name Is L'Claar"

The Gateway of the West was an enormous whirlpool, at least three hundred feet across. Even at its outer edges the water circled at a dizzying rate, quickly narrowing to create a dark, mysterious tunnel. The remnant of the raft to which Clive now clung was drawn inexorably toward the whirlpool by the implacable rush of the ocean.

He shook his head again and realized that he was not alone. The chunk of raft to which he was bound was at least ten feet long. Annie, Finnbogg, and Chang Guafe shared it with him. Annie's eyes were wide open, staring with horror at the vortex about to engulf them.

A wave washed over him, filling his eyes and mouth with water. Suddenly Clive felt the direction of travel change. Instead of moving forward, they were swept violently sideways as they were caught on the lip of the whirlpool. The speed of the water was breathtaking. Although he was bound securely by Shriek's webbing, Clive's instincts made him clutch the rail as the raft began to tip toward the center of the vortex. Clenched in the grip of the relentless water, they made their first circuit of the vortex. The center of the whirlpool looked to Clive like a dark, gaping mouth, waiting to swallow them.

Riding at a forty-five-degree angle, he looked across the center of the pool and saw another chunk of the raft. Several figures still clung to it. He tried to count, to see if the others were all there, but it was impossible.

He thought the roar of the water was going to split open his head.

Faster and faster the raft flew. With each circuit of the whirlpool they descended a little farther into the funnel. With each circuit their path grew shorter, tighter, the angle at which they were leaning sharper.

The roar of the water was deafening as they moved slowly down the dark tunnel. He looked up, but the sky had disappeared.

Clive's last conscious thought was that this was like being slowly swallowed. He heard Annie scream. Then he blacked out.

Clive Folliot woke to find his face pressed against wet sand. His head seemed to be filled with a roaring noise. At first he thought it was coming from inside him, an aftereffect of the battering he had just survived. But after a moment he realized it came from outside.

He moaned and rolled over. The air was filled with a cool, wet mist. Occasionally, larger drops spattered against his skin. He realized that his feet were still in the water.

He shook his head and rubbed his face. The fog began to clear from his brain. Wiping his hands down his cheeks, he looked forward and started back in alarm.

Not fifteen feet in front of him was an enormous column of water. This was the source of the deafening roar he heard.

The column spun rapidly, filling the air with mist. He looked up and caught his breath. The blue cylinder of water extended straight up for at least three hundred feet. At that point, still whirling, it began to spread, so that it formed a kind of huge, restless ceiling far above him. The turbulent waters stretched out until they met with some kind of rocky formation. Letting his eye follow the rock backward, Clive realized that it curved into a kind of wall, which had its base somewhere in the foliage behind him. The whole effect was that of a giant, rock-walled cylinder through the center of which ran the great whirlpool that had pulled them out of the third level and into what he assumed was the fourth level of the Dungeon.

The whirlpool beat the circular body of water just beyond his feet into a kind of frothing frenzy. He wondered if he leaped back in if the water would pull him down again to the fifth level. Considering the fact that every inch of his body seemed to be bruised, he decided that this was not the time to find out.

He heard a groan nearby. Turning his head, he saw Finnbogg pushing himself to his feet. The still form of Tomàs lay on the other side of him. Beyond the little sailor he could see Shriek. Were they all here? And if so, were they all alive? Fighting an urge to collapse back onto the sand, he pushed himself to his feet and walked toward the dwarf.

"Come on, old chap," he said, yelling to be heard above the roar of the water, "let's see if we can find the others."

Pausing to ascertain that Tomàs was breathing, and did not have any obvious injuries, they began to circle the swirling blue column. When he stared up at it again, Clive realized that it must actually curve outward. Here at the base, where it emptied into a circular pool about sixty feet across, the pillar itself was not more than thirty feet in diameter. The fact that it appeared almost exactly the same width at its distant top must mean it was actually considerably wider.

Clive paused to wipe some spray from his face. He realized that Shriek was lying face down in the dark sand, her eight limbs splayed around her as if to indicate the cardinal and ordinal directions on a compass. He hurried to her side, leaping over splintered pieces of the *Bold Endeavor* as he ran.

"Shriek," he called, shaking her by one of her upper shoulders. "Shriek, are you all right?"

She made no response. He paused, wondering how to discern whether she displayed any signs of life. He wasn't sure she even had a pulse. Her stiff, chitinous back would not show any signs of breath.

He shook her shoulder again, and felt a familiar tug

at his mind. He realized with a start how much he had missed that connection.

Here, she signaled feebly. *Need time. See to the others.*

His surge of relief bordered on joy. She must have read it, for she replied, *I am glad you still live, dear heart.* Then she seemed to flicker away. He paused. Was she all right, as she claimed? Or was she in trouble?

See to the others, she repeated.

He heard Finnbogg shouting with joy not far ahead of him. "Beloved Annie is all right," he cried. "Beloved Annie is well." As Clive continued around the circular beach he could see Annie sitting with her knees drawn up to her chest. Finnbogg was capering around her, his jowls flapping in his enthusiasm. She watched the dwarf with an expression that seemed to combine amusement and chagrin.

Not far beyond her Clive saw Wrecked Fred, looking truly wrecked. He broke into a trot.

"Hey, Grampa, aren't you going to say hello?" called Annie. Then she read the seriousness on his face. Turning in the direction he was running, she cried out and pushed herself to her feet.

"Is he all right?" she asked nervously, looking down at the crumpled form of the bearded man.

"He's alive," said Clive, who was kneeling at Fred's shoulder. "But that arm is definitely broken. We'll have to set it. If Shriek comes to, we'll have her give him an anesthetic like she gave me for my tooth."

"Drugs," said Annie. "He'll love it."

Limping and examining their wounds, the others began to arrive. To Clive's relief, except for Fred everyone was not only alive but ambulatory. Even Shriek was on her feet now, though she looked tired in a way that Clive had never seen before.

"I wonder if this entire level is so enclosed," he said, looking up at the cliffs and the roiling oceanic ceiling. "That seems to be the bottom of the third level right above us." He shivered. The vision made him feel entrapped, as if he were stuck in a cave. In fact, he realized, this area was very much like an enormous cave. He wondered if there were an opening somewhere in the rocky walls surrounding them.

Shriek anesthetized Fred, who seemed to be suffering from shock. Clive and Horace searched through the lush foliage surrounding the circular beach for some straight pieces of wood to use as splints. When they returned, they found that Chang Guafe had straightened and set the broken limb.

"You make a good doctor, for one so contemptuous of human frailty," said Clive, examining the cyborg's efforts.

"I am interested in how things work," he replied.

Unable to tear his own linenlike suit to make a binding, Clive removed Fred's vest.

"Not his vest," said Annie, her tone a strange combination of amusement and tenderness. "Use his shirt instead."

No need, sent Shriek. *It can be done with webbing.*

Thank you, replied Clive. Then he watched in admiration as the arachnid used her silk first to bind the arm and the splint together, and then to create a sling that would hold the arm in place.

Thanks to Shriek's anesthetic, Fred remained oblivious to the pain. Eventually he began singing about being "like a rolling stone." Clive realized it was a good thing that the "hippie," as Annie liked to call him, was not wearing one of Green's white suits. Otherwise he might just fade away to—well, to wherever it was the suits took you.

As Shriek was putting the final adjustments on the sling, Clive heard a rustling in the leaves behind them. He turned, and was astonished to see a very small girl—not more than six or seven by the look of her—step out onto the sand. Her skin was very pale, almost as white as the simple shift that was her only clothing. She had long black hair and large dark eyes.

"Are you the friends that were coming?" she asked.

"I beg your pardon?" said Clive.

"My name is L'Claar," she said, looking directly into his eyes. "I need to know if you are the friends of Sidi Bombay. He has been waiting for you. But he is almost gone. If you will follow me, I will lead you to him."

CHAPTER THIRTY-SEVEN

Welcome to Purgatory

Annie nudged Clive in the ribs. "Looks like you may actually keep a promise, Grampa," she whispered, referring to the vow he had taken back in the blue corridors beneath N'wrbb's castle.

He chose to ignore her.

"Where is Sidi Bombay?" he asked L'Claar.

"Probably with the worm," she replied solemnly. "It comes for him often now. He is deep within it."

A chill slithered along Clive's spine. The strange statement seemed even more eerie coming from this wide-eyed child. "I don't understand," he said. "What worm do you mean? Has Sidi been taken somewhere?"

"One of the great worms. But he is not really with it. It is a thing of the mind. His body is not far from here, in the Temple of Those Who Suffer. If you free him, we may be able to save him."

Horace had gone so white he might have been of the same race as Gram and 'Nrrc'kth. He knelt to face L'Claar. "Is Sidi still in pain?" he asked.

L'Claar nodded solemnly. "It is less now, because of the worm, and because so much has burned away. But the pain is still with him."

Horace closed his eyes and turned away.

"Is this temple far from here?" asked Clive.

L'Claar shook her head. "It is quite near."

"Can we enter it with no problem, or will it be guarded?"

"It is not hard to enter the temple. But the chamber where Sidi hangs is different. To reach that, we must wait until the city is asleep. Even then we will have to be careful. But we should be able to get in."

"Hangs?" asked Horace, his voice tight.

"In his egg," said L'Claar.

"What do you mean?"

"His *egg*," she said, with childish impatience at his stupidity.

The answer, and the tone in which she gave it, made Clive remember that she was indeed only a child—a fact he had almost lost sight of during this conversation.

"We'll see soon enough, Horace," he said gently. "For now, we are all tired and sore. Is there a place where we can rest, L'Claar, and perhaps get some food?"

The child hesitated. "I will take you to my home," she said at last. "Follow me."

Clive glanced at Fred. Remembering his own experience with Shriek's anesthetic, he said, "Our friend will not be able to travel on his own. We must arrange something."

L'Claar nodded, eyes wide, face as solemn as ever. Using more of Shriek's webbing, they lashed together some poles to create a travois on which to carry Fred. Finnbogg, short but powerful, volunteered to pull the contraption.

"Follow me," said L'Claar. She led them to a faint path that meandered through the undergrowth until it finally came to a narrow tunnel in the rock wall. When they emerged from the other side Clive looked up apprehensively. It was as he had feared: the sky was not more than a hundred yards away. Whatever that sky was, whatever it was made of, it seemed to be transfused with a dull glow. The light it shed was even, but dreary. Looking ahead, he saw that the sky and the land seemed to close together, in the same way that parallel railroad tracks meet in the distance. He felt entombed.

"Heepers!" said Annie, as she stepped out of the tunnel. "A brown-out!"

"That is where I live," said L'Claar, pointing to a walled city about a mile from where they stood.

Clive looked around. The landscape was stark and

severe, the barren soil seeming to sprout little more than boulders and upthrust rocks. The few trees and bushes he did see were weak and sickly-looking, a factor he guessed might be related to the light.

When everyone was out of the tunnel they started for the city.

"What is this place called?" Clive asked L'Claar. The child was walking beside him. Occasionally she would stop to pick up a smooth pebble, which she would put into a pocket that had been crudely stitched onto her white shift.

"The city is called Purgatory," she answered.

"I don't much like the sound of that, sah," Horace said softly.

"Why do they call it thus?" asked Clive.

L'Claar twisted her face, as if trying to recall exactly the content of some rather boring lessons. "According to the priests who run the city, the people who have been brought here were not wicked enough to go to Hell, but not good enough to go to Heaven. They say that when we died the Lord didn't know what to do with us, and so we were sent here to Purgatory to pay for our sins. If we behave properly, and wait long enough, eventually we will go to Heaven."

"Is this what you believe?" Clive asked gently.

The little girl laughed, and Clive was struck by how out-of-place the merry sound seemed in their dreary surroundings. "How can such a thing be true?" she asked. "Everyone knows the world is ruled by the three goddesses. They would never invent something as silly as this Purgatory of the priests."

"She is a demon," whispered Tomàs in awe. He crossed himself and began to finger his rosary. "You see?" he said, turning to Shriek. "I was right all along. This is the work of the Lord. He has brought us here to be tested, and to pay for our wicked ways on Earth."

"Shut up, Tomàs," said Chang Guafe.

"But the priests—"

"Whether something is believed by one fool or a hundred fools does not make it any more true. Stop your chatter."

"You will be very sorry," muttered Tomàs, as he began counting decades on his rosary. "The Lord will have His way."

"I have a feeling," Clive said to Horace, "that the situation here is much as it was on the island of the cannibals. The people who run this place were probably strongly religious back on Earth. Snatched up into this place that is obviously neither Heaven nor Hell, it would have been easy enough to decide that they had indeed been carried to Purgatory. If they came in a group—instead of alone, as did Tomàs—they would have based everything they did on that idea. Enough of them, and they could impose it on everyone."

He turned back to L'Claar. "Who runs things here? Do you have a king, or a governor of some kind?"

"The priests run things," she said. "They are in charge of Purgatory."

"Makes a certain amount of sense," Horace said grimly.

Tomàs scowled and increased the volume of his prayers.

"The most important thing to know," said L'Claar, "is that no one is allowed to leave. The priests say that because we are here by the will of the Lord, trying to escape is a sin. They say trying to leave will lead to eternal damnation."

"Just what we need," said Horace, "a whole city run by demented papists."

"*Madre de Dios!*" muttered Tomàs, appalled by the blasphemy.

Though the city was walled, no one challenged them as they approached the gates. At first Clive was afraid that they would attract undue attention as they walked through the city. However, after a while he realized that it was hard to stand out in a place where there was no such thing as standard garb, or even a standard kind of body. Like the city of Go-Mar, Purgatory was a great mixture of races, drawn from many worlds, many times.

Yet, from what L'Claar had said, one group—the religious leaders—must have gained sway.

"The temple is this way," said L'Claar, clutching Clive's

hand and leading him between a pair of stalls. A human woman was selling roast meat in the booth on his left. To his right something that resembled a hairy tree was selling vegetables. Coming around the booths, he found himself on a broad thoroughfare that led straight to what could only be the Temple of Those Who Suffer.

Clive was startled by the sight. He had become used to the crude and simple structures that seemed to prevail at the third level. But although its height was constricted by the low "sky," this temple was as impressive a piece of architecture as any of the great cathedrals he had seen on his tours of the European continent. Formed of white stone, with four great corner towers, it was fronted by a long pool from which two jets of water erupted at regular intervals. The red cobblestone road on which they stood was moderately busy, with individuals and small groups entering and exiting at the numerous cross streets. A steady stream of pedestrian traffic led to and from the temple doors.

As they drew closer, Clive saw that the edifice was carved with images of individuals in great torment. The carvings, which he estimated to be about ten feet tall, were framed by large ovals. They stretched in a ribbon of agony across the front of the temple, about twenty feet above the peak of the main doors.

"I thought we weren't going to go to the temple now," he said.

"I will take you inside so that you can see the upper portion," said L'Claar. "Later we will come back for Sidi."

As they mounted the steps of the temple, Clive could hear a dolorous chanting from within. When they entered the narthex he heard another sound, one that seemed so out-of-place that at first he thought he must be mistaken. But when they passed into the nave, he saw that his senses had not betrayed him, and it was all he could do to keep himself from crying out at the brutal sacrilege being conducted at the front of the temple.

"Careful," whispered Annie, putting a hand on his

elbow. "We're in Rome now, Grampa, so let's do as the Romans do."

Clive nodded. But he was unable to tear his gaze from the sight of a priest in flowing white robes lashing an old man strapped to a long wooden table. Even from where they stood Clive could see the lines of blood across the old man's back. The priest raised his arm and the lash whistled through the air once more. The old man cried out in pain—as did the people scattered among the pews, who sounded as if they had received the lash themselves.

Behind this bloody scene stood a choir of hooded monks. As Clive began to sort out the sounds—the whistle and crack of the lash, the cries of pain, and the voices of the monks—he realized that their words were a hymn in praise of a creator so merciful he allowed men to atone for their sins rather than simply consigning them to the eternal fires of damnation.

A line of people stood at the right of the dais. Clive wondered why they were there, until the priest set aside his lash and removed the old man's bonds. Moving slowly in his pain, the man climbed down from the table, then knelt to kiss his tormentor's feet. The priest reached down and gently drew the man to a standing position. He kissed him on both cheeks.

Clive hoped that this was the end of the ceremony. It was not. The priest turned and reached into a silver urn at his right side. Pulling out a double handful of white powder, he smeared it over the old man's back.

His scream echoed through the temple. The seated worshippers sighed in satisfaction.

But still it was not the end. As the old man hobbled away to the left, the next person in the line at the right, a dark-haired young woman, stepped forward. She dropped her robe, revealing a pair of round, full breasts. Then she mounted the table, where she lay face down in exactly the same position as the old man who had preceded her.

"For whom do you receive these lashes, my child?" asked the priest. Clive was shocked to realize that though his voice was deep and powerful, it was also oddly gentle.

"For my mother and my father," said the woman, "with the prayer that by this act they may be moved closer to the gates of Paradise."

The priest lifted the lash to his lips, kissed it, prayed over it, and set to work once more.

▪ CHAPTER THIRTY-EIGHT ▪

The Worms of Q'oorna

Clive had been appalled at the idea of L'Claar watching the perverted ritual in the temple—and even more appalled when he realized that to her it was an everyday occurrence. His heart ached as she led them from the temple, back along the boulevard, and then through a maze of alleys and side streets to a burnt-out building where she hesitated only slightly before sharing her secret: the dark, cool basement where she made her home.

"Is this really where you live?" Clive asked gently.

"That's a silly question," she replied, her voice utterly serious.

Annie snickered.

"But why?" asked Clive. "Surely there are people in this city who would take you in, care for you—"

"They would punish me," interrupted the child.

"Why?" asked Clive.

"So I could get to Heaven faster. And by helping me toward Heaven, they would also be moving along their own path. So I would be beaten often."

Clive could think of nothing to say.

The group huddled together in the damp room, their only light a dim glow provided by Chang Guafe.

After a while L'Claar offered them bread and fruit. When Clive insisted that they didn't want to eat her precious stores, she explained that food was no problem, since between begging and stealing she was always able to feed herself.

As they were eating, something scuttled across the

floor. Aside from the fact that it was completely hairless, the creature seemed remarkably similar to a rat.

Tomàs muttered and counted another decade on his rosary.

Clive was worried about the little sailor. He sensed that for all its perversity—or perhaps because of it—Tomàs was attracted to this place. He shivered and turned his attention back to L'Claar, who was leaning against Wrecked Fred.

As he looked at the child Clive felt a kind of despair come over him. It was bad enough that he and the others had been dragged to this hellhole. The idea of a child being brought here was unbearable. Worse, the sight of this abandoned waif brought to mind his own child, whom he had abandoned all unwittingly.

Had it—she—been born yet?

He shook his head. Of course she had been born; Annie was her descendant. But that meant the infant had grown to womanhood, given birth, died. How could that be? Surely it had been much less than a year since he had bidden farewell to Miss Annabella Leighton on that misty morning in London in 1868.

As usually happened when he tried to contemplate the nature of time as it related to the Dungeon, he succeeded only in making his head spin.

Annie stirred beside him. "How did you come here, L'Claar?" she asked gently.

"I came to Purgatory in my mother's womb," answered the child. "How she was brought here, I do not know. Two years after I was born, my mother was taken by a worm. I was sent to live with someone else."

She closed her eyes. "I did not like it there," she said. Her voice quivered a little, and Clive wondered what horrors were hidden behind those simple words.

"Like the spider woman, my mother and I could talk without talking. So when the worm returned, and left my mother in the Temple of Those Who Suffer, I knew it. She called to me, and I went to her. But I could not save her."

L'Claar was silent for a moment. Though her mouth

trembled, she did not give way to tears. Clive felt Annie's hand creep across the floor to grasp his.

"I was little then," said L'Claar, "not more than four cycles old. Now I go often to the Chamber of the Venerated Ones, to see if there are any souls that I can touch. Sometimes I can make their time easier. But I can never save them. I want to. But I do not know how."

Finally a single tear welled up at the lower edge of her left eye, rolled over the lashes, and trickled down her cheek. Yet her expression did not change. She gave no hint of seeking sympathy.

Finnbogg was snuffling outrageously.

"For a long time there was no one I could reach. Then one of the worms brought Sidi Bombay. He is good, and strong. I love him very much. We have to save him."

"What are these worms you speak of?" asked Horace.

L'Claar closed her eyes, and when she spoke Clive had the eerie feeling that it was not actually the child who was speaking, though who else it might be he could not say.

"The worms were the Lords of Q'oorna," she whispered hoarsely, "the ones who were here before all. They are the betrayed and the lost. They devour, and they mourn. They are the treasure and the enemy. They are the wanderers."

"What do they *look* like?" asked Horace.

L'Claar opened her eyes. "What difference does *that* make?" she asked, as if the question astonished her.

Clive thought it was time to turn the conversation in a more pragmatic direction. "What obstacles are we apt to encounter on the way to this chamber?" he asked.

"A priest and two soldiers guard the main entrance to the lower levels," she said. "We may meet some other priests in the hall. I think there will be another priest at the entrance to the chamber. I know a secret way to get in that I use when I don't want to be seen. But it's very small. I don't think you could squeeze through it."

"What kind of weapons do the soldiers have?" asked Shriek.

"Buzzers," said L'Claar.

"Buzzers?" asked Clive.

"Yes. You know—they point them at you, and they make a buzzing sound, and then you're not there anymore. You have to be careful around buzzers."

Clive shivered. "I think we'd best do some planning," he said to the others.

L'Claar closed her eyes again. "I'm tired," she said, leaning against Fred. The hippie put his good arm around her, and almost before Clive realized what was happening, the child was asleep. She looked more fragile than ever.

Clive thought about waking her but decided against it. He thought they had learned all they were apt to for the time being.

He discussed his ideas for dealing with what lay ahead with the others. To his surprise, they agreed with little argument.

And now I think we should all sleep, sent Shriek, in the format Clive recognized as her general message to all. *Or at least most of us. I fear we have a busy night ahead.*

"I will stand watch," said Chang Guafe. "I will wake you when the noises of the city have subsided."

Clive thanked the cyborg. He tried to rest, but sleep would not come easily. He felt that they were waiting at the edge of some great mystery. He felt, too, that they would be heading into great danger. Annie leaned against his shoulder, and soon her breathing was slow and regular. One by one the others fell asleep, until the only ones left awake were Horace, Clive, and, of course, the cyborg.

"It won't be long now, sah," said Horace, and though he whispered his voice was thick with excitement. "You were right, way back in those tunnels, when you said we'd cross Sidi Bombay's path again. But I'm worried, worried near sick. You can't get a straight answer out of the child, and for the life of me I don't know what we're going to find when she takes us to Sidi."

"I know what you mean, Sergeant Smythe," said Clive. "Her hints have been most maddening. And yet one hesitates to press her too hard. There is a kind of—fragility about her."

"Don't be sentimental, Folliot," said Chang Guafe. "If the child were fragile, she would not have survived."

Clive sighed. The cyborg was right, of course. But when he looked over at L'Claar, her face smooth and innocent as she lay sleeping in the crook of Fred's arm, it was difficult to think of her as a tough survivor of street life.

"Just another of the Dungeon's little mysteries, sah," said Horace.

"I guess you're right, Sergeant Smythe."

Clive closed his eyes, uneasy at what lay ahead, but comforted by the presence of good friends. He did not really expect to sleep, but the strain of the day's adventures overcame him, and he quickly fell into an almost deathlike slumber.

He opened his eyes again when he felt a metallic tentacle tapping on his forehead. He wondered if the cyborg, which he had always thought of as humorless, considered this amusing.

As if in answer, Chang Guafe lifted the tentacle and caused the end of it to glow. "Rise and shine," he said, repeating the words he had often heard Horace use in the morning.

Clive still wasn't sure if the mechanical man was actually trying to make a joke. He thought about asking, but considering the way conversations with the cyborg usually went, he decided to hold the question for a more propitious time.

"I don't think we should do this," Tomàs said. "The priests will not like it."

"Tomàs," Clive said firmly, "this is *not* the Purgatory your religion speaks of. It is simply another level of the Dungeon—hellish enough, I grant you. But I am convinced that the creatures who made it are flesh and blood, even as you and I. Just because some men have decided what we should believe does not mean we have to believe it."

"An accurate assessment of all religion," said the cyborg.

Clive was contemplating his retort when L'Claar broke in with a request that they begin their journey.

"Kid's the only one with her eye on the ball," said Annie.

Following L'Claar's lead, they traveled quietly through the darkened streets. It was cold, and except for the occasional still figure of some homeless wretch sleeping in a doorway, there was no one else abroad.

The glowing sky was now dim and nearly black. Clive had difficulty seeing. L'Claar, however, seemed to move with quiet assurance.

"Do they lock the gates of the city at night?" he whispered, as they walked along the empty boulevard leading to the temple.

"Why would they do that?" she asked.

"You said that the priests consider escape a great sacrilege; I thought they might want to keep everyone inside the city."

"They don't care if people escape from the city," replied L'Claar. "They do not want them to escape from the Dungeon itself. Did you know it is against the law to speak that name here? The priests consider it heresy, and bring people who insist on using it before the Inquisition. Despite their lies, most of us know that there are many levels here. Anyway, I think the real reason the priests worry about escape is that there is a way out of the Dungeon beneath the city."

Clive drew up short, nearly causing Shriek to trip over him.

"A way out?" he hissed incredulously.

"So some of them have told me," she said. "The priests are fond of me, because I worship so piously in the Chamber of the Venerated Ones. Some of them tell me things."

"But where is this exit?" asked Clive.

"They do not tell me that much! All they say is that it is beneath the city. Who knows. Maybe they are lying anyway."

Clive's head was swirling. A way out!

"Another priest told me," continued L'Claar, "that

no one knows where the gate will take you. 'It is a way out,' he said. 'But a way out to where?' "

Clive felt his heart sink. As much as he wanted to escape the Dungeon, it made no sense to go through a door that would take him to—well, to Shriek's home, for example. It might be an improvement for her. But hardly for him.

He remained silent until they reached the temple. The great building was dark. Its doors, however, had been left unlocked.

"Any may seek sanctuary here at any time," said L'Claar, in reply to Clive's whispered question. "It is the lower levels that are more heavily guarded."

In the dim light provided by Guafe she led them through the nave, past the altar where the ritual flagellations had been performed earlier that day, to a curtained door at the back of the apse. It was locked, but Chang Guafe made quick work of that by inserting one of his metallic tentacles in the keyhole and jiggering the tumblers.

"The 'borg would have made a great sneak thief," whispered Annie, as the door swung open.

"Shhh," cautioned L'Claar. She stepped forward.

They began their descent into the bowels of the temple.

CHAPTER THIRTY-NINE

The Venerated Ones

L'Claar put out a hand to stay their progress.

They stood in a narrow corridor. Walls, floor, and ceiling were all made of smoothly polished black stone. Dim blue lights shone in recessed niches, evenly spaced about twenty paces apart. Clive wondered how they worked.

The temple seemed to be slowly changing as they moved deeper within it. Like the city of Purgatory itself, the upper structure had seemed to Clive as though it came from an era earlier than his own expanding world of exploration and scientific discovery. But here at the lower levels that sense no longer held. Little things—the lights, something about the very feel of the walls—seemed to speak of a different level of scientific knowledge.

And yet the transition was slow. He wondered if the priesthood that served in the temple was arranged in a hierarchy, such that the more advanced you were, the deeper you were allowed to go in the temple.

L'Claar interrupted his thoughts. "Soon we will come to a wider corridor," she said. "It is but a short distance from there to the guards."

Clive nodded, and motioned for Shriek and Horace to join him.

It is time, he sent to the spider woman.

She acknowledged the message, then used her lower arms, both the old one and the still somewhat spindly new one, to pluck a pair of spikes from her belly. These she handed to Clive and Horace.

Be careful! she thought at them sharply. *If you accidentally prick yourselves, you will be unconscious for hours.*

Clive nodded, and wished her luck. She turned and scuttled up the wall. Pressing herself to the ceiling, she began to creep along the corridor. The combination of high ceiling and low light rendered her nearly invisible.

"We're ready," Clive said softly. He marveled at the way L'Claar simply nodded and walked on. *How did she come to be so brave?* he wondered.

Perhaps she no longer cares, sent Shriek. He knew from her tone as much as her words that the message was for his mind only. It carried a quality of feeling he had not experienced for some time.

I have missed you, my friend, he responded warmly.

And I you. But this is no time to speak of what has been. We can discuss our differences later. For now, you need what my eyes will tell you. I am going to peer around the corner. I will be back in a moment.

He tapped L'Claar on the shoulder, motioned for her to stop for a moment, and waited for Shriek's report.

It came mostly in pictures, which he translated as follows: *To the right of the corner, about a hundred paces as you walk, a priest sits in a large alcove. He is armed with what appears to be a thick wooden staff. However, it would be foolish to assume that it is merely a staff. Beyond the priest the corridor is closed by a pair of wooden doors.*

Clive hoped L'Claar had been accurate when she told them there would be only two guards on the other side of the door. He wondered why whoever was in charge of the temple would post the priest outside the door, and the guards inside, and decided there were two possible reasons: either the main purpose of the guards was to keep people *in* rather than out, or else they were hidden behind the priest in order to try to maintain some image of ecclesiastical order.

Let us proceed as planned, he sent to Shriek.

His heart leaped at her response: *It shall be as you wish, O Folliot.*

Leaving the others at the corner, Clive and Horace began walking toward the priest. They moved slowly, so as not to alarm him—the same reason they had decided, earlier on, to leave most of the group hidden. All they were trying to do at this point was keep him from noticing Shriek as she scuttled along the ceiling of the corridor.

The priest stood up as soon as he saw Clive and Horace enter the corridor. Horace began to speak to him in one of the obscure dialects he had mastered during his travels, trying to hold the man's attention without actually saying anything.

The priest looked puzzled, but not worried. He held his staff braced before him.

When they were but ten paces away, Shriek dropped from the ceiling like the wrath of God. She had her webbing around the priest's head before he knew what hit him. Horace and Clive, racing past her, stood ready to slip the drugged spikes she had given them into the guards as soon as they stepped through the door.

The battle was swift and silent; the surprised guards did little more than sigh as they crumpled to the floor. After that it was a matter of but moments to strip the clothing from the three men.

Shriek went back to summon the others. Without shedding the mysterious suit that Green had given him, Clive donned the uniform of one of the guards. Wrecked Fred took the other uniform, though with his arm in a sling he was not entirely convincing as a soldier on duty. As planned, Horace took the priest's clothing. When he had finished slipping into the clerical garb he passed his hand over his face in a gesture Clive had first seen when the sergeant appeared to him in the guise of a Chinese mandarin back on the *Empress Philippa*.

The others cried out in surprise. Even Clive, who had seen this before, was surprised at the transformation in his old friend's face. He wondered how much of the effect was due to Horace's native ability, and how much came from the implants he had received on that fateful journey to Tibet.

"Take their buzzers," said L'Claar, pointing to the tubes the guards had been holding, which had fallen to the floor when Clive and Horace rendered them unconscious.

Clive picked up the tubes. He examined them curiously. "How do they work?" he asked.

"I do not know," said L'Claar. "But they are very powerful. Anyway, you will not look like a guard if you are not carrying one."

He thrust the tube through the loop in his belt that L'Claar said was meant to hold the weapon. Then he passed the other "buzzer" to Fred.

In grudging deference to Clive's wishes, Shriek refrained from killing the unconscious men. They left them in the alcove, thoroughly bound by the arachnid's webbing.

With L'Claar in the lead once more, they moved on. Clive decided they must have appeared fairly convincing as an official group, for the three priests they passed did no more than nod in their direction.

They descended another broad flight of stairs.

"This is not the only route to the chamber," said L'Claar, in answer to a question from Horace. "There is another way, broader and more direct. Everyone in Purgatory knows that route, for it is open to worshippers every third day. Because it is so well known, that way is much more carefully guarded."

"None of the priests seem surprised to see you," said Fred.

L'Claar actually smiled. "They call me the little priestess," she replied, "because of my devoted attendance in the chamber."

Except for occasional questions for L'Claar, they traveled in silence. Clive noticed that it was getting very warm.

He was just wondering how much farther they had to go when L'Claar touched his arm. "Here," she whispered. They were facing a rather sharp curve in the passage. "The chamber is not far ahead. We must wait here while Horace goes ahead to take care of the priest at the door."

Shriek passed a spike to Horace. Handling it with caution, he slipped the potent weapon into his sleeve. Then he continued around the curve.

Clive held himself alert, ready for any indication of trouble from ahead. After a moment he heard voices.

The first was that of the priest on guard: "Hoy, brother. What brings you here at this time of night?"

"I have a message from above," said Horace, finessing the fact that he had no idea what the priest's superiors might be called.

"Is there trouble?" asked the other.

"They did not read me the message," said Horace, in a tone guaranteed to make the other feel slightly foolish. "They merely asked me to bring it to you."

A brief cry, the sound of someone crumpling to the floor, and then Horace reappeared at the curve, motioning for them to follow him.

They set out at once. It was but a short distance to the wooden door where the now-unconscious priest had stood guard.

"He would have let me in if I had come alone," L'Claar said wistfully. "He was one of the ones who called me the little priestess."

"War is hell, sweetheart," said Fred, taking her by the hand. "Let's go see about your friend."

Clive swung open the sturdy wooden door and led them into a vision so hellish it was easy to believe the city above really was Purgatory.

The floor of the room was covered with more than an inch of some mucuslike substance, thick, clinging, and slimy. From the walls and the ceiling, all of which were festooned with thick strands of a yellow, weblike substance, hung hundreds of gelatinous egg sacs. The sacs seemed almost alive in the way they twitched and writhed. The whole was lit by a dim yellow light, which seemed to come from the walls themselves.

"What is this?" asked Clive, his voice thick with disgust. "Where is Sidi Bombay?"

"He's in one of the eggs," said L'Claar, in the tone of voice she used to answer foolish questions.

Annie put her hand on the child's shoulder. "How did he get here?" she asked. Her voice was trembling.

"A worm brought him," said the child. Her expression indicated that she was thoroughly sick of stupid questions. "This is the Chamber of the Venerated Ones. It is where I found my mother, though it was too late to save her. Everyone here was swallowed by a Q'oornan worm as it journeyed between the worlds. Here they suffer. Here they are tested. Most will die, but a few will find union with the worms."

"But what is it all about?" asked Horace. "Why are they called the Venerated Ones?"

"Because they suffer so terribly," said L'Claar. "The priests say that the people in the sacs are special souls, chosen to bear the weight of others' sins. Their suffering is so great that it moves everyone closer to Paradise. This is why they are held in a place of high honor."

"Nasty!" Finnbogg said vehemently, pulling his foot up from the clinging ooze in which they stood. "Nasty, nasty stuff. Bad smell hurts Finnbogg's nose."

Clive could understand that. He could barely tolerate the powerful odor of the chamber himself. For Finnbogg's delicate nose it had to be nearly overwhelming.

He began to walk around the hellacious chamber, using the short buzzer he had taken from the priest to push aside the clinging strands of yellowed webbing. Through the translucent sides of the yellow sacs he could occasionally see a figure writhing in torment. Some of them were vaguely human; others were not. The postures looked familiar, and in a few moments he recognized them as ones that were carved into the outer wall of the temple.

The atmosphere of the chamber seemed weighted with suffering.

"That one is Sidi Bombay," said L'Claar, slipping her hand into Clive's and pointing to a sac far to the right of where he stood.

He approached the spot slowly, with a kind of horrified awe. Through the translucent amber walls of the sac he could see the outlines of a man.

L'Claar stared at the sac almost reverently. Tears stood in the corners of her eyes.

"I cannot reach him," she whispered. "I want to tell him we are here. But he is deep within the worm. He is far away."

Clive reached inside the guard's clothing to draw his own knife. Heedless of the sacrilege, he reached forward and slashed open the sac containing Sidi Bombay.

He jumped back with a cry of disgust as a gush of rank liquid came spurting out of the sac. His cry changed to one of astonishment as he studied what had come tumbling through the sundered membrane and now lay twitching at his feet.

· CHAPTER FORTY ·

The Harvest of Souls

At first, Clive did not understand that the twitching figure lying in the puddle of reeking fluid spreading around his feet was truly Sidi Bombay. What had changed, what made his former guide so difficult to recognize, was that the time in the egg appeared to have stripped his years away from him.

The Sidi Bombay whom Clive had first met back in Africa had been gaunt and wrinkled, nearly an old man. The dark-skinned man he now beheld was smooth-skinned, round of limb, and had not a touch of white in his hair.

"What has happened to him?" cried Horace. "What's happened to Sidi Bombay?"

"The worm has been devouring his past," said L'Claar. She had rushed to Sidi's side. Now she knelt beside him, heedless of the revolting layer of mucus that covered the floor. She stroked his forehead with her tiny hand. "The priests say the worms feast on what a person is, what he has done, seen, experienced. In return, they make the person part of them. That Sidi was being used as food for the mind of the creature he was linked with means the linkage was truly successful." Her voice held an unmistakable note of pride. "Such a thing is very rare. It means Sidi would have been greatly valued when the Harvest came. The saints have use for one such as him, though I do not know what it is."

She looked around nervously. "They would know he was here, waiting for the Harvest. They will be very angry when they find what has happened. The wrath of the saints is said to be great indeed."

Sidi began to blink. Suddenly his body spasmed. The scream that came ripping out of him seemed to echo endlessly from the chamber walls. The other egg sacs writhed as if in sympathy. His eyes still closed, he reached forward. He seemed to be trying to clutch something elusive. He began to shake and weep.

"What's happening?" demanded Horace.

"It is the severing of the connection," whispered L'Claar. "He is no longer in union with the worm. Something very deep in him is being torn away."

She leaned over the writhing man and whispered in his ear. Clive could not hear her words, but slowly Sidi's shaking began to lessen. His eyes fluttered, opened, then opened wider still. He closed them, as if shutting out something impossible, then opened them once again.

"It's you!" he said. His voice was weak. He looked at her again. "You are not as I expected," he whispered.

"But I am here," she answered.

He closed his eyes and his large, dark hand tightened on hers. Another spasm racked his body.

"Where have I been?" he moaned. "I feel like part of me is missing—like there's a hole right through the center of me."

"You were with the worm," said L'Claar.

Sidi opened his eyes and gazed at the child. Then he noticed his own arm, extending from between her clasped hands. He looked down at his body.

"What has happened to me?" he cried.

Suddenly the fact that Sidi was naked penetrated Clive's consciousness. Stripping off the guard's tunic he had been wearing, he laid it over Sidi's waist and legs.

"The perfect Victorian," whispered Annie, but her tone seemed less deriding than ironically affectionate.

"You appear to be quite rejuvenated," said Horace, struggling to keep his voice light. He knelt at Sidi's left side, opposite L'Claar. "Do you remember how it happened?"

"I was so far away," murmured Sidi. "I saw such strange things, went to so many distant places. Yet I don't seem to remember them. Where have they gone, L'Claar?"

"Never mind that, old chap," said Horace, stroking his friend's brow. "It's all over now. We've found you. You're back with us, back where you belong."

"Belong?" Sidi asked distantly, and Clive could tell that, for the moment at least, there was nowhere that Sidi Bombay belonged. It was as if his soul had wandered free of his body, and wasn't quite sure how to find its way back in.

"There now, Sidi," said Horace. "You just rest a bit. We've come to take you away from this. You remember me, don't you? Your old mate, Horace—your blood brother."

His voice seemed almost desperate.

Sidi's eyes flickered open again. "I remember," he whispered. "But it's as though I'm seeing it through some kind of fog. Everything is so dim and hazy."

"Do you remember how you came here?" asked Annie.

Sidi hesitated, then nodded. "It was after the battle on the bridge," he said softly. "I remember using the mechanical claws we had taken from that other creature to climb the tentacles of the monster worm. They were slimy, and the way they slid back and forth beneath my hands and my legs, I don't know how I held on as long as I did. When I finally got above them, I realized it had been pointless. The thing just stretched its mouth forward—it was like a long tube—and sucked me in."

A shudder rippled through his body.

"Even inside I hacked and slashed with the claw, but it did no good. Soon I found myself moving through a kind of fleshy tunnel. It squeezed me and pulled me, kneading me like I was a piece of dough. No matter how I struggled, it pulled me on and on. It was dark! It was so dark, Horace. I have never experienced such darkness. And then—"

Sidi paused, and a thin stream of tears seeped out from beneath his closed eyelids. His voice was thick with the pain of the memory.

"And then I came out into a thick fluid that seemed to burn the flesh right off me. I screamed and screamed, but no sound came out. I don't know how I was breathing. Maybe I wasn't. It was so dark. I was in such pain. After a while, things began to push against me in the darkness, prodding me, caressing me—licking me."

Annie moved closer to Clive. He slipped his arm around her.

"After a while I realized something had enclosed me. Though it was still dark, sometimes I saw things in my mind. I don't understand them, can barely remember the images. I do seem to remember traveling through smooth blue tunnels for a long time."

Clive felt an idea poking at the back of his mind. But it wouldn't come out in the open where he could examine it.

"Then, later, I felt an enormous pressure, as if I was being squeezed through a small hole. And then there was nothing but darkness and pain, until L'Claar came to me."

He squeezed her hand.

"This is most intriguing," Chang Guafe said tonelessly. "This creature—which you described to me as having your brother's face when you first told me of your adventures, Folliot—seems to encase the creatures it swallows in these membranes. Then it brings them here and excretes them. Why? Surely not as mere waste—this place is too much like a nest for that to make sense. But what can be the purpose behind it? Perhaps as food for its young?"

Clive was angered by the cyborg's detachment. But his speculations gave him a renewed awareness of what was surrounding him. A dark rage began to surge within him as he looked around the hellish chamber. Strung amid the webbing were hundreds of sacs, twitching in the dim amber light. And in each of those sacs some living creature—some man or woman, or even some alien—was suffering as Sidi Bombay had suffered.

He moved to the nearest sac.

"What are you doing?" asked Annie.

Before he could answer, the thing in the sac lurched

sideways. Clive winced in disgust as the slimy membranes brushed against his face. Through the translucent yellow envelope he could see the creature in the sac writhing in agony.

Without another moment's thought he raised his knife and slashed open the sac. Hot liquid gushed out, and with it a bundle of raw, liver-colored flesh that might once have been a man but certainly was no longer. It landed with a soft *plop* in the mucus and lay there twitching in misery, banging the lump that must once have been its head up and down against the floor. An opening that was probably a mouth seemed to strain to scream, though no sound came out.

Clive felt his stomach lurch, and a hot curl of acid came biting at the back of his throat. Closing his eyes, he ran the wretched thing through. If it was murder, then it was murder. He could not call himself a man and let such suffering go on.

"Horace, help me!" he cried. "We have to put an end to this atrocity."

Without waiting for a response, he moved to the next sac and slashed it open. The creature that fell out immediately wrapped a tentacle around Clive's leg. It was screaming even as it wrenched his foot toward its mouth. Clive slipped and fell into the noxious mucus. His stomach churning in disgust, he wrenched himself forward and lashed out with his knife, slashing through the creature's face. It died screaming.

Clive shuddered. He was trying to decide whether to open the next sac when the decision was taken out of his hands by the arrival of a saint and twelve priests.

They entered through a hole in the floor, which appeared in the center of the chamber as if by magic. A platform carried the thirteen men swiftly and silently into the room. One man—the saint, as Clive later learned—was dressed in a hooded white robe, bound at the waist with a crimson sash. He had long black hair and eyes that looked like they could stop a locomotive in its tracks.

"You will cease this sacrilege instantly," he commanded.

"This chamber belongs to the Saints of Purgatory. The Venerated Ones are not to be touched."

Clive was trembling with rage. "This is unholy," he said. "How can you condone such a thing?"

He began to move toward the next sac.

"I think you do not understand," said the saint. He withdrew his hand from his sleeve, revealing a slender shaft, about the thickness of a man's thumb and perhaps three times as long.

Clive's first reaction was amusement. Was this simpleminded priest no better than a jungle mystic, to think he could stop them with his religious version of a magic wand?

He started forward. The priest made a slight gesture with his hand and a bolt of energy struck the floor in front of Clive. He heard only a slight sizzling noise. But where the bolt struck the floor it had seared a hole the size of his fist. Mucus oozed over the edges, filling the hole even as he watched.

"Buzzers," L'Claar said simply.

Before Clive could respond, another dozen priests appeared at the door where his own group had entered. All of them were armed with the same kind of weapons.

"I know we've gotten in trouble this way before," Clive said quietly. "But I think we'd better do as they say."

Even so, it was difficult when the priests, gesturing with their weapons, gathered them into a knot and marched them out of the chamber. For a moment Clive thought they were going to lose Horace.

"No," he said. "I'll not go unless we take Sidi Bombay with us."

"Do not be a fool," said the saint. "The Venerated One has been severely traumatized. He must be treated properly, or his usefulness will be over."

He loosed another bolt from his buzzer, drilling a hole in the floor about a hand's width from where Horace knelt beside Sidi Bombay.

"That is my last warning," said the saint. "If not for the fact that the Inquisition will want to deal with this blasphemy, I would cheerfully destroy you now. Give me any more reason, and I may decide I would rather deal with the Inquisitor's questions than with any further delays."

"Pragmatism," said the cyborg. "Survive now, have a chance later. Die now, and you decrease your chances considerably."

Horace stood and crossed to join the others.

"I am sorry to see that you are a part of this, little priestess," one of the men said to L'Claar. "You realize there will be no mercy for you."

"I know that," said L'Claar, her voice flat with the acceptance of someone who has long ago learned to accept pain as inevitable.

"Brother Daniel, will you take charge of the prisoners?" asked the man in white.

"Yes, your holiness," said a tall, slender man with a sour face.

"Your holiness?" asked Tomàs, his voice quivering.

"I am one of the saints," said the man in white. Then, as surely as a fencer spotting a weakness in an opponent's guard, he added, "and I am sore displeased with your actions on this day."

Tomàs cried out in despair and clutched his rosary.

Brother Daniel issued a command, and the prisoners were herded out of the chamber and into the hall, where they began to travel through what seemed an endless maze of corridors. Finally they reached a narrow corridor lined with solid-looking metal doors. One of the priests opened a door on the right-hand side. Using their buzzers, the others forced the captives through the door.

Brother Daniel took the trouble to spit in Clive's face as he was entering the cell. "Blasphemer," he said. The door slammed shut, leaving them in the dark—a condition Chang Guafe was willing to alleviate on an irregular basis.

Several slow, unhappy hours later a small panel slid aside, revealing an opening covered by a sturdy grate.

"You are being held for high treason," said a solemn voice from the other side of the door. "You are to be brought before the next session of the Grand Inquisition, which will begin in three days' time."

"What are we—" began Clive. But the little panel slid shut, leaving them in the dark once more.

After a while another man came. His voice, which they heard this time through a small flap at the bottom of the door, sounded old and tired.

"Now don't try anything fancy with me," he said, sliding a pan of tepid water through the flap. "I ain't got a key, so it won't do you no good anyhow. Quite a mess you've gotten yourself into," he continued cheerfully, following up the water with a pan of thin gruel.

"I'd do it again, given the chance," Clive said sullenly.

"Heroes," said Annie, though she uttered the word so neutrally he had no idea what she actually meant by it.

"The Grand Inquisitor will be glad to hear you say that," said the man. "It'll make his job easier."

"What kind of trial is it to be?" asked Clive. "Will we have a jury?"

"What's a jury?" asked the old man.

When Clive explained, the man broke out laughing and said, "Not likely. Trials here take place before the Grand Inquisitor, and he don't need no jury to help him make up his mind. We have a new one, just this short time ago, and a harsh judge he is too, from what I hear tell. Bishop Neville, they call him, and I doubt he'll have much mercy on the likes of you."

CHAPTER FORTY-ONE

Bishop Neville

If unraveling mysteries were an activity sufficient for mind and body alike, Clive Folliot's little band would have had more than enough to keep them occupied for the three days of their incarceration.

To begin with, there was the matter of Sidi Bombay and the maddeningly oblique replies L'Claar gave them to most of their questions about that whole situation. It was only because they now knew a little more that they were able to ask questions which garnered any significant new information.

Then there was the matter of Neville—or "Bishop Neville," as the Grand Inquisitor was called.

"Is there no end to my brother's gall?" Clive had seethed, shortly after the man who gave them this bit of information had gone scuffling off along the corridor.

"Now don't be too harsh on the lad, sah," said Horace. "To begin with, you don't know that it's him. It could be just some bizarre coincidence. He's not the only Neville in the world, you know."

"Well, his name seems to pop up more often than 'John Smith' here in this damnable Dungeon," Clive said hotly. But he knew Horace was right. It was too early to become overly exercised on the matter. He really didn't know whether his brother was actually in charge of the Inquisition they were about to face.

The matter was further confused during one of the periods when Chang Guafe was providing some light for their little cell and Clive decided, with a degree of perversity he did not quite understand himself, to flip through the maddening little journal that had been his only communication with Neville since his reckless brother had disappeared in the African bush nearly two years before.

He was both appalled and delighted to discover a new message:

Clive—I think I've got the devils licked. I know I told you to ignore any further messages, because the journal had been tainted. Fortunately, you can cancel that warning.

Heed, instead, this new instruction. Beware the priests of the fourth level! They preach a strange creed of salvation through punishment; they are nearly demented in their pursuit of their beliefs, and it is easier to offend them than you can imagine. Avoid falling into their clutches at all costs.

Things are developing at a fantastic pace. Hurry and catch me, for I have much to tell you.

As ever, Neville

"Well, that's an encouragin' bit of news," said Horace after Clive had read it aloud. "Don't do that which we've already done, because we'll be in bloody all if we do!"

"Oh, but it is good news," said Clive. "Don't you see—it means we can trust the journal again. Neville's advice was at least correct in this instance, if a bit late. And he says he has the problem licked."

"Are you simpleminded or simply too good-hearted to recognize treachery when it slaps you in the face?" asked Tomàs, in a tone of voice somewhat sharper than he generally used with Clive.

"What do you mean?" asked Clive, a little belligerently.

"I mean what better way would there be for someone who wanted to gain your trust then to do so by giving you a genuinely useful message in your brother's name? Just because the words are true this time does not mean that the intent behind them is good. And how useful is a message that tells us something we already know anyway?"

"Maybe I just didn't read the book in time," Clive said uncertainly. "We've been fairly busy of late."

But it was too late; his faith in the message had already been destroyed. It might indeed be genuine. The book might be trusted once again—more valuable than ever, now that he was aware of the past treachery, which would explain such messages as the disastrous adjuration to ring the gong in the Black Tower, an action that had brought them under attack by the forces waiting to be roused by that sound.

But there was no way to know for certain. Every message would now be suspect, every piece of information a two-edged blade. He thrust the book back into his suit with a sigh of disgust.

Was anything ever what it seemed in this damnable Dungeon?

And thus they passed the time, bickering among themselves, worrying about what had happened to Sidi Bombay now that he had been taken by the saints, and even, in their more tranquil moments, remembering their past adventures, recounting the stories to one another as old friends who meet after a long absence and share a drink and memories of days gone by.

Both Horace and L'Claar were particularly distraught over the fact that Sidi was in the hands of the saints. Though Horace was generally fairly stoic over the matter, L'Claar often grew tearful about it. When this happened, Wrecked Fred would gather her into his arms and rock her, crooning ridiculous songs about monkeys and bears. From the number and variety of these little ditties Clive suspected Fred was making them up as he went along, simply to amuse himself while he soothed the child.

Chang Guafe spent innumerable hours trying to validate Annie's earlier comment that he would have made a fine sneak thief. However, he was at no time able to find a combination of tentacles that would open their prison door—primarily, Clive suspected, because there was no keyhole on this side of the door.

In fact, the blank nature of the cell was their greatest discomfort. It was so narrow that no more than three of them could stand shoulder to shoulder across its width at the same time. It was furnished with only one small iron bench, so short that only L'Claar or Finnbogg could lie down on it, and the poor dwarf was so broad he couldn't use it with any comfort anyway. A round hole in the corner of the room was the only place for them to relieve themselves, a fact that made Clive profoundly uncomfortable, and also most appreciative of the darkness.

He appreciated the dark even more on the occasion that Shriek reached out to communicate with him privately. He was sitting against the wall, his arms around his knees, contemplating what L'Claar had said earlier about the exit from the Dungeon rumored to be hidden somewhere beneath the temple. When he had questioned her about it again, she had admitted that many people believed the exit would take you back to wherever you came from.

He could not help but fantasize about the idea. Could he but find it and return home to a world that seemed suddenly more dear than ever he could have imagined, home to Annabella Leighton and their child—and, of course, at that point the fantasy went awry, for to return would be to create some twist in the shape of time and history that had led to the birth of User Annie.

Nothing simple, he thought bitterly, just before things got more complicated than ever.

Clive, I wish to communicate with you.

He was startled; he could not recall that Shriek had ever addressed him by his given name.

What is it, great warrior? he asked, feeling a surge of genuine fondness for the arachnid despite the gap that had existed between them since their adventure on the island of the cannibals.

She did not answer for a time, and Clive began to wonder if she had fallen asleep. *Shriek?* he asked.

I am here, she sent. *But I am uncertain of what I want to say.*

That is not like you, he replied gently.

I have experienced much that is new to me since I met you, Clive.

There it was again; his given name.

We have all experienced new things here in the Dungeon, he answered.

What I am feeling now is stranger to me than any of those things. I have faced danger and adventure in many forms. My world is a strange and sometimes fearful place, though I love it very much. But I have never met anyone like you before, a spirit so simple—please do not take the word amiss—a spirit so simple and sweet, so loyal and daring. Do you know how the rest of us feel about you, Clive?

He felt his cheeks grow warm, and hoped Chang Guafe would not choose this moment to suddenly illuminate their cell.

I suppose it changes from day to day, he thought lightly.

At one level. Sometimes we are angry with you, or frustrated, or find you unbearably silly. No! Do not defend yourself. There is no need. Because beyond that is the fact that we have all come to love you. Do not argue, dear heart, for I know this to be true. Little is truly hidden from me, you know. And I think I love you most of all, Clive. That is why I was so angry with you. Because in loving you I had come to expect too much of you. And also, that feeling was frightening to me. To be angry gave me a great wall to use against the feelings you created in me. You are a man of the world, Clive Folliot. What does one do with such ridiculous feelings as these?

All the time he was receiving this message Clive was trying desperately not to think, for fear that he would offend this dear, horrifying friend with some unguarded reaction. But it was hard, for underneath the rest of the message he could sense a yearning for physical closeness that he knew he could never reciprocate.

Alas, wily Shriek knew her man too well for him to escape by hiding.

You once asked if no one had any privacy on my world, sent Shriek. *I made light of your discomfort. But now I see its source, and I apologize. Perhaps because of what we are, perhaps because of the way we communicate, the emotions of my people are more simple and direct. I have never before sensed or experienced the kind of complicated and subtle feelings that you have created in me. Now I wish that I, too, could hide from you. I would not have you know of my desires, for I know you well enough to know that you could never return them, not if you spent a lifetime trying to overcome the horror and the revulsion that the idea creates in you. O Folliot, I once said to you weep not for Shriek. But now weep if you will, for I am caught in a web not of my own making, tied to you by strands of a kind I never meant to weave. Yes, weep for Shriek, who loves you so, and in the instant of expressing that love, knows every bit of your reaction, and is sliced to the core of her being, and knows no way to escape your precious, bitter knife.*

And as when she was in Ma-sand and he had been overwhelmed by her desire, now he was swept by her despair, and he did indeed weep, laying his head on his knees and trying to keep the sound to himself while the tears rolled freely along the white suit that could not absorb them.

Clive was asleep when the company of priests and guards came to escort them to the Inquisition. He wondered if they were vastly cautious by nature, or if they had somehow divined the powers contained within their little group, for they opened the small panel and, holding one of the weapons called buzzers against it, ordered Shriek and Chang Guafe to press their faces to the back wall. Opening the door a crack, they took L'Claar and informed the others that at the first sign of resistance the child would be destroyed. One by one the others were taken from the cell, and with each the warning was renewed: resistance from one would result in death for all.

They reversed the direction of their earlier journey, returning to the upper levels of the temple, which Clive now understood to be a structure far larger than even its imposing outer structure had initially led him to suspect. As they left the lower levels the glowing blue lights were replaced by torches, and again he had that sense of somehow moving through time, as if they were returning to an earlier, less technically advanced era.

When they reached the Great Hall of the Inquisition the flickering light of the torches was barely sufficient to light the room. Tormented grotesques leered from the shadowy corners of the vaulted ceiling.

The hall was lined with priests in black robes, who began to chant in a solemn, doleful manner as the prisoners were led among them.

At the end of the room was a great judicial bench, approached by several broad steps. On each step stood a burly guard clutching a sword and a whip.

Clive wondered if the priests actually used their buzzers at this level, or if they were reserved for the lower regions of the temple. Of course, since he knew that both of the priests guarding him were armed with the lethal weapons, he could always test the question just by trying to run. He decided that in this case ignorance was, if not actually bliss, at least preferable to a tangible demonstration of the truth.

Suddenly a trumpet sounded. The chanting ceased. A hush fell over the great chamber as the Grand Inquisitor entered. He was wrapped in a black robe, and an enormous hood engulfed his face. Strain as he might, Clive could not tell if it was indeed his brother hidden beneath that dark cowl. Even so, his pulse began to pound. Was it possible that after all this time Neville truly was here, right in front of him? But what mad twist could have landed him in the role of Grand Inquisitor for this demented religion? And if it truly was Neville, what would he do when Clive and his friends stood before him?

The Inquisition began.

Clive soon realized that theirs was not the only case to be heard this day. As other, less serious, matters were brought before the Inquisition, he began to suspect that they were being saved for the main event.

To his enormous frustration, the Inquisitor—Bishop Neville—never once drew back his hood, or even spoke, but only sat, listening to the evidence, and then nodding in agreement with the man Clive had come to think of as the persecuting priest. Flagellations and worse were handed out in abundance for crimes of greed and passion as the morning, or evening, or whatever it was wore on. It seemed there was not one of the seven deadly sins to which some resident of Purgatory had not laid claim, and the priests appeared to have a network of spies and informants that was most efficient in searching out such behavior. Clive decided that life here in Purgatory was probably even more unpleasant than he had originally expected.

He began to sweat, though he couldn't tell if this was due to nervousness or to an actual increase in the temperature.

Bored and terrified at the same time, he began to reach out to Shriek, hesitated, and realized that of course thought was faster than regret, so the line of communication was already open.

But she was still and calm, and sent him fond greetings and amusingly acerbic comments on the demeanor of both the priests and the unfortunate sinners who had been brought before them.

He appreciated her as he never had before.

"Clive Folliot, approach the bench."

His mind went blank for a moment, then spilled over with so many stray thoughts they were stepping on each other's toes. Was he being called up on his own, without the others? He had thought they would be tried as a group. How did they know his name? He was sure that no one had ever asked him. Of course, if it really *was* Neville under that hood, then they would automatically know who he was, but if it was Neville then why was he on trial anyway, unless Neville was powerless to prevent it, which didn't seem likely, and anyway—

The mad jumble of thoughts was interrupted by the voice of the priest: "Clive Folliot, you stand accused of blasphemy and heresy. You did with willful intent enter the most sacred area in all of Purgatory, where you attacked and killed two of those whom we most venerate, and prematurely released another soul who was on the road to Heaven. This was witnessed by many priests. There is no question of your guilt, only of the nature and duration of the torture that will lead to your death, a torture that will do you no good, as your soul is surely consigned to the nether regions of Hell already. It is the recommendation of this court—"

"Wait!" said Clive, and the outburst was so unexpected that the priest actually halted in his tirade long enough for Clive to step forward and begin to speak.

"Do I not have the option of defending myself before sentencing?" he asked.

The priest began to object, but the Inquisitor waved his hand, indicating that Clive be allowed to speak.

He hesitated. Now that he had the floor, what could he possibly say?

He bowed his head, then looked up. "Your holiness," he said, wondering whom he was actually addressing, "my friends and I have traveled a great distance and suffered extreme hardship in search of two men. One is my brother, with whom I have had many differences. Yet he is blood of my blood, and flesh of my flesh, and I swore an oath to our father that I would try to find him. Along the way we lost a good man, honest and true, whom we found once more in the chamber below."

"Motive is of no concern," interrupted the persecutor.

"Let me speak," Clive said savagely.

Again the Inquisitor waved his hand.

Clive's throat was dry, his hands trembling. He was well aware that these might be the last words he ever spoke. He pressed on now not to buy time, or with any hope of saving himself or the others, for all that seemed impossibly lost. He spoke only because it might be his last chance, and there were things he had to say.

"For a long time I wanted only two things: the love of my father, and of my brother. Yet after a time I realized that they were the very things most likely to be forever denied to me. My father, you see, has always blamed me for the death of my mother. He has told me this from his own lips, and told me too of the hatred he bore me because of it. My brother was the favored one, the golden child. He could do no wrong. Everything came easily to him. Despite the fact that we were twins, I always seemed to lag behind. I was never as fast, as strong, as smart.

"Yet, despite the fact that he had so much, and I had

so little, my brother never took pity on me. More often, he tormented me. For a long time I hated him for that, though now I understand that it was only his childish reflection of an attitude he learned from our father.

"Even more, I can now see that harshness as a gift. For though I was not as strong, as fast, as smart, still his torments hardened me. They made me a survivor. I do not think I would have lived through the last months had I not been tempered by my brother's contempt."

He paused, then rushed on before the priest could interrupt.

"The thing is, I have already had my time in Purgatory, and have no wish to remain here any longer if death is now my fate. But if this is my last chance to speak, then I need to say that I have finally learned to forgive my brother for what was between us in the past. Despite my vow to our father, the true reason I have sought him for these last months is because he is my brother, and I love him."

And then he bowed his head, because he was finished.

A startled squeak from the persecutor caused him to look up again.

The Inquisitor had risen. He stepped around the great judicial bench and walked down the broad stairs until he stood on the first step, less than ten feet from where Clive stood.

Reaching up, he began to draw back his hood.

It was just about then that all hell broke loose.

CHAPTER FORTY-TWO

Worm

It began with the assassination of the Grand Inquisitor.

"Death to the traitor!" yelled a voice from the back of the chamber. "Death to the pawns of the outsiders!"

Clive heard a noise like bacon being slapped against a hot griddle. The figure in front of him sighed and crumpled to the floor like a leaf falling from a tree. Clive started to run forward, but was grabbed from behind by several pairs of hands.

"Let me go!" he cried, struggling against them. "I must see to him!"

But the entire hall had erupted in a sort of grand melee, as if the assassination had been but the prelude to some long-planned revolution. A mass of struggling men, clerics and guards and others with no identifying insignia of any kind, swept between Clive and the fallen Inquisitor, blocking his view of both the man and the strange thing that he thought he had seen behind the judicial bench just before the assassination.

"Let me go!" he cried again.

"You'll go nowhere but straight to hell!" snarled a familiar voice. Clive turned and saw that the persecutor had drawn a buzzer from somewhere in his robes. He had it aimed directly at Clive, and it was clear that he intended to carry out a summary execution.

But now there was another interruption, and even the battle raging around them ground to a halt as a low rumble, deep and powerful, more powerful by the moment it seemed, caused the floor to shake and bits of stone to crumble from the ceiling.

Clive held his breath as the intensity of the earth quake, for so he assumed it to be, continued to increase. The whole room was vibrating now. Great cracks appeared in the floor, and men who had been caught in life-and-death battles but instants before were crying out in terror and trampling over one another as they tried to flee the room.

And then the cries of terror and the raw scent of fear increased tenfold, as the true source of the shaking was revealed when the stone floor shattered as though a volcano were erupting beneath it and the broad head of one of the great worms of Q'oorna came thrusting into the room.

Purgatory had turned to hell indeed, and the screams that echoed through the vast chamber could easily have been those of lost souls.

For Clive, the creature was no less terrifying for the fact that he was seeing it a second time. This time, however, it did not wear his brother's face. It was simply a great blind thrust of muscle, still surging up through the hole it had created. Its tentacles—hundreds of the things, it seemed—thrashed wildly about, flinging men fifty feet and more to leave a streak of blood and brains as they slid down the stone walls into which they crashed.

And still the great length of the body flowed out of the hole, and the wrath of the worm expressed itself in a roar of anger that threatened to split Clive's skull.

He clapped his hands to his ears, then discarded all dignity and screamed in terror as the worm snatched him up and pulled him forward. He struggled desperately, but was suddenly still when he came face to face with the awesome realization that the worm was rescuing him, a thing he understood when it drew him within the ring of tentacles and deposited him next to Shriek, next to Annie, next to all his dear friends, and most of all next to a smiling Sidi Bombay, who had somehow summoned this creature and brought it to put an end to their trial, and likely to the Inquisition altogether.

The cries of the dying, the sizzle of weapons, the

rumble of falling stones seemed to combine in a mad symphony of death as the worm pivoted around the hole, sweeping priests and sinners before it without discrimination.

And then suddenly it withdrew, slipping back into the hole from which it had erupted. Clive could not be sure, but he thought he heard the great arched roof collapsing above them. He saw a familiar blue tunnel around them, the same kind of tunnel through which they had wandered so long beneath N'wrbb's castle, and recognized it at last for what it was: the mark of passage of the great worms of Q'oorna.

He blinked in astonishment as they seemed to drift through three floors of stone in less time than it takes to draw a breath.

The worm came to rest in an enormous chamber.

It was blue throughout, smooth as tile, though Clive now understood that it was not tile, was not anything made by man.

And then the worm was still.

"Off!" cried Sidi Bombay. "Off, off while we can, or there's no telling where it will take us." Scrambling through the thicket of tentacles, he slid to the floor. The others were close behind. No sooner had L'Claar jumped into Fred's good arm than the tentacles began to swirl, and with a speed that seemed impossible for something of that size the worm shot forward and disappeared *through* the wall.

For a moment no one said a thing. Suddenly Clive began to laugh, a rich, uproarious sound that echoed from the blue walls of the chamber. First Horace joined him, then Sidi, and soon all but Chang Guafe had succumbed to a kind of hysteria that Clive quickly recognized as nothing more than a way of relieving an almost impossible accumulation of tensions.

Clive finally came to his senses when he realized he was holding Annie, who was giggling convulsively, in a fashion entirely too intimate for someone who was his direct descendant.

Slowly the group regained its sobriety. Clive strode forward and clasped Sidi Bombay by the shoulders.

"By God, it is good to have you back with us," he exclaimed.

"It is good to be back," said Sidi. "And I have much to tell you. But before I say most of it, we should quit this place, which will not be safe for us much longer."

"Where are we?" asked Clive, staring around the blue chamber in a kind of awe.

"This is a wormhole. It lies beneath the Temple of Those Who Suffer, though the priests are not aware that it is here. The 'saints,' however—who are connected with the priests only in the fact that they have them fooled into doing much of their dirty work—will probably arrive before long. They are not happy with any of us.

"The worms are very powerful, and very useful for those who know how to tap that power. They can travel through time and space. But they were betrayed long ago, by a race that had first claimed to befriend them and then found a way to cloud their minds and harness their power. They are the only creatures who can move from level to level within the Dungeon at will. However, at certain places others can use their tunnels as points of passage, albeit perilous ones.

"All this I learned from the saints while I was in their grasp. They spoke freely in front of me, for I feigned unconsciousness, as if I were still in the grip of the worm. And indeed, much of the time I was, for I was summoning it to me with all the power of our connection."

Sidi paused, and seemed to fold in on himself like a moonflower at dawn.

"I am much different," he said, "in ways I do not begin to understand. I am afraid, and confused. I can sense things—I know, for example, that the blue circle on the wall ahead of us, not far from where my worm disappeared, will lead us to the fifth level of the Dungeon.

"I know, too, that the circle to the left leads out of the Dungeon altogether."

"I told you!" L'Claar said triumphantly.

They stood looking at one another uncomfortably.

"I will be going ahead," Clive said at last. "For if my

brother still lives, I am convinced that he will be found still deeper within this mystery."

"Was that Neville beneath that robe or not?" demanded Annie.

"I don't know," said Clive. "I think perhaps it was, at least for part of the time. But I wonder if my brother hasn't pulled another switch. I saw something very strange today: just after the Inquisitor was killed, and before the battle blocked my view, I spotted someone who might well have been Neville darting away from the back of the judicial bench."

On an impulse, he reached into his clothing and withdrew the journal. Flipping through its pages he found a new message. It was but two words long: *Follow me!*

Tomàs snorted. "That journal is the devil's work," he said. "You cannot trust anything you read in there."

"And yet we must all make a choice about where we are going to go next," said Sidi, "and it must be made quickly, for the saints will be here soon. As for me, I have unfinished business in the Dungeon. I will be going with Clive Folliot."

"As will I," said Horace.

"And I," said Shriek.

Tomàs shrugged. "I think you are all *muy estupido*. I think the priests were right all along—this is the will of God, and one should not try to escape. But—" again he shrugged, as if accepting the implacable will of destiny, "I am with you."

"I still seek my vengeance," said Chang Guafe.

Finnbogg was wringing his hands.

Annie and Fred looked at the others with a kind of misery. "I want to go home," Annie said desperately, almost apologetically.

"I understand," said Clive. He cursed himself for not being able to urge her any more firmly. If he was a proper great-great-grandfather he would just pick her up and throw her through that hole, back to where she would be safe, and have done with it.

Finnbogg had no such reservations.

"Do not go!" he wailed, throwing himself at Annie's

feet. "Stay with Finnbogg and Clive. Finnbogg love Annie."

"And Annie love Finnbogg," she said softly. "But Annie must go home."

While Annie was trying to disengage herself from Finnbogg, L'Claar had turned to stare at the hole with a look of hopeless longing.

"I don't know where home is," she said at last.

Fred reached down to stroke her hair. Then he picked her up in his good arm. Carrying her, he followed the group to the opening Sidi claimed would lead out of the Dungeon, back home.

Annie hesitated. "Well, I guess this is goodbye, Grampa," she said, placing a hand on Clive's chest. "I hope you find that crazy brother of yours someday. I can't say I hope that you actually get out of here. You understand—"

She stopped as something caught in her throat.

"I understand," said Clive.

She slid her hand up to his shoulder. But as he was bending to kiss her the saints came marching in.

Clive spun at the sound of their arrival. They had entered at the far side of the chamber, so they were still a great distance away. But they were at least twenty in number, and every one of them that Clive could see was holding a buzzer. Immediately the saints began to run toward the little band. The energy shots of the buzzers struck and spattered on the blue walls around them.

"Get out!" said Clive to Annie. "Go while you can!"

But Finnbogg was clinging to her feet, and so Fred reached the hole first. Clutching L'Claar to his chest, he leaped into the opening.

Man and child disappeared.

The hole flared green. Then it, too, vanished from sight.

Annie tore herself free from Finnbogg's grasp. "Damn!" she screamed. She ran to the wall and began pounding her hands against the blank, blue space. "Oh damn, damn, damn!"

"Finnbogg sorry!" moaned the dwarf, clutching his head in misery. "Finnbogg sorry, Annie!"

"Shut up and move!" yelled Clive. He grabbed Annie by the arm and dragged her away from the wall.

A spatter of energy struck the floor by their feet.

"Come on," he ordered. "We have to get out of here! Now!"

Annie nodded. Hands linked, Finnbogg at their heels, they raced toward the blue hole Sidi Bombay had said would lead them to the next level of the Dungeon. The others had already gone through. But unlike the way home, this hole had not disappeared.

"Damn!" Annie said again.

Clive pulled her to him. Sweeping her into his arms, he leaped forward.

The world exploding into blue, they escaped Purgatory, and began their descent into the inferno.

The following drawings are from Major Clive Folliot's private sketchbook, which was mysteriously left on the doorstep of *The London Illustrated Recorder and Dispatch*, the newspaper that provided financing for his expedition. There was no explanation accompanying the parcel, save for an enigmatic inscription in the hand of Major Folliot himself.

Again, I have been caught up in this puzzling search, leaving me with little time to record the idiosyncracies of this journey. I pause as briefly as the exploits allow me to attempt to send to you additional images of my encounters with the fantastic within the enclave of the Dungeon.

I pray that my visual journal of these phenomena reaches your abode and illuminates the peculiarities of this world. How far from Britain I must be!

CHANG GUAFE — A VERY ROUGH
APPROXIMATION OF
'HIS' INHUMAN
VISAGE.

A TAVERN IN GO-MAR
LESS FRIENDLY THAN
IT LOOKED...

THE CAVE OF CERBERUS·WITH ITS STONE WATCHDOG.

THE
TRAPDOOR
TO THE
CAVE OF
THE
FINNBOGGI

KA THE MERMAN
THOUGH HIS PEOPLE HAVE SOME DISTURBING
CUSTOMS, HE WAS A LOYAL FRIEND.

GREEN HAVEN — A FABULOUS RESIDENCE, HOME TO THE MYSTERIOUS MAN KNOWN AS 'GREEN'.

THE GIANT SNAKE OF THE ISLAND
OF TONADANO, ATTACKING MY
DESCENDANT, ANNIE.

R STURDY VESSEL, THE BOLD ENDEAVOR

WRECKED FRED —
A STRANGE MAN FRO[M]
ANNIES OWN TIME.

THE CHURCH OF THE HOLY
CANNIBAL AND ITS PRIES[T].

GUR-NANN-LORD
OF HIS OWN
ISLAND, AND
PROTECTOR
OF OUR
GRAM.

THE POISONOUS FLYING FISH
THAT ATTACKED OUR RAFT.

THE KRAKEN

THE WATERSPOUT
THROUGH WHICH WE
CAME TO
LEVEL FOUR.

THE EGG SACS
OF THE GREAT
WORMS OF Q'OORNA